JULIET TAKES A BREATH

Published by

BOOM! BOX™

Logo Design by
Jillian Crab

Designer
Marie Krupina

Assistant Editor
Kenzie Rzonca

Editor
Shannon Watters

BOOM! BOX™

BOOM! Studios, 5670 Wilshire Boulevard, Suite 400, Los Angeles, CA 90036-5679. Printed in China. First Printing.

ISBN: 978-1-68415-611-5, eISBN: 978-1-64668-023-8

JULIET TAKES A BREATH ™

Written by

Gabby Rivera

Illustrated & Adapted for Comics by

Celia Moscote

Colored by

James Fenner

Lettered by

DC Hopkins

Cover by

Celia Moscote

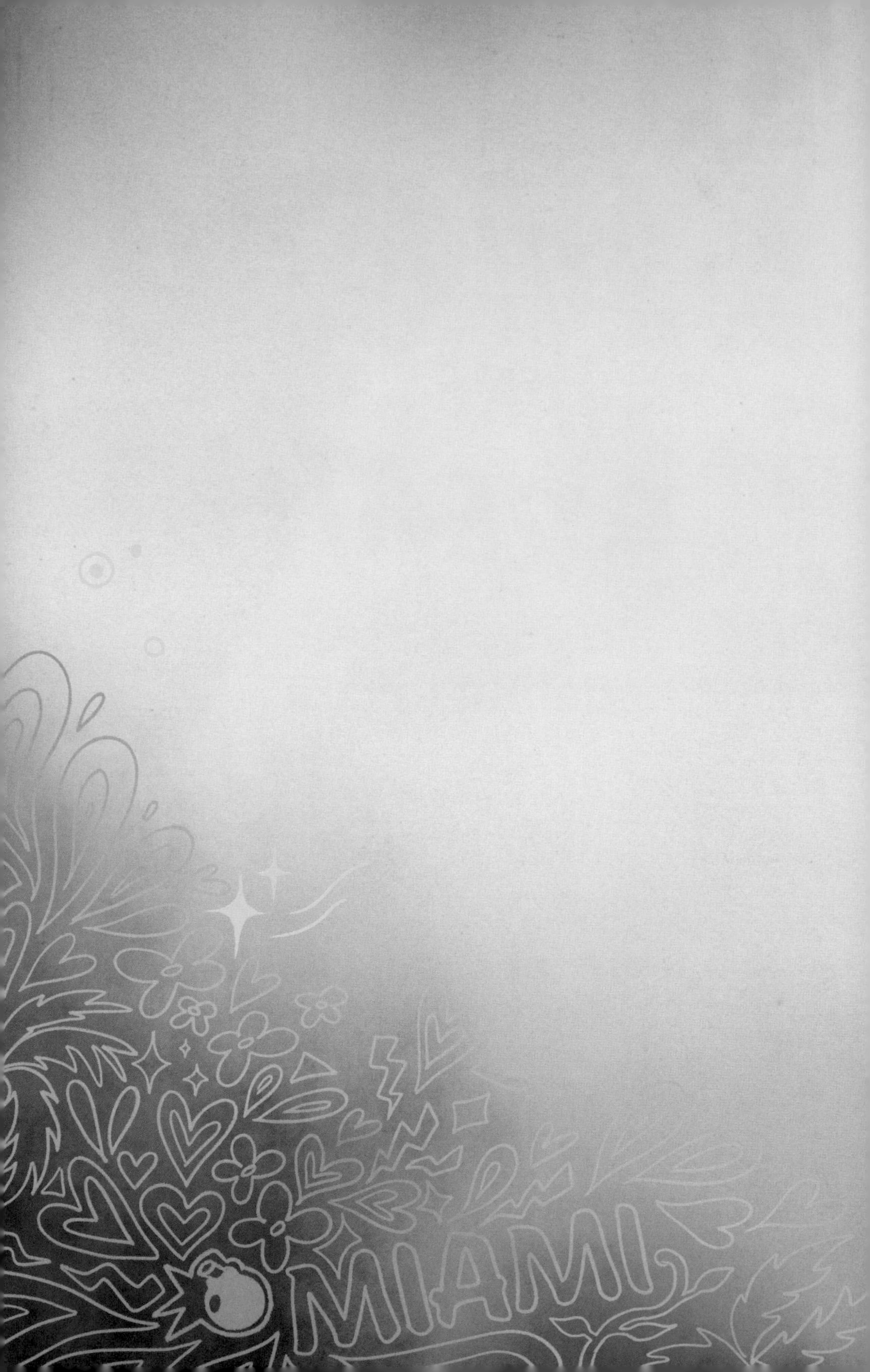
MIAMI

Juliet Palante (Juliet.Palante@zmail.com)   ☐ Sent - Juliet Palante   10:09 AM
Subject: A Big Important Professional (Fan) Letter
To: contact@ragingflower.com

Dear Harlowe,

Hi, my name is Juliet Palante. I've been reading your book **Raging Flower: Empowering Your Pussy by Empowering Your Mind.** No lie, I started reading it so that I could make people uncomfortable on the subway.

I'm writing to you because this book of yours, this magical labia manifesto, has become my bible. It's definitely a reading from the book of white lady feminism and yet, there are moments where I see my round brown ass in your words. I wanted more of that, Harlowe, more representation, more acknowledgment, more room to breathe the same air as you. "We are all women. We are all of the womb. It is in that essence of the moon that we share sisterhood"—that's you. You wrote that and I highlighted it, wondering if that was true.

If you don't know my life and my struggle, can we be sisters? Can a white lady like you make room for me? Or do I need to just push you out of the way?

I hope it's okay that I say this to you. I don't mean any disrespect, but if you can question the patriarchy, then I can question you, I think. I don't really know how this feminism stuff works, anyway. I've only taken one women's studies class and that was legit because a cutie on my floor signed up for it.

I read **Raging Flower,** and now I dream of raised fists and solidarity marches led by matriarchs fueled by café con leche where I can march alongside cigar-smoking doñas and Black Power dykes and all the world's weirdos and no one is left out.
And no one is living a lie.

Is that the world you live in? I read that you live in Portland, Oregon. No one I know has ever been there; most people I know have never left the Bronx. And I get it, I'm BX Puerto Rican all day with a big family that loves me so much.

But damn if this place and the people here don't wear me down. Some days it feels like we argue to be louder than the trains that rumble us home. There aren't even enough trees to absorb the chaos and breathe out some peace.

I'll trade you pancakes for peace. I heard that you're writing another book. I can help with that. Seriously, some of my best friends are libraries.

If there's room in your world for a nerdy asthmatic baby-dyke from the Bronx, you should write me back. Everybody needs a hand, especially when it comes to fighting the good fight.

Punani Power Forever,
Juliet Milagros Palante

PS: How do you take your coffee? This will help me decide if we're compatible social justice superheroes or not.

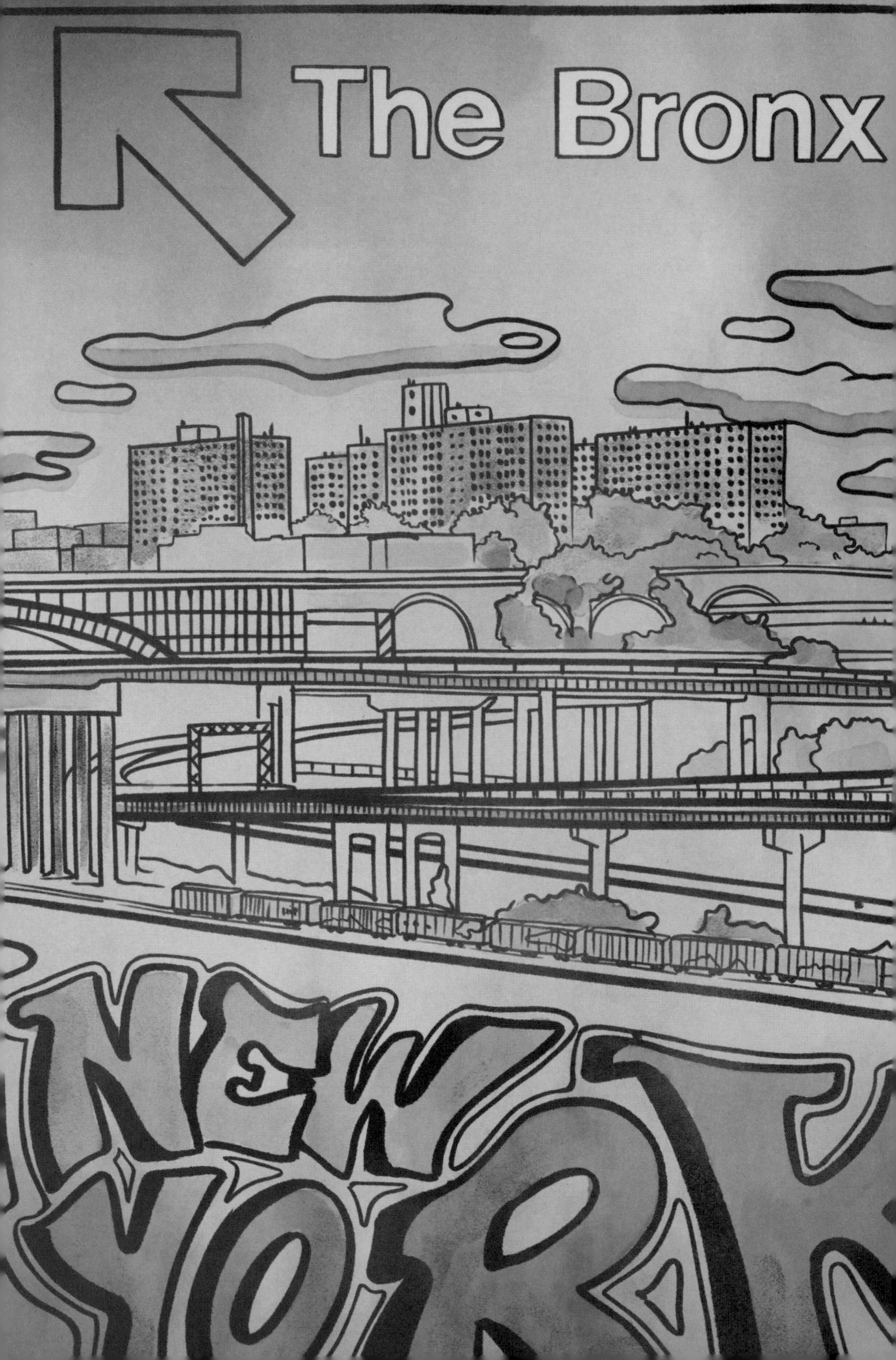
The Bronx

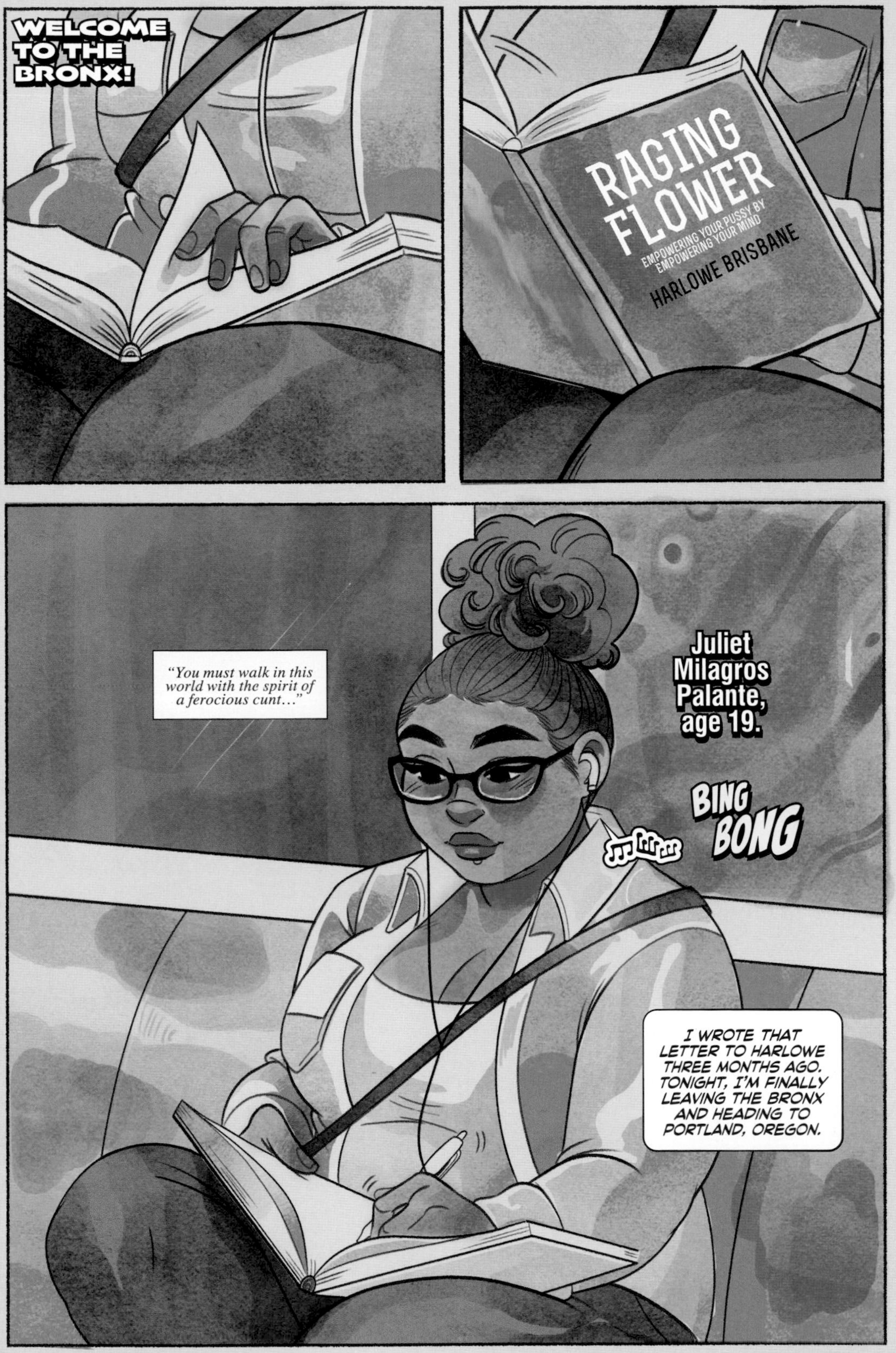
WELCOME TO THE BRONX!
RAGING FLOWER
EMPOWERING YOUR PUSSY BY EMPOWERING YOUR MIND
HARLOWE BRISBANE
"You must walk in this world with the spirit of a ferocious cunt…"
Juliet Milagros Palante, age 19.
BING BONG
I WROTE THAT LETTER TO HARLOWE THREE MONTHS AGO. TONIGHT, I'M FINALLY LEAVING THE BRONX AND HEADING TO PORTLAND, OREGON.

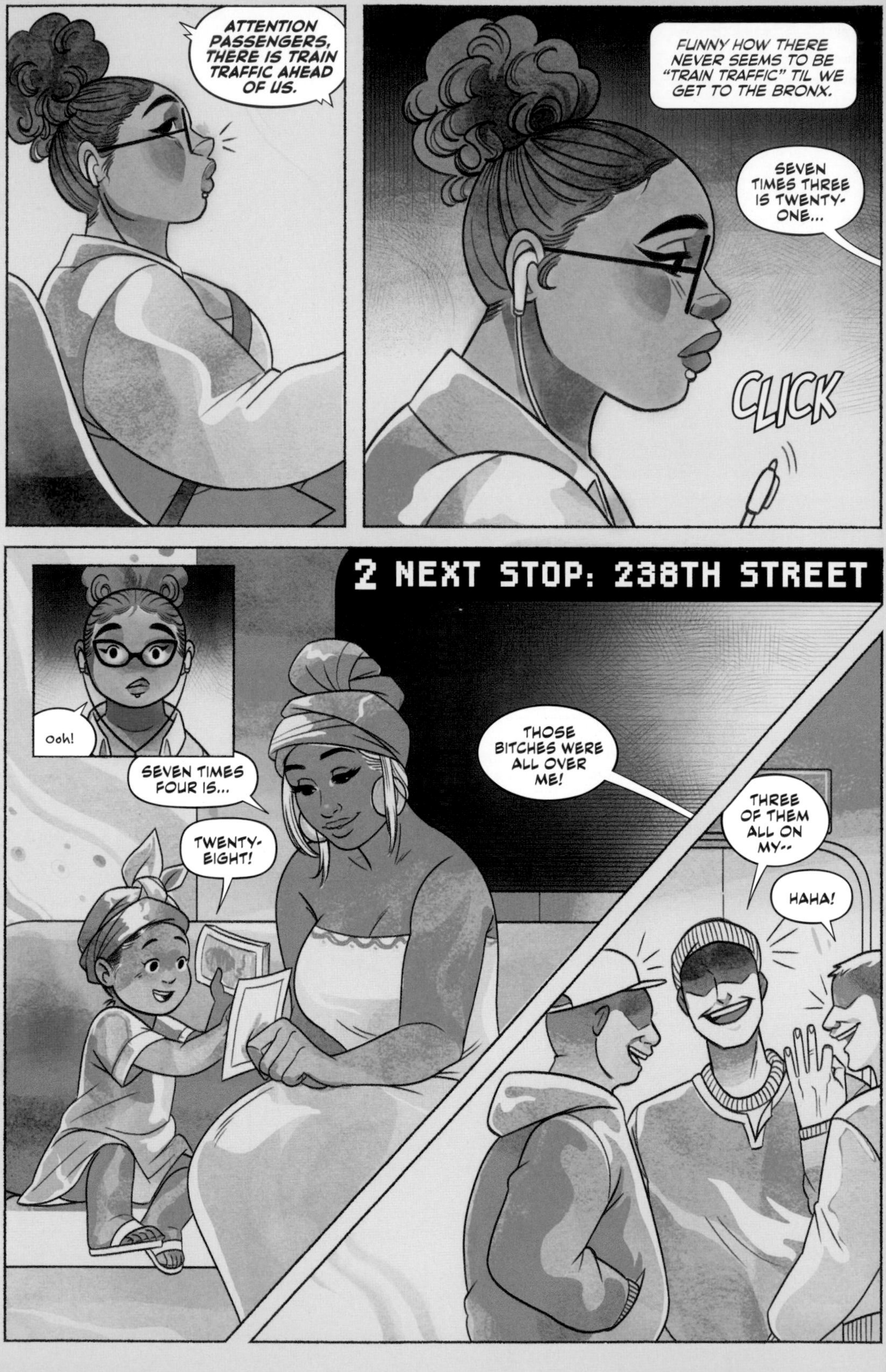
ATTENTION PASSENGERS, THERE IS TRAIN TRAFFIC AHEAD OF US.
FUNNY HOW THERE NEVER SEEMS TO BE "TRAIN TRAFFIC" TIL WE GET TO THE BRONX.
SEVEN TIMES THREE IS TWENTY-ONE...
CLICK
2 NEXT STOP: 238TH STREET
Ooh!
SEVEN TIMES FOUR IS...
TWENTY-EIGHT!
THOSE BITCHES WERE ALL OVER ME!
THREE OF THEM ALL ON MY--
HAHA!

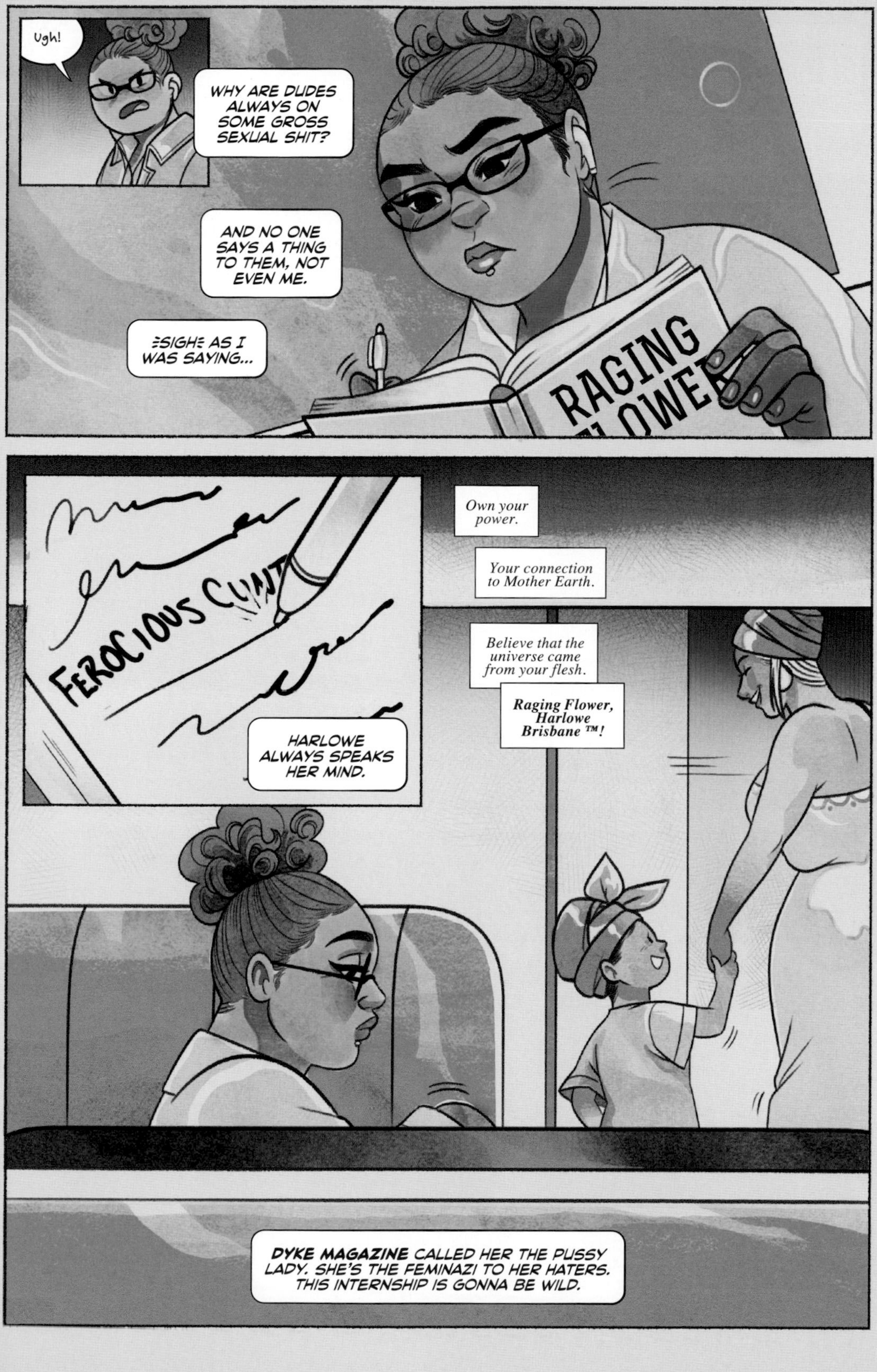
Ugh!
WHY ARE DUDES ALWAYS ON SOME GROSS SEXUAL SHIT?
AND NO ONE SAYS A THING TO THEM, NOT EVEN ME.
=SIGH= AS I WAS SAYING...
RAGING FLOWE
FEROCIOUS CUNT
HARLOWE ALWAYS SPEAKS HER MIND.
Own your power.
Your connection to Mother Earth.
Believe that the universe came from your flesh.
Raging Flower, Harlowe Brisbane ™!
DYKE MAGAZINE CALLED HER THE PUSSY LADY. SHE'S THE FEMINAZI TO HER HATERS. THIS INTERNSHIP IS GONNA BE WILD.

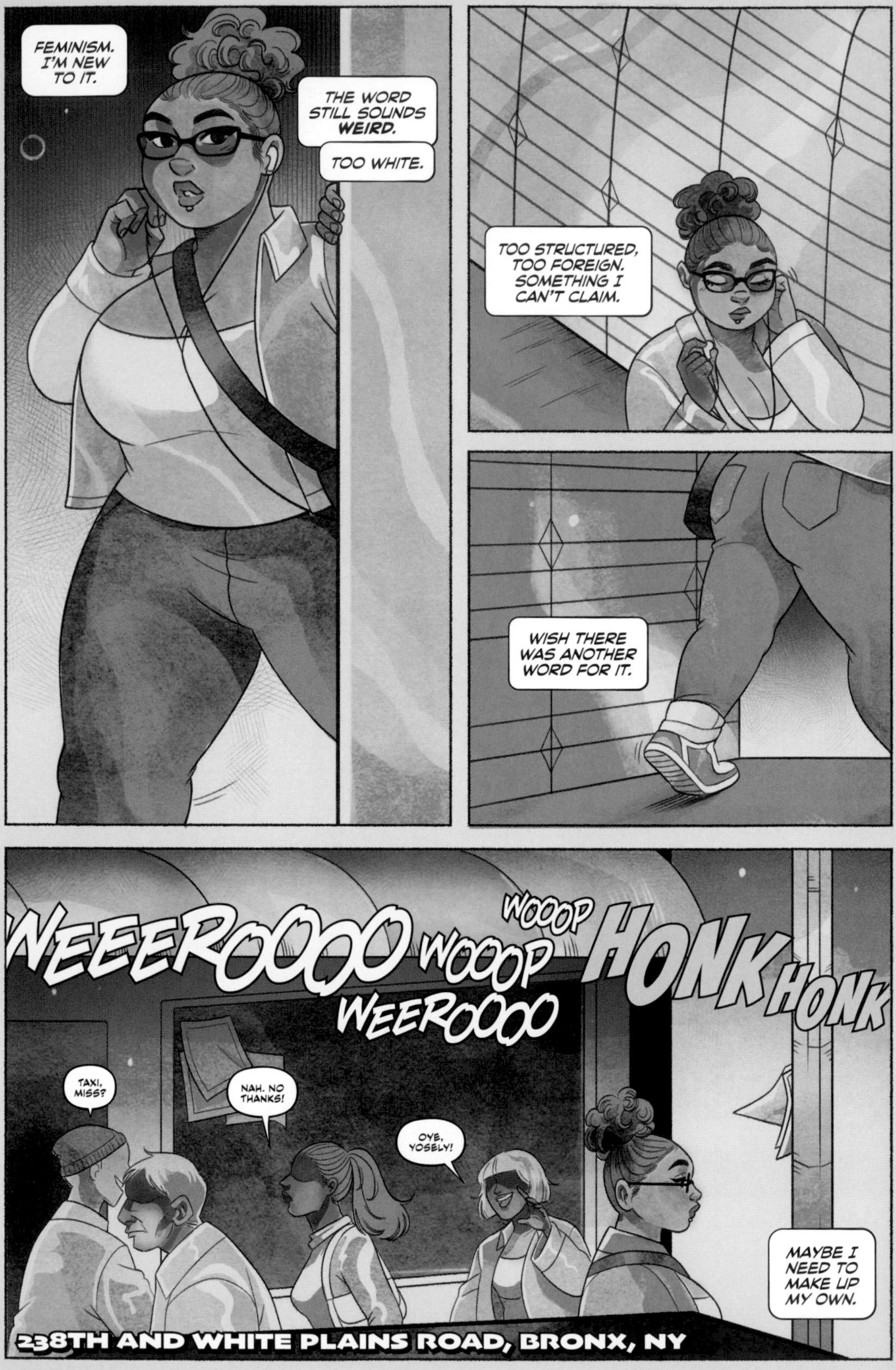
FEMINISM. I'M NEW TO IT.
THE WORD STILL SOUNDS **WEIRD.**
TOO WHITE.
TOO STRUCTURED, TOO FOREIGN. SOMETHING I CAN'T CLAIM.
WISH THERE WAS ANOTHER WORD FOR IT.
WEEEROOOO WOOOP WOOOP WEEROOOO HONK HONK
TAXI, MISS?
NAH. NO THANKS!
OYE, YOSELY!
MAYBE I NEED TO MAKE UP MY OWN.
238TH AND WHITE PLAINS ROAD, BRONX, NY

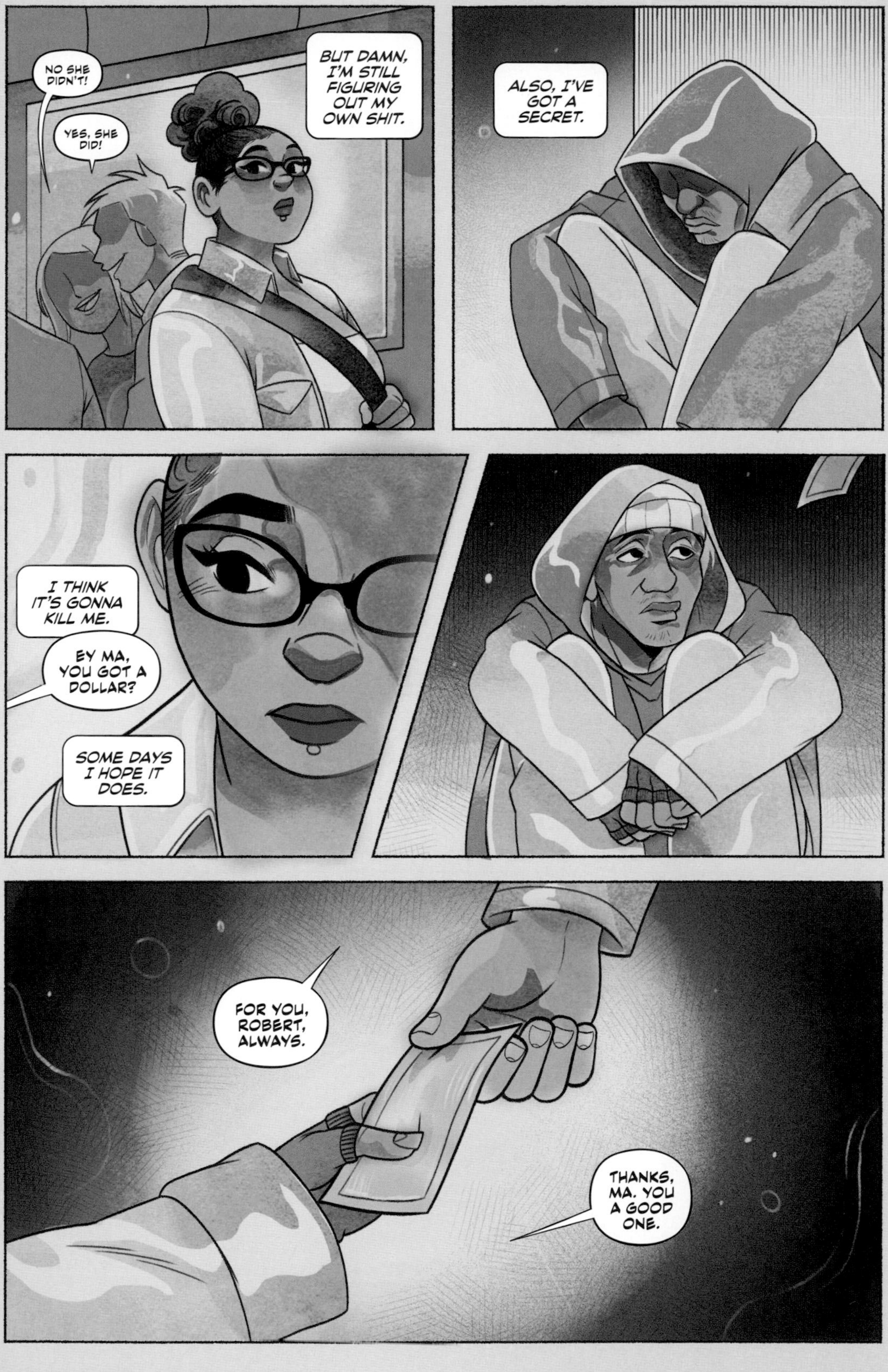
NO SHE DIDN'T!
YES, SHE DID!
BUT DAMN, I'M STILL FIGURING OUT MY OWN SHIT.
ALSO, I'VE GOT A SECRET.
I THINK IT'S GONNA KILL ME.
EY MA, YOU GOT A DOLLAR?
SOME DAYS I HOPE IT DOES.
FOR YOU, ROBERT, ALWAYS.
THANKS, MA. YOU A GOOD ONE.

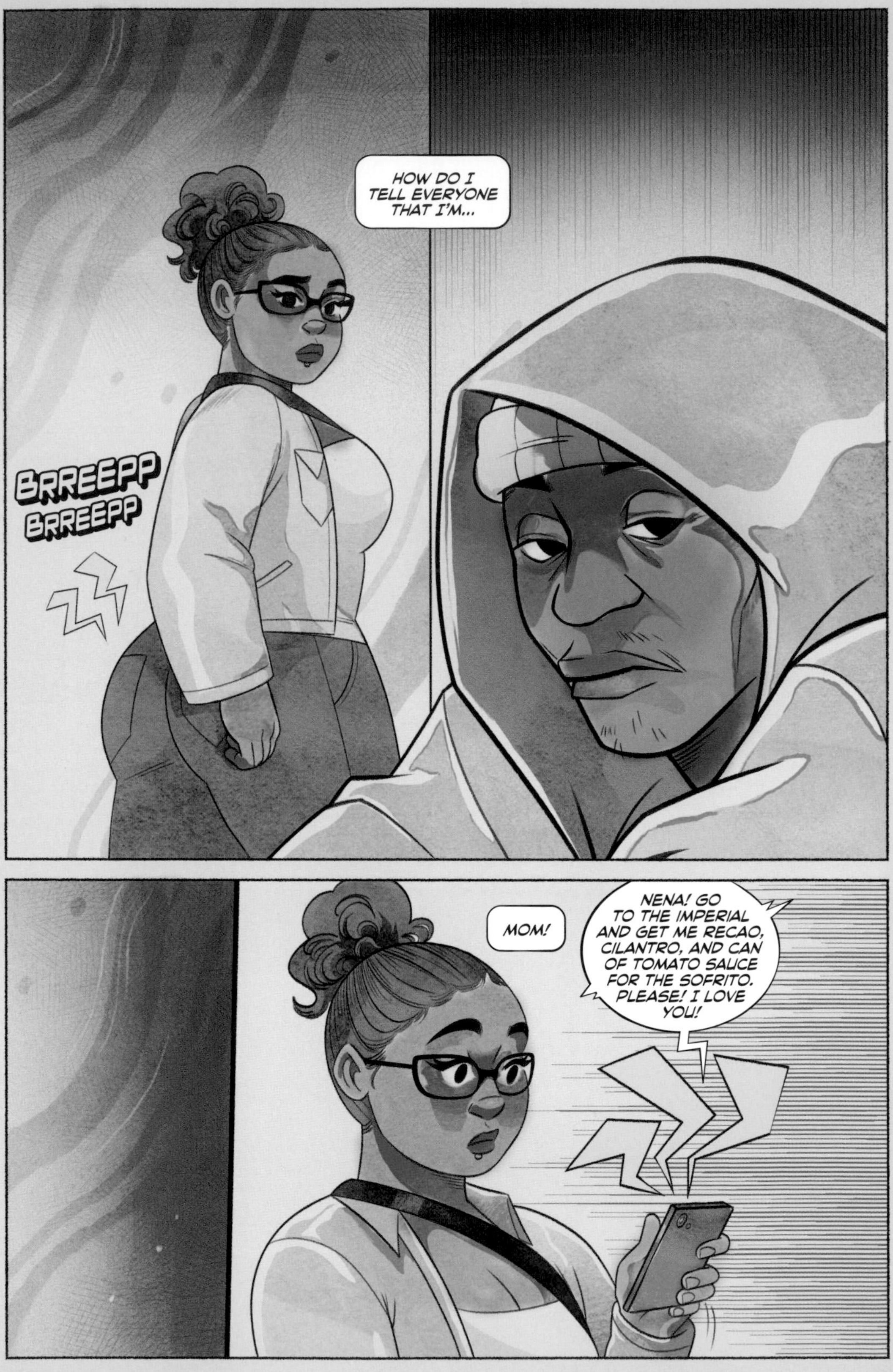
HOW DO I TELL EVERYONE THAT I'M...
BRREEPP BRREEPP
MOM!
NENA! GO TO THE IMPERIAL AND GET ME RECAO, CILANTRO, AND CAN OF TOMATO SAUCE FOR THE SOFRITO. PLEASE! I LOVE YOU!

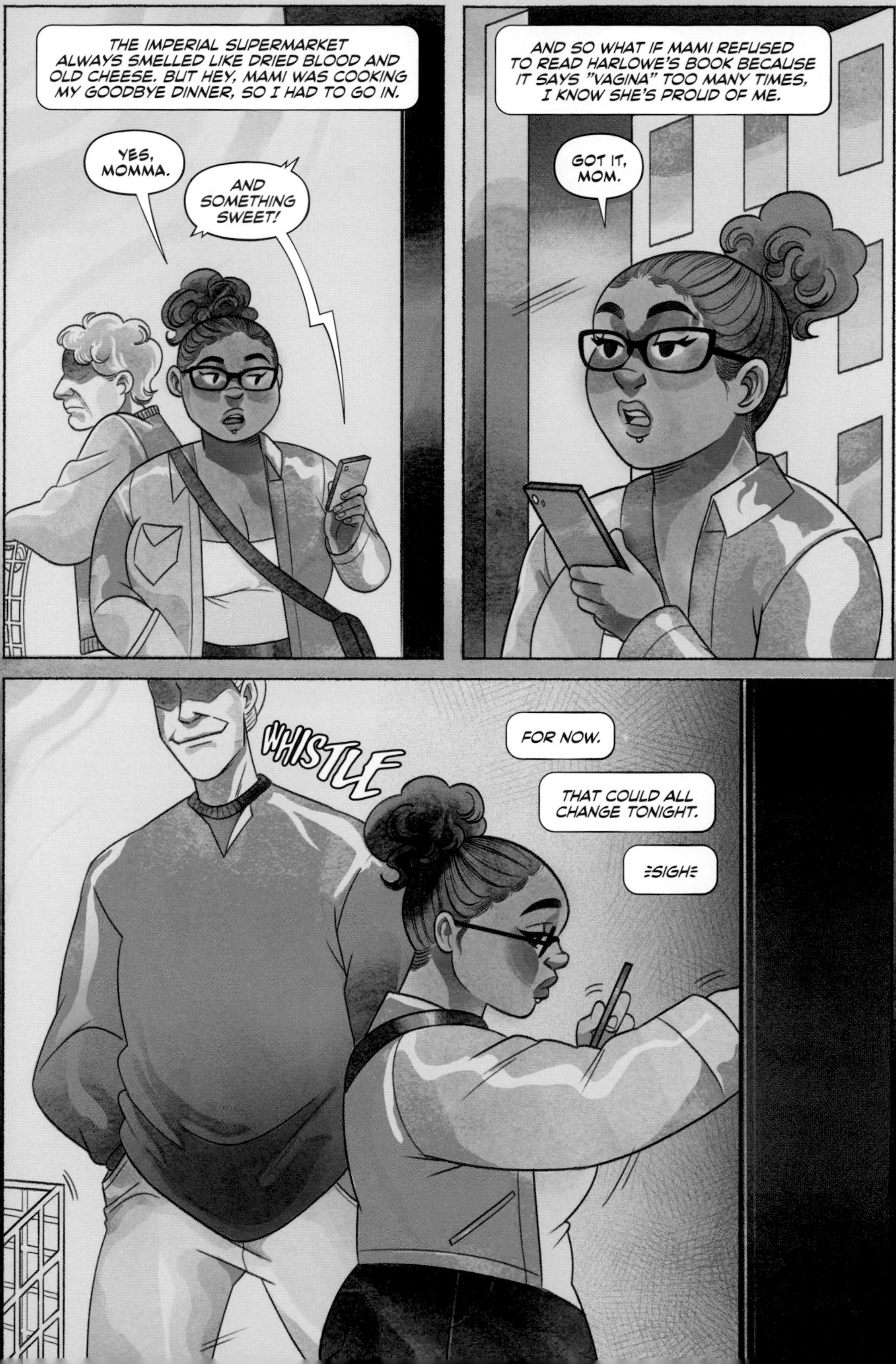
THE IMPERIAL SUPERMARKET ALWAYS SMELLED LIKE DRIED BLOOD AND OLD CHEESE. BUT HEY, MAMI WAS COOKING MY GOODBYE DINNER, SO I HAD TO GO IN.
YES, MOMMA.
AND SOMETHING SWEET!
AND SO WHAT IF MAMI REFUSED TO READ HARLOWE'S BOOK BECAUSE IT SAYS "VAGINA" TOO MANY TIMES, I KNOW SHE'S PROUD OF ME.
GOT IT, MOM.
WHISTLE
FOR NOW.
THAT COULD ALL CHANGE TONIGHT.
SIGH

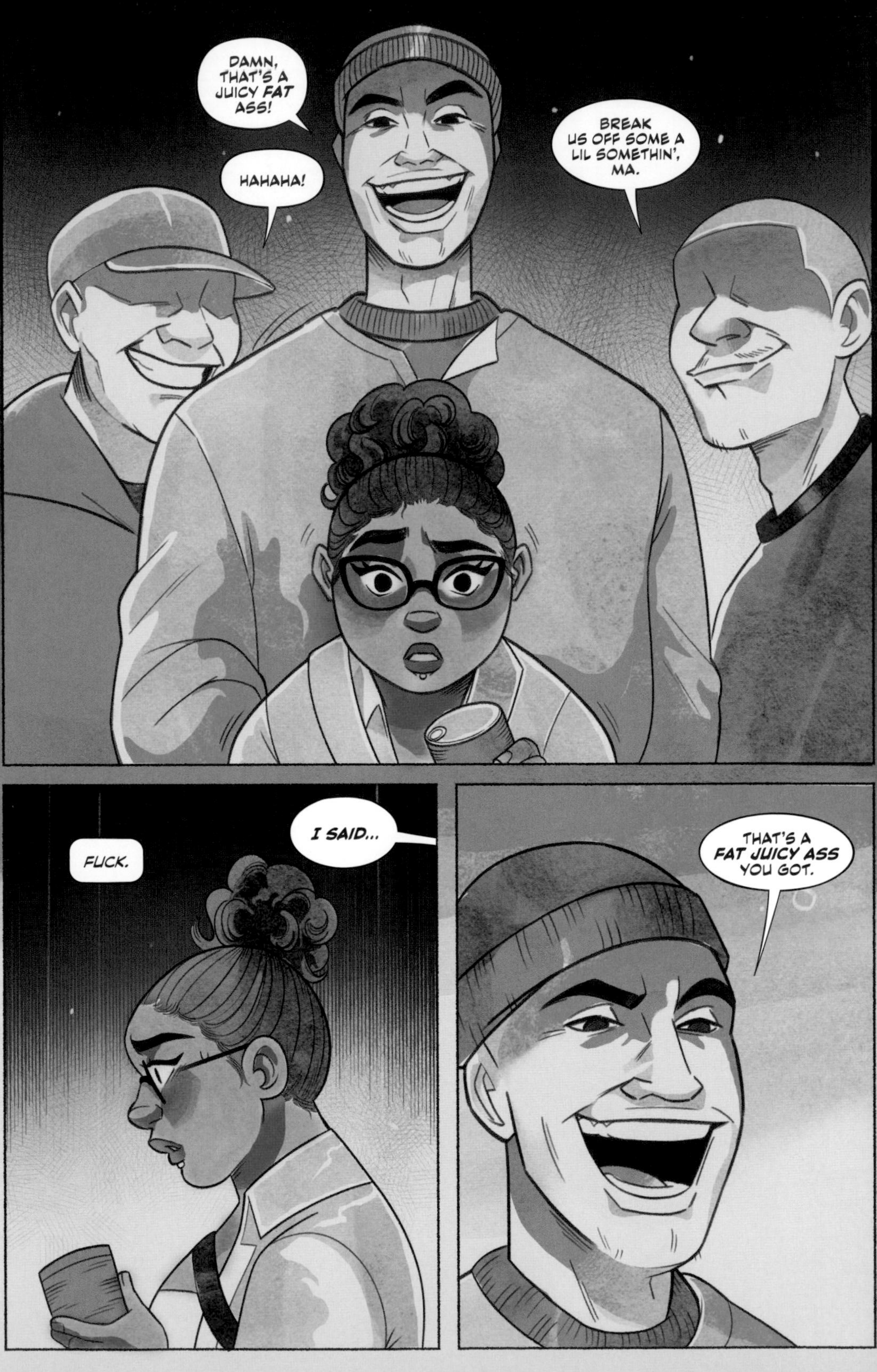
DAMN, THAT'S A JUICY *FAT* ASS!
HAHAHA!
BREAK US OFF SOME A LIL SOMETHIN', MA.
FUCK.
I SAID...
THAT'S A **FAT JUICY ASS** YOU GOT.

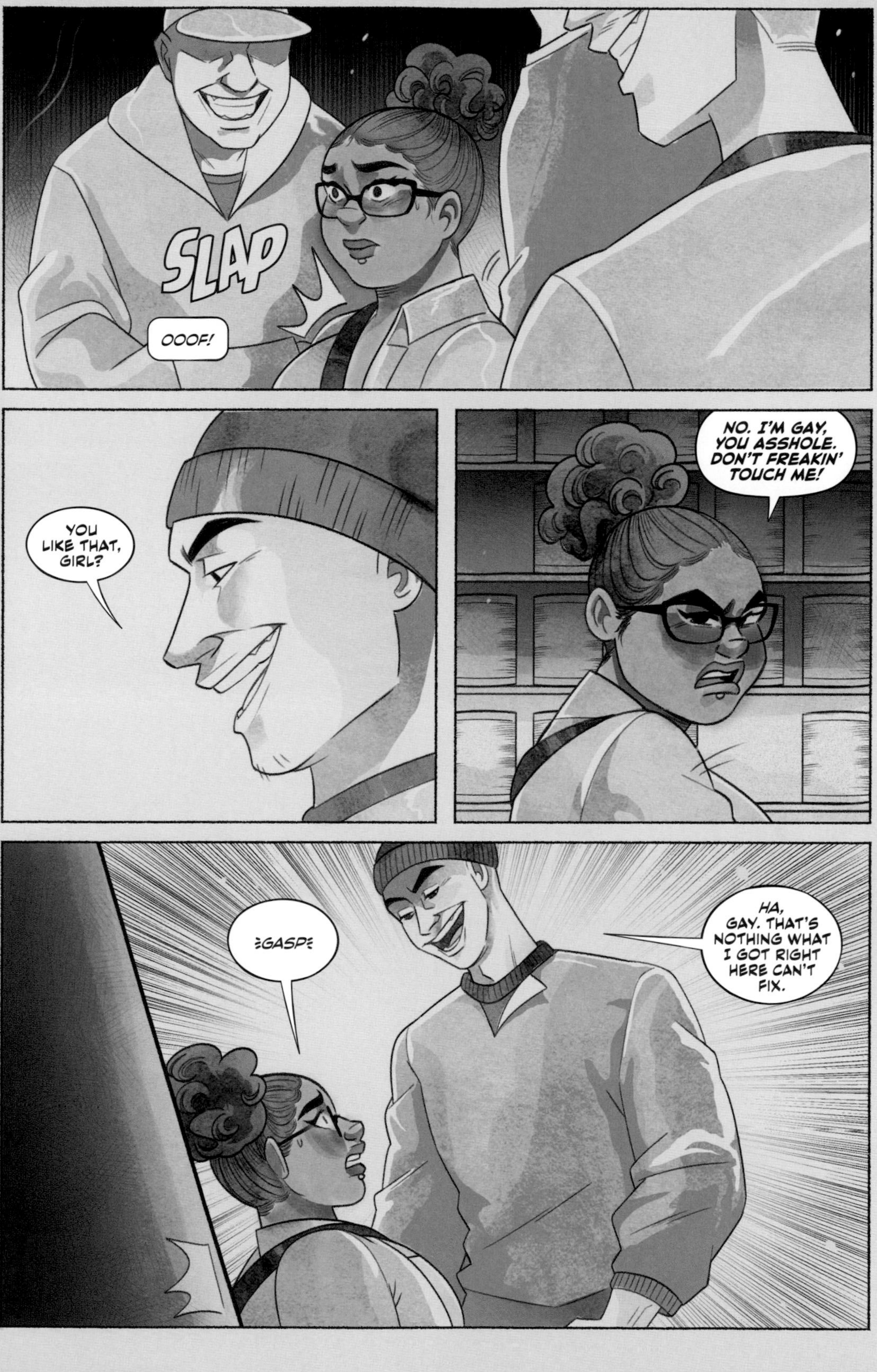
SLAP
OOOF!
YOU LIKE THAT, GIRL?
NO. I'M GAY, YOU ASSHOLE. DON'T FREAKIN' TOUCH ME!
GASP
HA, GAY. THAT'S NOTHING WHAT I GOT RIGHT HERE CAN'T FIX.

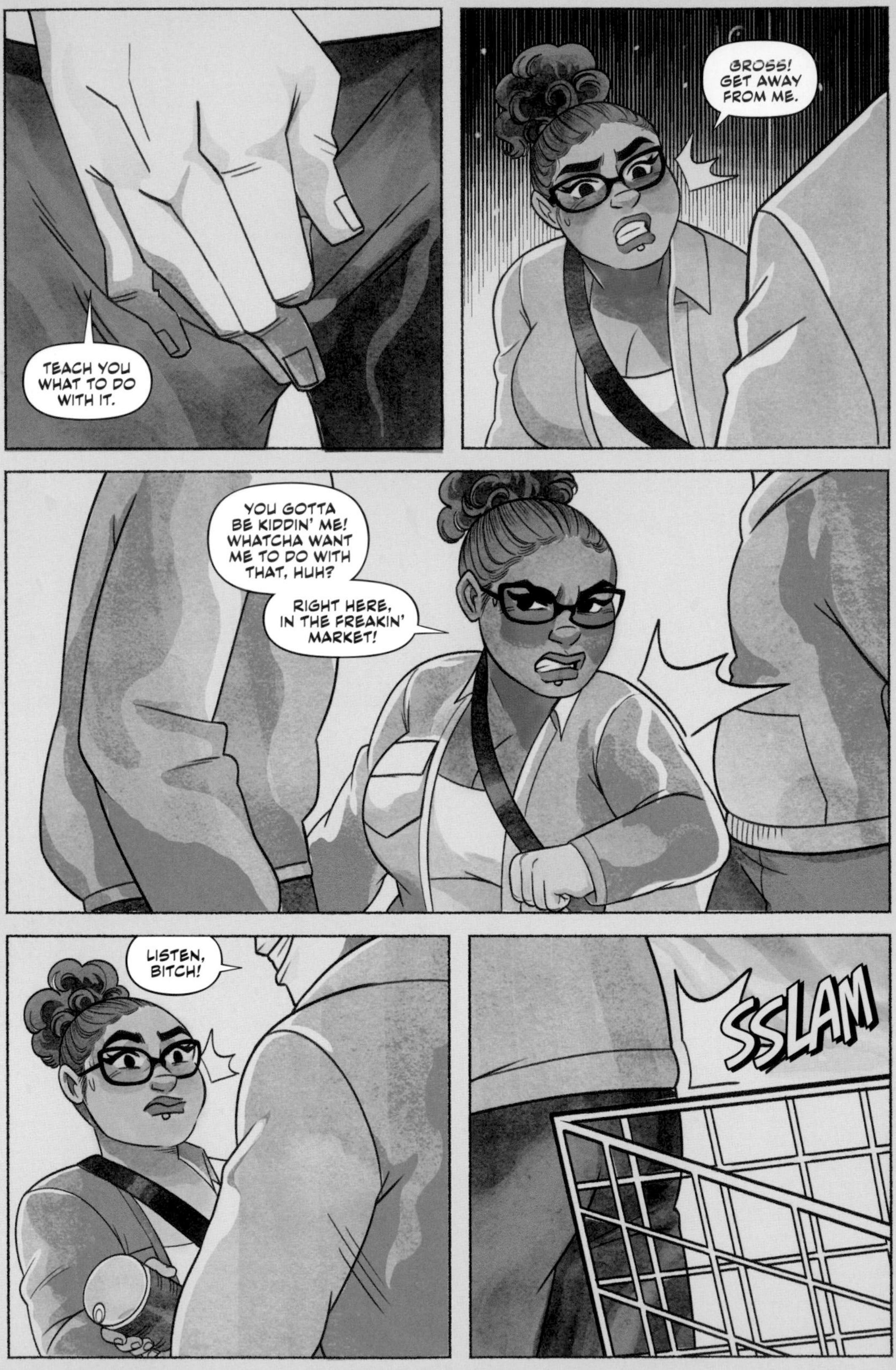
TEACH YOU WHAT TO DO WITH IT.
GROSS! GET AWAY FROM ME.
YOU GOTTA BE KIDDIN' ME! WHATCHA WANT ME TO DO WITH THAT, HUH?
RIGHT HERE, IN THE FREAKIN' MARKET!
LISTEN, BITCH!
SSLAM

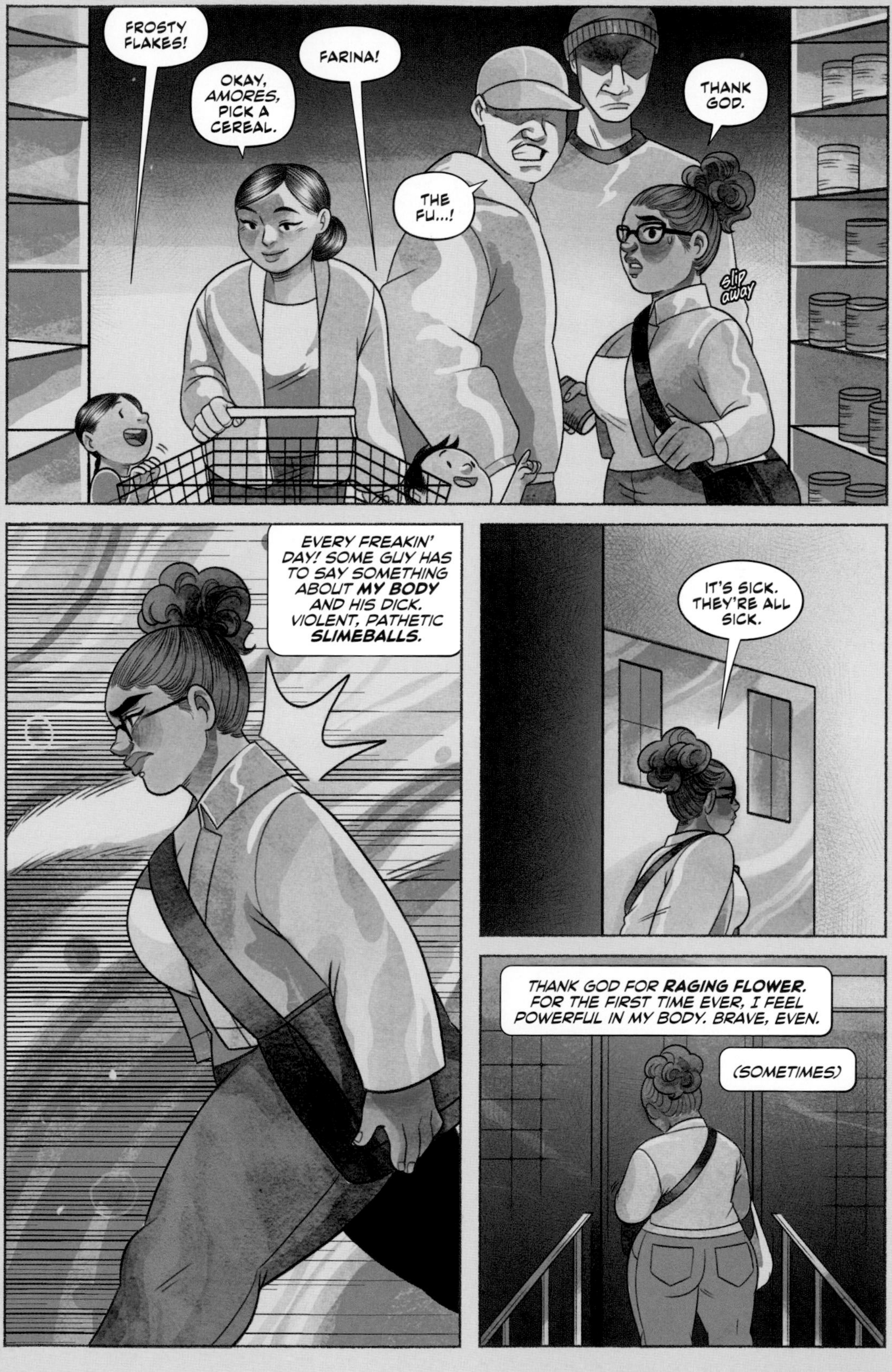
FROSTY FLAKES!
OKAY, AMORES, PICK A CEREAL.
FARINA!
THE FU...!
THANK GOD.
slip away
EVERY FREAKIN' DAY! SOME GUY HAS TO SAY SOMETHING ABOUT **MY BODY** AND HIS DICK. VIOLENT, PATHETIC **SLIMEBALLS.**
IT'S SICK. THEY'RE ALL SICK.
THANK GOD FOR **RAGING FLOWER.** FOR THE FIRST TIME EVER, I FEEL POWERFUL IN MY BODY. BRAVE, EVEN.
(SOMETIMES)

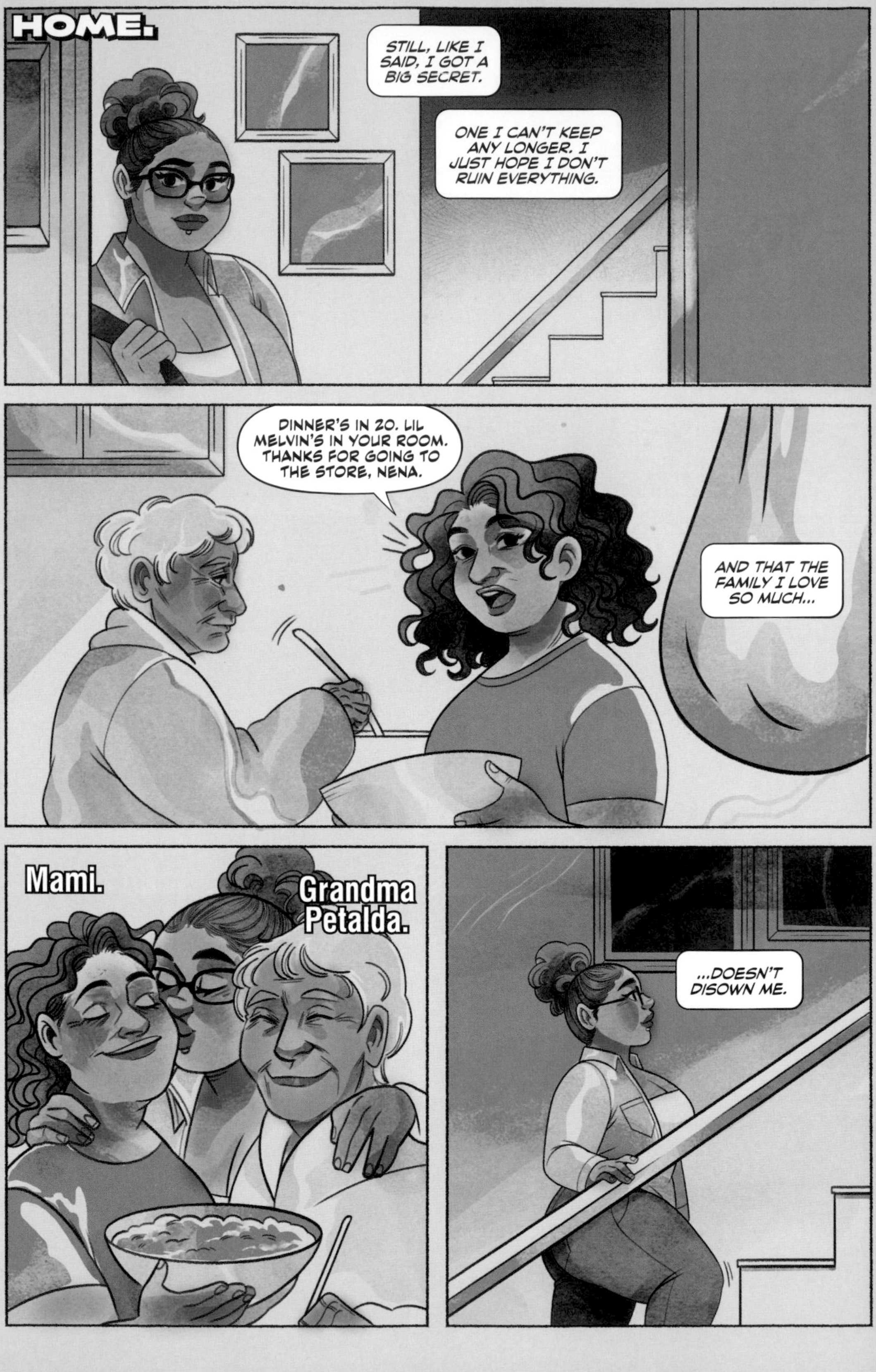
HOME.
STILL, LIKE I SAID, I GOT A BIG SECRET.
ONE I CAN'T KEEP ANY LONGER. I JUST HOPE I DON'T RUIN EVERYTHING.
DINNER'S IN 20. LIL MELVIN'S IN YOUR ROOM. THANKS FOR GOING TO THE STORE, NENA.
AND THAT THE FAMILY I LOVE SO MUCH...
Mami.
Grandma Petalda.
...DOESN'T DISOWN ME.

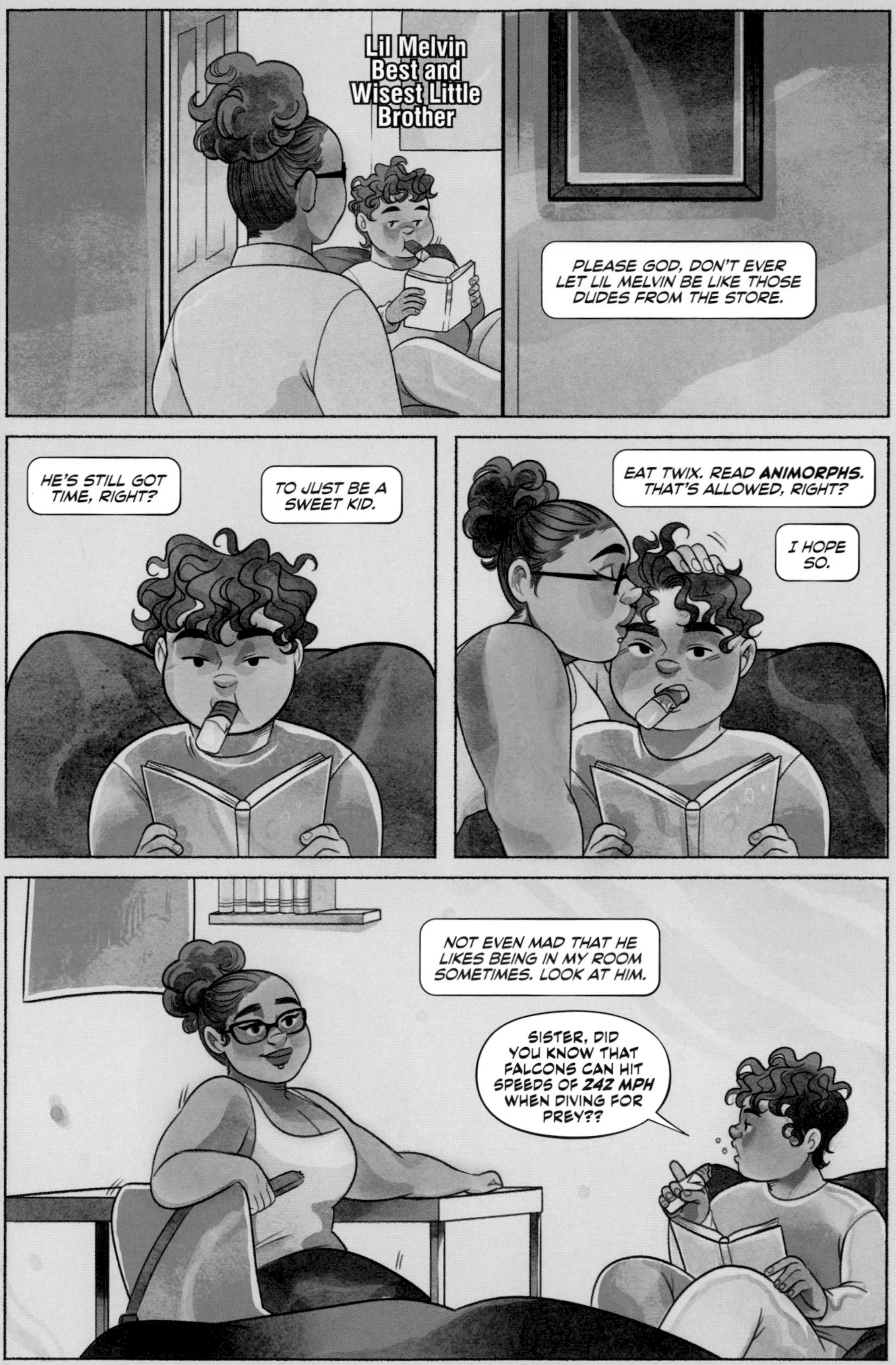
Lil Melvin
Best and
Wisest Little
Brother
PLEASE GOD, DON'T EVER LET LIL MELVIN BE LIKE THOSE DUDES FROM THE STORE.
HE'S STILL GOT TIME, RIGHT?
TO JUST BE A SWEET KID.
EAT TWIX. READ ANIMORPHS. THAT'S ALLOWED, RIGHT?
I HOPE SO.
NOT EVEN MAD THAT HE LIKES BEING IN MY ROOM SOMETIMES. LOOK AT HIM.
SISTER, DID YOU KNOW THAT FALCONS CAN HIT SPEEDS OF 242 MPH WHEN DIVING FOR PREY??

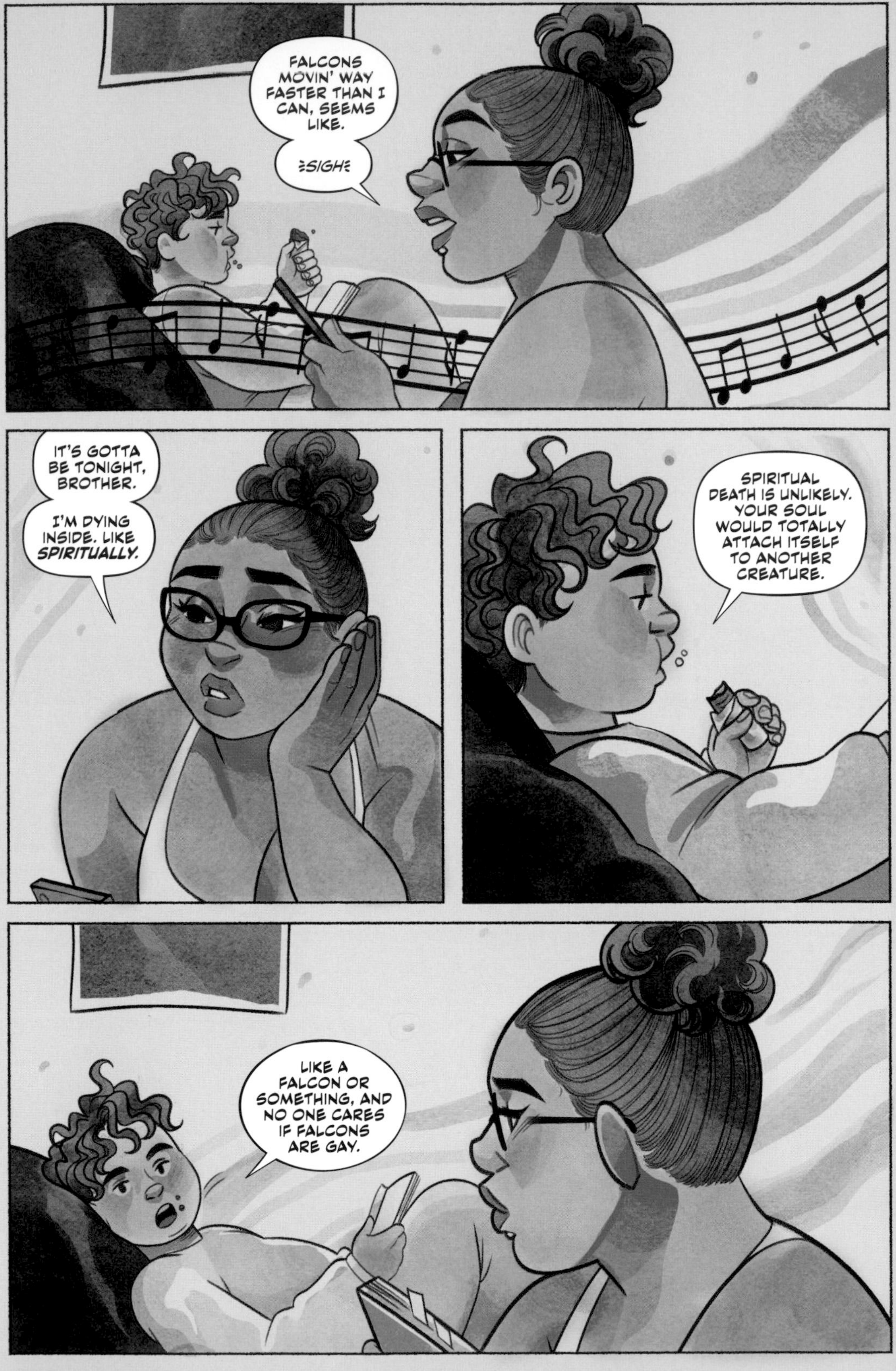
FALCONS MOVIN' WAY FASTER THAN I CAN, SEEMS LIKE.
≷SIGH≶
IT'S GOTTA BE TONIGHT, BROTHER.
I'M DYING INSIDE. LIKE *SPIRITUALLY.*
SPIRITUAL DEATH IS UNLIKELY. YOUR SOUL WOULD TOTALLY ATTACH ITSELF TO ANOTHER CREATURE.
LIKE A FALCON OR SOMETHING, AND NO ONE CARES IF FALCONS ARE GAY.

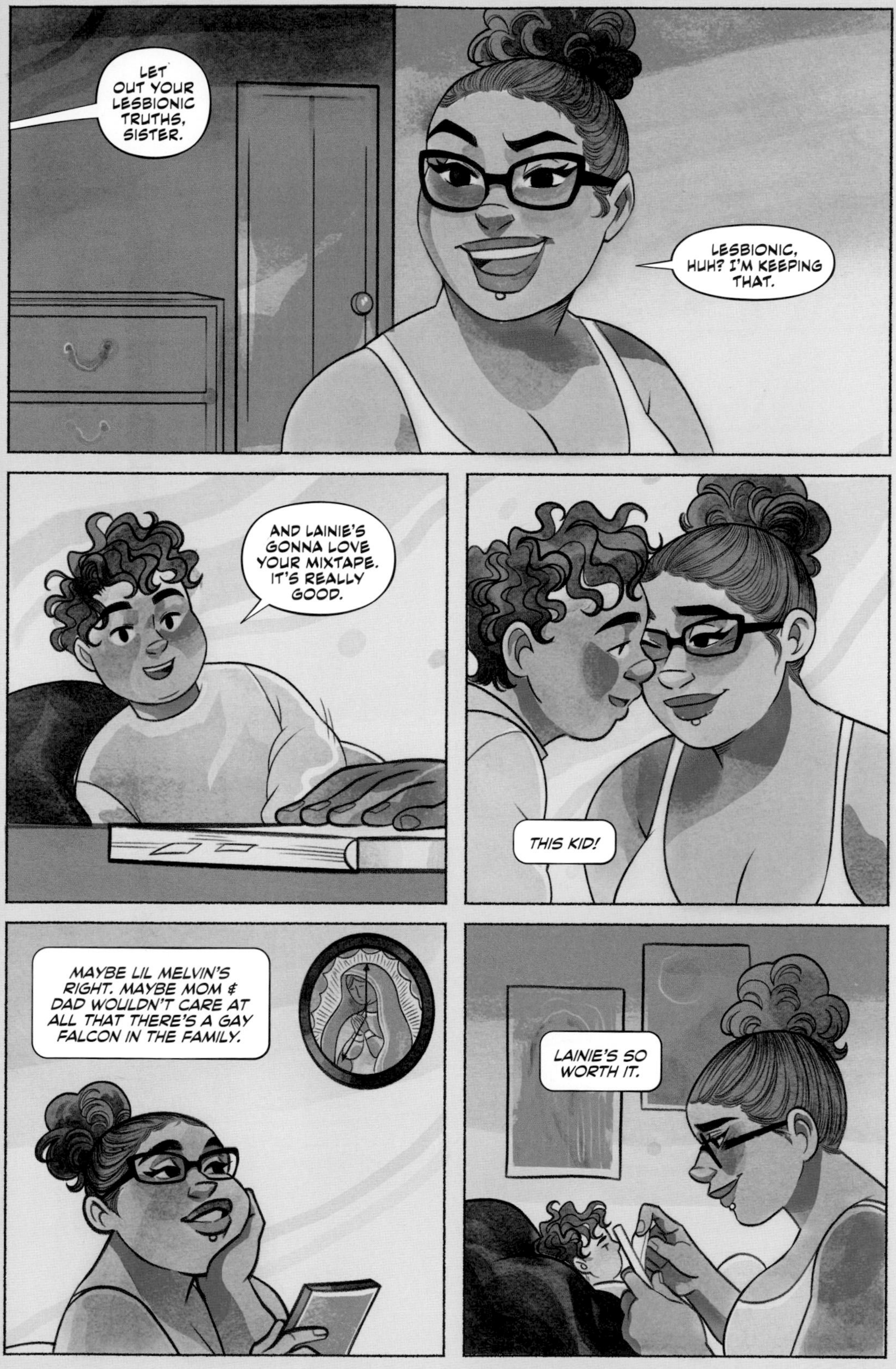
LET OUT YOUR LESBIONIC TRUTHS, SISTER.
LESBIONIC, HUH? I'M KEEPING THAT.
AND LAINIE'S GONNA LOVE YOUR MIXTAPE. IT'S REALLY GOOD.
THIS KID!
MAYBE LIL MELVIN'S RIGHT. MAYBE MOM & DAD WOULDN'T CARE AT ALL THAT THERE'S A GAY FALCON IN THE FAMILY.
LAINIE'S SO WORTH IT.

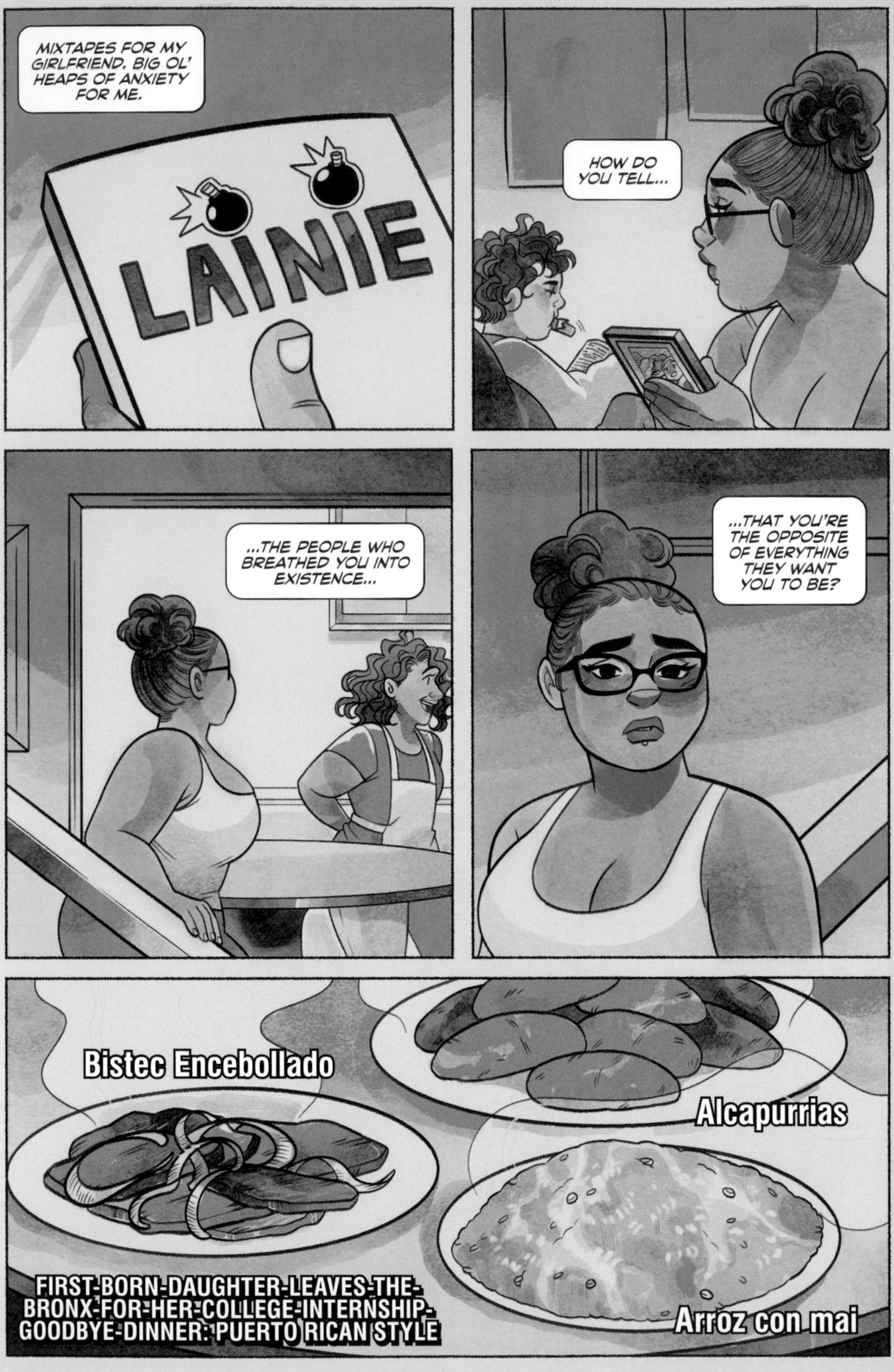
MIXTAPES FOR MY GIRLFRIEND. BIG OL' HEAPS OF ANXIETY FOR ME.
LAINIE
HOW DO YOU TELL...
...THE PEOPLE WHO BREATHED YOU INTO EXISTENCE...
...THAT YOU'RE THE OPPOSITE OF EVERYTHING THEY WANT YOU TO BE?
Bistec Encebollado
Alcapurrias
FIRST-BORN-DAUGHTER-LEAVES-THE-BRONX-FOR-HER-COLLEGE-INTERNSHIP-GOODBYE-DINNER: PUERTO RICAN STYLE
Arroz con mai

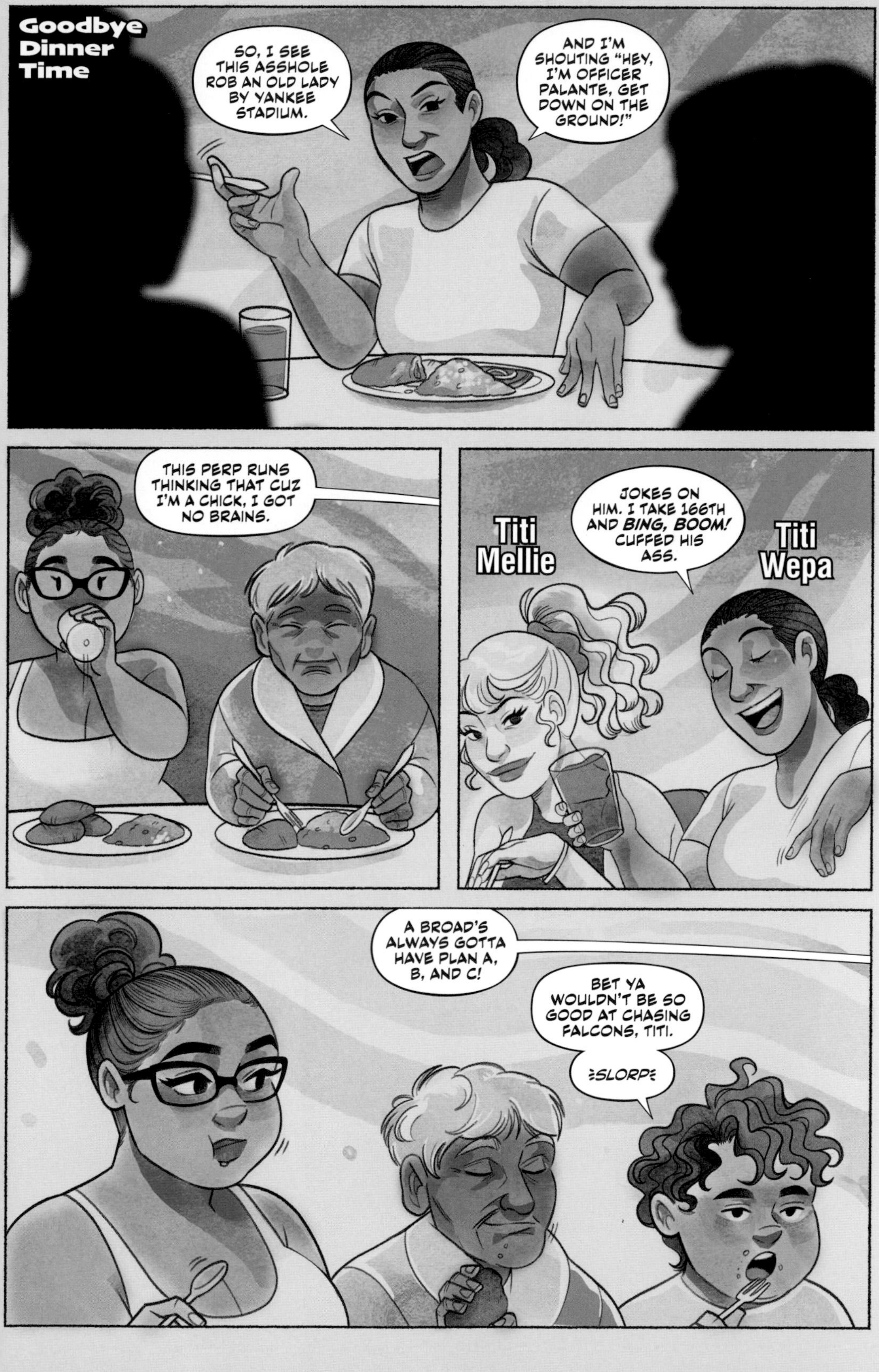

Goodbye Dinner Time
SO, I SEE THIS ASSHOLE ROB AN OLD LADY BY YANKEE STADIUM.
AND I'M SHOUTING "HEY, I'M OFFICER PALANTE, GET DOWN ON THE GROUND!"
THIS PERP RUNS THINKING THAT CUZ I'M A CHICK, I GOT NO BRAINS.
JOKES ON HIM. I TAKE 166TH AND *BING, BOOM!* CUFFED HIS ASS.
Titi Mellie
Titi Wepa
A BROAD'S ALWAYS GOTTA HAVE PLAN A, B, AND C!
BET YA WOULDN'T BE SO GOOD AT CHASING FALCONS, TITI.
SLORP

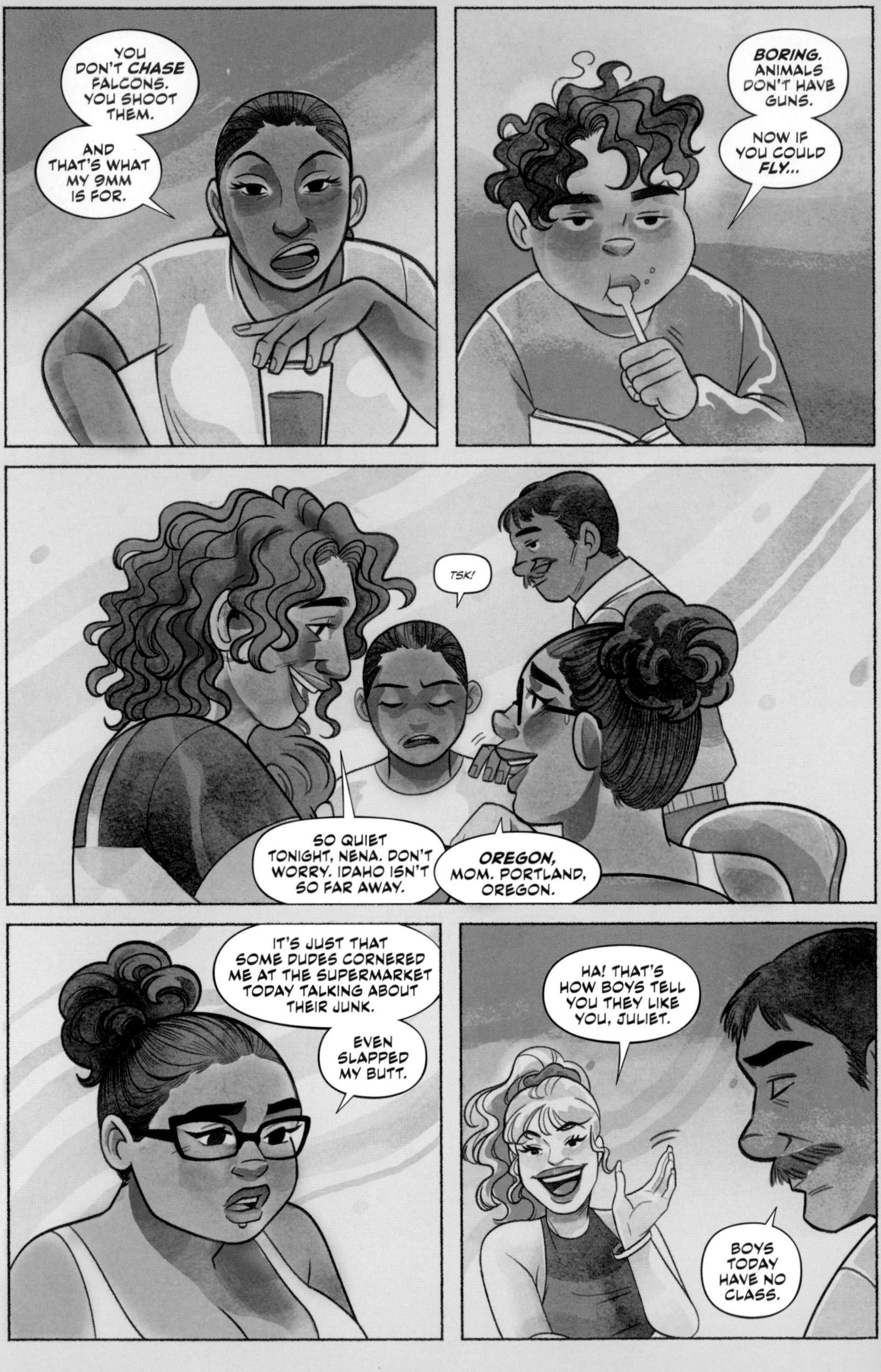

YOU DON'T *CHASE* FALCONS. YOU SHOOT THEM.
AND THAT'S WHAT MY 9MM IS FOR.
BORING. ANIMALS DON'T HAVE GUNS.
NOW IF YOU COULD *FLY...*
TSK!
SO QUIET TONIGHT, NENA. DON'T WORRY. IDAHO ISN'T SO FAR AWAY.
OREGON, MOM. PORTLAND, OREGON.
IT'S JUST THAT SOME DUDES CORNERED ME AT THE SUPERMARKET TODAY TALKING ABOUT THEIR JUNK.
EVEN SLAPPED MY BUTT.
HA! THAT'S HOW BOYS TELL YOU THEY LIKE YOU, JULIET.
BOYS TODAY HAVE NO CLASS.

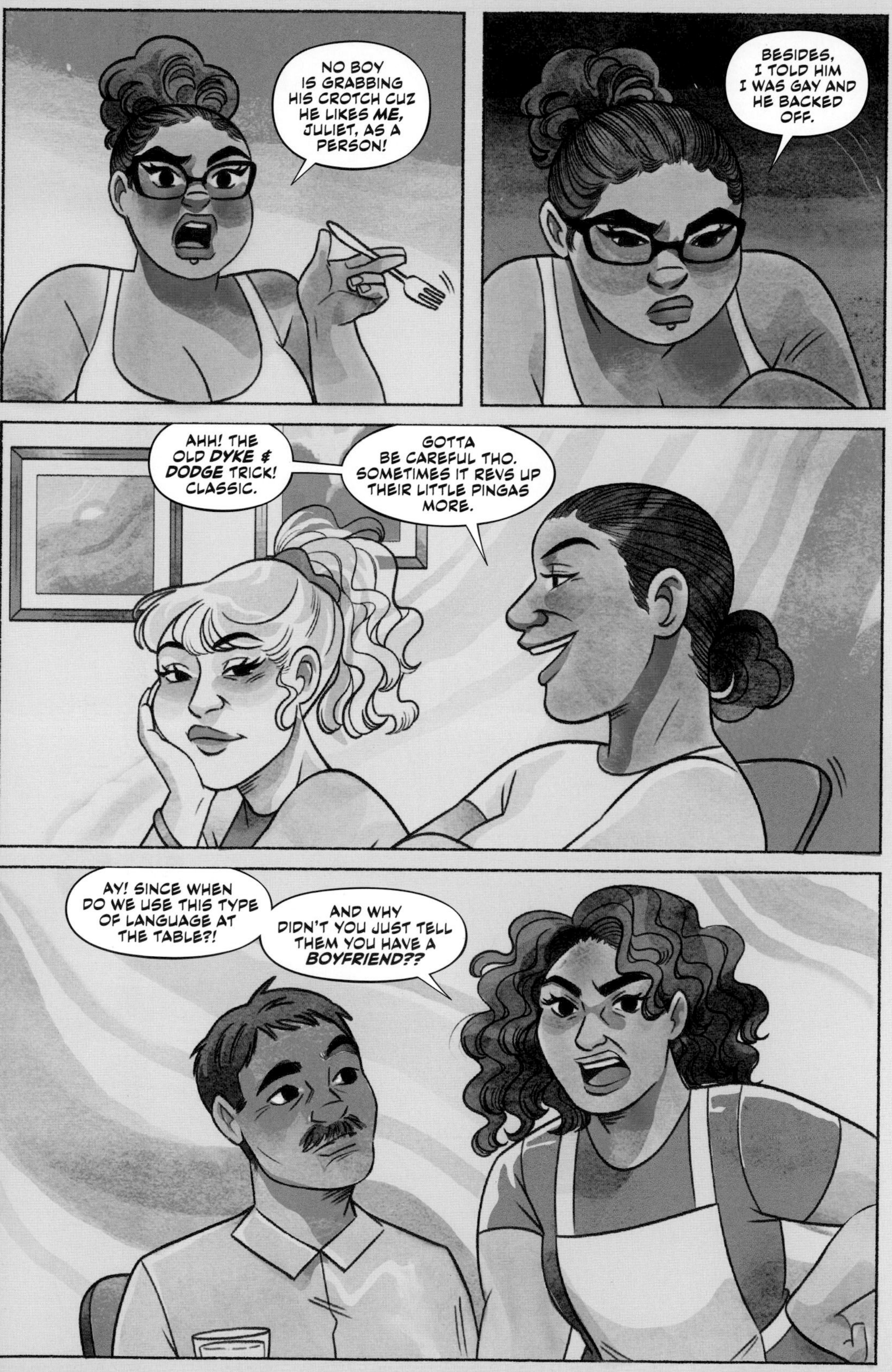
NO BOY IS GRABBING HIS CROTCH CUZ HE LIKES *ME,* JULIET, AS A PERSON!
BESIDES, I TOLD HIM I WAS GAY AND HE BACKED OFF.
AHH! THE OLD *DYKE & DODGE* TRICK! CLASSIC.
GOTTA BE CAREFUL THO. SOMETIMES IT REVS UP THEIR LITTLE PINGAS MORE.
AY! SINCE WHEN DO WE USE THIS TYPE OF LANGUAGE AT THE TABLE?!
AND WHY DIDN'T YOU JUST TELL THEM YOU HAVE A *BOYFRIEND??*

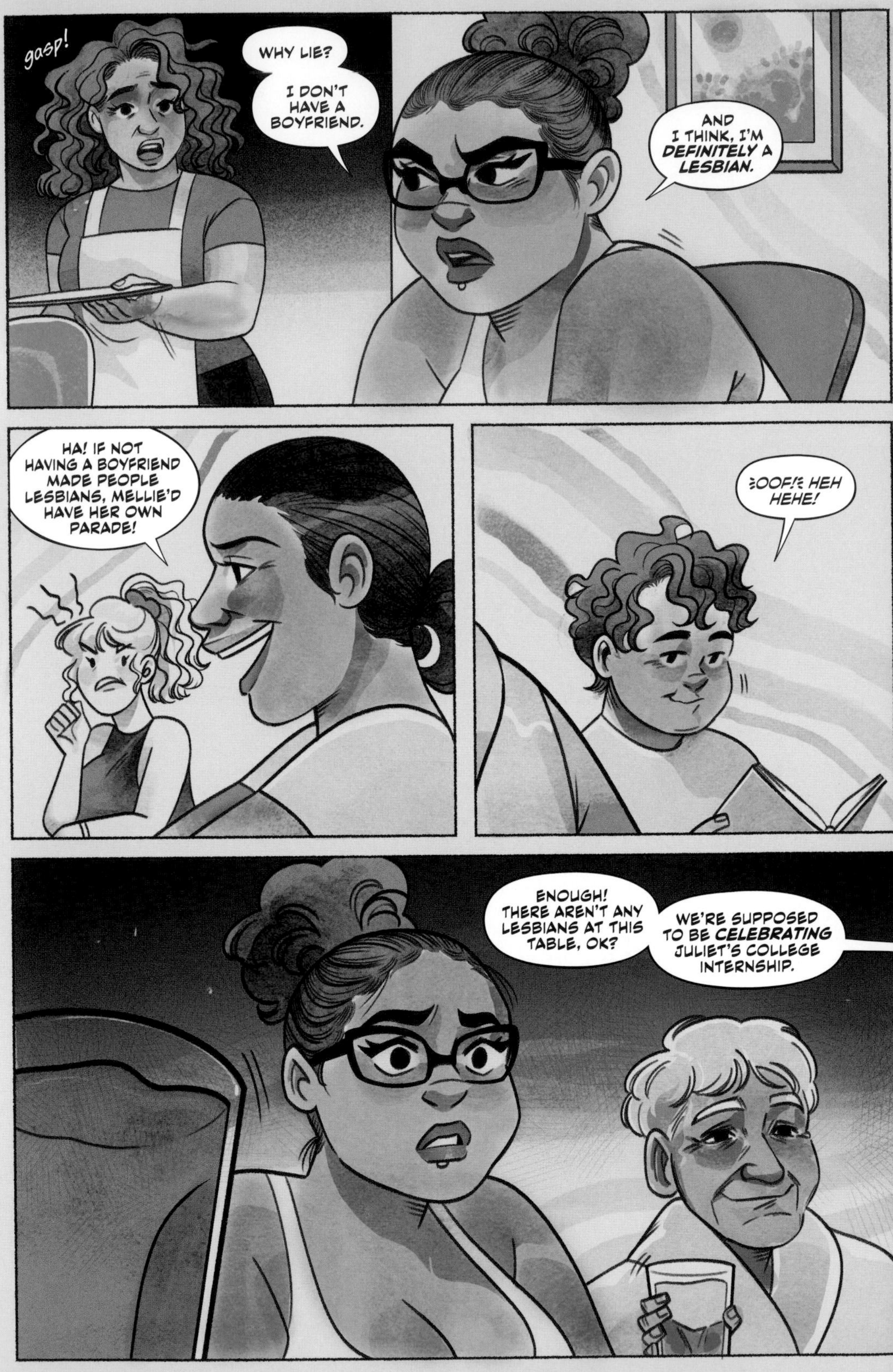
gasp!
WHY LIE?
I DON'T HAVE A BOYFRIEND.
AND I THINK, I'M DEFINITELY A LESBIAN.
HA! IF NOT HAVING A BOYFRIEND MADE PEOPLE LESBIANS, MELLIE'D HAVE HER OWN PARADE!
OOF! HEH HEHE!
ENOUGH! THERE AREN'T ANY LESBIANS AT THIS TABLE, OK?
WE'RE SUPPOSED TO BE CELEBRATING JULIET'S COLLEGE INTERNSHIP.

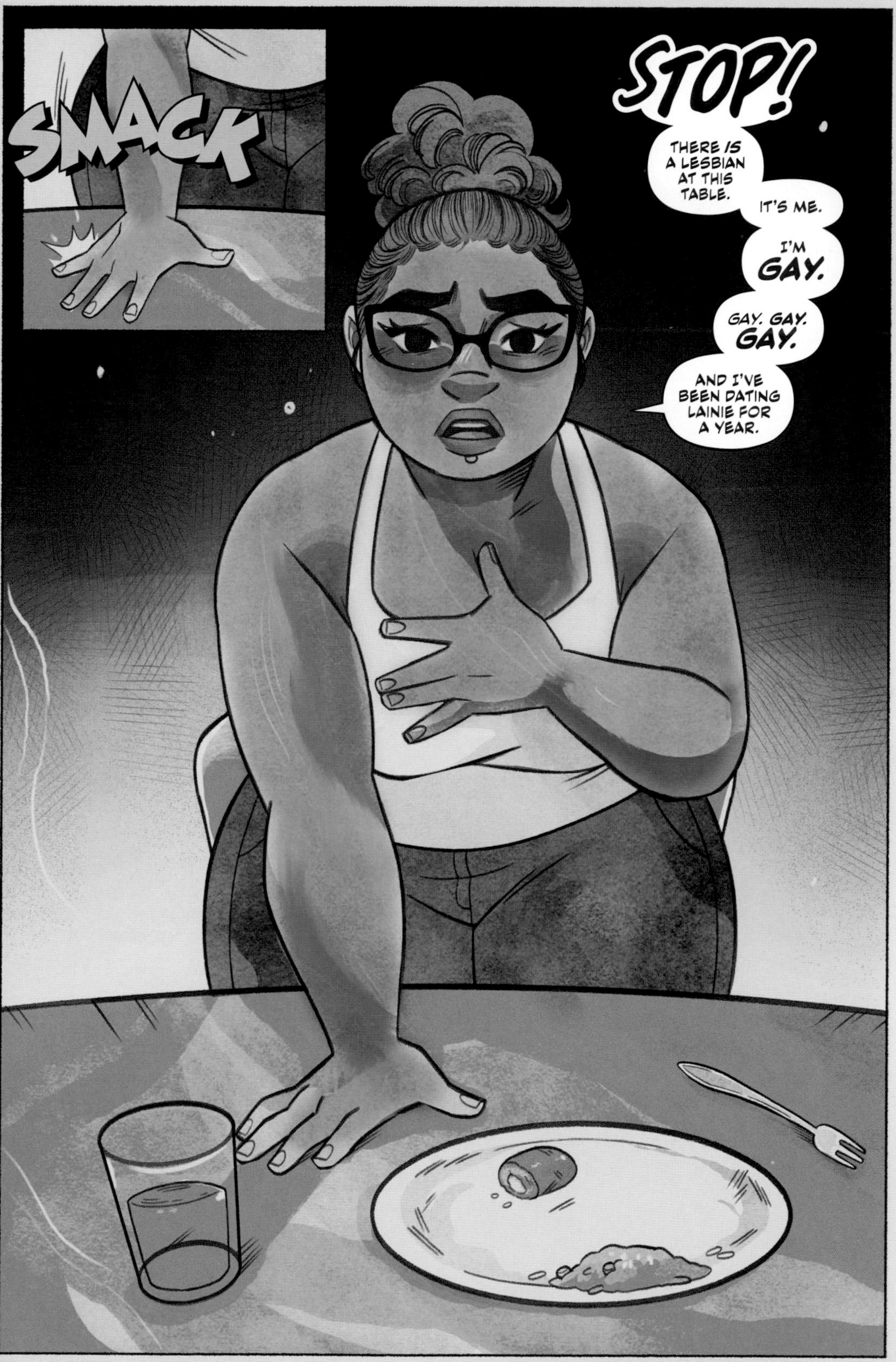
SMACK
STOP!
THERE IS A LESBIAN AT THIS TABLE.
IT'S ME.
I'M GAY.
GAY. GAY. GAY.
AND I'VE BEEN DATING LAINIE FOR A YEAR.

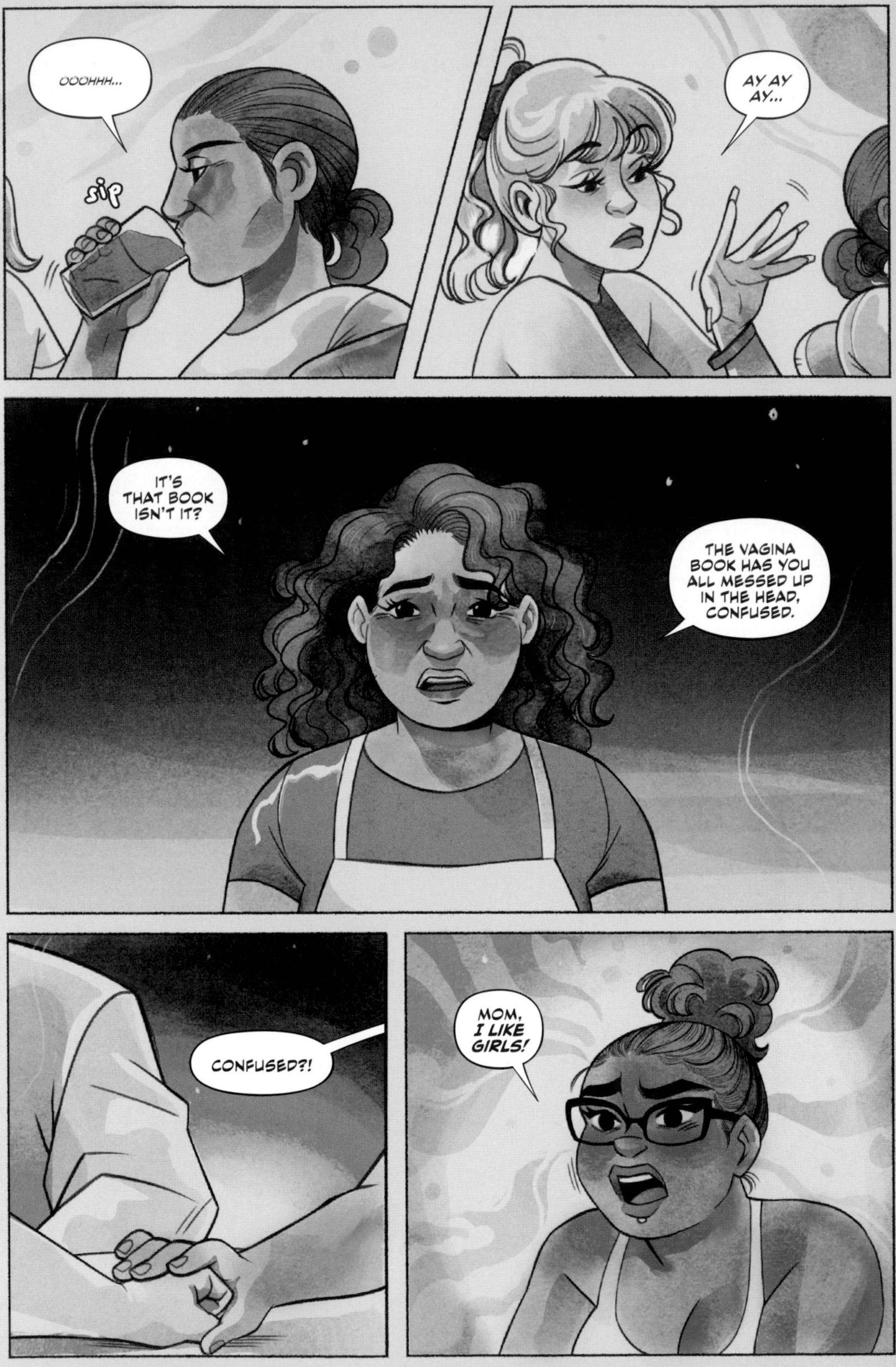
OOOHHH...
sip
AY AY AY...
IT'S THAT BOOK ISN'T IT?
THE VAGINA BOOK HAS YOU ALL MESSED UP IN THE HEAD, CONFUSED.
CONFUSED?!
MOM, I LIKE GIRLS!

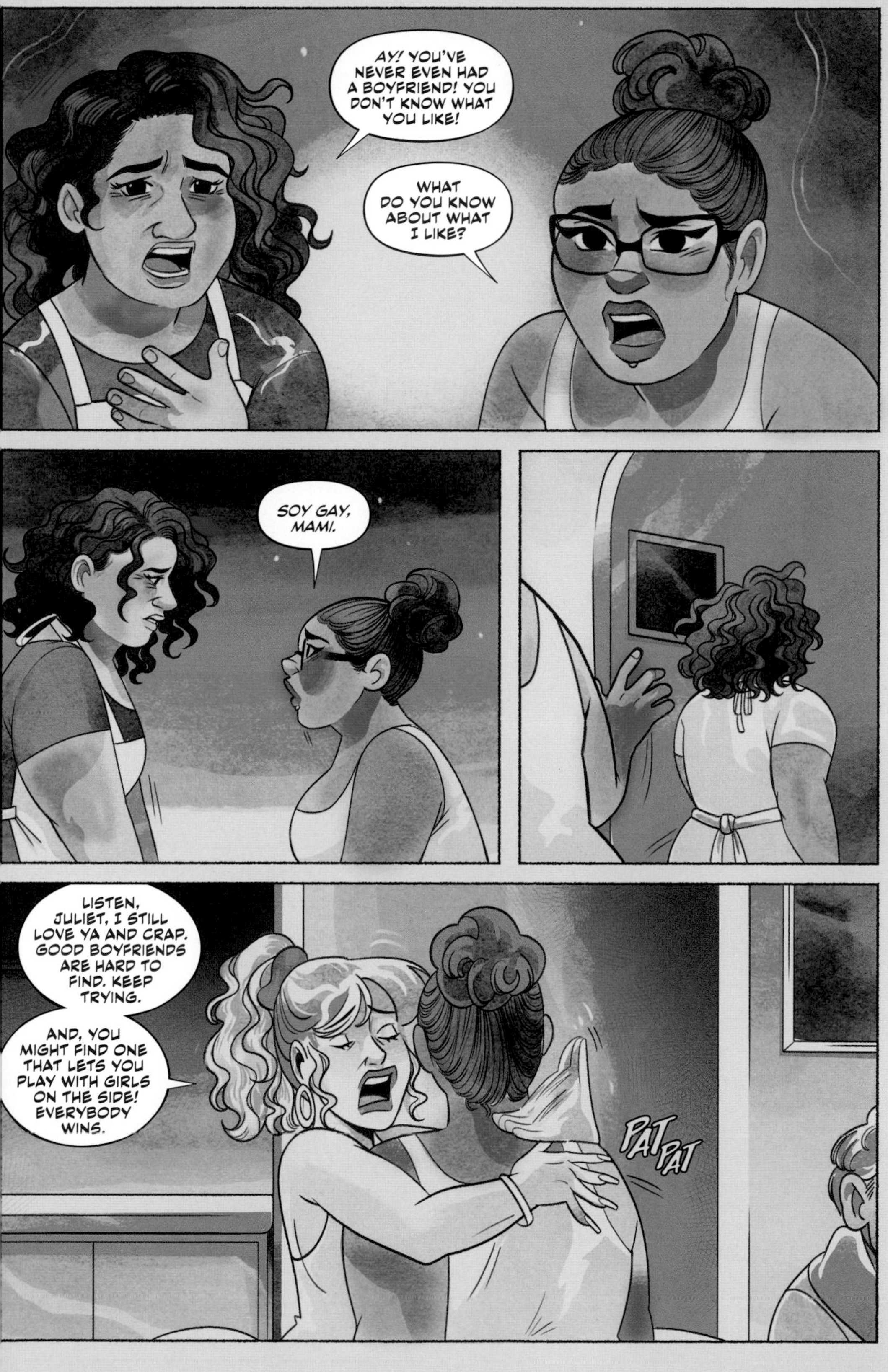
AY! YOU'VE NEVER EVEN HAD A BOYFRIEND! YOU DON'T KNOW WHAT YOU LIKE!
WHAT DO YOU KNOW ABOUT WHAT I LIKE?
SOY GAY, MAMI.
LISTEN, JULIET, I STILL LOVE YA AND CRAP. GOOD BOYFRIENDS ARE HARD TO FIND. KEEP TRYING.
AND, YOU MIGHT FIND ONE THAT LETS YOU PLAY WITH GIRLS ON THE SIDE! EVERYBODY WINS.
PAT PAT

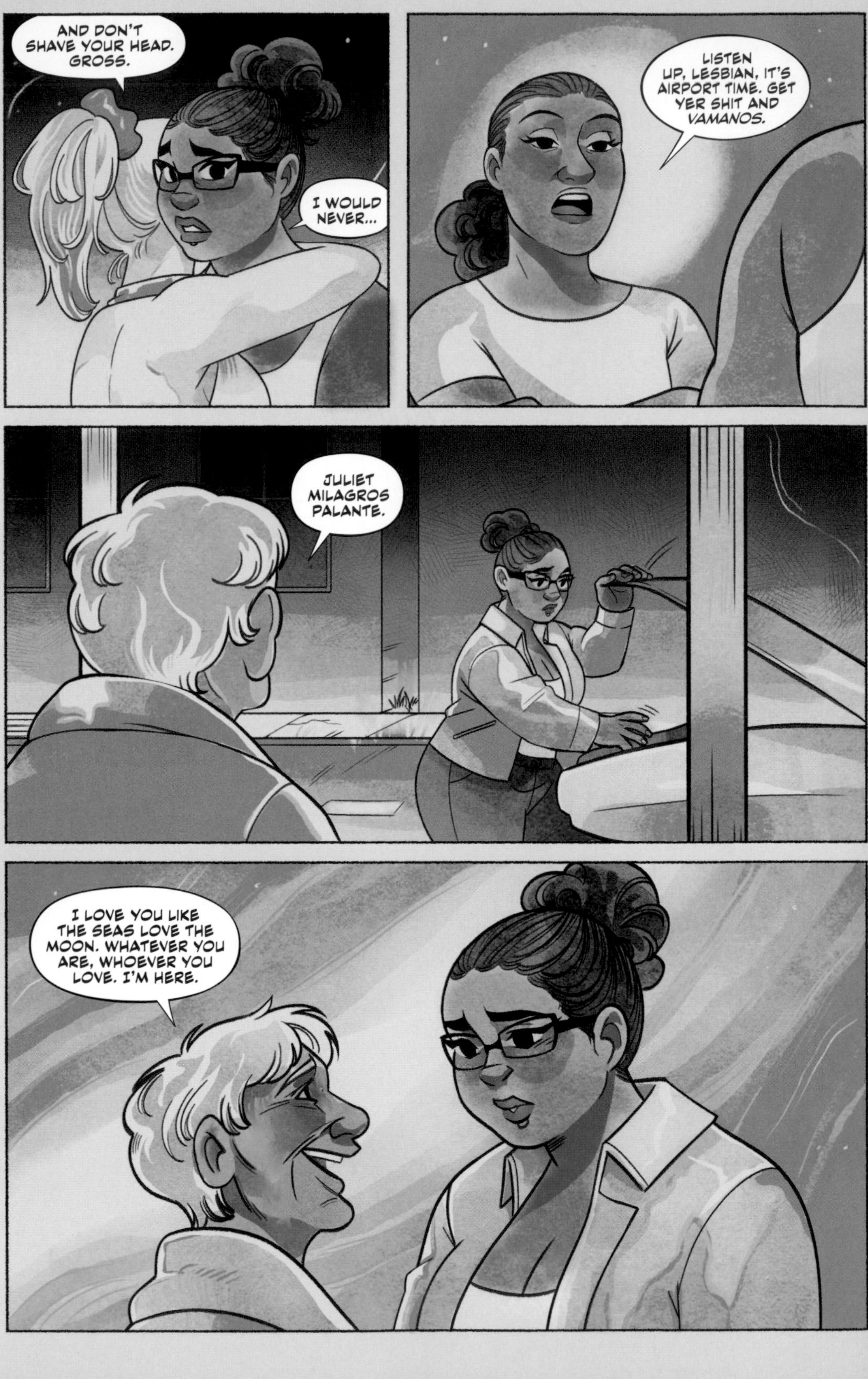
AND DON'T SHAVE YOUR HEAD. GROSS.
I WOULD NEVER...
LISTEN UP, LESBIAN, IT'S AIRPORT TIME. GET YER SHIT AND VAMANOS.
JULIET MILAGROS PALANTE.
I LOVE YOU LIKE THE SEAS LOVE THE MOON. WHATEVER YOU ARE, WHOEVER YOU LOVE. I'M HERE.

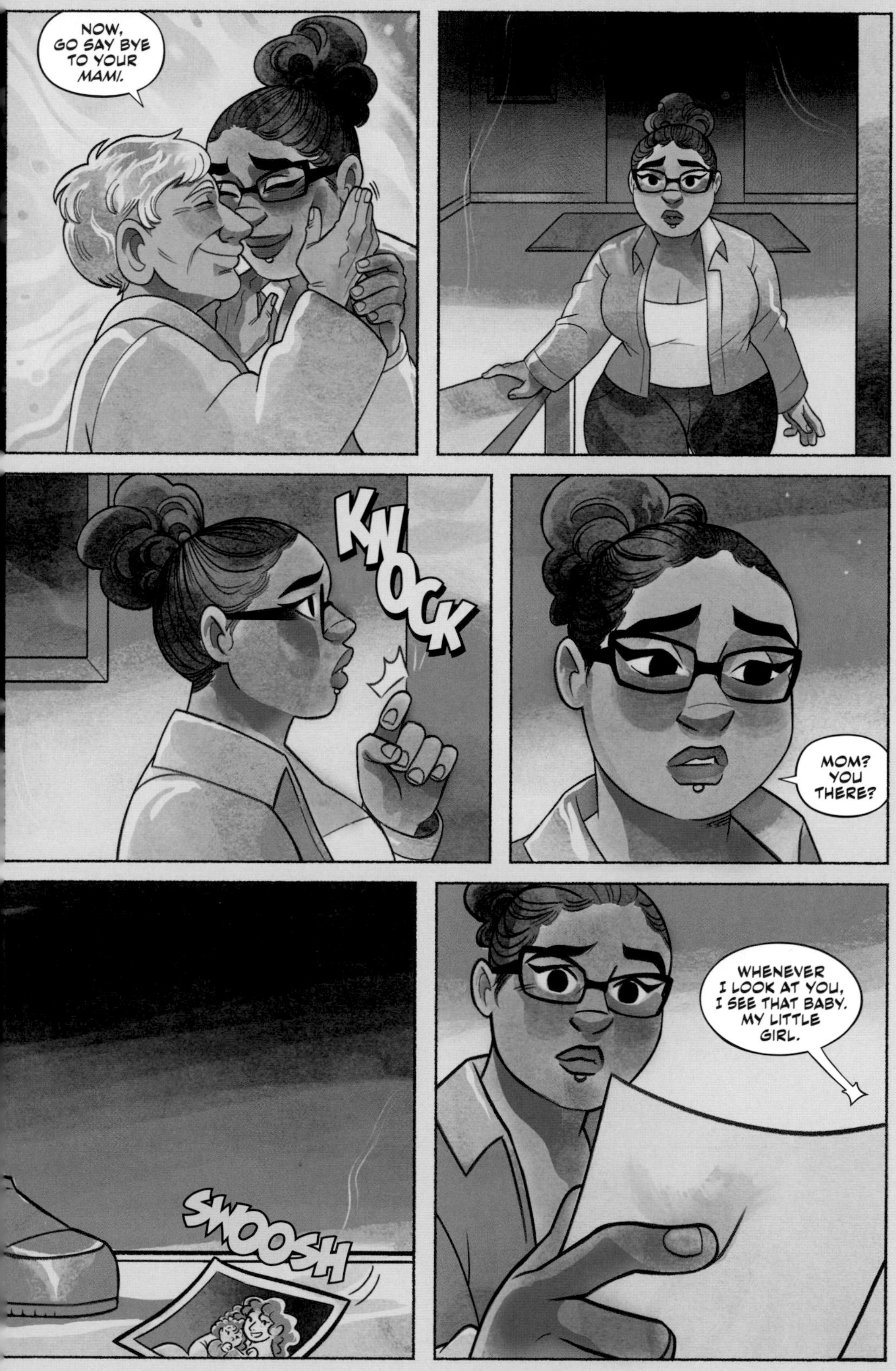
NOW, GO SAY BYE TO YOUR MAMI.
KNOCK
MOM? YOU THERE?
SWOOSH
WHENEVER I LOOK AT YOU, I SEE THAT BABY. MY LITTLE GIRL.

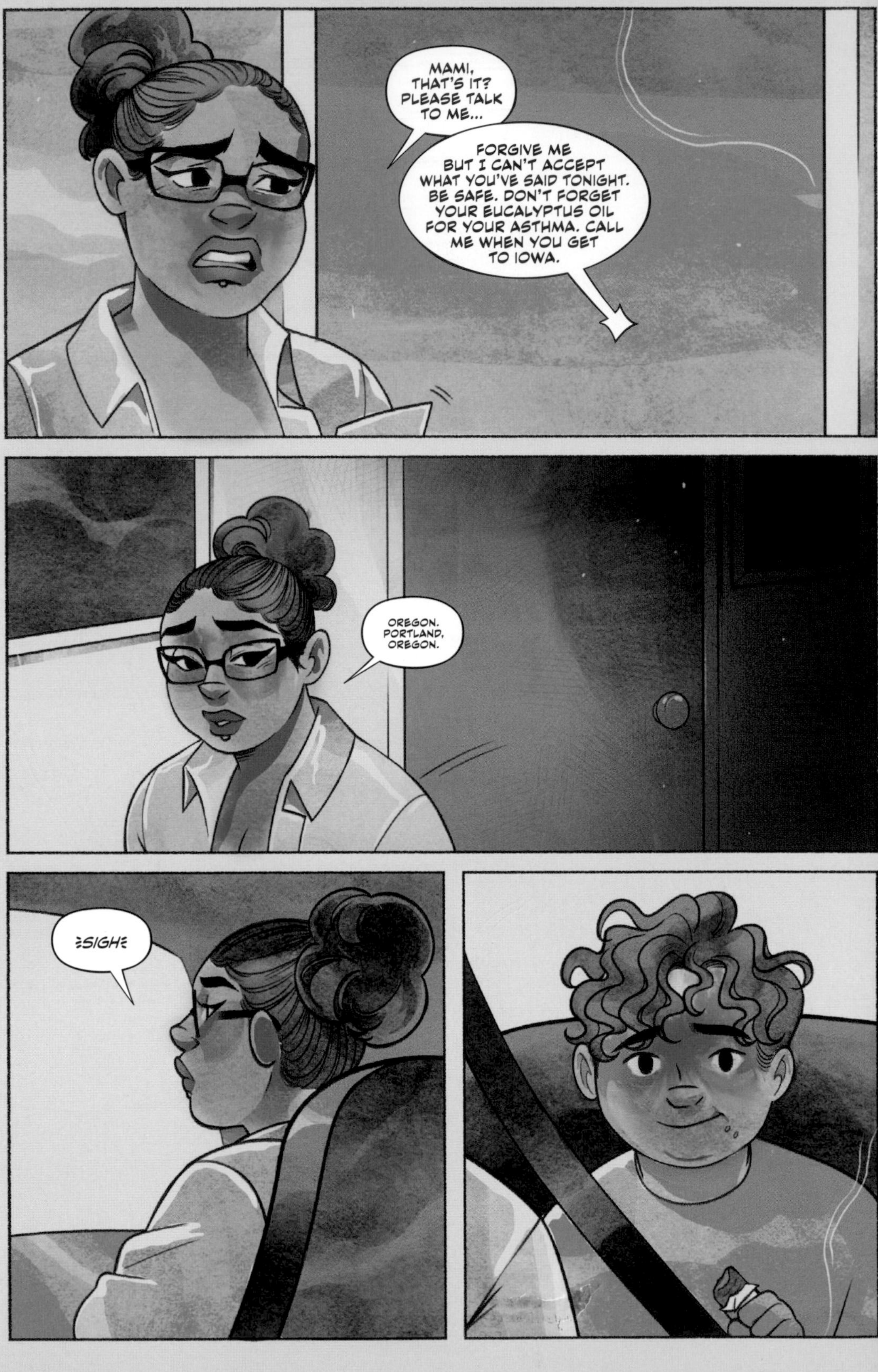
MAMI, THAT'S IT? PLEASE TALK TO ME...
FORGIVE ME BUT I CAN'T ACCEPT WHAT YOU'VE SAID TONIGHT. BE SAFE. DON'T FORGET YOUR EUCALYPTUS OIL FOR YOUR ASTHMA. CALL ME WHEN YOU GET TO IOWA.
OREGON. PORTLAND, OREGON.
SIGH

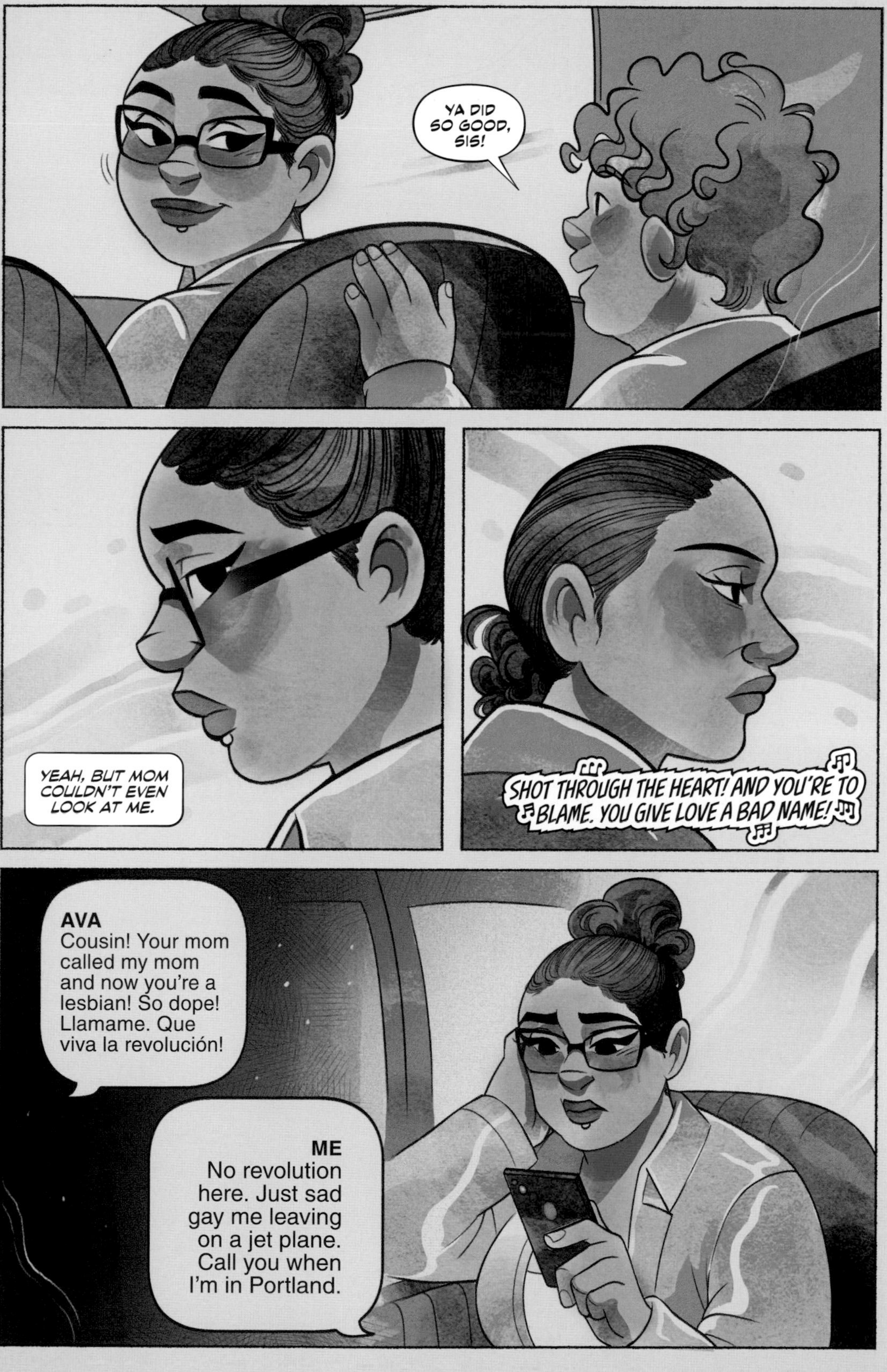
YA DID SO GOOD, SIS!
YEAH, BUT MOM COULDN'T EVEN LOOK AT ME.
SHOT THROUGH THE HEART! AND YOU'RE TO BLAME. YOU GIVE LOVE A BAD NAME!
AVA
Cousin! Your mom called my mom and now you're a lesbian! So dope! Llamame. Que viva la revolución!
ME
No revolution here. Just sad gay me leaving on a jet plane. Call you when I'm in Portland.

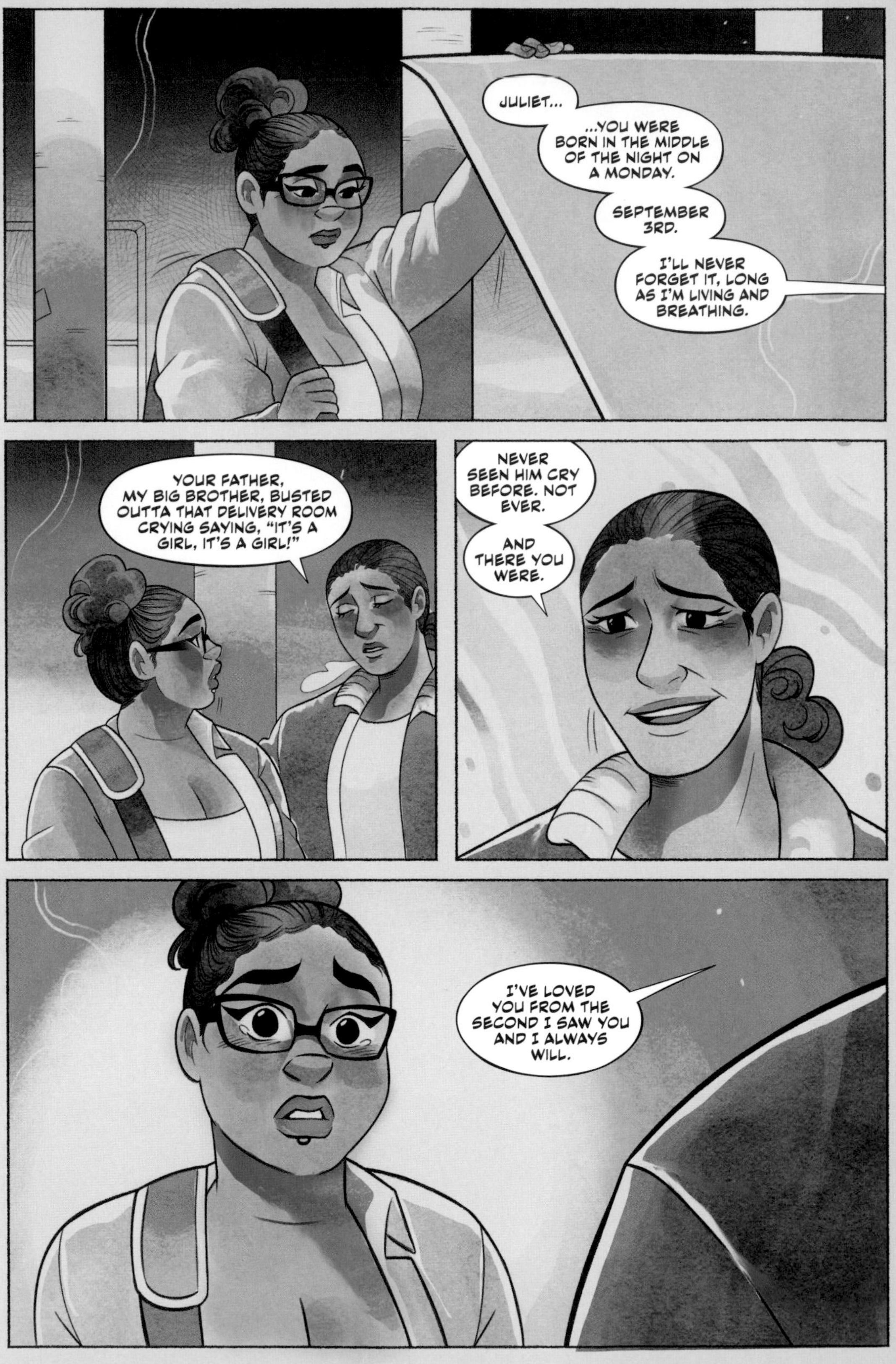
JULIET...
...YOU WERE BORN IN THE MIDDLE OF THE NIGHT ON A MONDAY.
SEPTEMBER 3RD.
I'LL NEVER FORGET IT, LONG AS I'M LIVING AND BREATHING.
YOUR FATHER, MY BIG BROTHER, BUSTED OUTTA THAT DELIVERY ROOM CRYING SAYING, "IT'S A GIRL, IT'S A GIRL!"
NEVER SEEN HIM CRY BEFORE. NOT EVER.
AND THERE YOU WERE.
I'VE LOVED YOU FROM THE SECOND I SAW YOU AND I ALWAYS WILL.

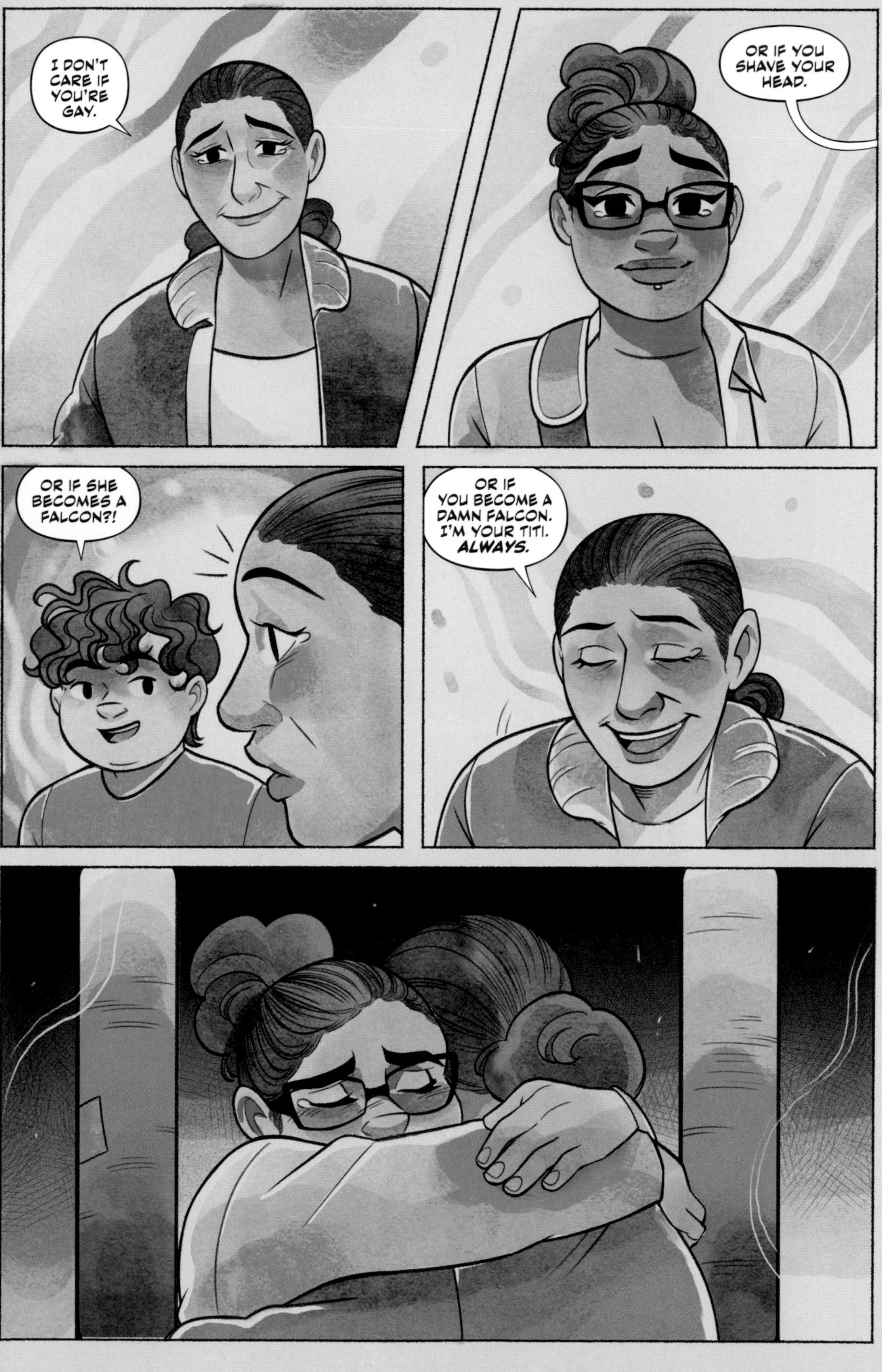
I DON'T CARE IF YOU'RE GAY.
OR IF YOU SHAVE YOUR HEAD.
OR IF SHE BECOMES A FALCON?!
OR IF YOU BECOME A DAMN FALCON. I'M YOUR TITI. *ALWAYS.*

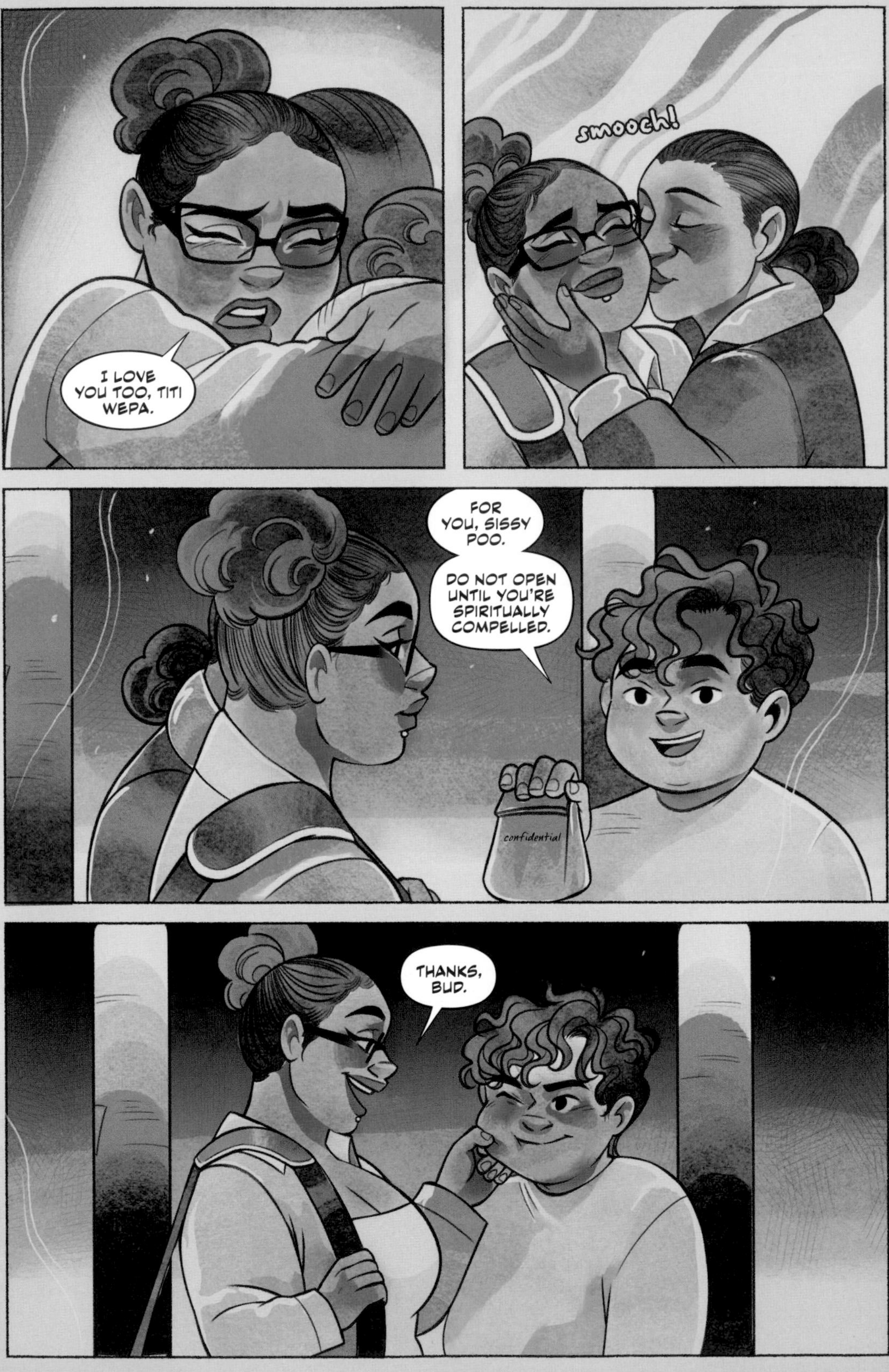
I LOVE YOU TOO, TITI WEPA.
smooch!
FOR YOU, SISSY POO.
DO NOT OPEN UNTIL YOU'RE SPIRITUALLY COMPELLED.
confidential
THANKS, BUD.

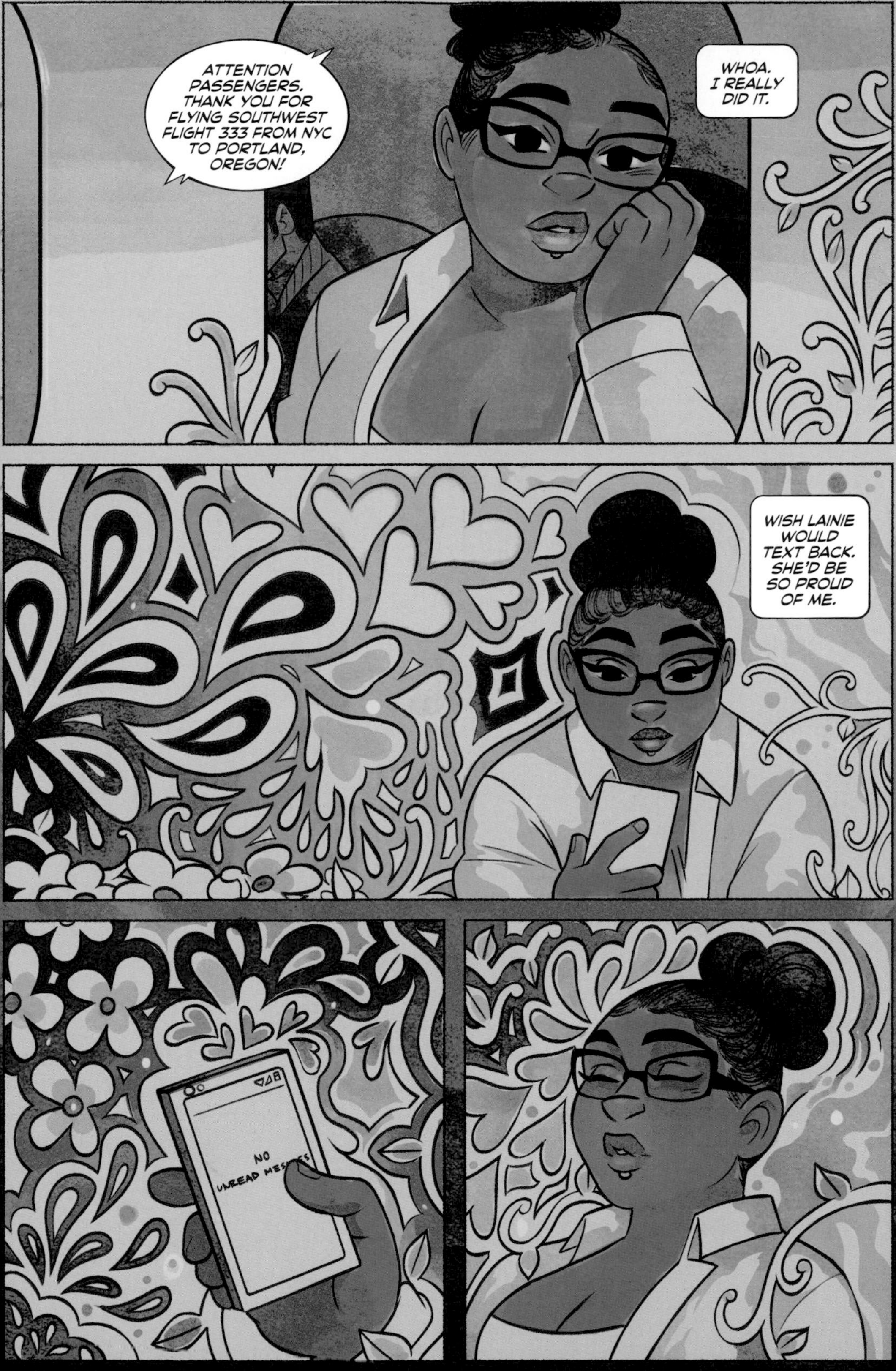
ATTENTION PASSENGERS. THANK YOU FOR FLYING SOUTHWEST FLIGHT 333 FROM NYC TO PORTLAND, OREGON!
WHOA. I REALLY DID IT.
WISH LAINIE WOULD TEXT BACK. SHE'D BE SO PROUD OF ME.
NO
UNREAD

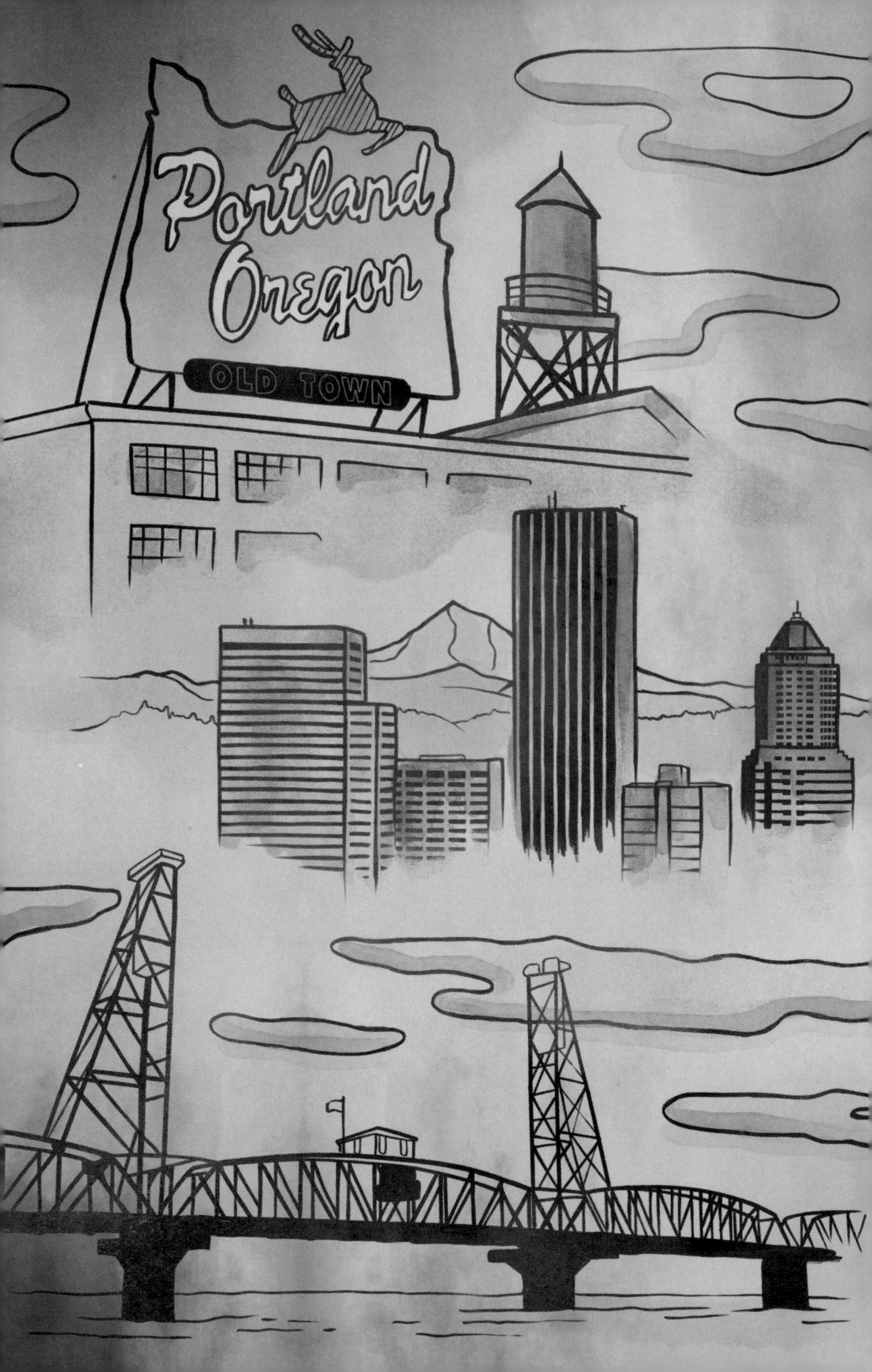
Portland Oregon
OLD TOWN

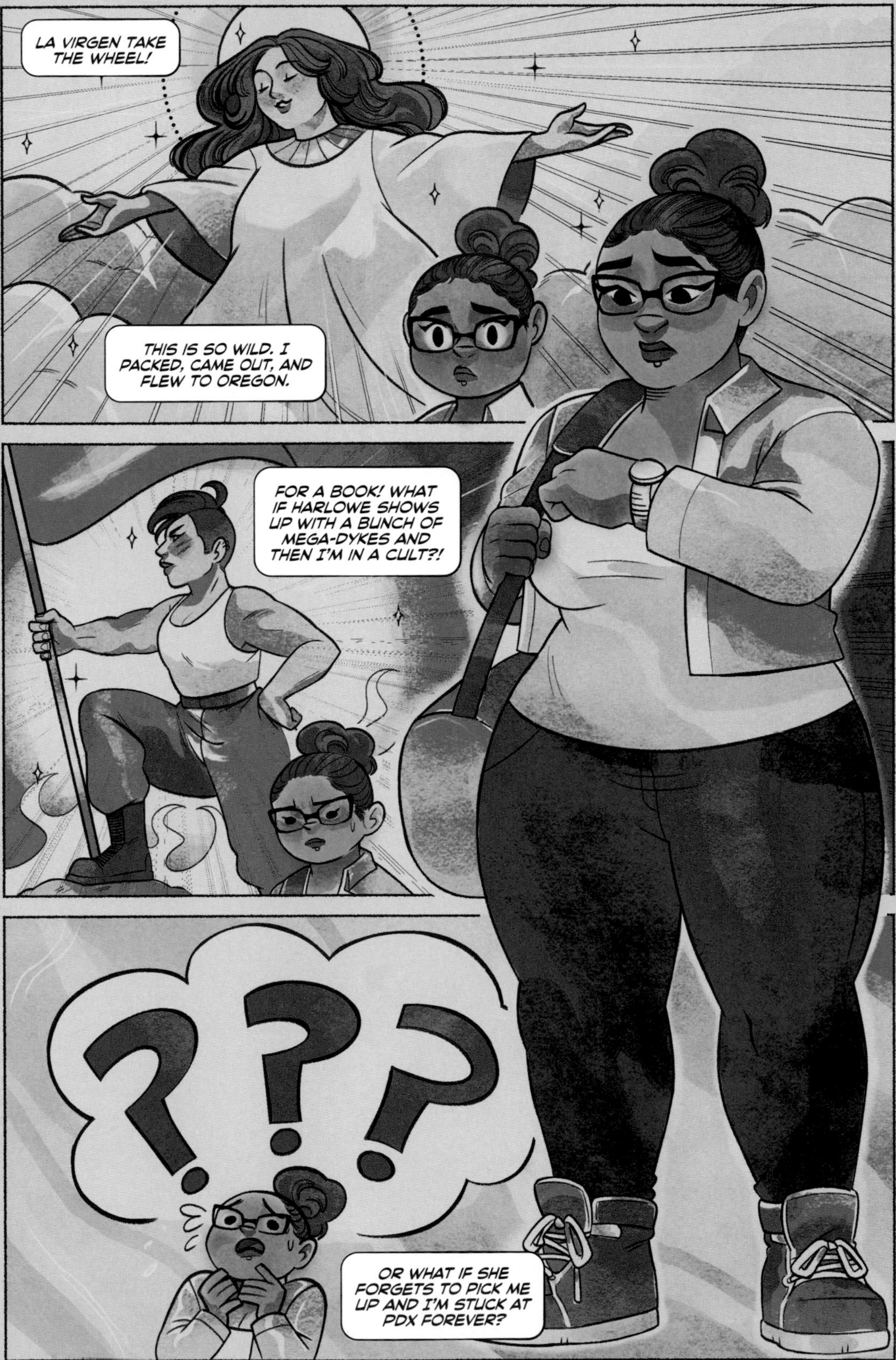
LA VIRGEN TAKE THE WHEEL!
THIS IS SO WILD. I PACKED, CAME OUT, AND FLEW TO OREGON.
FOR A BOOK! WHAT IF HARLOWE SHOWS UP WITH A BUNCH OF MEGA-DYKES AND THEN I'M IN A CULT?!
???
OR WHAT IF SHE FORGETS TO PICK ME UP AND I'M STUCK AT PDX FOREVER?

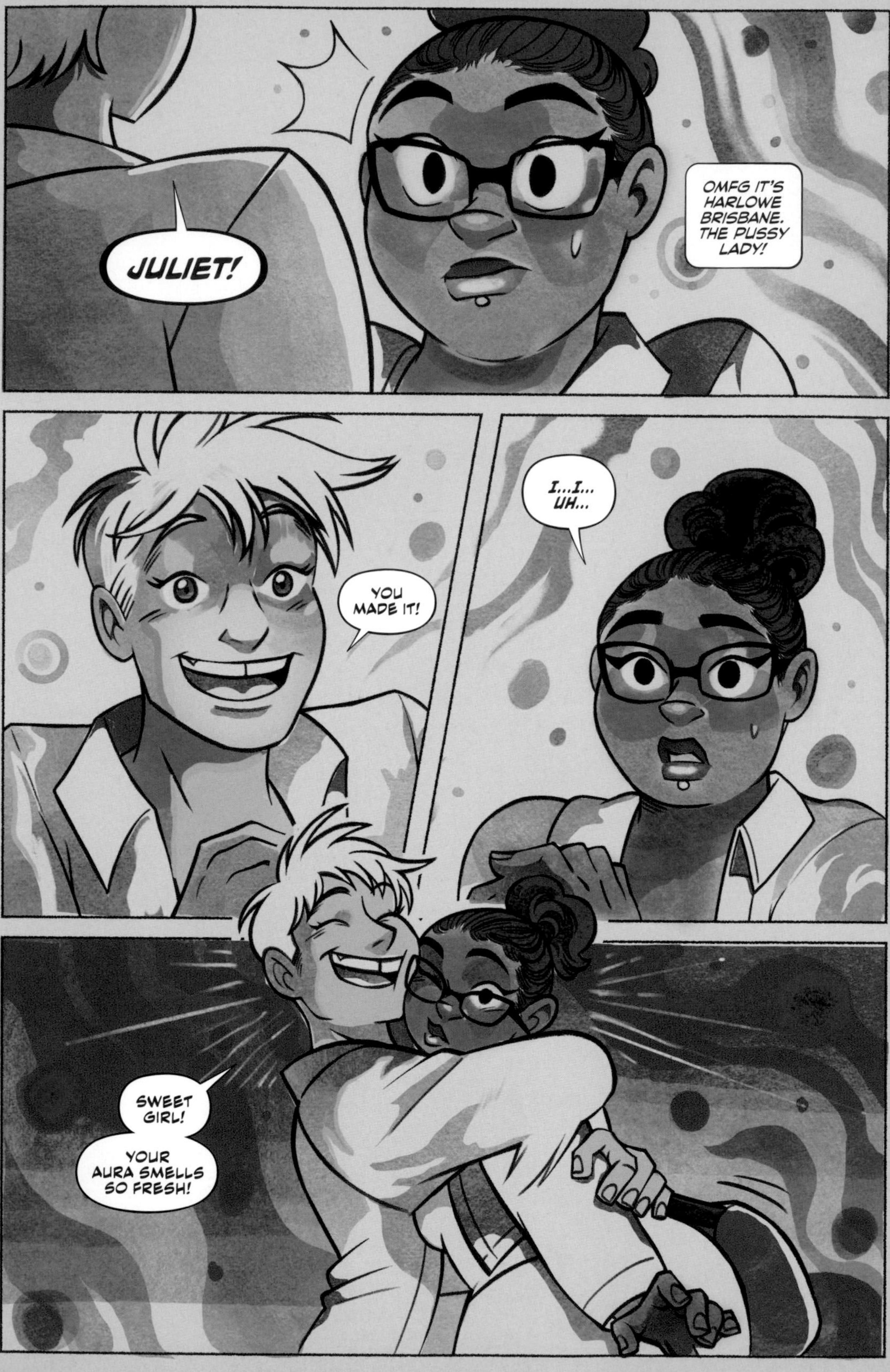
JULIET!
OMFG IT'S HARLOWE BRISBANE. THE PUSSY LADY!
YOU MADE IT!
I...I... UH...
SWEET GIRL!
YOUR AURA SMELLS SO FRESH!

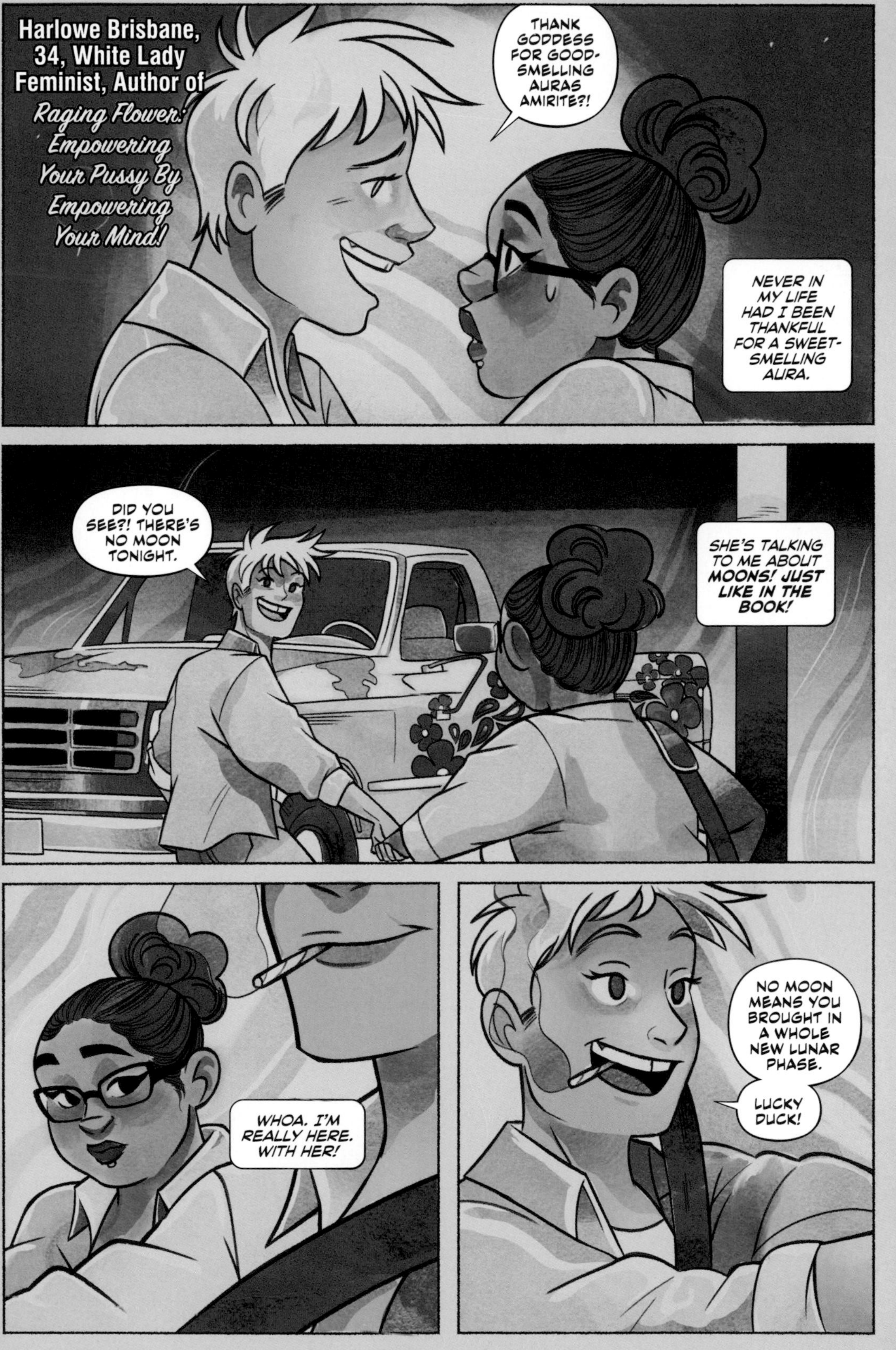
Harlowe Brisbane, 34, White Lady Feminist, Author of *Raging Flower: Empowering Your Pussy By Empowering Your Mind!*
THANK GODDESS FOR GOOD-SMELLING AURAS AMIRITE?!
NEVER IN MY LIFE HAD I BEEN THANKFUL FOR A SWEET-SMELLING AURA.
DID YOU SEE?! THERE'S NO MOON TONIGHT.
SHE'S TALKING TO ME ABOUT MOONS! JUST LIKE IN THE BOOK!
WHOA. I'M REALLY HERE. WITH HER!
NO MOON MEANS YOU BROUGHT IN A WHOLE NEW LUNAR PHASE.
LUCKY DUCK!

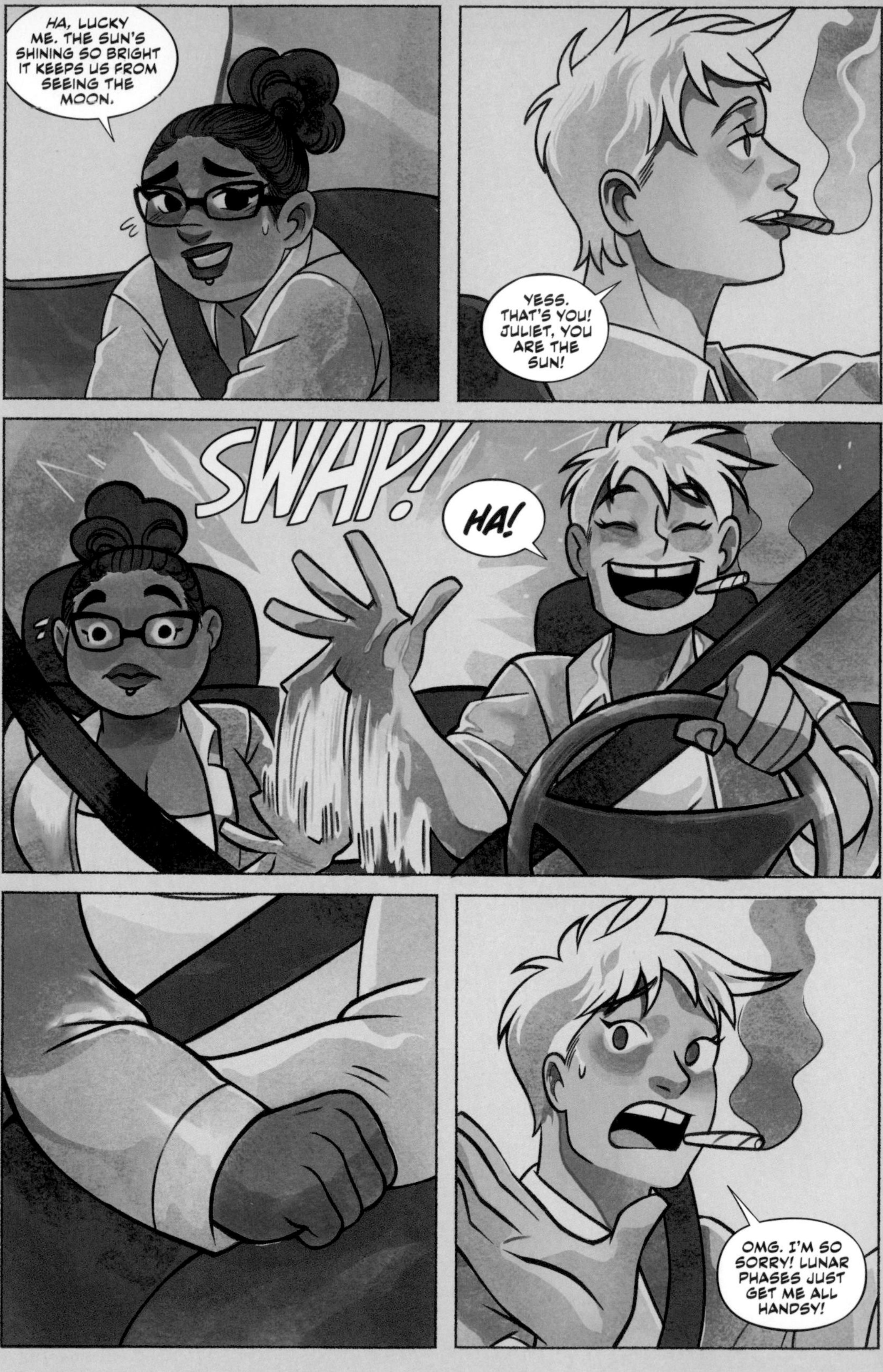
HA, LUCKY ME. THE SUN'S SHINING SO BRIGHT IT KEEPS US FROM SEEING THE MOON.
YESS. THAT'S YOU! JULIET, YOU ARE THE SUN!
SWAP!
HA!
OMG. I'M SO SORRY! LUNAR PHASES JUST GET ME ALL HANDSY!

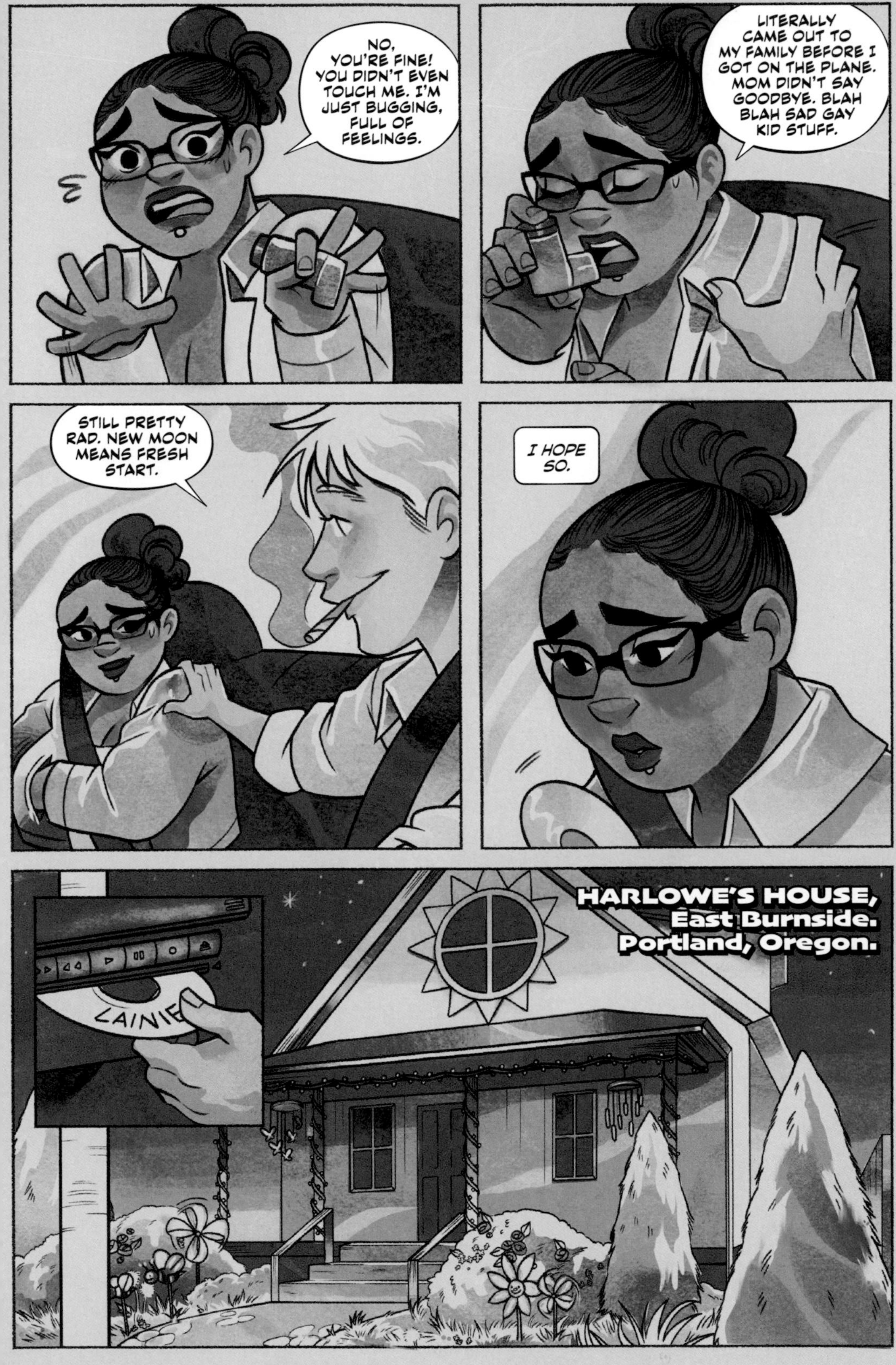
NO, YOU'RE FINE! YOU DIDN'T EVEN TOUCH ME. I'M JUST BUGGING, FULL OF FEELINGS.
LITERALLY CAME OUT TO MY FAMILY BEFORE I GOT ON THE PLANE. MOM DIDN'T SAY GOODBYE. BLAH BLAH SAD GAY KID STUFF.
STILL PRETTY RAD. NEW MOON MEANS FRESH START.
I HOPE SO.
LAINIE
HARLOWE'S HOUSE, East Burnside. Portland, Oregon.

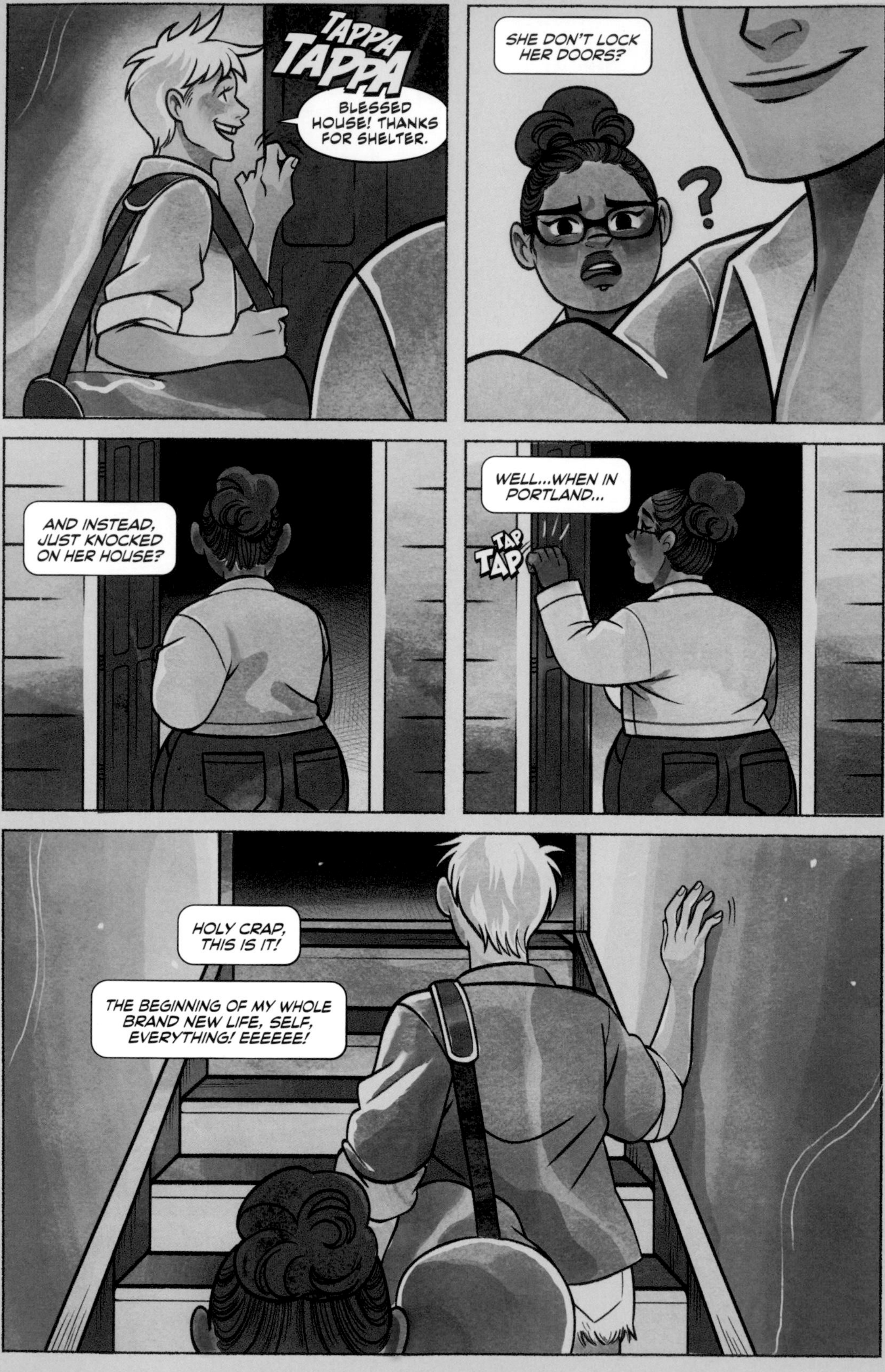
TAPPA TAPPA
BLESSED HOUSE! THANKS FOR SHELTER.
SHE DON'T LOCK HER DOORS?
?
AND INSTEAD, JUST KNOCKED ON HER HOUSE?
WELL...WHEN IN PORTLAND...
TAP TAP
HOLY CRAP, THIS IS IT!
THE BEGINNING OF MY WHOLE BRAND NEW LIFE, SELF, EVERYTHING! EEEEEE!

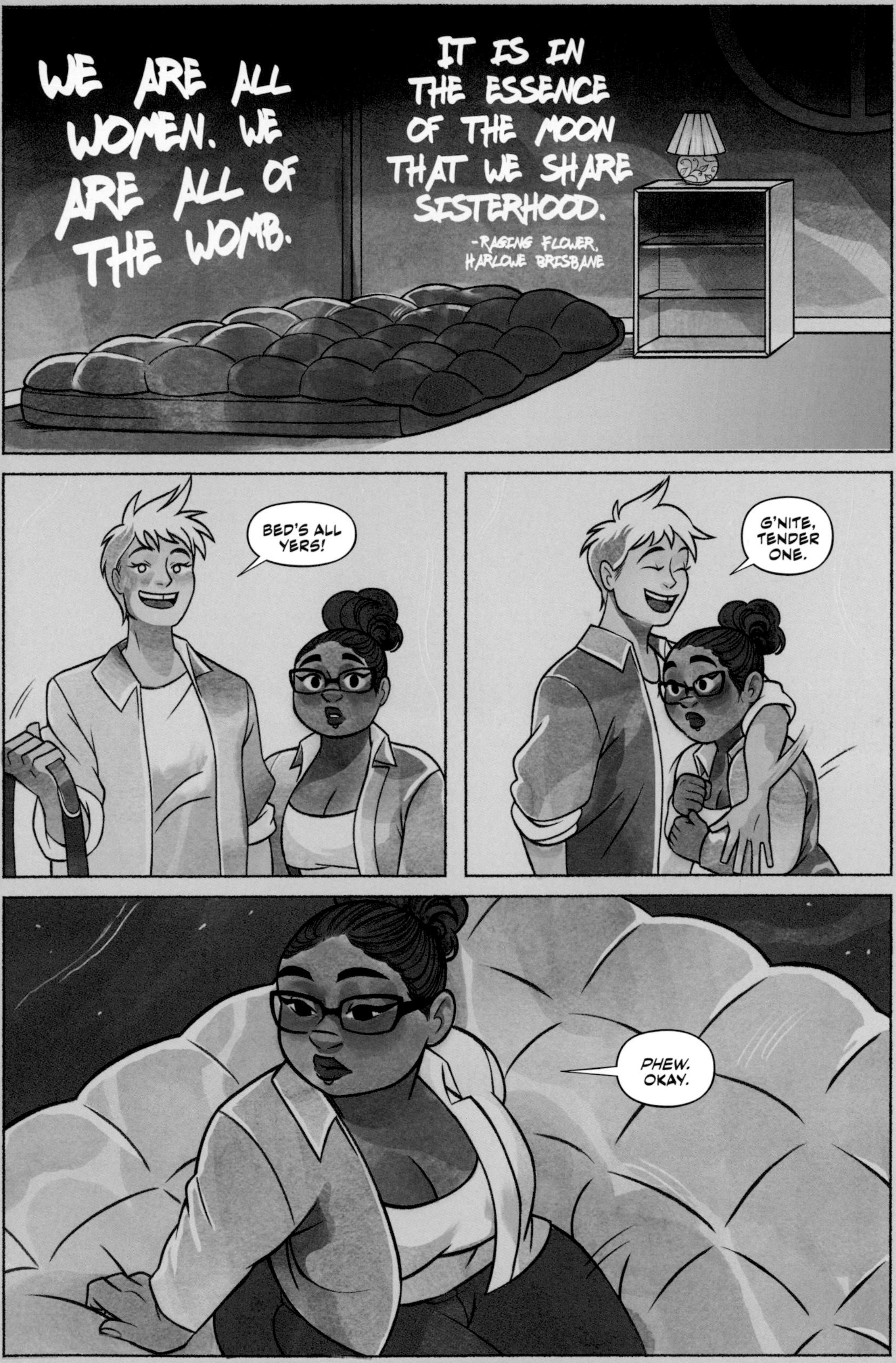
WE ARE ALL WOMEN. WE ARE ALL OF THE WOMB.
IT IS IN THE ESSENCE OF THE MOON THAT WE SHARE SISTERHOOD.
-RAGING FLOWER, HARLOWE BRISBANE
BED'S ALL YERS!
G'NITE, TENDER ONE.
PHEW. OKAY.

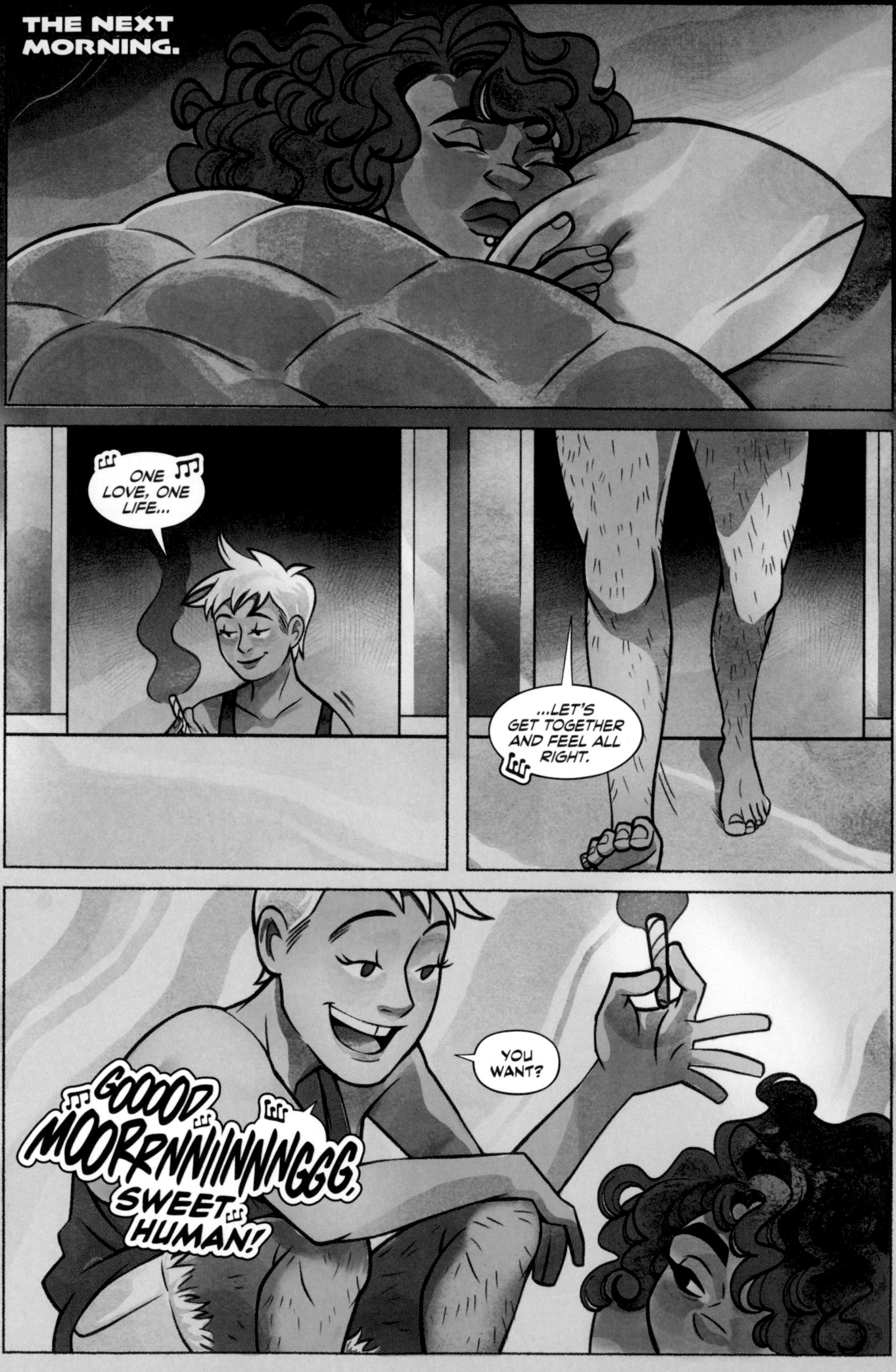
THE NEXT MORNING.
ONE LOVE, ONE LIFE...
...LET'S GET TOGETHER AND FEEL ALL RIGHT.
GOOOOOD MOORRNNIINNNGGG, SWEET HUMAN!
YOU WANT?

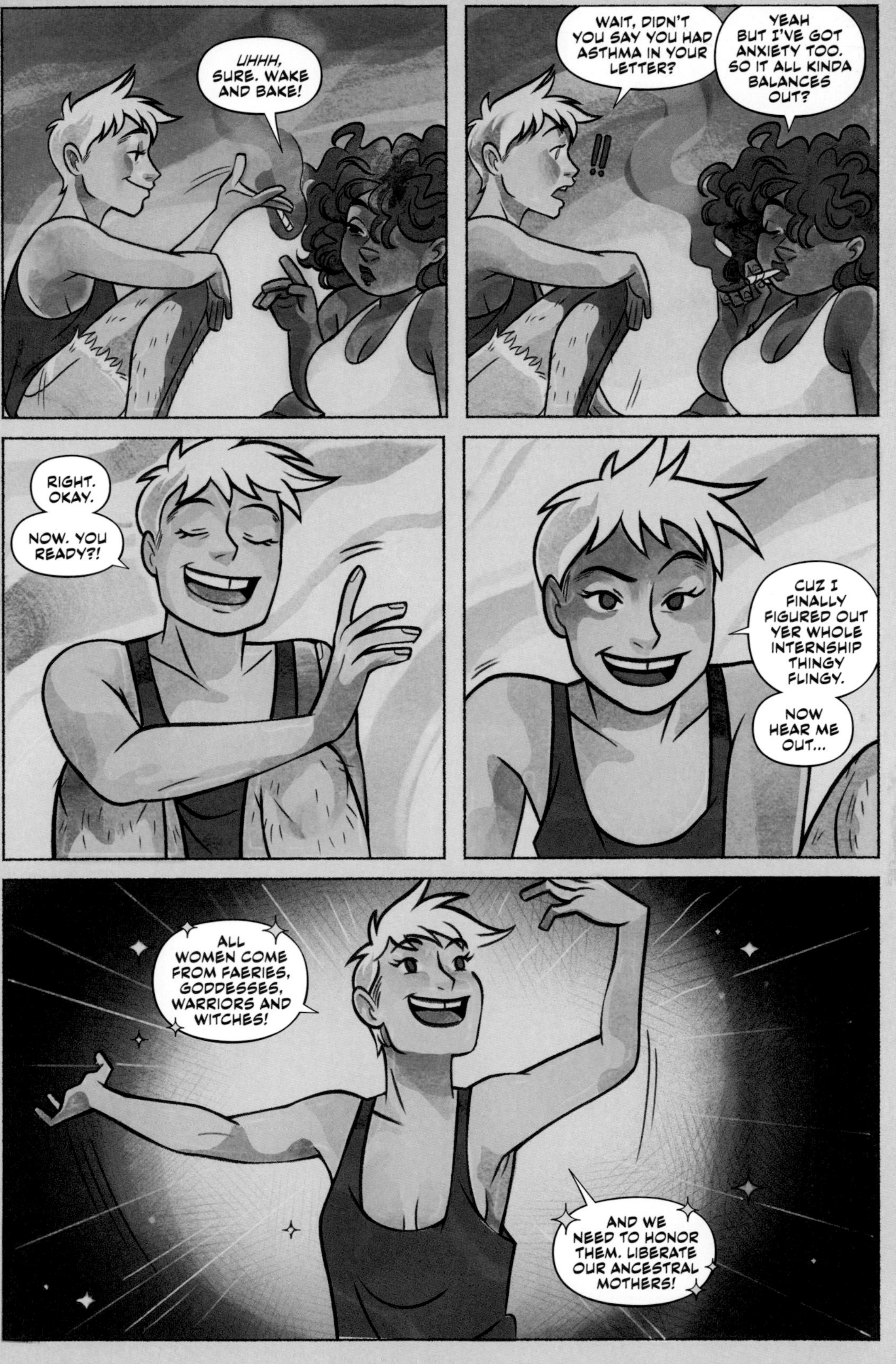
UHHH, SURE. WAKE AND BAKE!
WAIT, DIDN'T YOU SAY YOU HAD ASTHMA IN YOUR LETTER?
YEAH BUT I'VE GOT ANXIETY TOO. SO IT ALL KINDA BALANCES OUT?
!!
RIGHT. OKAY.
NOW. YOU READY?!
CUZ I FINALLY FIGURED OUT YER WHOLE INTERNSHIP THINGY FLINGY.
NOW HEAR ME OUT...
ALL WOMEN COME FROM FAERIES, GODDESSES, WARRIORS AND WITCHES!
AND WE NEED TO HONOR THEM. LIBERATE OUR ANCESTRAL MOTHERS!

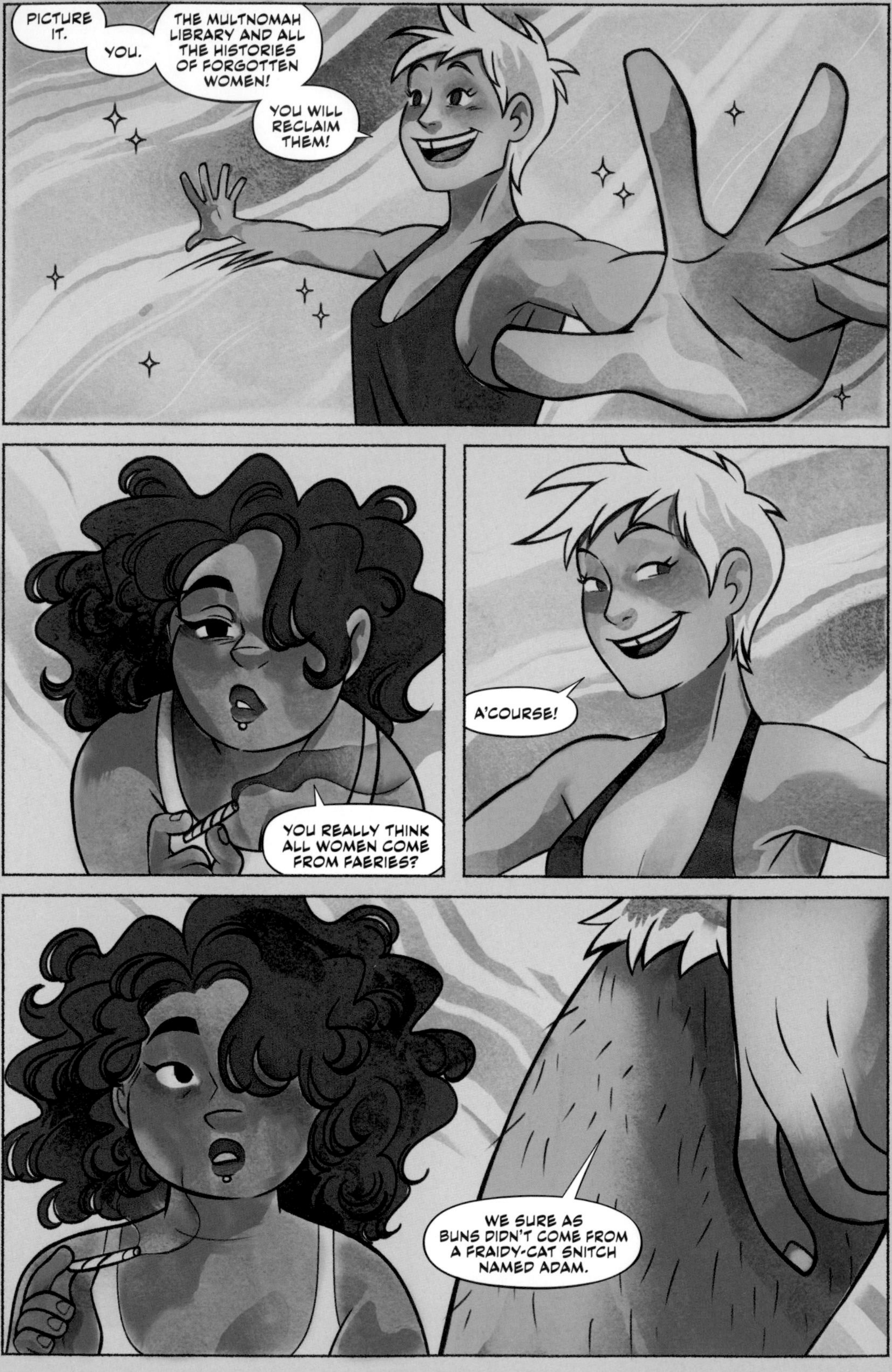
PICTURE IT.
YOU.
THE MULTNOMAH LIBRARY AND ALL THE HISTORIES OF FORGOTTEN WOMEN!
YOU WILL RECLAIM THEM!
YOU REALLY THINK ALL WOMEN COME FROM FAERIES?
A'COURSE!
WE SURE AS BUNS DIDN'T COME FROM A FRAIDY-CAT SNITCH NAMED ADAM.

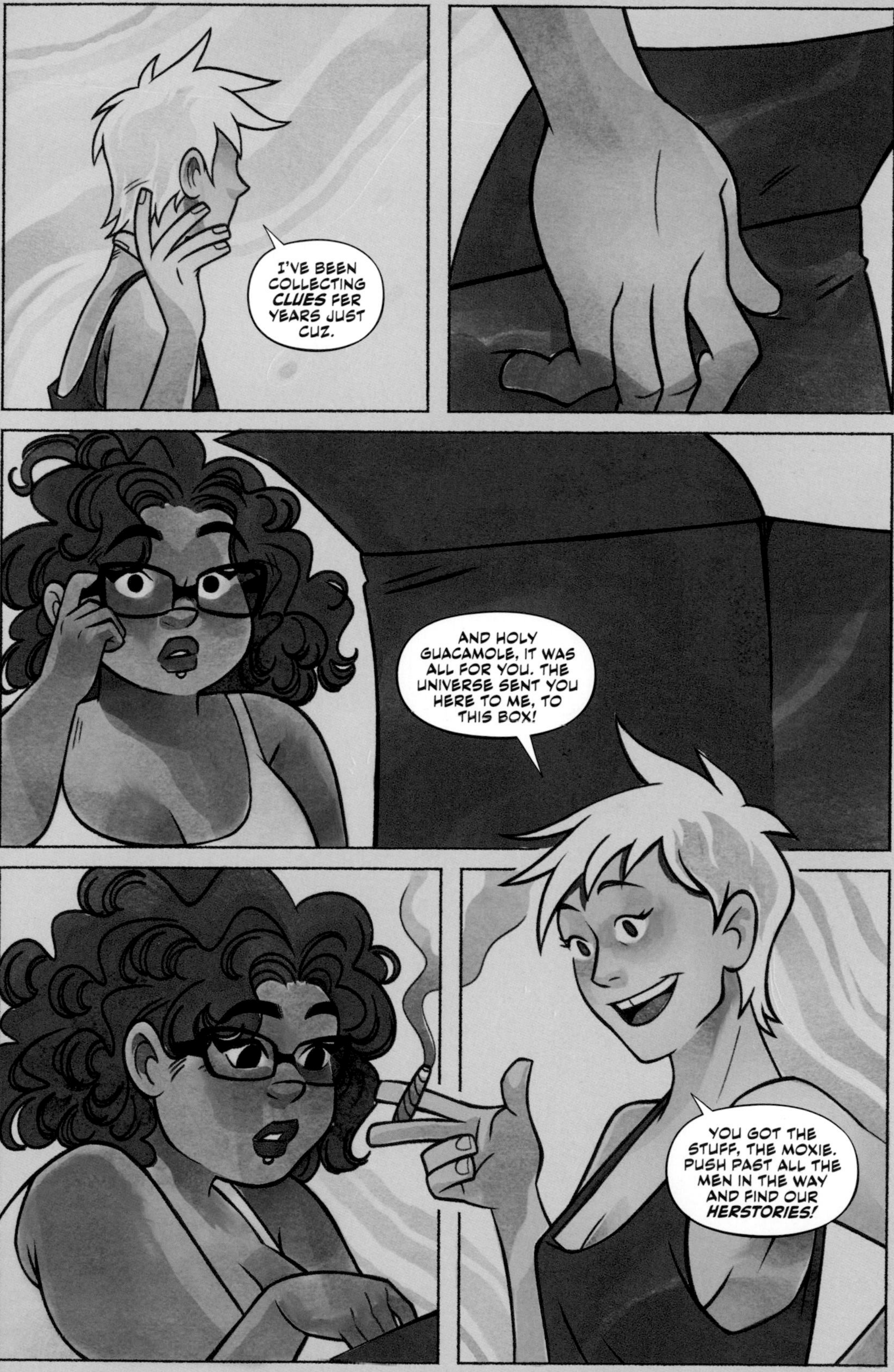
I'VE BEEN COLLECTING *CLUES* FER YEARS JUST CUZ.
AND HOLY GUACAMOLE, IT WAS ALL FOR YOU. THE UNIVERSE SENT YOU HERE TO ME, TO THIS BOX!
YOU GOT THE STUFF, THE MOXIE. PUSH PAST ALL THE MEN IN THE WAY AND FIND OUR *HERSTORIES!*

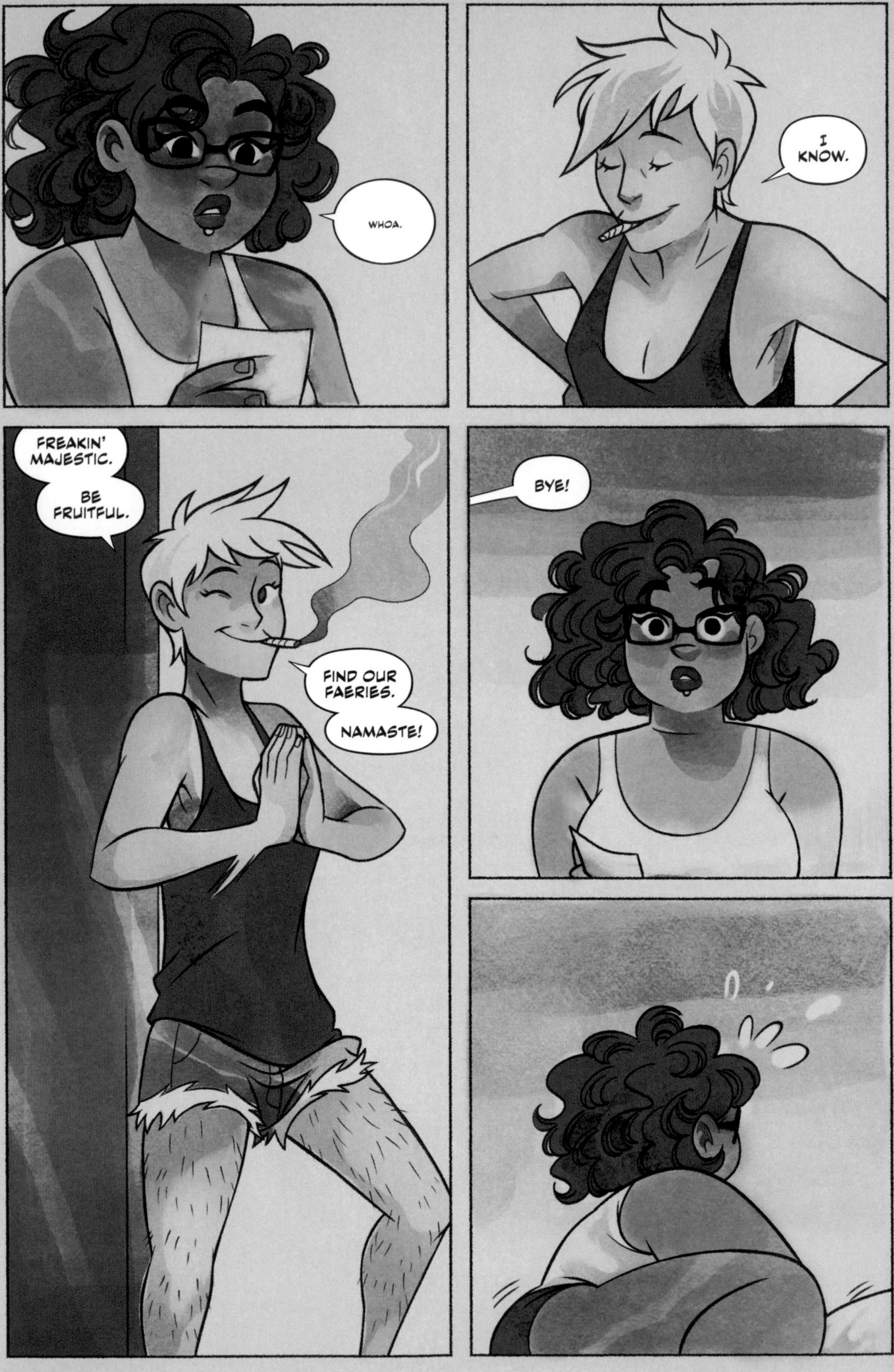
WHOA.
I KNOW.
FREAKIN' MAJESTIC.
BE FRUITFUL.
FIND OUR FAERIES.
NAMASTE!
BYE!

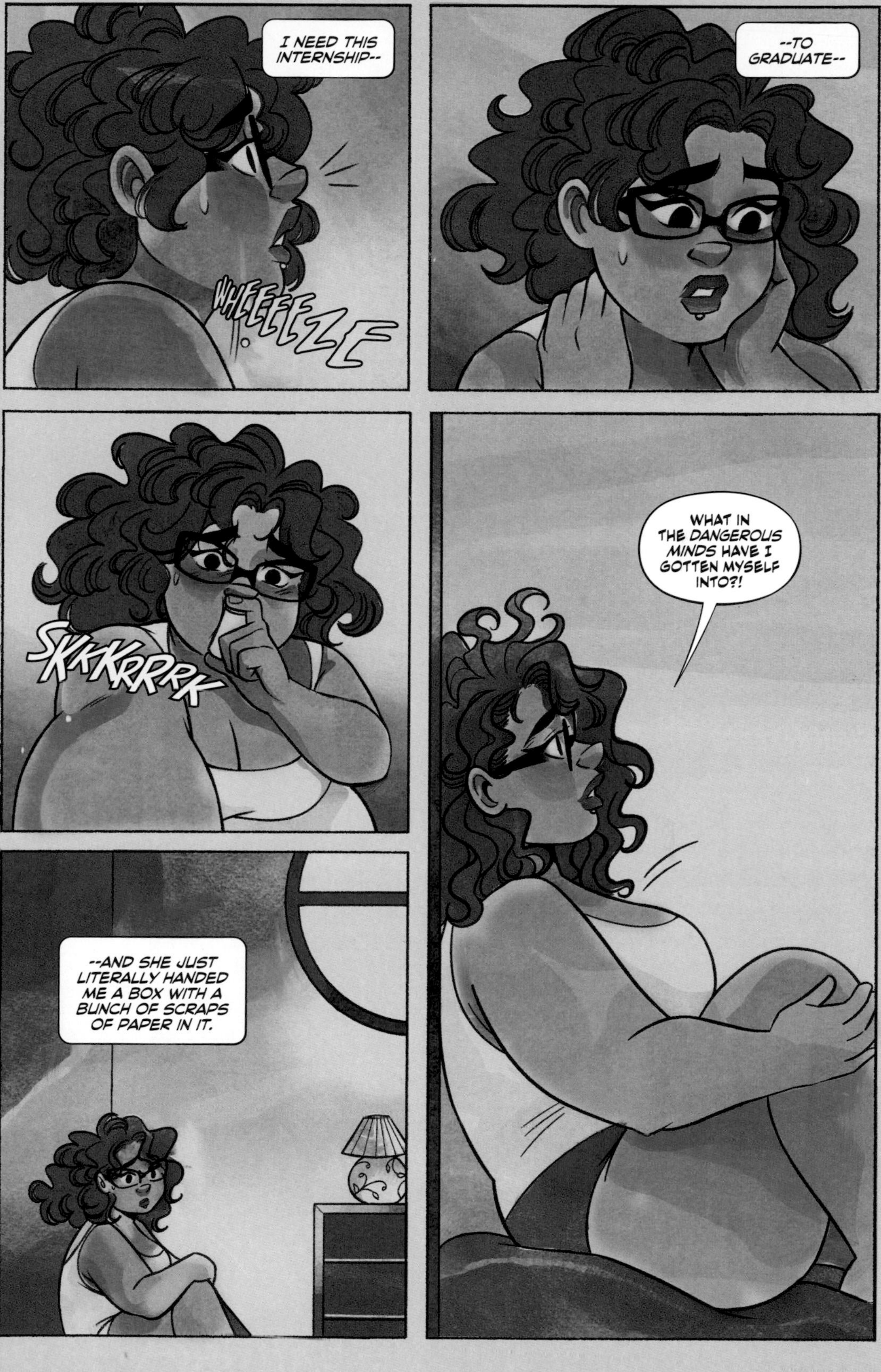
I NEED THIS INTERNSHIP--
WHEEEEEZE
--TO GRADUATE--
SKKKRRRRK
--AND SHE JUST LITERALLY HANDED ME A BOX WITH A BUNCH OF SCRAPS OF PAPER IN IT.
WHAT IN THE *DANGEROUS MINDS* HAVE I GOTTEN MYSELF INTO?!

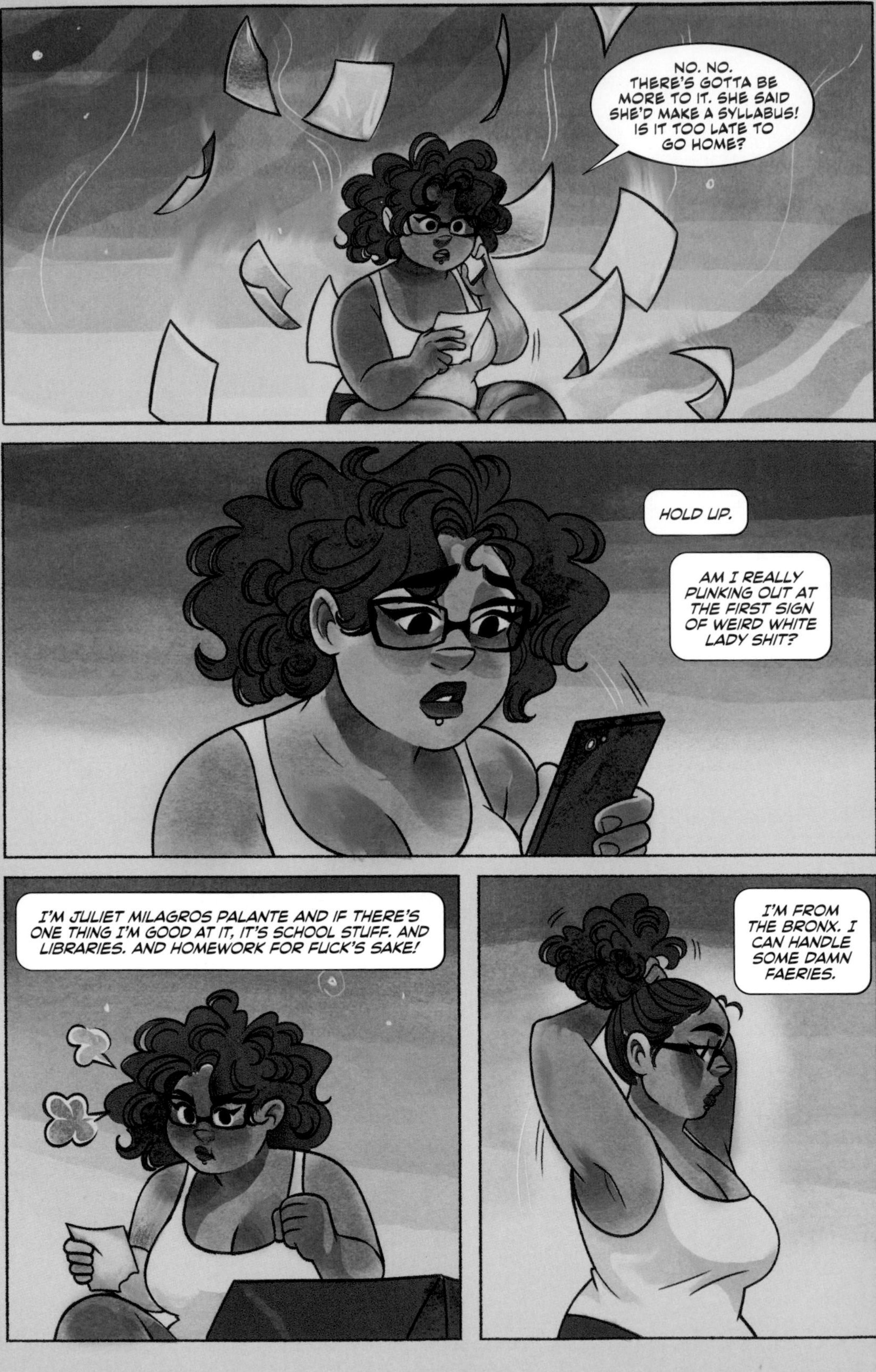
NO. NO. THERE'S GOTTA BE MORE TO IT. SHE SAID SHE'D MAKE A SYLLABUS! IS IT TOO LATE TO GO HOME?
HOLD UP.
AM I REALLY PUNKING OUT AT THE FIRST SIGN OF WEIRD WHITE LADY SHIT?
I'M JULIET MILAGROS PALANTE AND IF THERE'S ONE THING I'M GOOD AT IT, IT'S SCHOOL STUFF. AND LIBRARIES. AND HOMEWORK FOR FUCK'S SAKE!
I'M FROM THE BRONX. I CAN HANDLE SOME DAMN FAERIES.

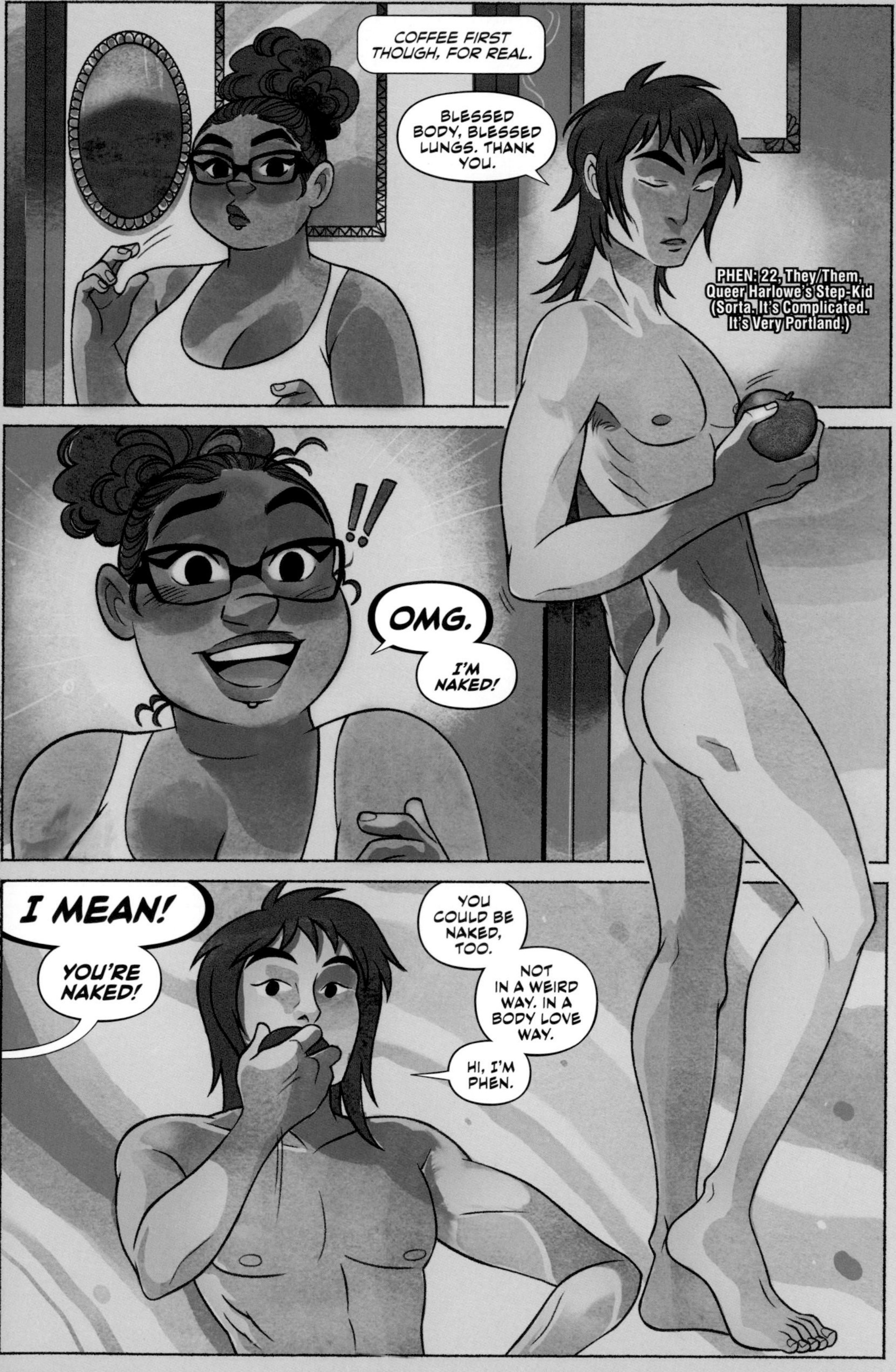
COFFEE FIRST THOUGH, FOR REAL.
BLESSED BODY, BLESSED LUNGS. THANK YOU.
PHEN: 22, They/Them, Queer Harlowe's Step-Kid (Sorta. It's Complicated. It's Very Portland.)
!!
OMG.
I'M NAKED!
I MEAN!
YOU'RE NAKED!
YOU COULD BE NAKED, TOO.
NOT IN A WEIRD WAY. IN A BODY LOVE WAY.
HI, I'M PHEN.

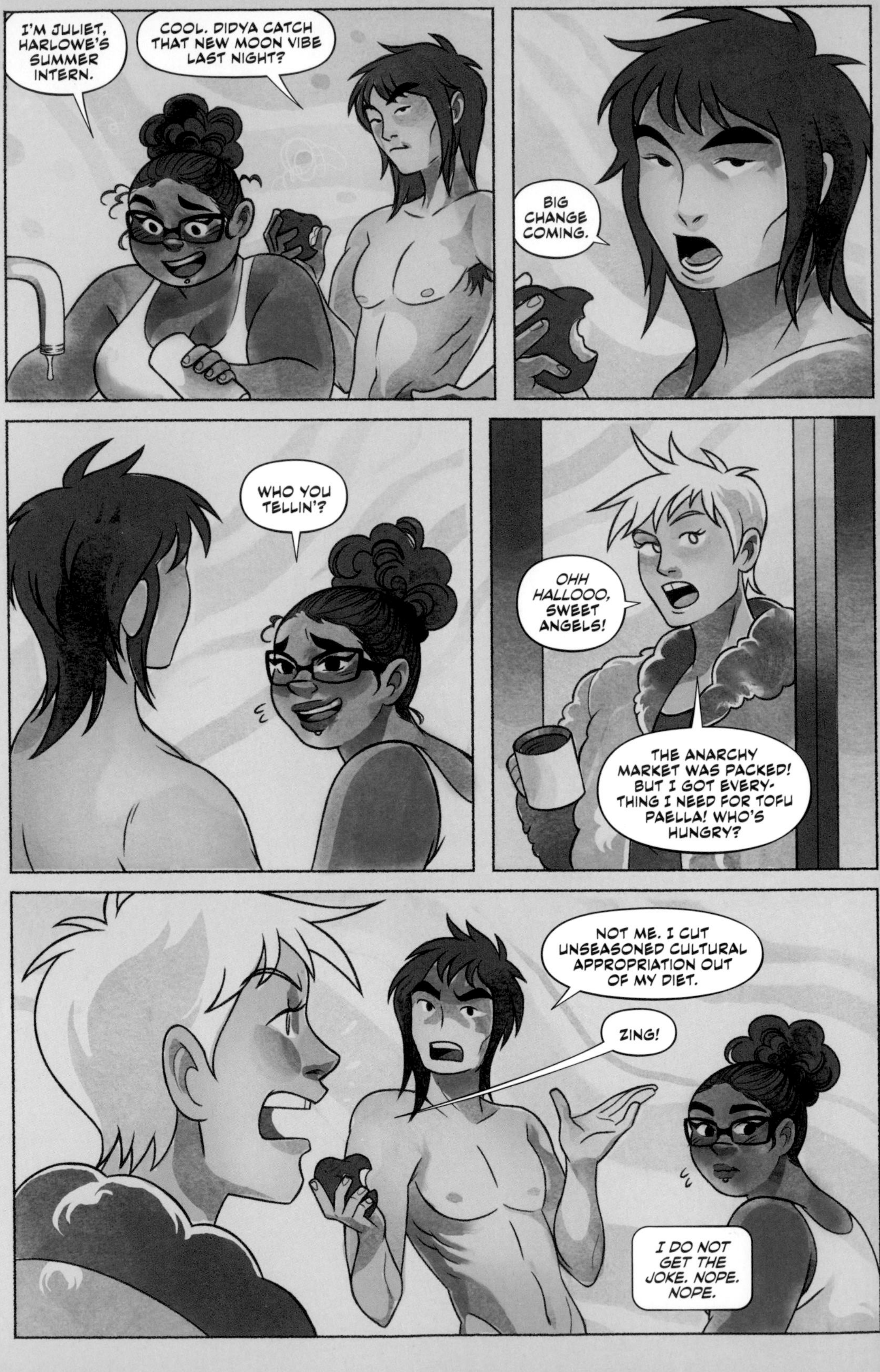
I'M JULIET, HARLOWE'S SUMMER INTERN.
COOL. DIDYA CATCH THAT NEW MOON VIBE LAST NIGHT?
BIG CHANGE COMING.
WHO YOU TELLIN'?
OHH HALLOOO, SWEET ANGELS!
THE ANARCHY MARKET WAS PACKED! BUT I GOT EVERY-THING I NEED FOR TOFU PAELLA! WHO'S HUNGRY?
NOT ME. I CUT UNSEASONED CULTURAL APPROPRIATION OUT OF MY DIET.
ZING!
I DO NOT GET THE JOKE. NOPE. NOPE.

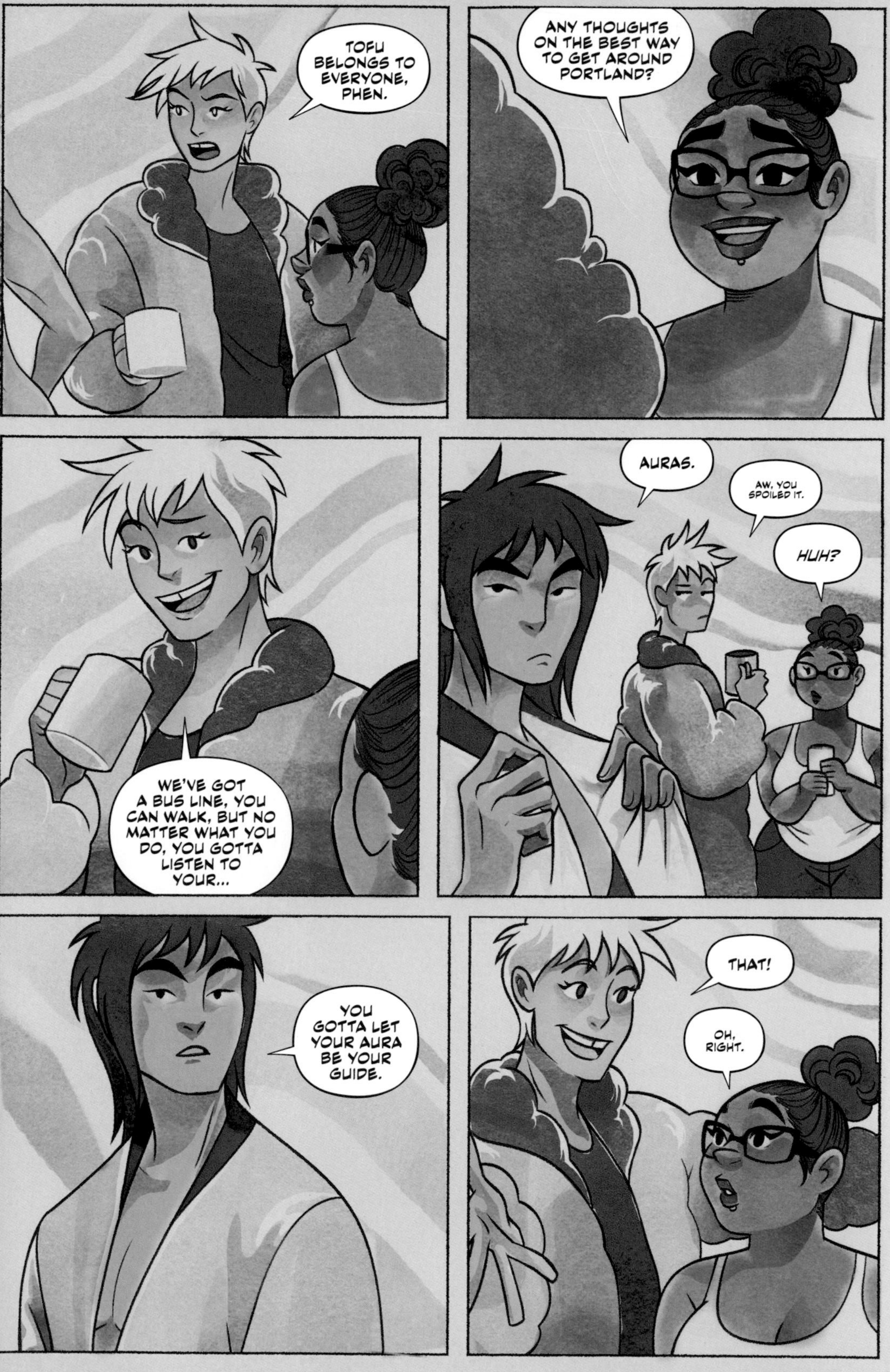
TOFU BELONGS TO EVERYONE, PHEN.
ANY THOUGHTS ON THE BEST WAY TO GET AROUND PORTLAND?
WE'VE GOT A BUS LINE, YOU CAN WALK, BUT NO MATTER WHAT YOU DO, YOU GOTTA LISTEN TO YOUR...
AURAS.
AW, YOU SPOILED IT.
HUH?
YOU GOTTA LET YOUR AURA BE YOUR GUIDE.
THAT!
OH, RIGHT.

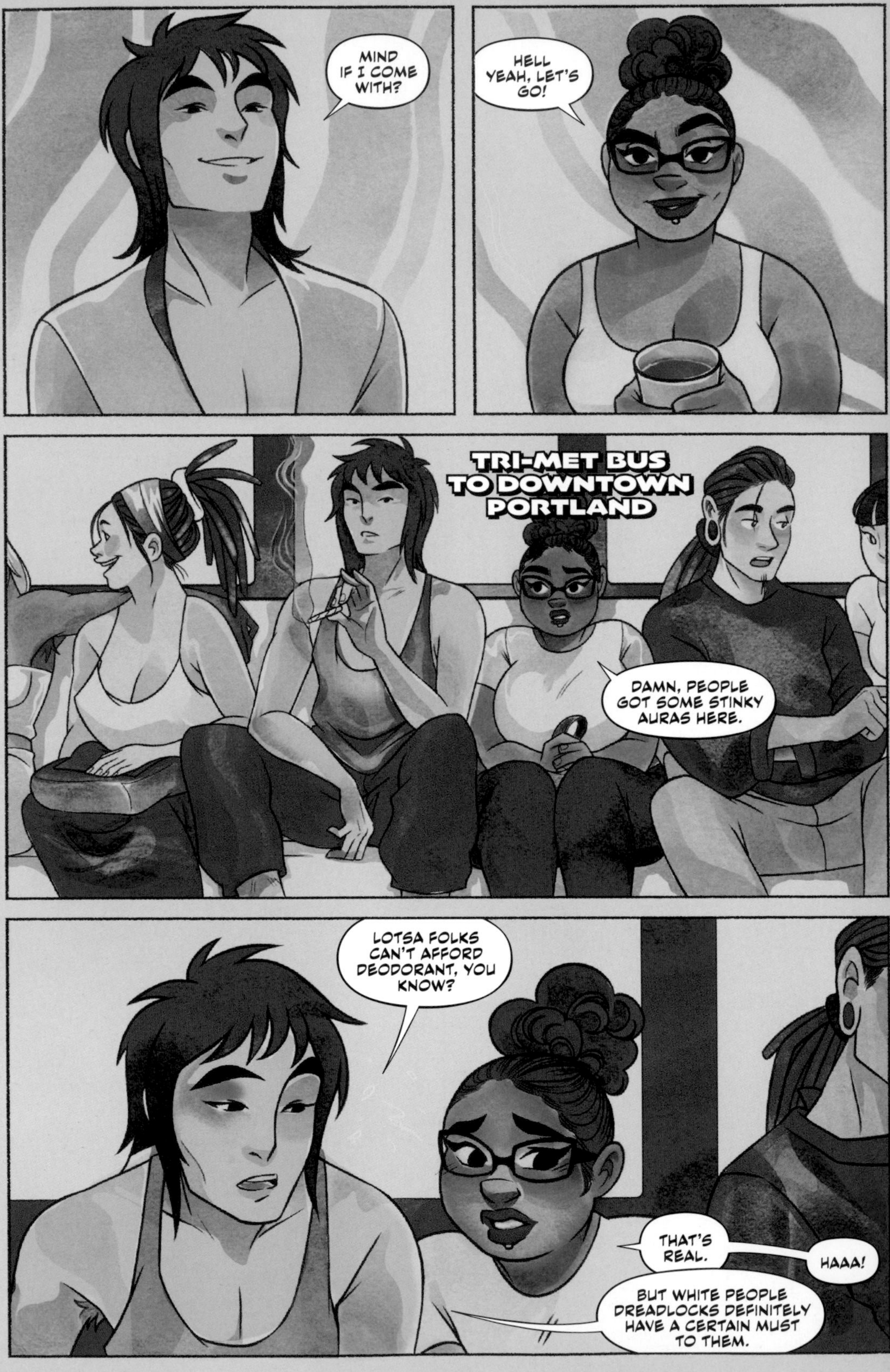
MIND IF I COME WITH?
HELL YEAH, LET'S GO!
TRI-MET BUS TO DOWNTOWN PORTLAND
DAMN, PEOPLE GOT SOME STINKY AURAS HERE.
LOTSA FOLKS CAN'T AFFORD DEODORANT, YOU KNOW?
THAT'S REAL.
HAAA!
BUT WHITE PEOPLE DREADLOCKS DEFINITELY HAVE A CERTAIN MUST TO THEM.

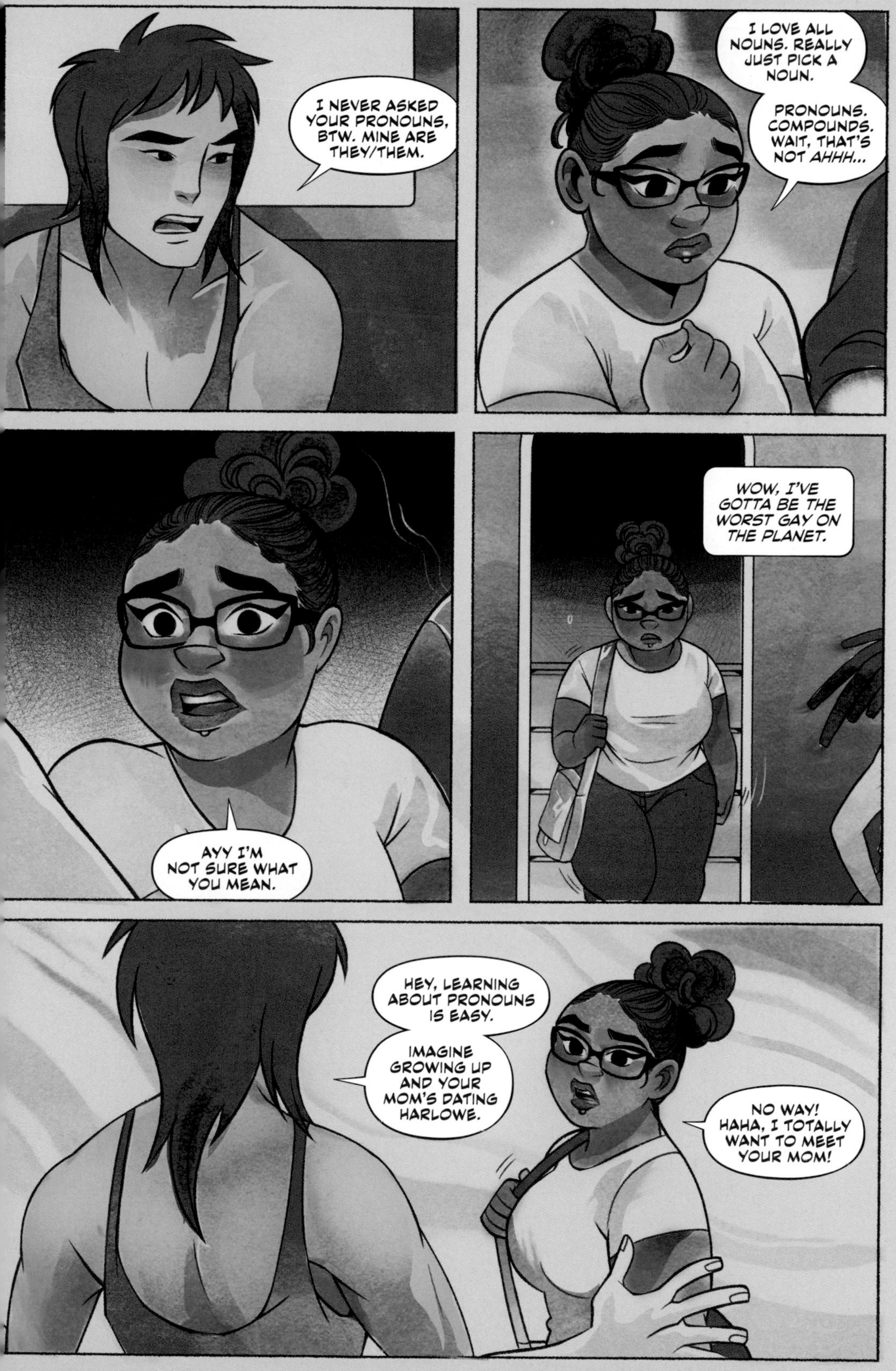
I NEVER ASKED YOUR PRONOUNS, BTW. MINE ARE THEY/THEM.
I LOVE ALL NOUNS. REALLY JUST PICK A NOUN.
PRONOUNS. COMPOUNDS. WAIT, THAT'S NOT *AHHH*...
AYY I'M NOT SURE WHAT YOU MEAN.
WOW, I'VE GOTTA BE THE WORST GAY ON THE PLANET.
HEY, LEARNING ABOUT PRONOUNS IS EASY.
IMAGINE GROWING UP AND YOUR MOM'S DATING HARLOWE.
NO WAY! HAHA, I TOTALLY WANT TO MEET YOUR MOM!

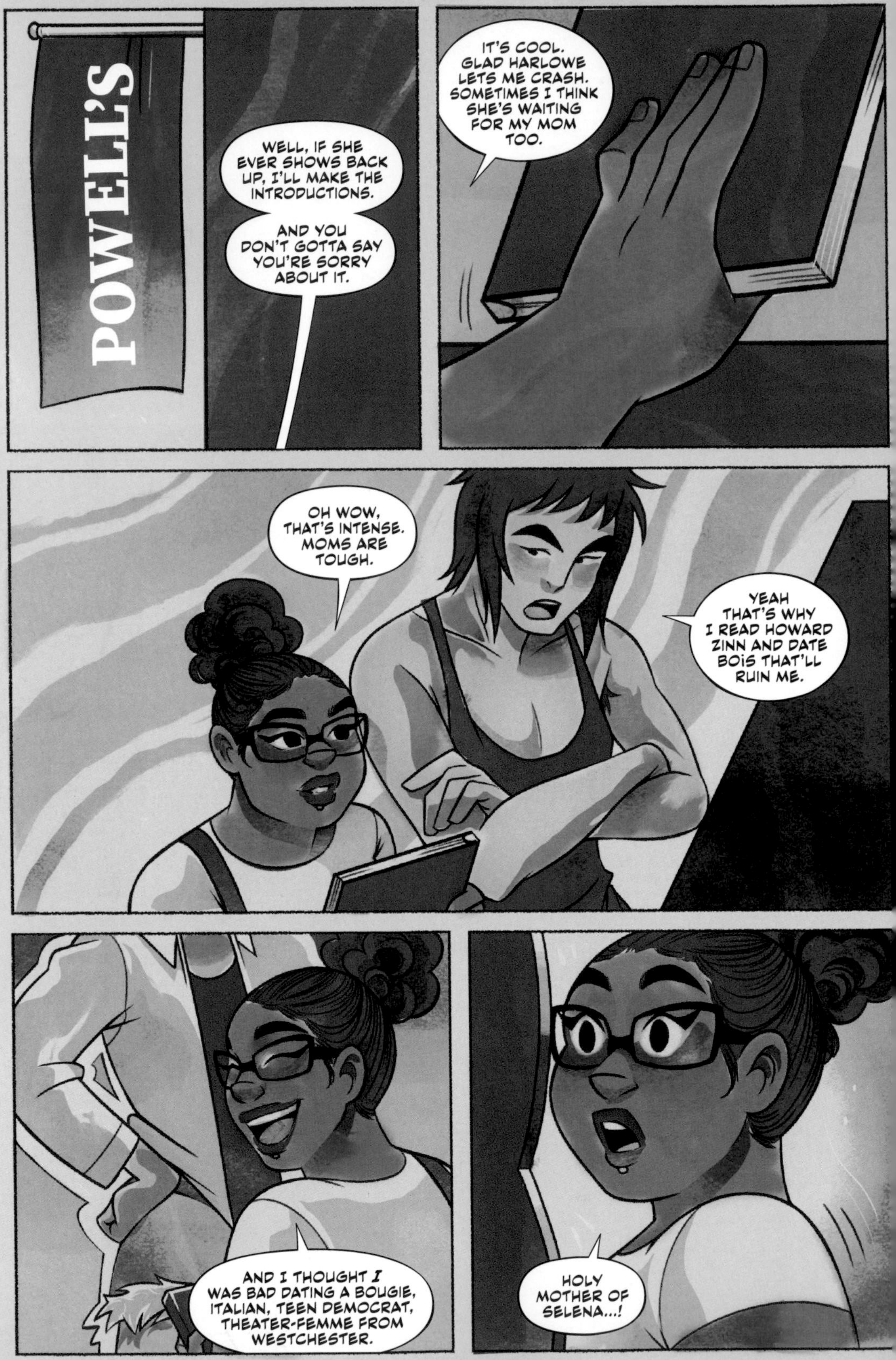
POWELL'S
WELL, IF SHE EVER SHOWS BACK UP, I'LL MAKE THE INTRODUCTIONS.
AND YOU DON'T GOTTA SAY YOU'RE SORRY ABOUT IT.
IT'S COOL. GLAD HARLOWE LETS ME CRASH. SOMETIMES I THINK SHE'S WAITING FOR MY MOM TOO.
OH WOW, THAT'S INTENSE. MOMS ARE TOUGH.
YEAH THAT'S WHY I READ HOWARD ZINN AND DATE BOIS THAT'LL RUIN ME.
AND I THOUGHT *I* WAS BAD DATING A BOUGIE, ITALIAN, TEEN DEMOCRAT, THEATER-FEMME FROM WESTCHESTER.
HOLY MOTHER OF SELENA...!

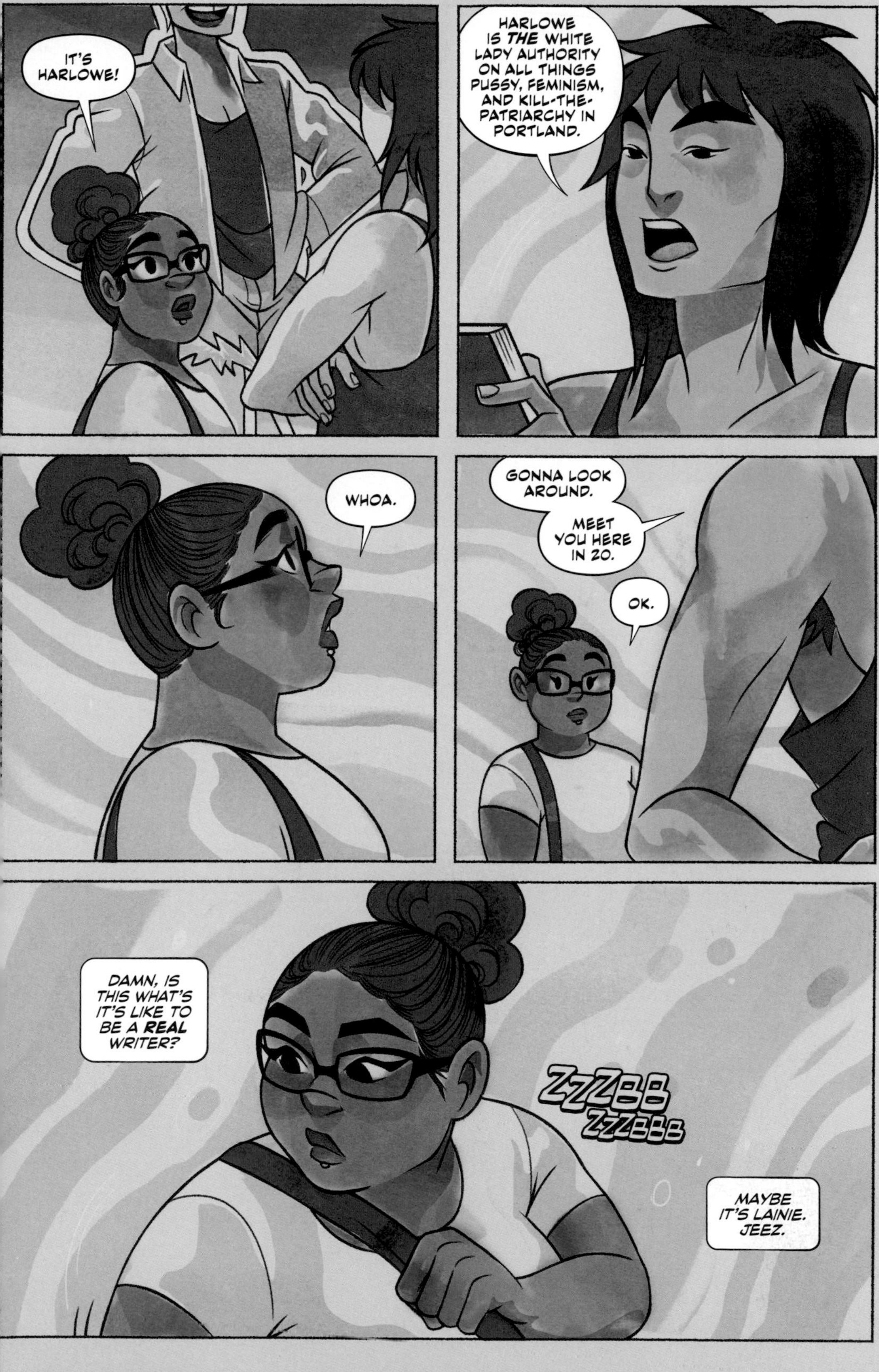
IT'S HARLOWE!
HARLOWE IS *THE* WHITE LADY AUTHORITY ON ALL THINGS PUSSY, FEMINISM, AND KILL-THE-PATRIARCHY IN PORTLAND.
WHOA.
GONNA LOOK AROUND.
MEET YOU HERE IN 20.
OK.
*DAMN, IS THIS WHAT'S IT'S LIKE TO BE A **REAL** WRITER?*
ZZZBBB
ZZZBBB
MAYBE IT'S LAINIE. JEEZ.

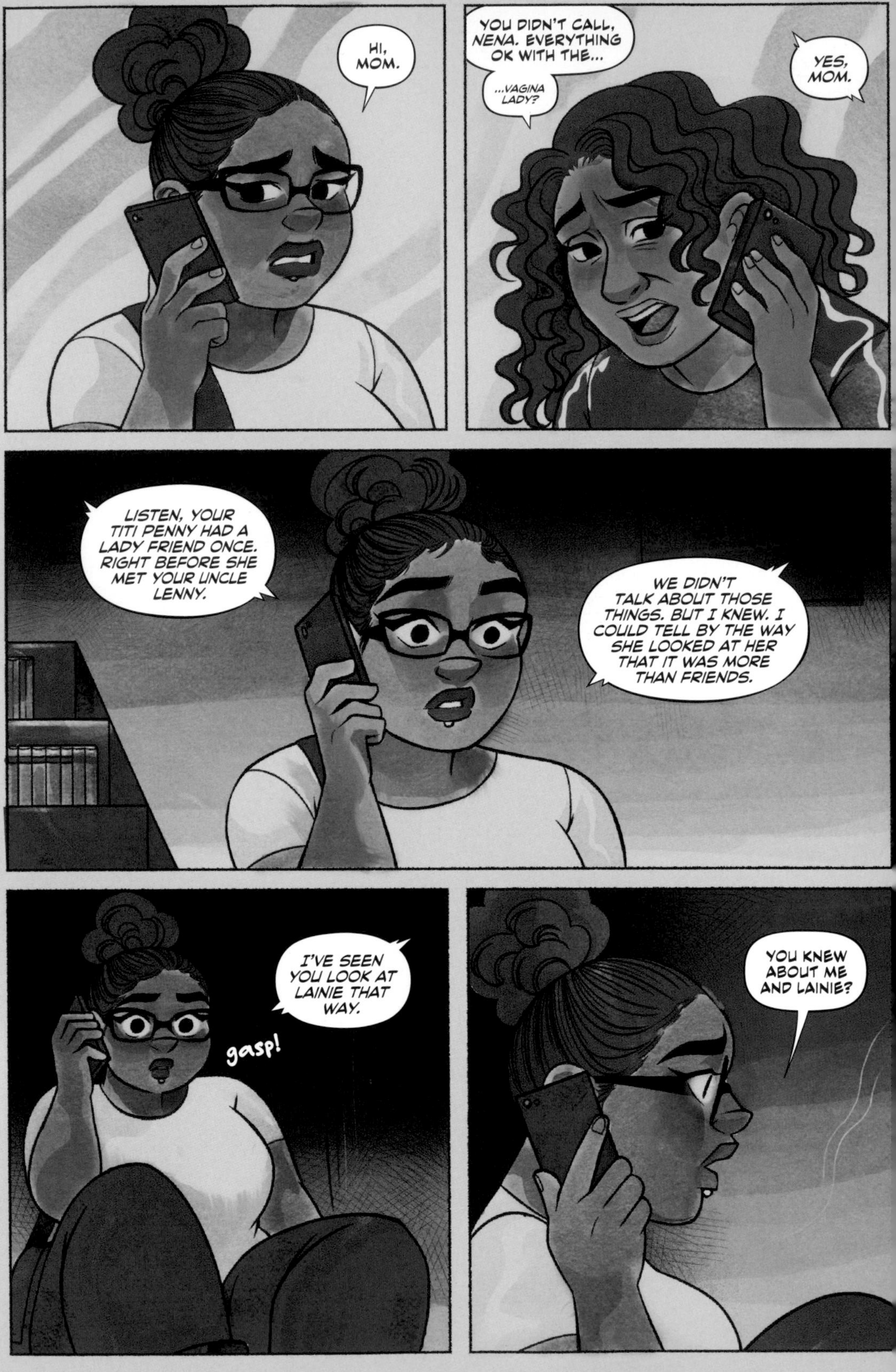
HI, MOM.
YOU DIDN'T CALL, NENA. EVERYTHING OK WITH THE...
...VAGINA LADY?
YES, MOM.
LISTEN, YOUR TITI PENNY HAD A LADY FRIEND ONCE. RIGHT BEFORE SHE MET YOUR UNCLE LENNY.
WE DIDN'T TALK ABOUT THOSE THINGS. BUT I KNEW. I COULD TELL BY THE WAY SHE LOOKED AT HER THAT IT WAS MORE THAN FRIENDS.
I'VE SEEN YOU LOOK AT LAINIE THAT WAY.
gasp!
YOU KNEW ABOUT ME AND LAINIE?

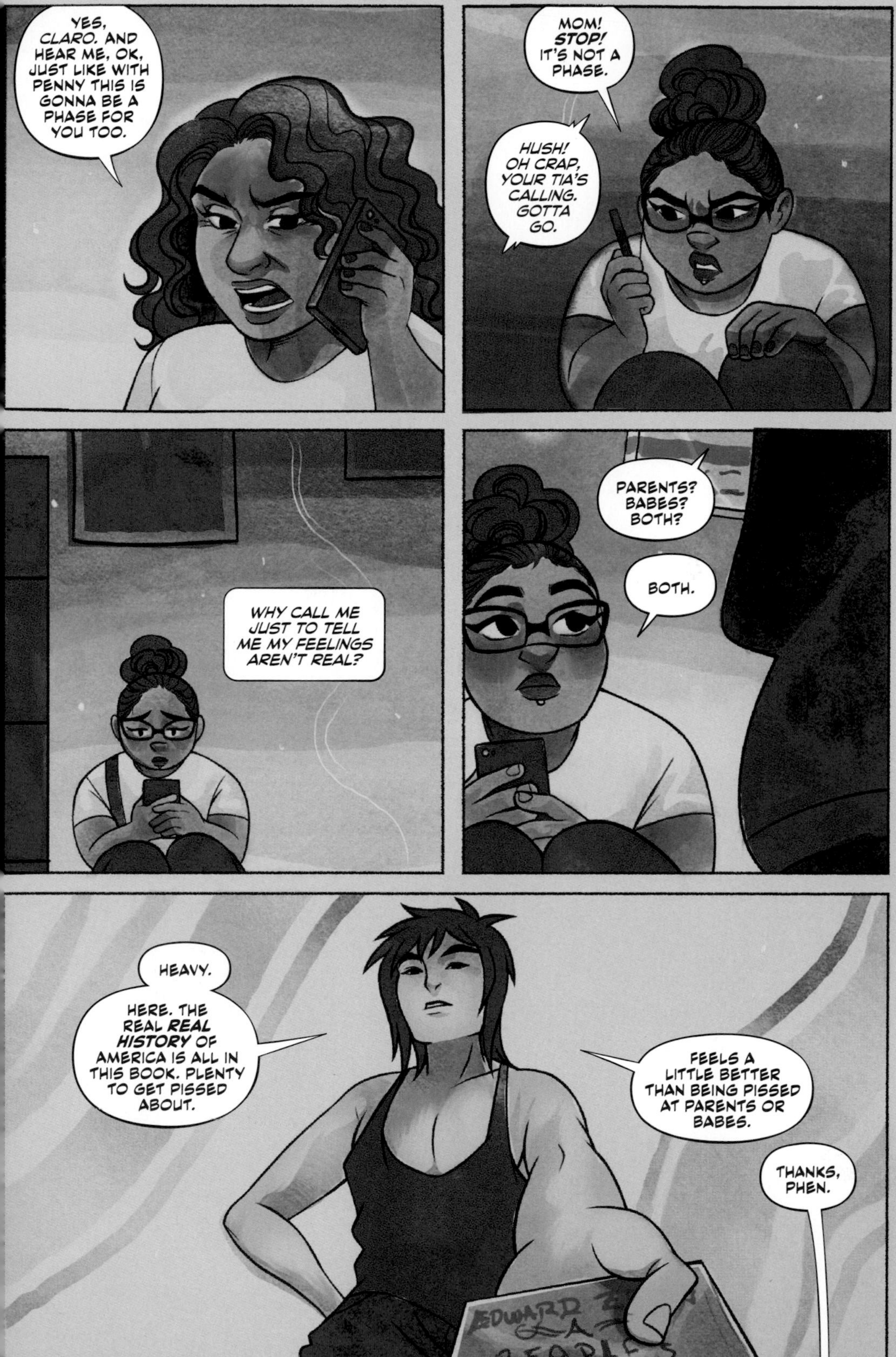
YES, CLARO. AND HEAR ME, OK, JUST LIKE WITH PENNY THIS IS GONNA BE A PHASE FOR YOU TOO.
MOM! STOP! IT'S NOT A PHASE.
HUSH! OH CRAP, YOUR TIA'S CALLING. GOTTA GO.
WHY CALL ME JUST TO TELL ME MY FEELINGS AREN'T REAL?
PARENTS? BABES? BOTH?
BOTH.
HEAVY.
HERE. THE REAL REAL HISTORY OF AMERICA IS ALL IN THIS BOOK. PLENTY TO GET PISSED ABOUT.
FEELS A LITTLE BETTER THAN BEING PISSED AT PARENTS OR BABES.
THANKS, PHEN.

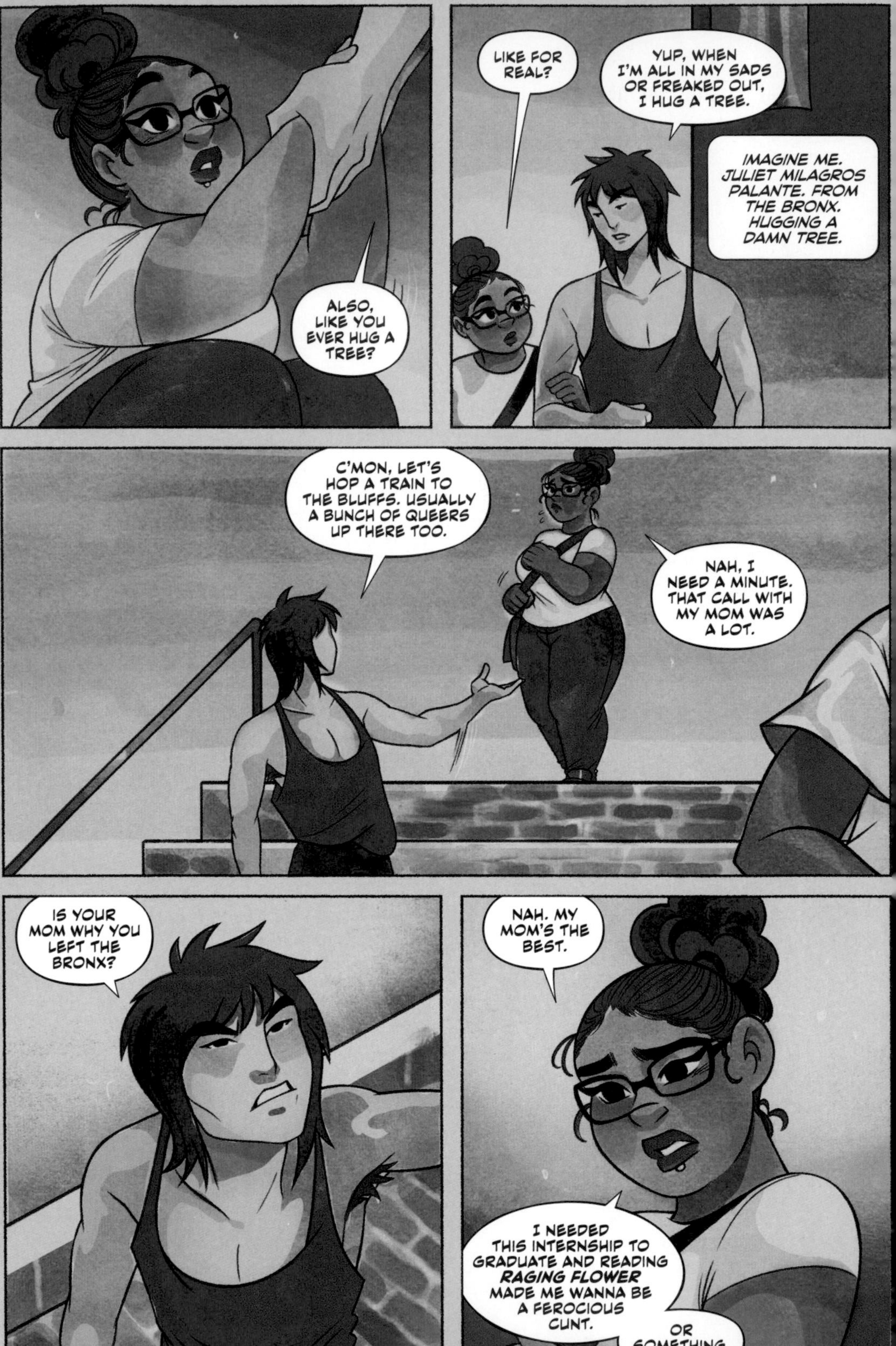
ALSO, LIKE YOU EVER HUG A TREE?
LIKE FOR REAL?
YUP, WHEN I'M ALL IN MY SADS OR FREAKED OUT, I HUG A TREE.
IMAGINE ME. JULIET MILAGROS PALANTE. FROM THE BRONX. HUGGING A DAMN TREE.
C'MON, LET'S HOP A TRAIN TO THE BLUFFS. USUALLY A BUNCH OF QUEERS UP THERE TOO.
NAH, I NEED A MINUTE. THAT CALL WITH MY MOM WAS A LOT.
IS YOUR MOM WHY YOU LEFT THE BRONX?
NAH. MY MOM'S THE BEST.
I NEEDED THIS INTERNSHIP TO GRADUATE AND READING *RAGING FLOWER* MADE ME WANNA BE A FEROCIOUS CUNT.
OR SOMETHING.

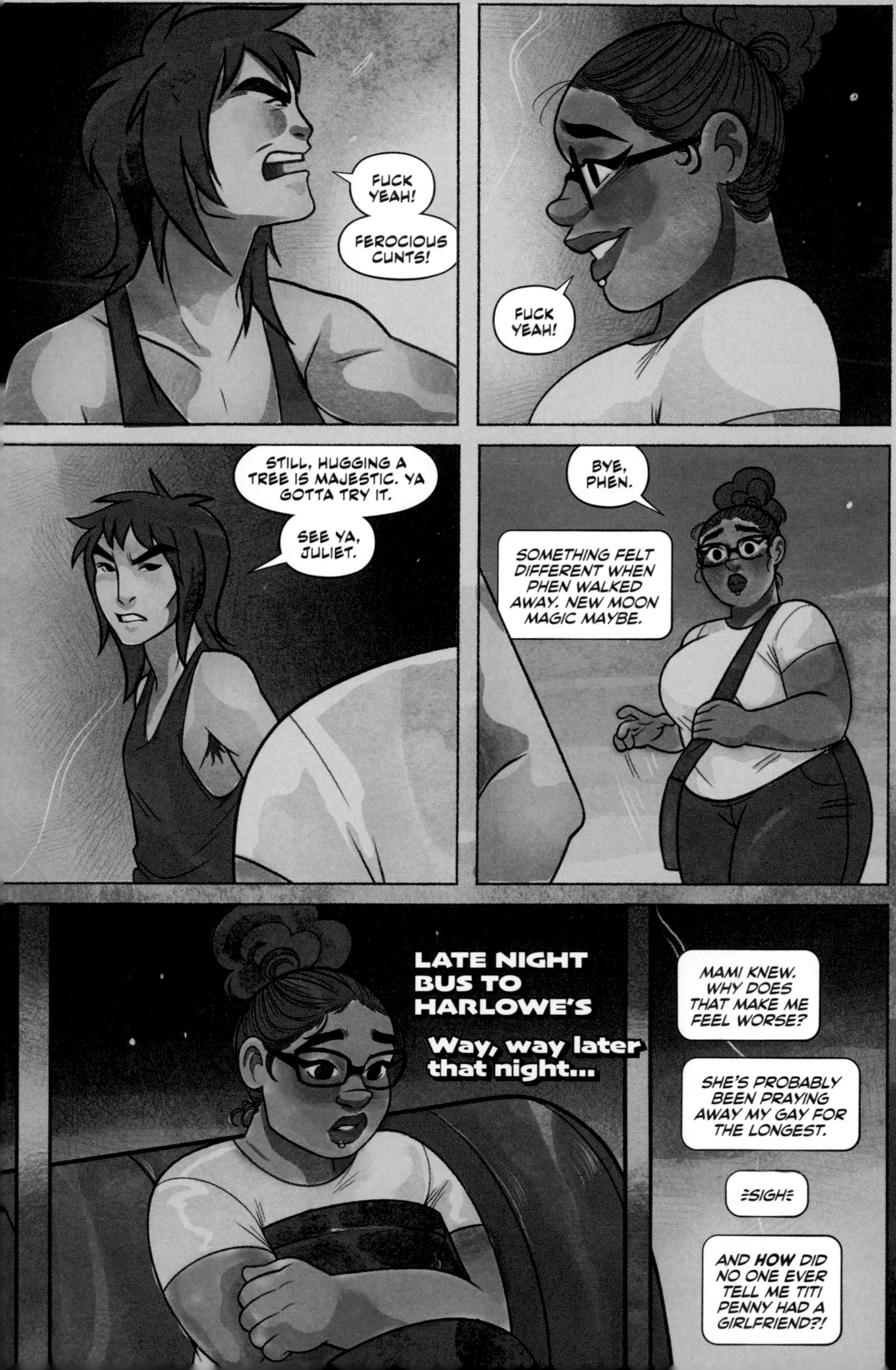
FUCK YEAH!
FEROCIOUS CUNTS!
FUCK YEAH!
STILL, HUGGING A TREE IS MAJESTIC. YA GOTTA TRY IT.
SEE YA, JULIET.
BYE, PHEN.
SOMETHING FELT DIFFERENT WHEN PHEN WALKED AWAY. NEW MOON MAGIC MAYBE.
LATE NIGHT BUS TO HARLOWE'S
Way, way later that night...
MAMI KNEW. WHY DOES THAT MAKE ME FEEL WORSE?
SHE'S PROBABLY BEEN PRAYING AWAY MY GAY FOR THE LONGEST.
SIGH
AND HOW DID NO ONE EVER TELL ME TITI PENNY HAD A GIRLFRIEND?!

HARLOWE'S FRONT STEPS

DANGIT! I TOTALLY FORGOT TO TALK TO SOMEONE ABOUT HARLOWE'S READING. UGH!

TERRIBLE GAY AND TERRIBLE ASSISTANT.

PHEN, WHAT ARE YOU DOING UP?

LEAN

WHAT'S WITH ALL THE BAGS? ARE YOU GOING SOMEWHERE?

YUP! THE OREGON COASTAL TRAIL.

LITERALLY YES. THE UNIVERSE KNOWS ALL! GO FORTH, PHEN.

HUNDREDS OF SPECIES OF TREES. IMAGINE ALL THE HUGS THEY HAVE TO GIVE.

AND YOU KNOW, MAYBE LIKE, THIS IS MY PATH. JULIET'S ON HERS.

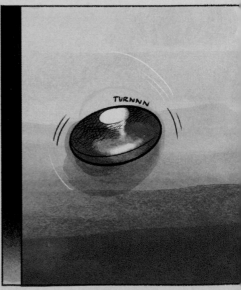

TURNNN

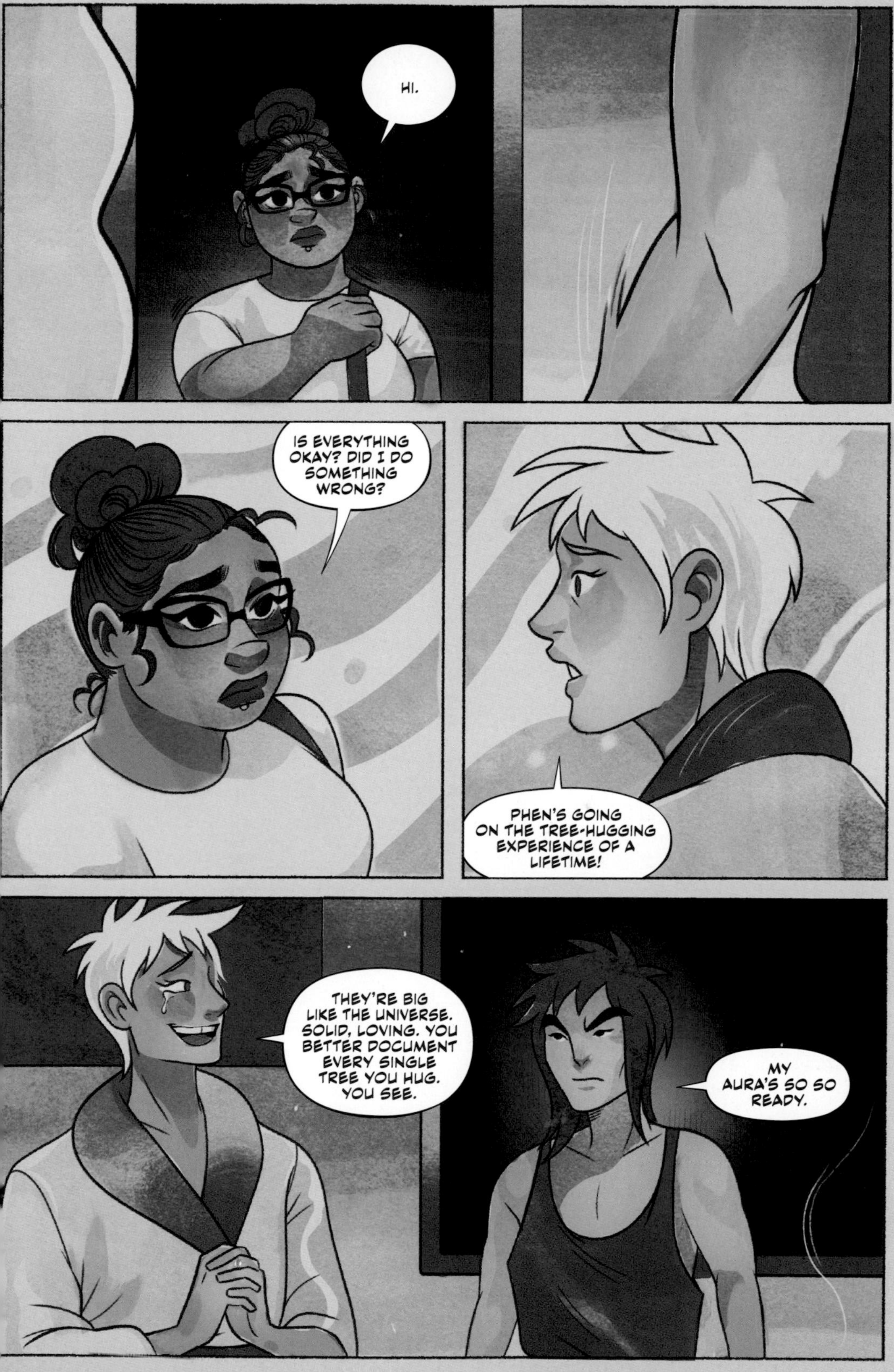
HI.
IS EVERYTHING OKAY? DID I DO SOMETHING WRONG?
PHEN'S GOING ON THE TREE-HUGGING EXPERIENCE OF A LIFETIME!
THEY'RE BIG LIKE THE UNIVERSE. SOLID, LOVING. YOU BETTER DOCUMENT EVERY SINGLE TREE YOU HUG. YOU SEE.
MY AURA'S SO SO READY.

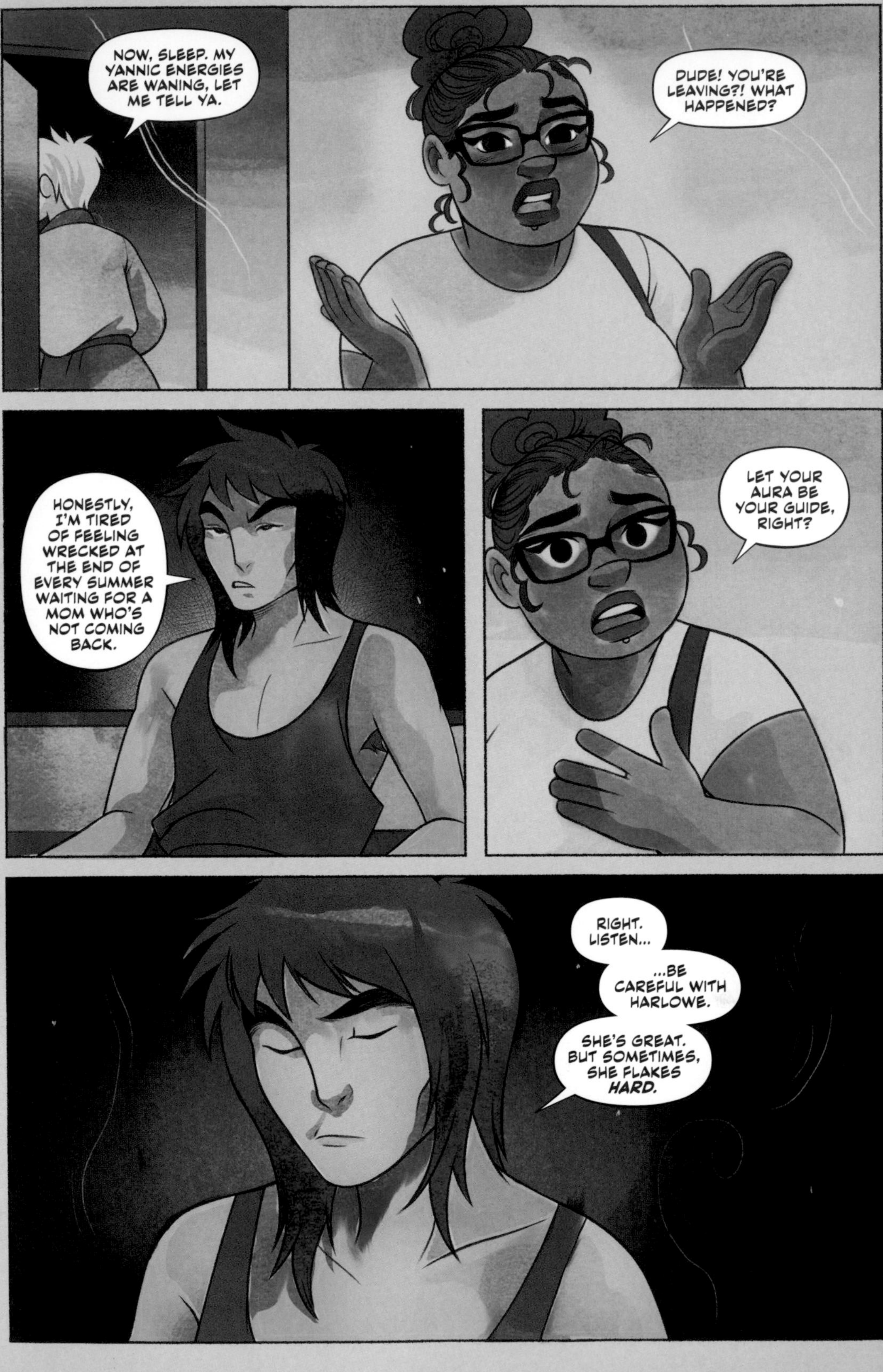
NOW, SLEEP. MY YANNIC ENERGIES ARE WANING, LET ME TELL YA.
DUDE! YOU'RE LEAVING?! WHAT HAPPENED?
HONESTLY, I'M TIRED OF FEELING WRECKED AT THE END OF EVERY SUMMER WAITING FOR A MOM WHO'S NOT COMING BACK.
LET YOUR AURA BE YOUR GUIDE, RIGHT?
RIGHT. LISTEN...
...BE CAREFUL WITH HARLOWE.
SHE'S GREAT. BUT SOMETIMES, SHE FLAKES ***HARD.***

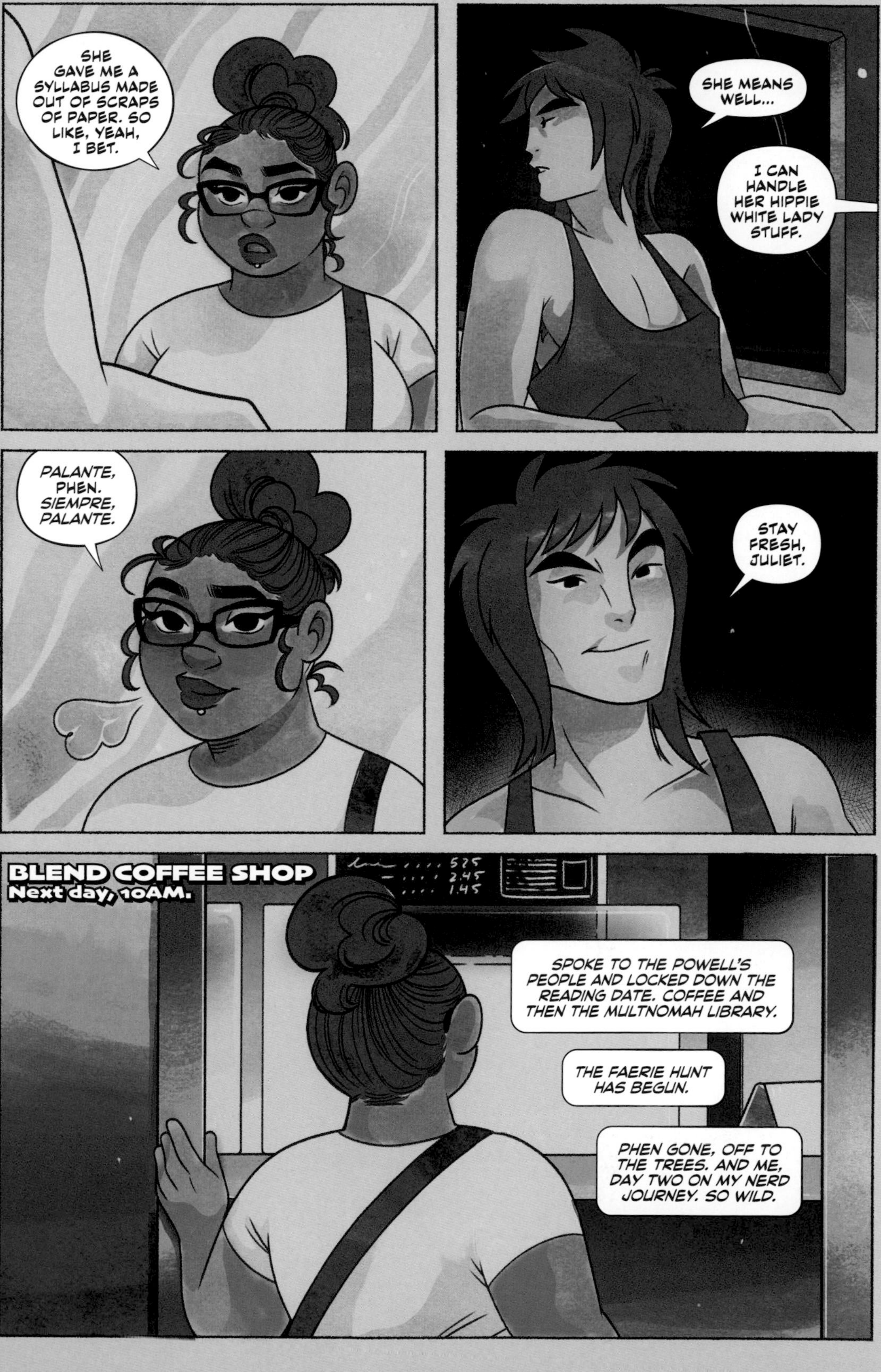
SHE GAVE ME A SYLLABUS MADE OUT OF SCRAPS OF PAPER. SO LIKE, YEAH, I BET.
SHE MEANS WELL...
I CAN HANDLE HER HIPPIE WHITE LADY STUFF.
PALANTE, PHEN. SIEMPRE, PALANTE.
STAY FRESH, JULIET.
BLEND COFFEE SHOP
Next day, 10AM.
SPOKE TO THE POWELL'S PEOPLE AND LOCKED DOWN THE READING DATE. COFFEE AND THEN THE MULTNOMAH LIBRARY.
THE FAERIE HUNT HAS BEGUN.
PHEN GONE, OFF TO THE TREES. AND ME, DAY TWO ON MY NERD JOURNEY. SO WILD.

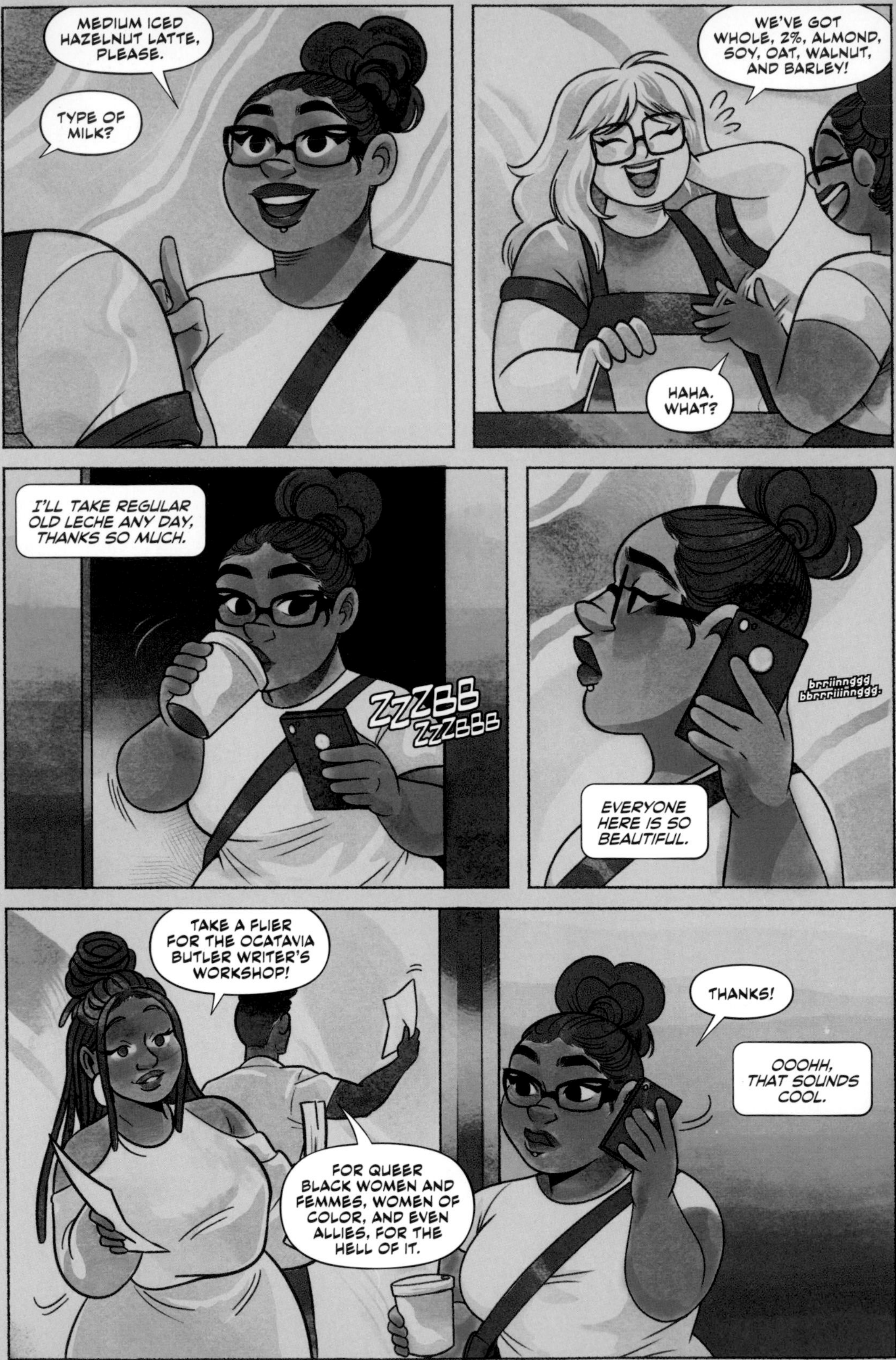

MEDIUM ICED HAZELNUT LATTE, PLEASE.
TYPE OF MILK?
WE'VE GOT WHOLE, 2%, ALMOND, SOY, OAT, WALNUT, AND BARLEY!
HAHA. WHAT?
I'LL TAKE REGULAR OLD LECHE ANY DAY, THANKS SO MUCH.
ZZZBB
ZZZBBB
brriinnggg
bbrrrriiinnggg.
EVERYONE HERE IS SO BEAUTIFUL.
TAKE A FLIER FOR THE OCATAVIA BUTLER WRITER'S WORKSHOP!
FOR QUEER BLACK WOMEN AND FEMMES, WOMEN OF COLOR, AND EVEN ALLIES, FOR THE HELL OF IT.
THANKS!
OOOHH, THAT SOUNDS COOL.

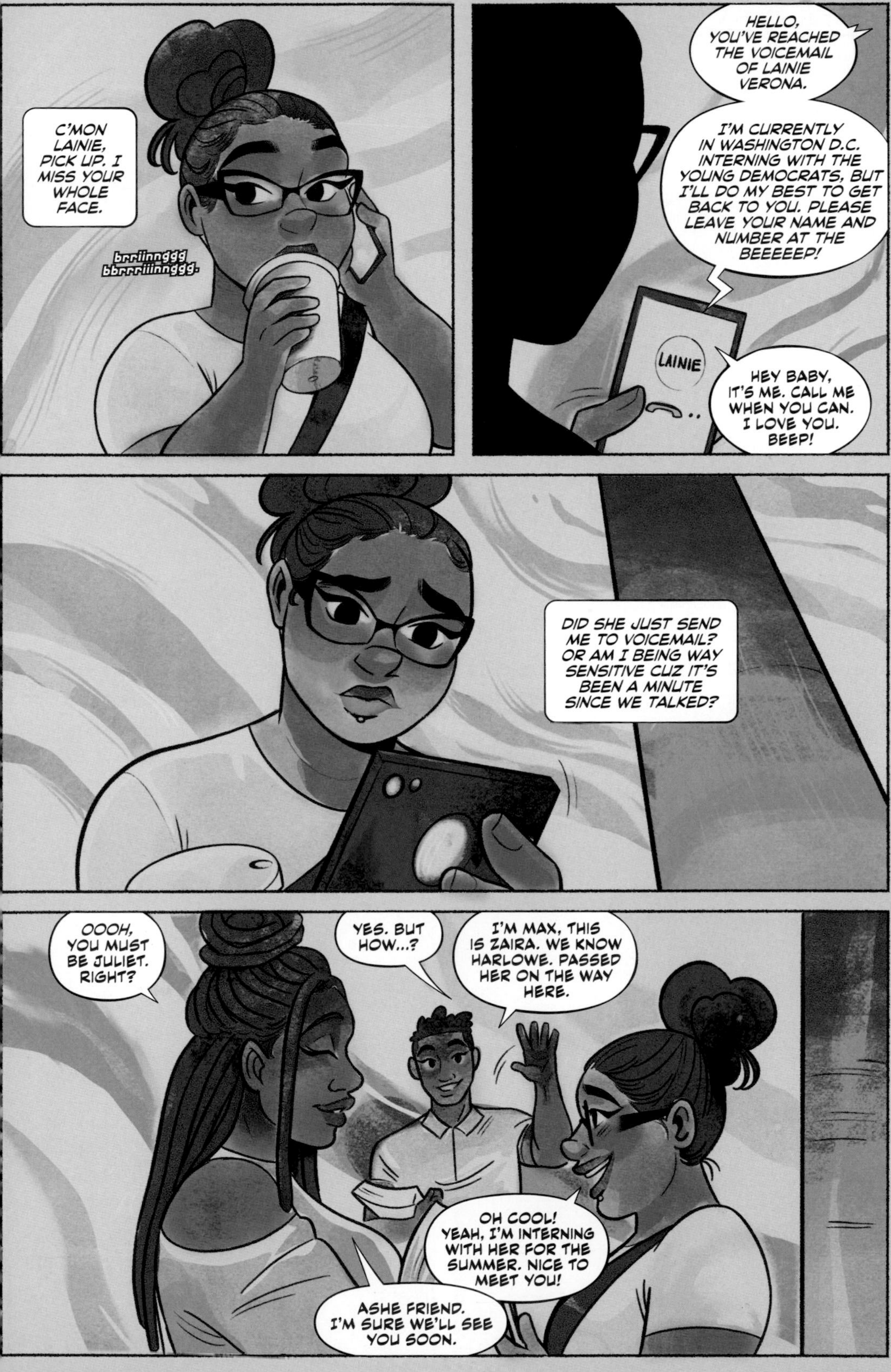
C'MON LAINIE, PICK UP. I MISS YOUR WHOLE FACE.
brriinnggg bbrrriiinnggg.
HELLO, YOU'VE REACHED THE VOICEMAIL OF LAINIE VERONA.
I'M CURRENTLY IN WASHINGTON D.C. INTERNING WITH THE YOUNG DEMOCRATS, BUT I'LL DO MY BEST TO GET BACK TO YOU. PLEASE LEAVE YOUR NAME AND NUMBER AT THE BEEEEEP!
LAINIE
HEY BABY, IT'S ME. CALL ME WHEN YOU CAN. I LOVE YOU. BEEP!
DID SHE JUST SEND ME TO VOICEMAIL? OR AM I BEING WAY SENSITIVE CUZ IT'S BEEN A MINUTE SINCE WE TALKED?
OOOH, YOU MUST BE JULIET. RIGHT?
YES. BUT HOW...?
I'M MAX, THIS IS ZAIRA. WE KNOW HARLOWE. PASSED HER ON THE WAY HERE.
OH COOL! YEAH, I'M INTERNING WITH HER FOR THE SUMMER. NICE TO MEET YOU!
ASHE FRIEND. I'M SURE WE'LL SEE YOU SOON.

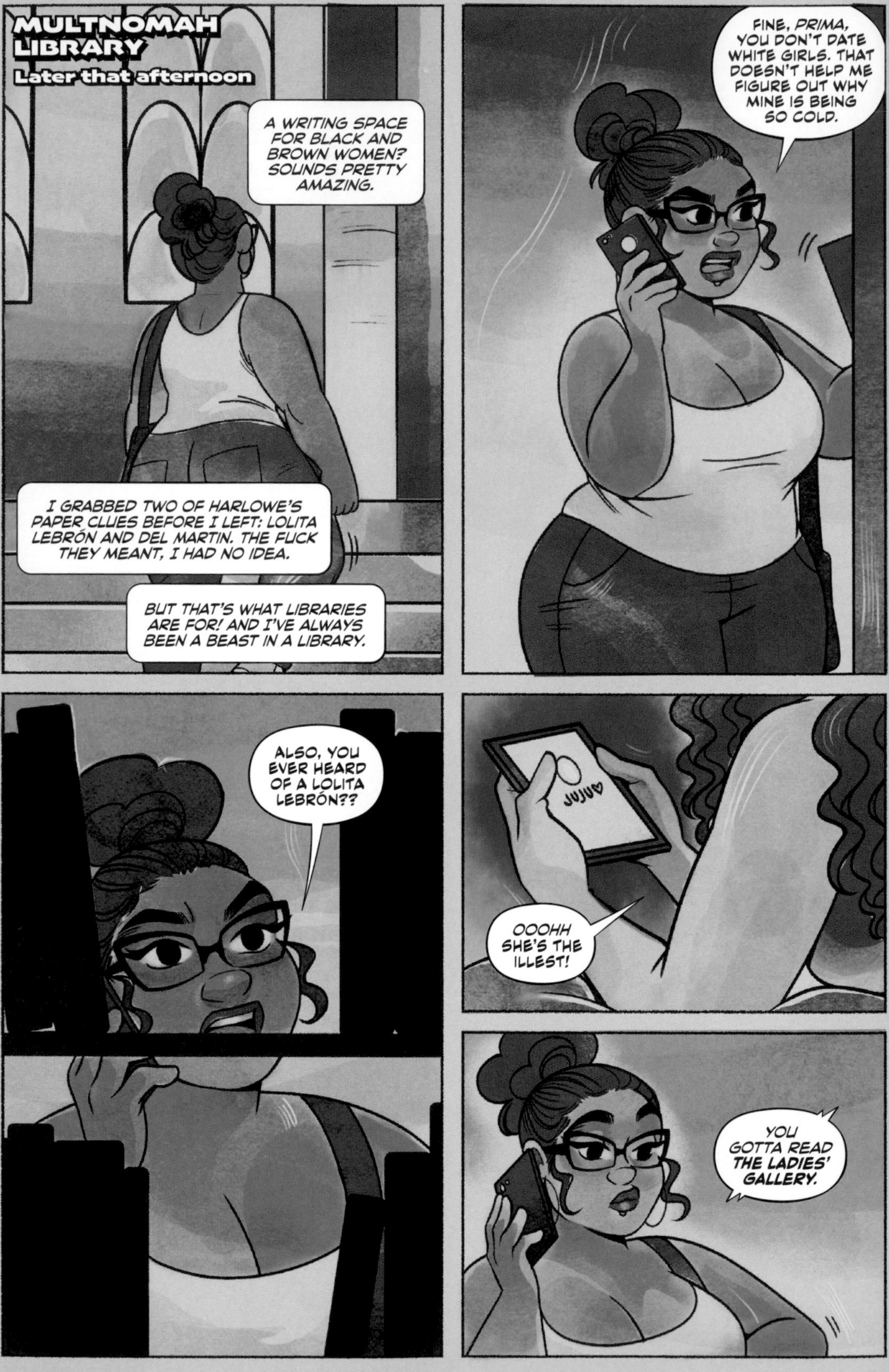
MULTNOMAH LIBRARY
Later that afternoon
A WRITING SPACE FOR BLACK AND BROWN WOMEN? SOUNDS PRETTY AMAZING.
I GRABBED TWO OF HARLOWE'S PAPER CLUES BEFORE I LEFT: LOLITA LEBRÓN AND DEL MARTIN. THE FUCK THEY MEANT, I HAD NO IDEA.
BUT THAT'S WHAT LIBRARIES ARE FOR! AND I'VE ALWAYS BEEN A BEAST IN A LIBRARY.
FINE, *PRIMA*, YOU DON'T DATE WHITE GIRLS. THAT DOESN'T HELP ME FIGURE OUT WHY MINE IS BEING SO COLD.
ALSO, YOU EVER HEARD OF A LOLITA LEBRÓN??
JUJU♡
OOOHH SHE'S THE ILLEST!
YOU GOTTA READ ***THE LADIES' GALLERY.***

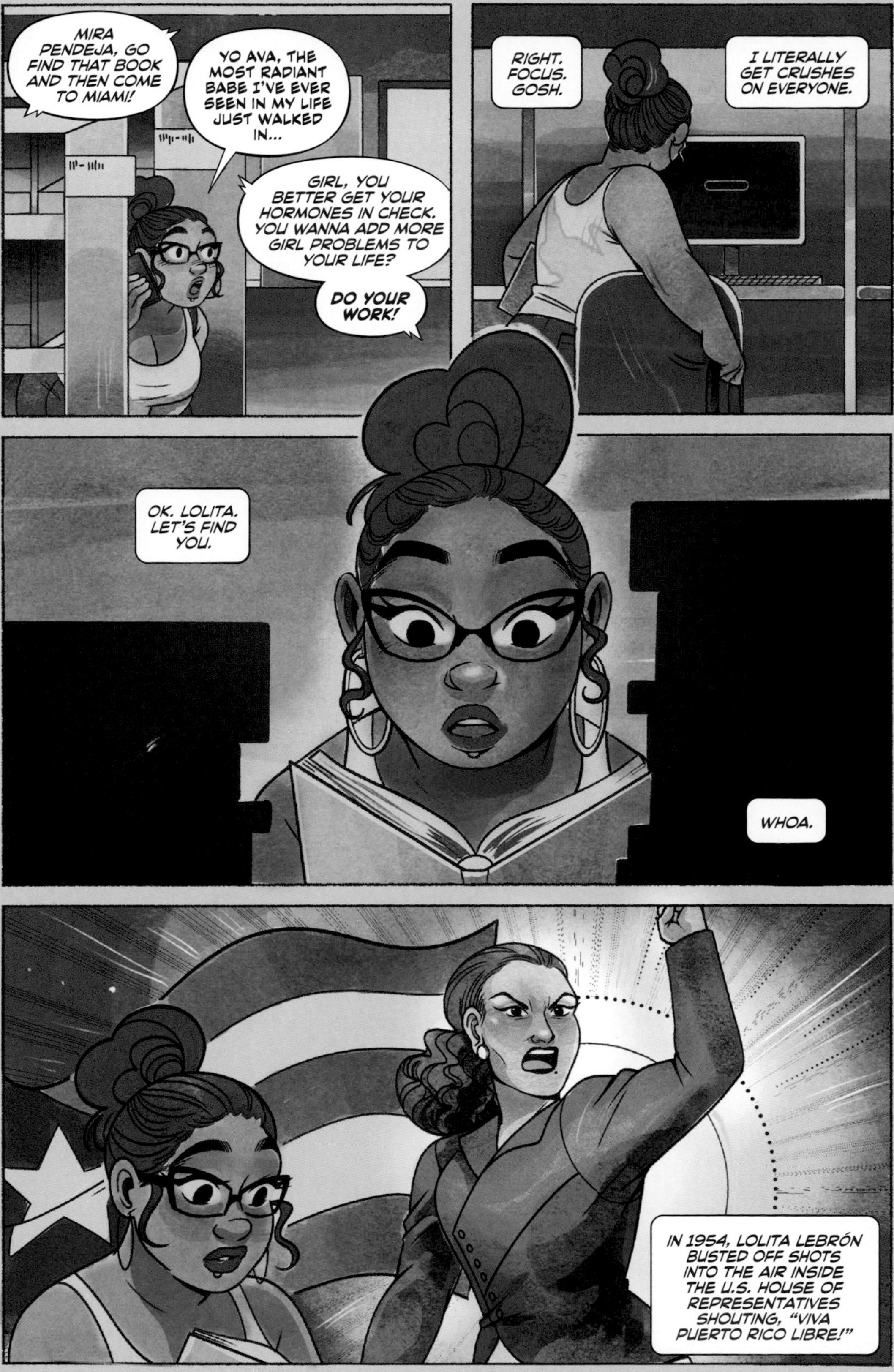
MIRA PENDEJA, GO FIND THAT BOOK AND THEN COME TO MIAMI!
YO AVA, THE MOST RADIANT BABE I'VE EVER SEEN IN MY LIFE JUST WALKED IN...
GIRL, YOU BETTER GET YOUR HORMONES IN CHECK. YOU WANNA ADD MORE GIRL PROBLEMS TO YOUR LIFE?
DO YOUR WORK!
RIGHT. FOCUS. GOSH.
I LITERALLY GET CRUSHES ON EVERYONE.
OK. LOLITA. LET'S FIND YOU.
WHOA.
IN 1954, LOLITA LEBRÓN BUSTED OFF SHOTS INTO THE AIR INSIDE THE U.S. HOUSE OF REPRESENTATIVES SHOUTING, "VIVA PUERTO RICO LIBRE!"

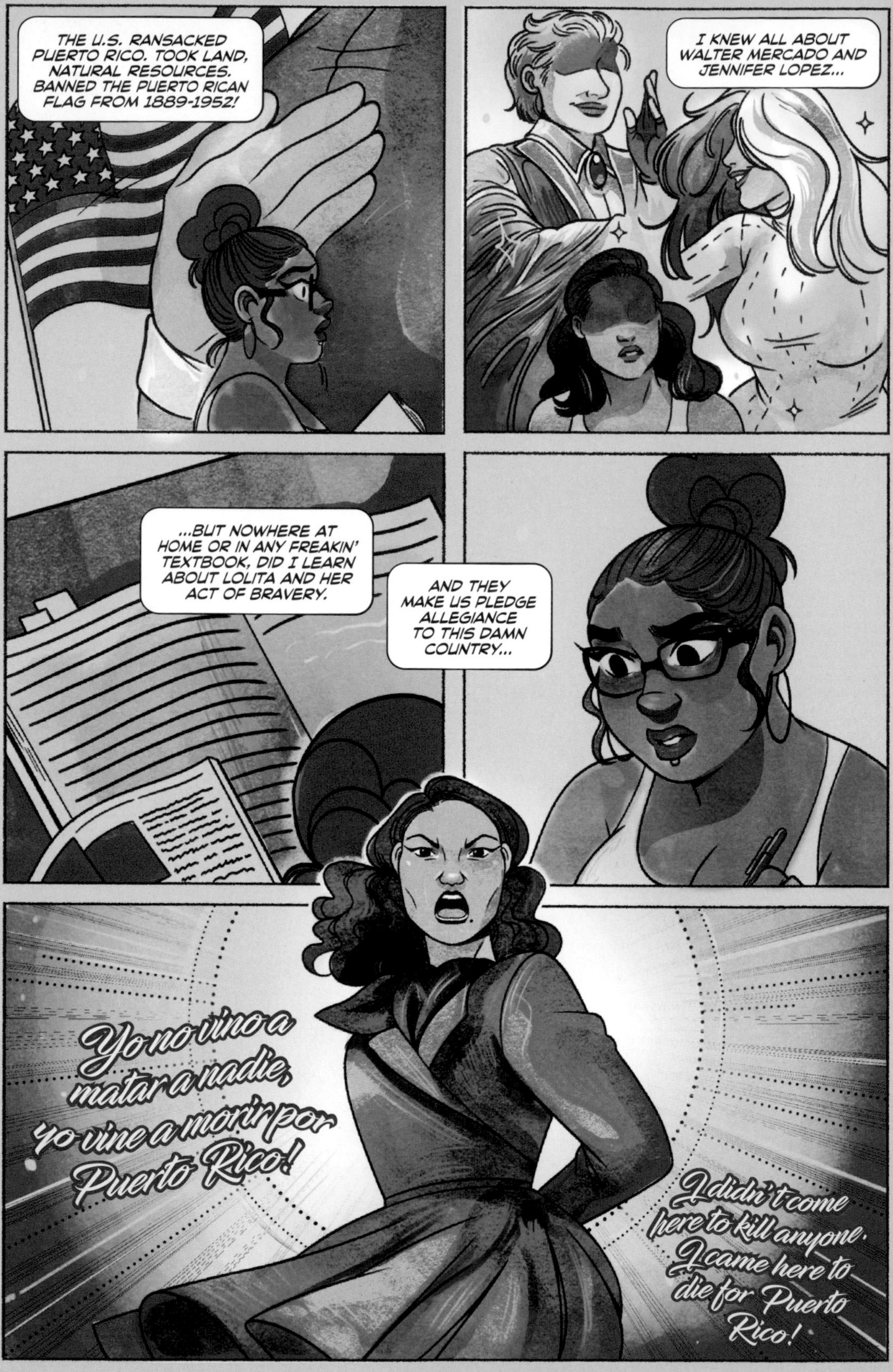
THE U.S. RANSACKED PUERTO RICO. TOOK LAND, NATURAL RESOURCES. BANNED THE PUERTO RICAN FLAG FROM 1889-1952!
I KNEW ALL ABOUT WALTER MERCADO AND JENNIFER LOPEZ...
...BUT NOWHERE AT HOME OR IN ANY FREAKIN' TEXTBOOK, DID I LEARN ABOUT LOLITA AND HER ACT OF BRAVERY.
AND THEY MAKE US PLEDGE ALLEGIANCE TO THIS DAMN COUNTRY...
Yo no vino a matar a nadie, yo vine a morir por Puerto Rico!
I didn't come here to kill anyone. I came here to die for Puerto Rico!

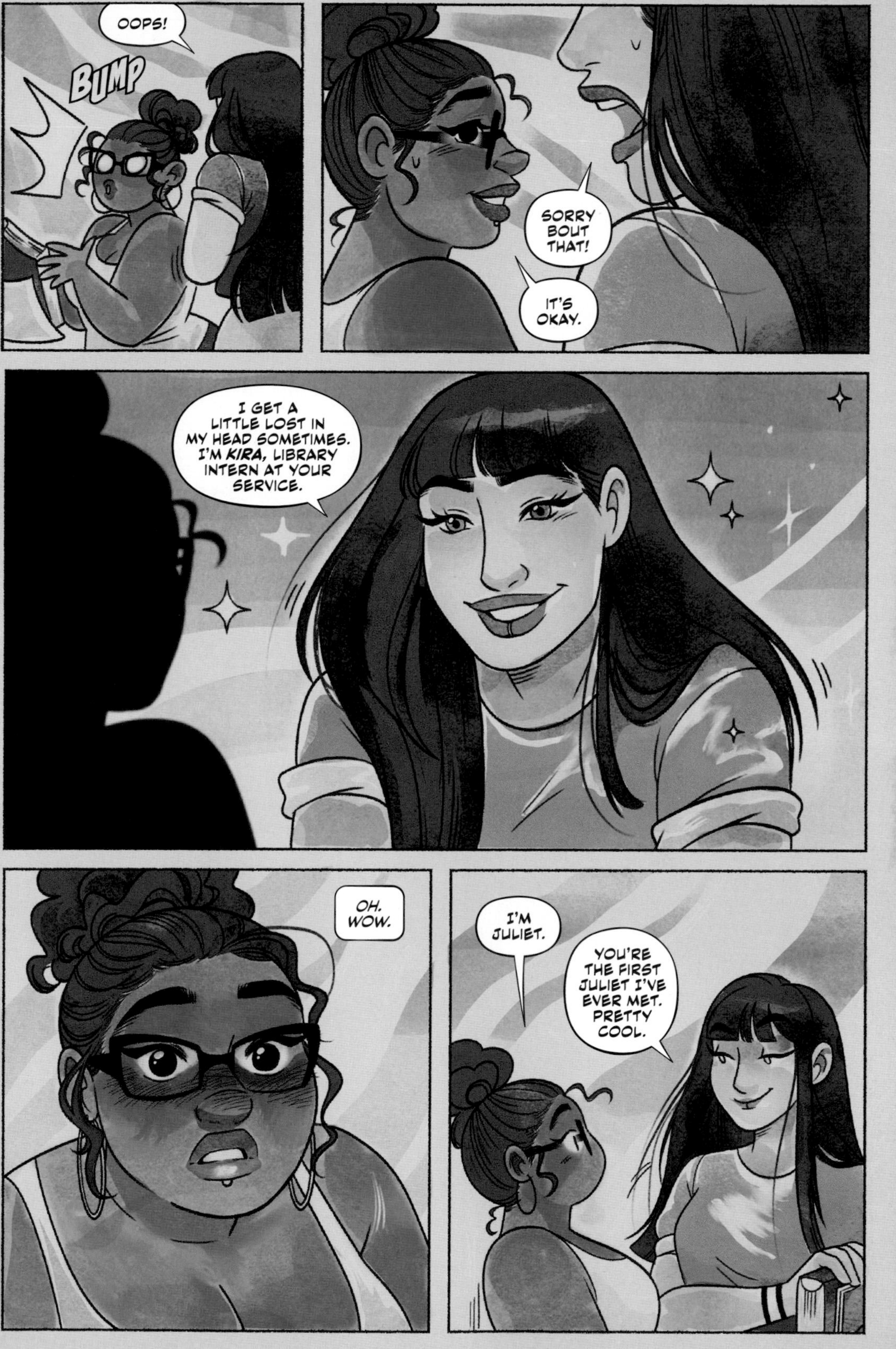
OOPS!
BUMP
SORRY BOUT THAT!
IT'S OKAY.
I GET A LITTLE LOST IN MY HEAD SOMETIMES. I'M KIRA, LIBRARY INTERN AT YOUR SERVICE.
OH. WOW.
I'M JULIET.
YOU'RE THE FIRST JULIET I'VE EVER MET. PRETTY COOL.

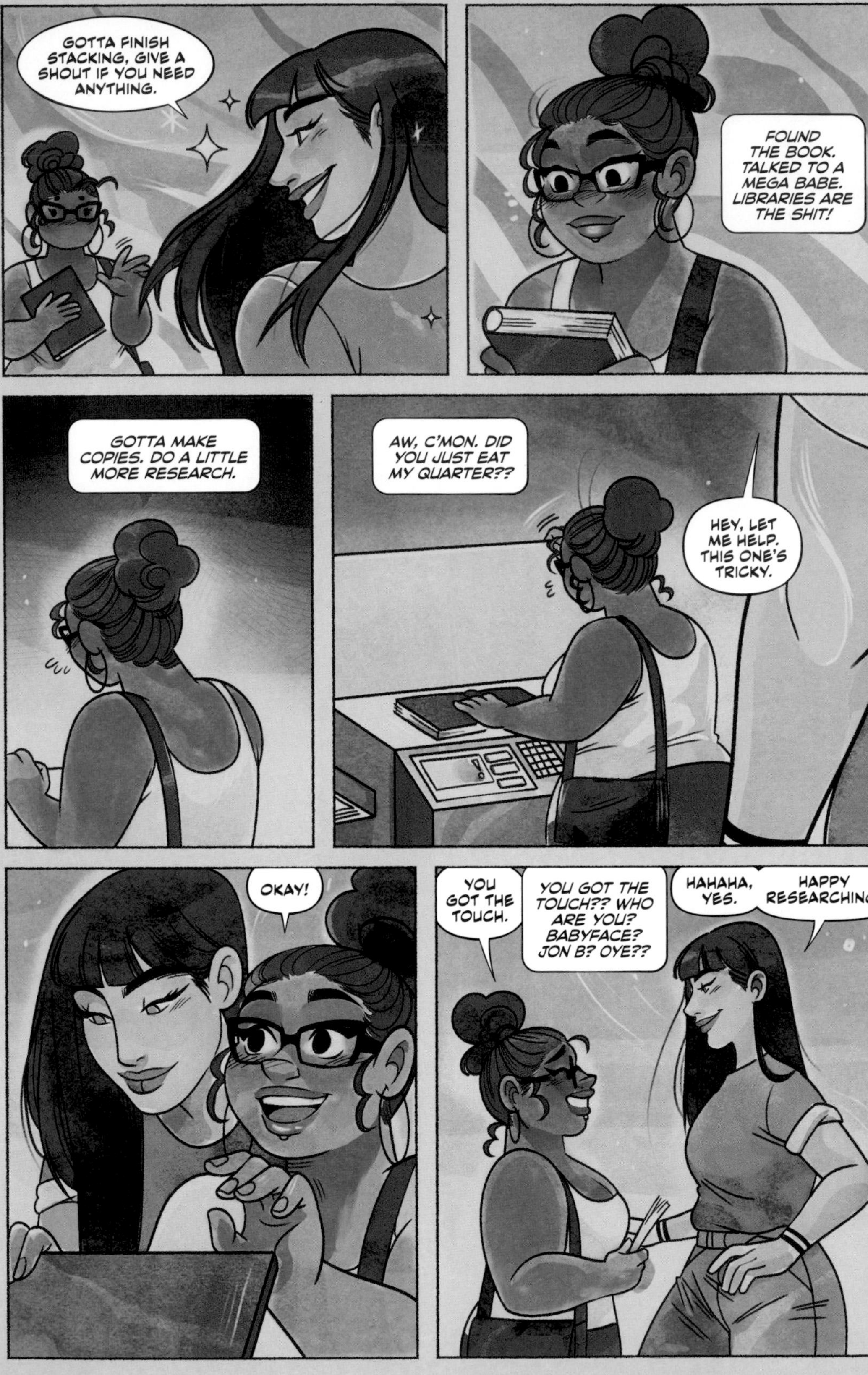
GOTTA FINISH STACKING, GIVE A SHOUT IF YOU NEED ANYTHING.
FOUND THE BOOK. TALKED TO A MEGA BABE. LIBRARIES ARE THE SHIT!
GOTTA MAKE COPIES. DO A LITTLE MORE RESEARCH.
AW, C'MON. DID YOU JUST EAT MY QUARTER??
HEY, LET ME HELP. THIS ONE'S TRICKY.
OKAY!
YOU GOT THE TOUCH.
YOU GOT THE TOUCH?? WHO ARE YOU? BABYFACE? JON B? OYE??
HAHAHA, YES.
HAPPY RESEARCHING!

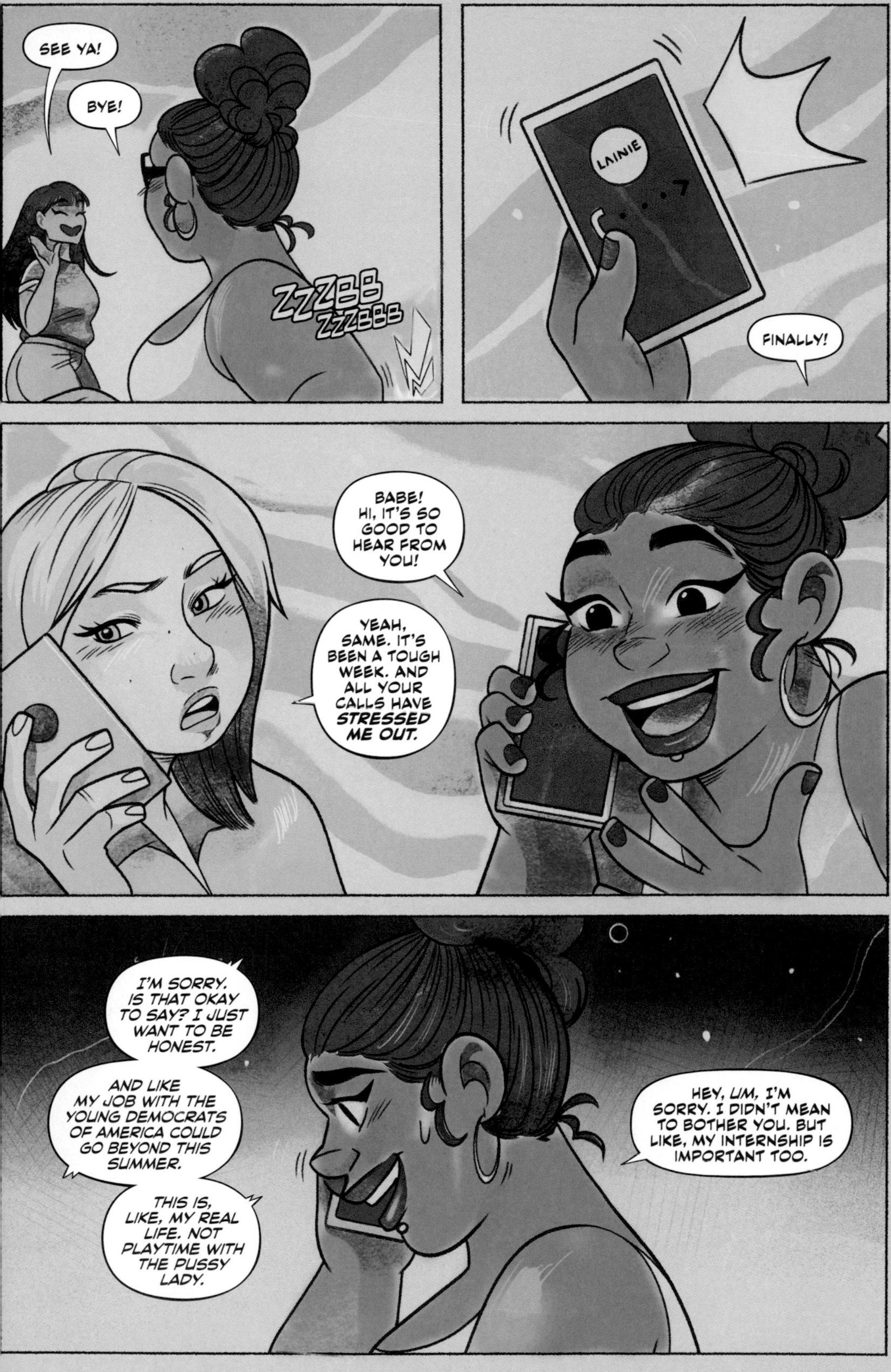
SEE YA!
BYE!
ZZZBBB ZZZBBB
LAINIE
FINALLY!
BABE! HI, IT'S SO GOOD TO HEAR FROM YOU!
YEAH, SAME. IT'S BEEN A TOUGH WEEK. AND ALL YOUR CALLS HAVE STRESSED ME OUT.
I'M SORRY. IS THAT OKAY TO SAY? I JUST WANT TO BE HONEST.
AND LIKE MY JOB WITH THE YOUNG DEMOCRATS OF AMERICA COULD GO BEYOND THIS SUMMER.
THIS IS, LIKE, MY REAL LIFE. NOT PLAYTIME WITH THE PUSSY LADY.
HEY, UM, I'M SORRY. I DIDN'T MEAN TO BOTHER YOU. BUT LIKE, MY INTERNSHIP IS IMPORTANT TOO.

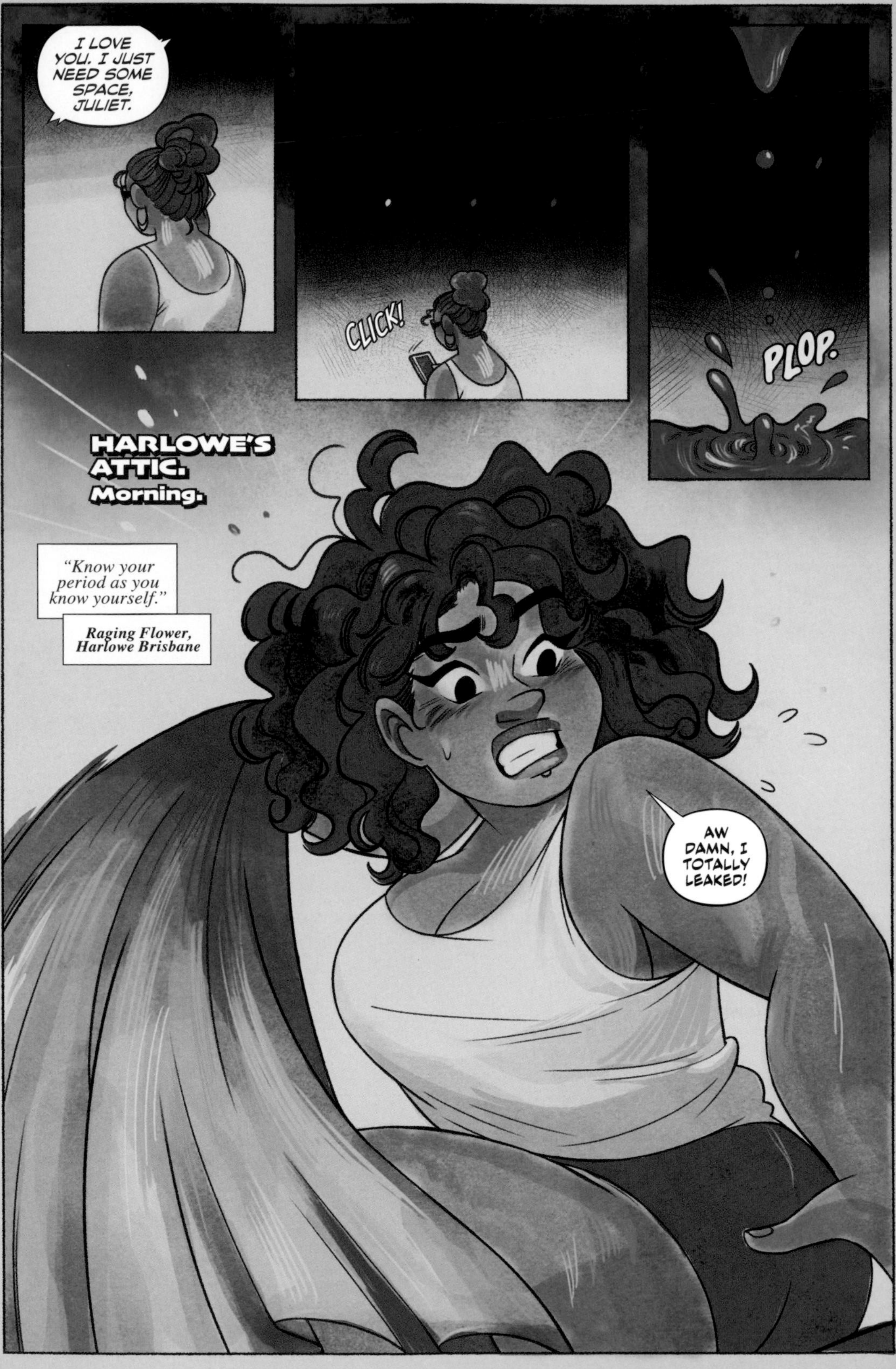
I LOVE YOU. I JUST NEED SOME SPACE, JULIET.
CLICK!
PLOP.
HARLOWE'S ATTIC. Morning.
"Know your period as you know yourself."
Raging Flower, Harlowe Brisbane
AW DAMN, I TOTALLY LEAKED!

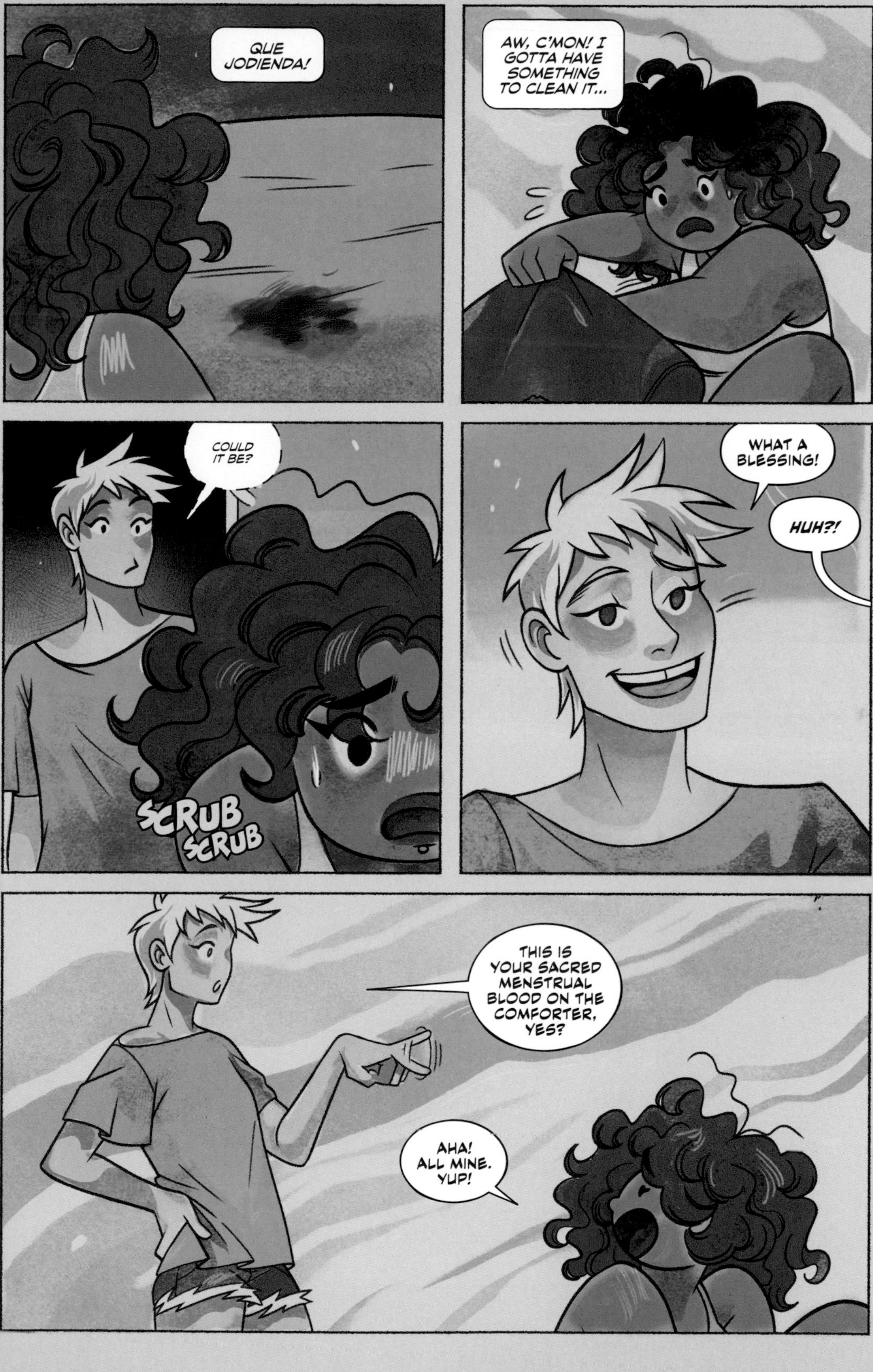
QUE JODIENDA!
AW, C'MON! I GOTTA HAVE SOMETHING TO CLEAN IT...
COULD IT BE?
SCRUB SCRUB
WHAT A BLESSING!
HUH?!
THIS IS YOUR SACRED MENSTRUAL BLOOD ON THE COMFORTER, YES?
AHA! ALL MINE. YUP!

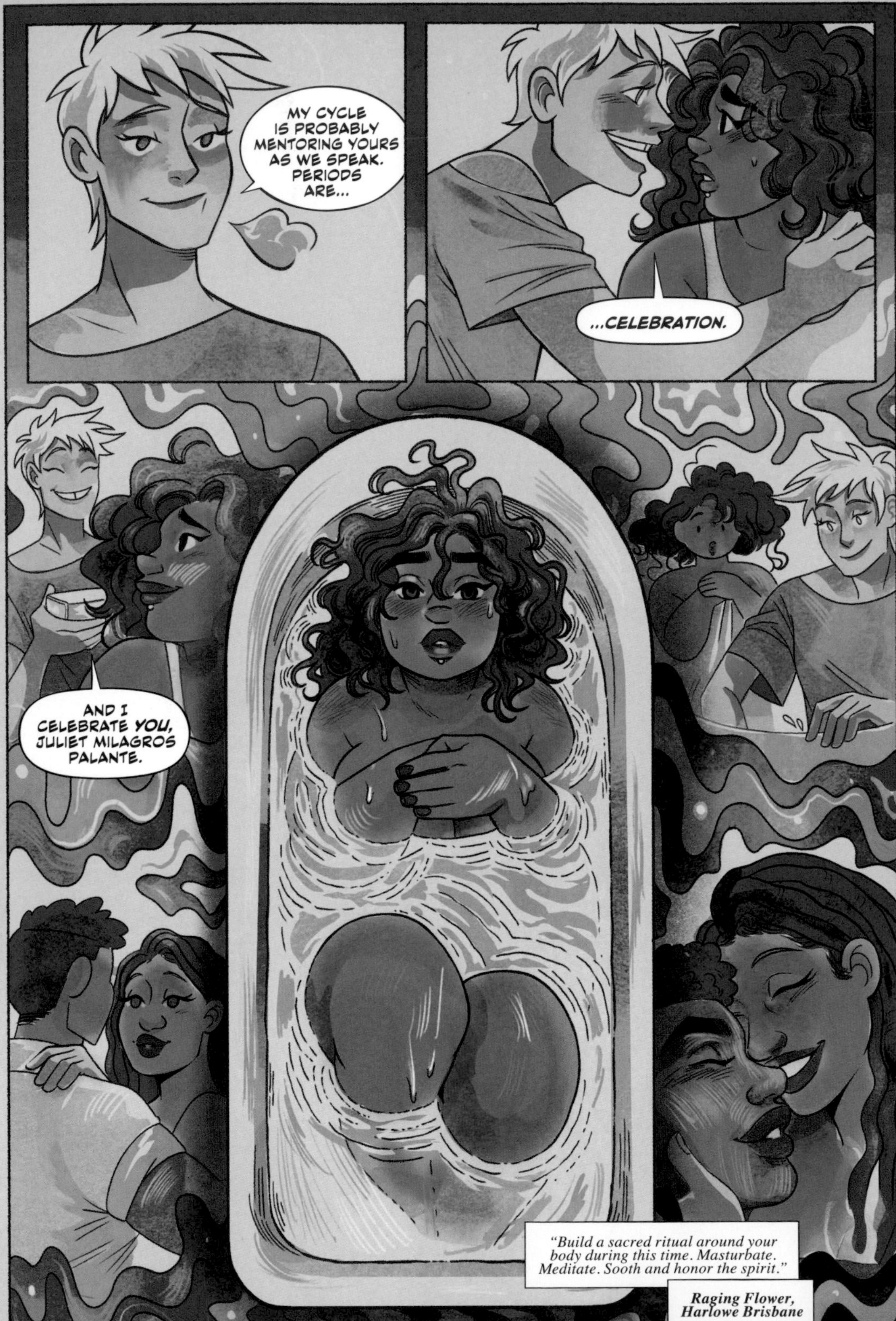
MY CYCLE IS PROBABLY MENTORING YOURS AS WE SPEAK. PERIODS ARE...
...CELEBRATION.
AND I CELEBRATE YOU, JULIET MILAGROS PALANTE.
"Build a sacred ritual around your body during this time. Masturbate. Meditate. Sooth and honor the spirit."
Raging Flower, Harlowe Brisbane

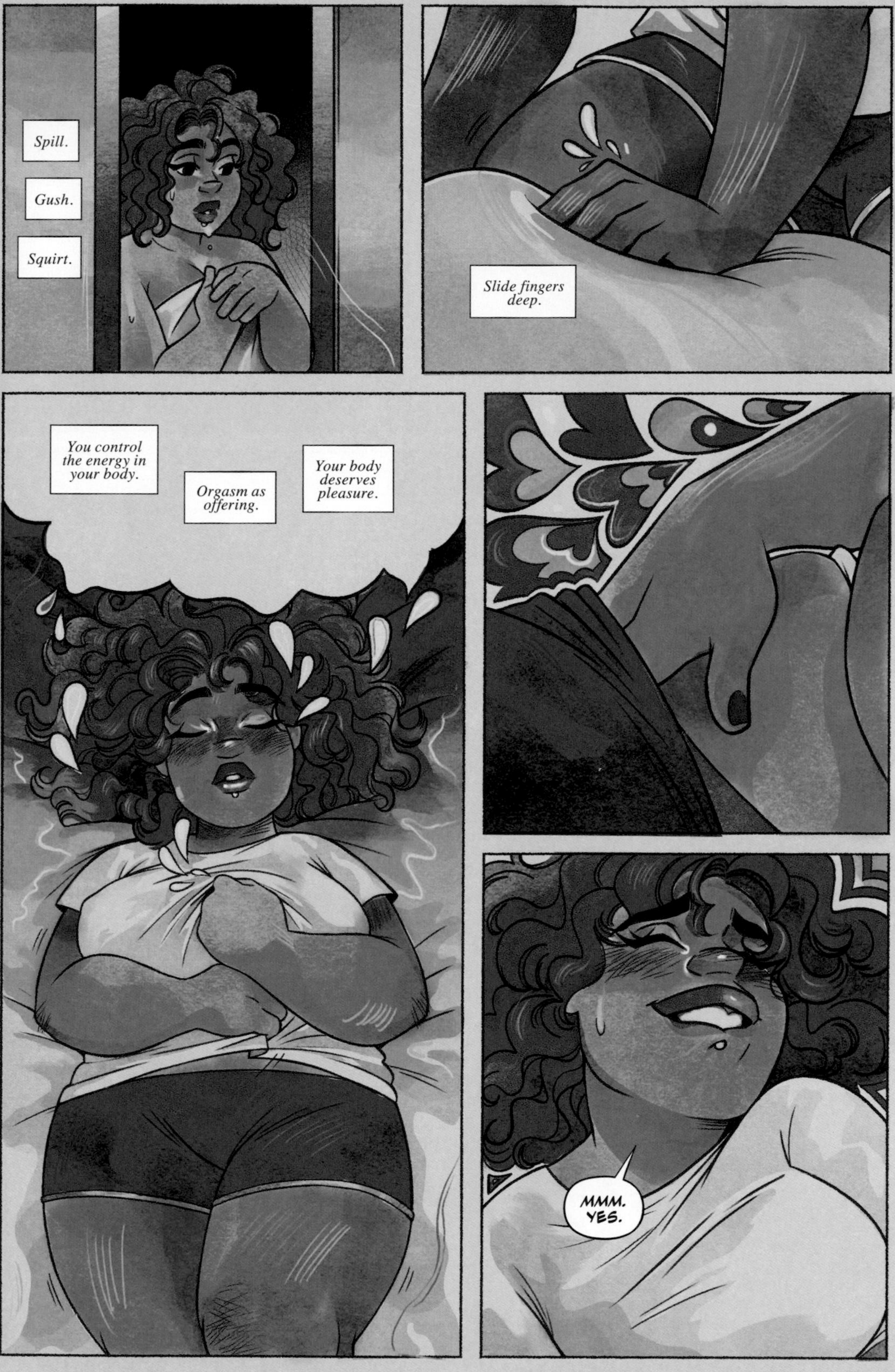
Spill.
Gush.
Squirt.
Slide fingers deep.
You control the energy in your body.
Orgasm as offering.
Your body deserves pleasure.
MMM. YES.

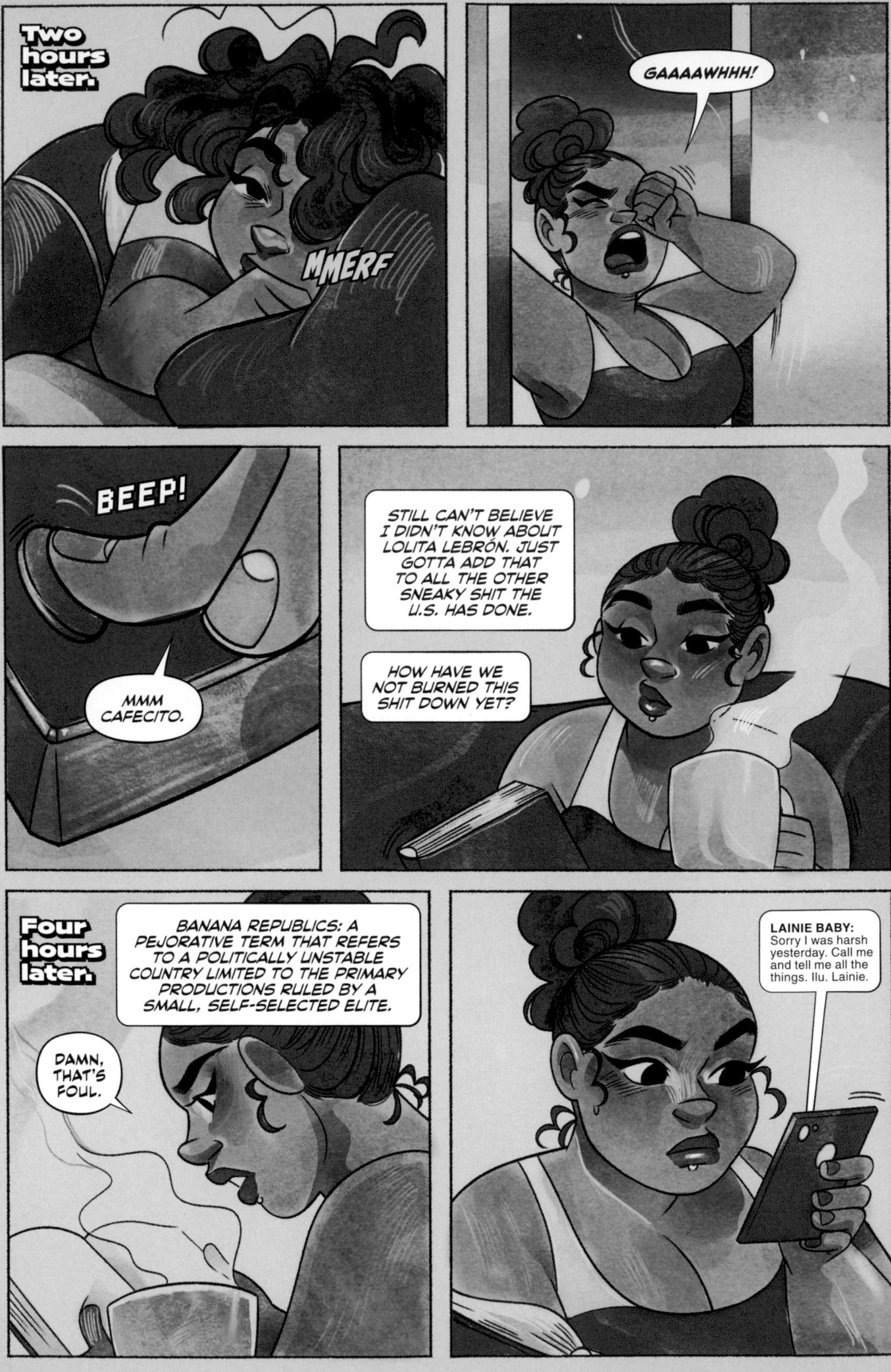
Two hours later.
MMERF
GAAAAWHHH!
BEEP!
MMM CAFECITO.
STILL CAN'T BELIEVE I DIDN'T KNOW ABOUT LOLITA LEBRÓN. JUST GOTTA ADD THAT TO ALL THE OTHER SNEAKY SHIT THE U.S. HAS DONE.
HOW HAVE WE NOT BURNED THIS SHIT DOWN YET?
Four hours later.
BANANA REPUBLICS: A PEJORATIVE TERM THAT REFERS TO A POLITICALLY UNSTABLE COUNTRY LIMITED TO THE PRIMARY PRODUCTIONS RULED BY A SMALL, SELF-SELECTED ELITE.
DAMN, THAT'S FOUL.
LAINIE BABY:
Sorry I was harsh yesterday. Call me and tell me all the things. Ilu. Lainie.

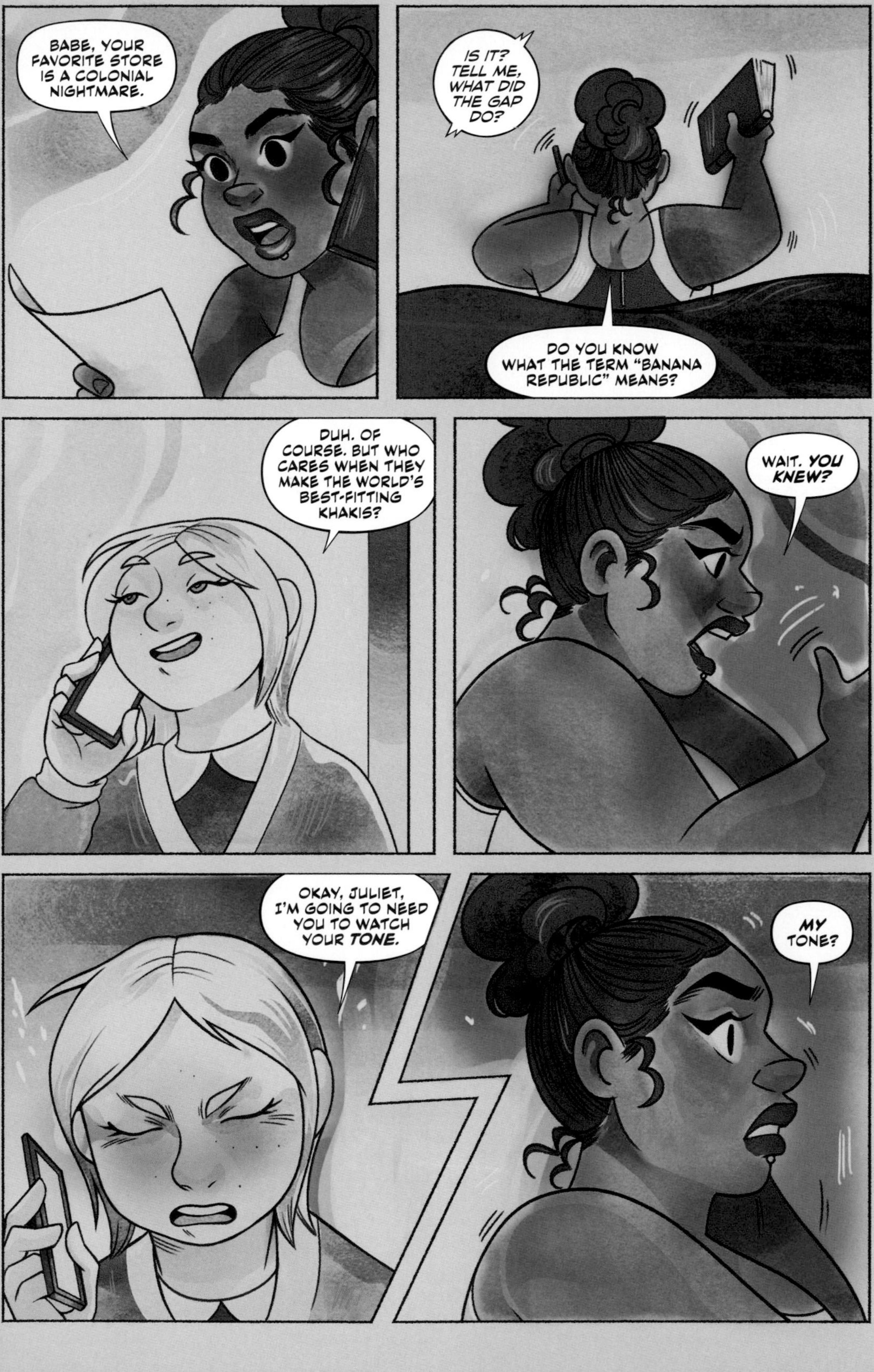
BABE, YOUR FAVORITE STORE IS A COLONIAL NIGHTMARE.
IS IT? TELL ME, WHAT DID THE GAP DO?
DO YOU KNOW WHAT THE TERM "BANANA REPUBLIC" MEANS?
DUH. OF COURSE. BUT WHO CARES WHEN THEY MAKE THE WORLD'S BEST-FITTING KHAKIS?
WAIT. *YOU KNEW?*
OKAY, JULIET, I'M GOING TO NEED YOU TO WATCH YOUR *TONE.*
MY TONE?

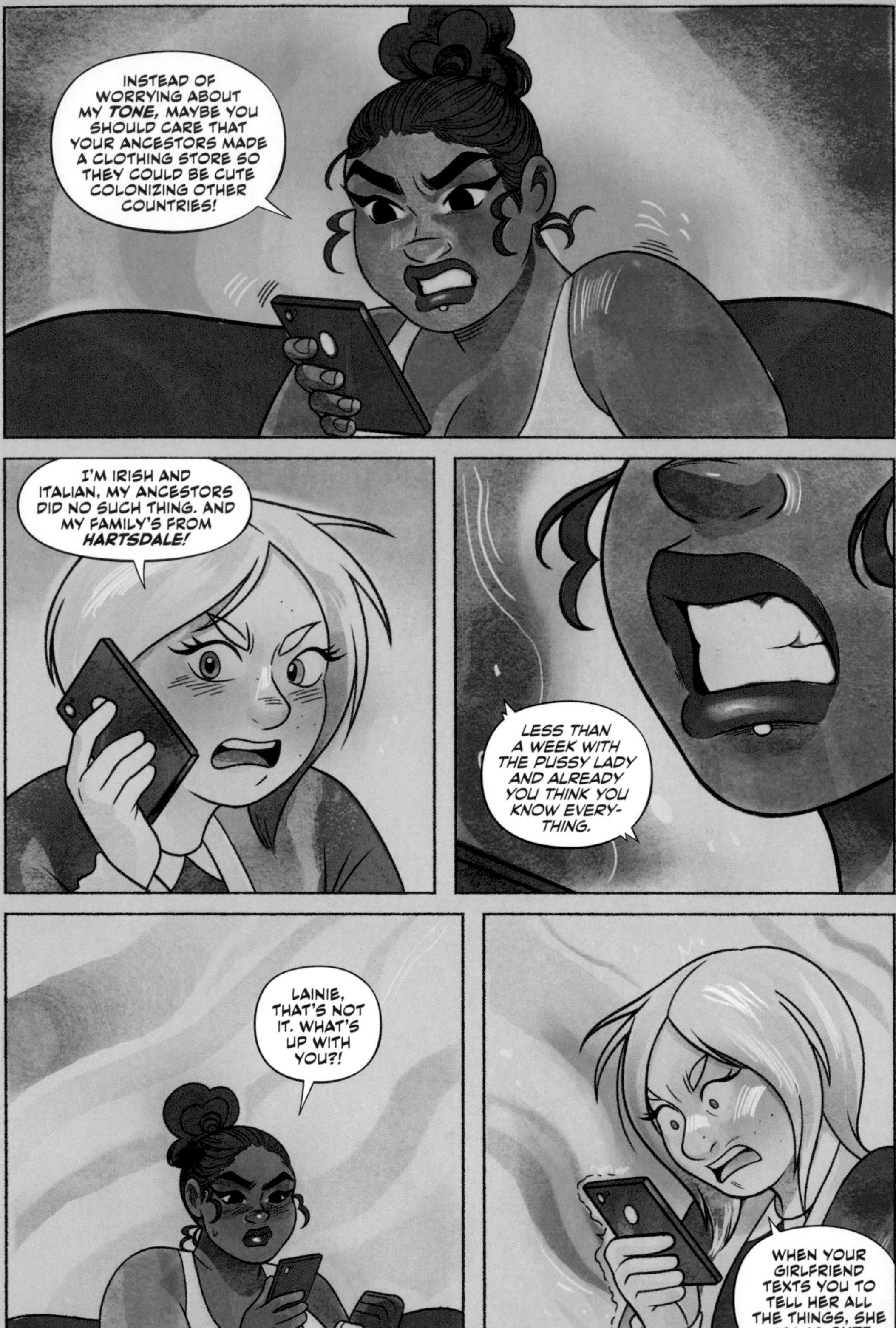
INSTEAD OF WORRYING ABOUT MY TONE, MAYBE YOU SHOULD CARE THAT YOUR ANCESTORS MADE A CLOTHING STORE SO THEY COULD BE CUTE COLONIZING OTHER COUNTRIES!
I'M IRISH AND ITALIAN, MY ANCESTORS DID NO SUCH THING. AND MY FAMILY'S FROM HARTSDALE!
LESS THAN A WEEK WITH THE PUSSY LADY AND ALREADY YOU THINK YOU KNOW EVERY-THING.
LAINIE, THAT'S NOT IT. WHAT'S UP WITH YOU?!
WHEN YOUR GIRLFRIEND TEXTS YOU TO TELL HER ALL THE THINGS, SHE MEANS CUTE THINGS.

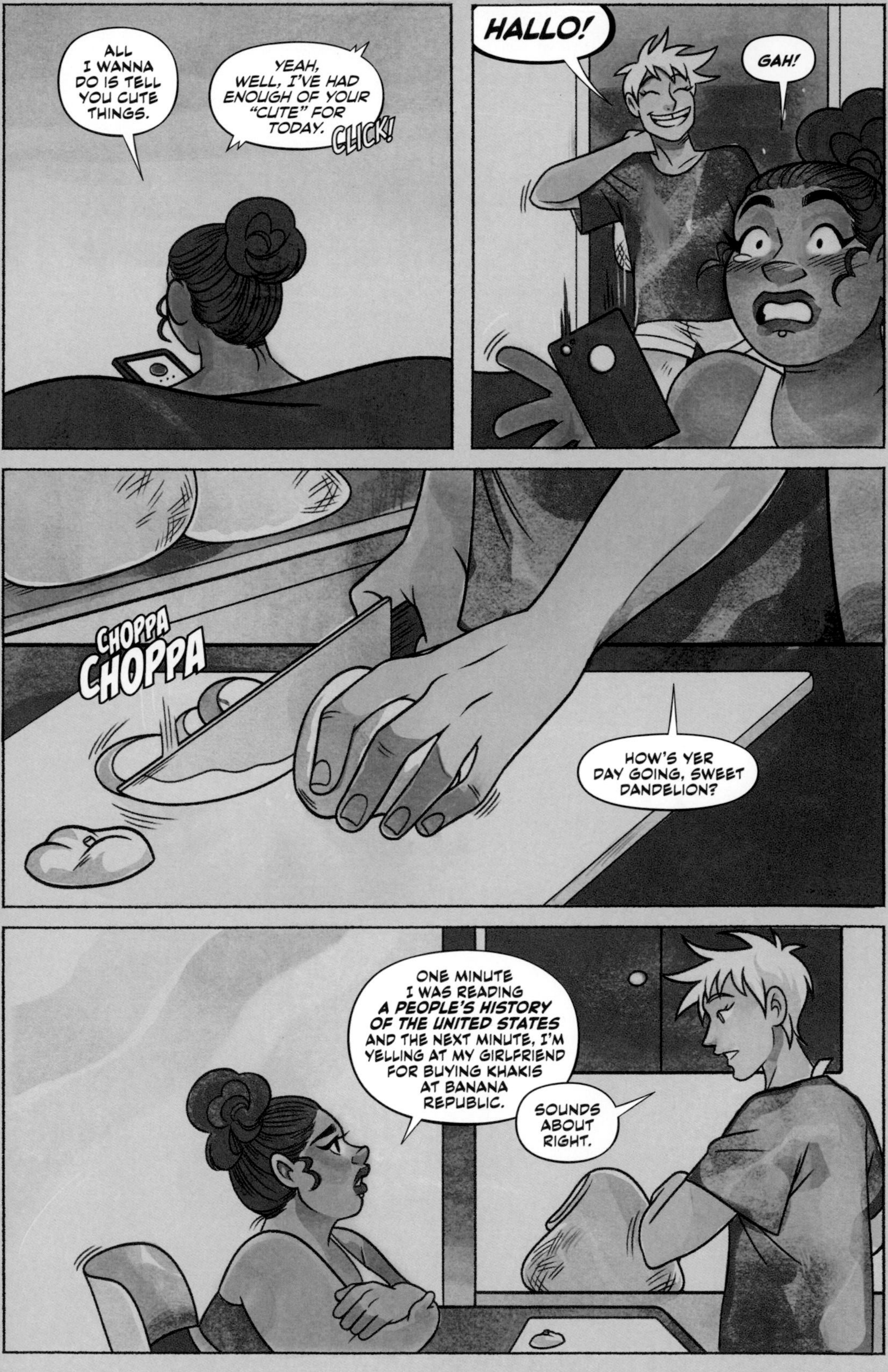
ALL I WANNA DO IS TELL YOU CUTE THINGS.
YEAH, WELL, I'VE HAD ENOUGH OF YOUR "CUTE" FOR TODAY.
CLICK!
HALLO!
GAH!
CHOPPA CHOPPA
HOW'S YER DAY GOING, SWEET DANDELION?
ONE MINUTE I WAS READING *A PEOPLE'S HISTORY OF THE UNITED STATES* AND THE NEXT MINUTE, I'M YELLING AT MY GIRLFRIEND FOR BUYING KHAKIS AT BANANA REPUBLIC.
SOUNDS ABOUT RIGHT.

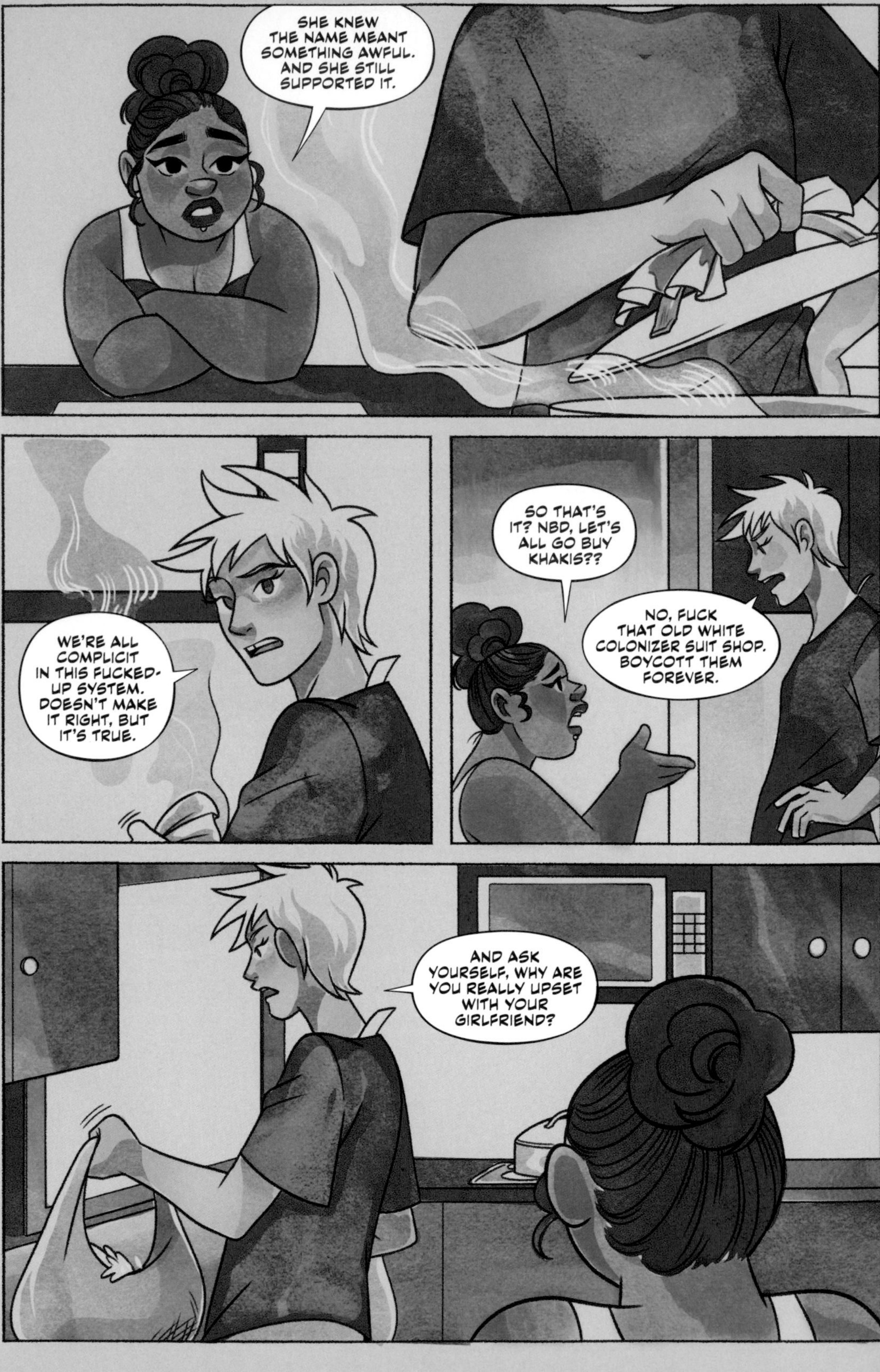
SHE KNEW THE NAME MEANT SOMETHING AWFUL. AND SHE STILL SUPPORTED IT.
WE'RE ALL COMPLICIT IN THIS FUCKED-UP SYSTEM. DOESN'T MAKE IT RIGHT, BUT IT'S TRUE.
SO THAT'S IT? NBD, LET'S ALL GO BUY KHAKIS??
NO, FUCK THAT OLD WHITE COLONIZER SUIT SHOP. BOYCOTT THEM FOREVER.
AND ASK YOURSELF, WHY ARE YOU REALLY UPSET WITH YOUR GIRLFRIEND?

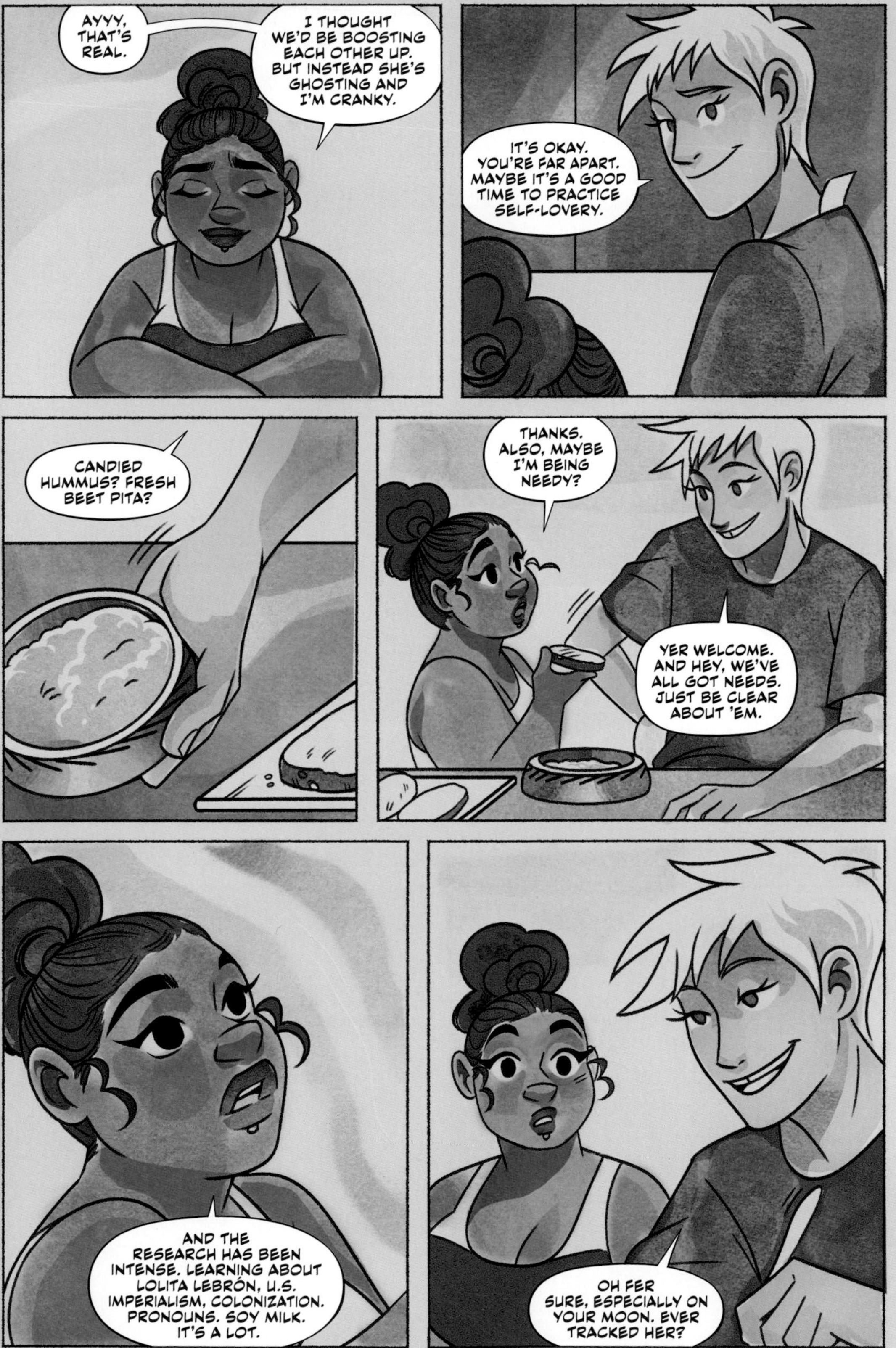
AYYY, THAT'S REAL.
I THOUGHT WE'D BE BOOSTING EACH OTHER UP. BUT INSTEAD SHE'S GHOSTING AND I'M CRANKY.
IT'S OKAY. YOU'RE FAR APART. MAYBE IT'S A GOOD TIME TO PRACTICE SELF-LOVERY.
CANDIED HUMMUS? FRESH BEET PITA?
THANKS. ALSO, MAYBE I'M BEING NEEDY?
YER WELCOME. AND HEY, WE'VE ALL GOT NEEDS. JUST BE CLEAR ABOUT 'EM.
AND THE RESEARCH HAS BEEN INTENSE. LEARNING ABOUT LOLITA LEBRÓN, U.S. IMPERIALISM, COLONIZATION. PRONOUNS. SOY MILK. IT'S A LOT.
OH FER SURE, ESPECIALLY ON YOUR MOON. EVER TRACKED HER?

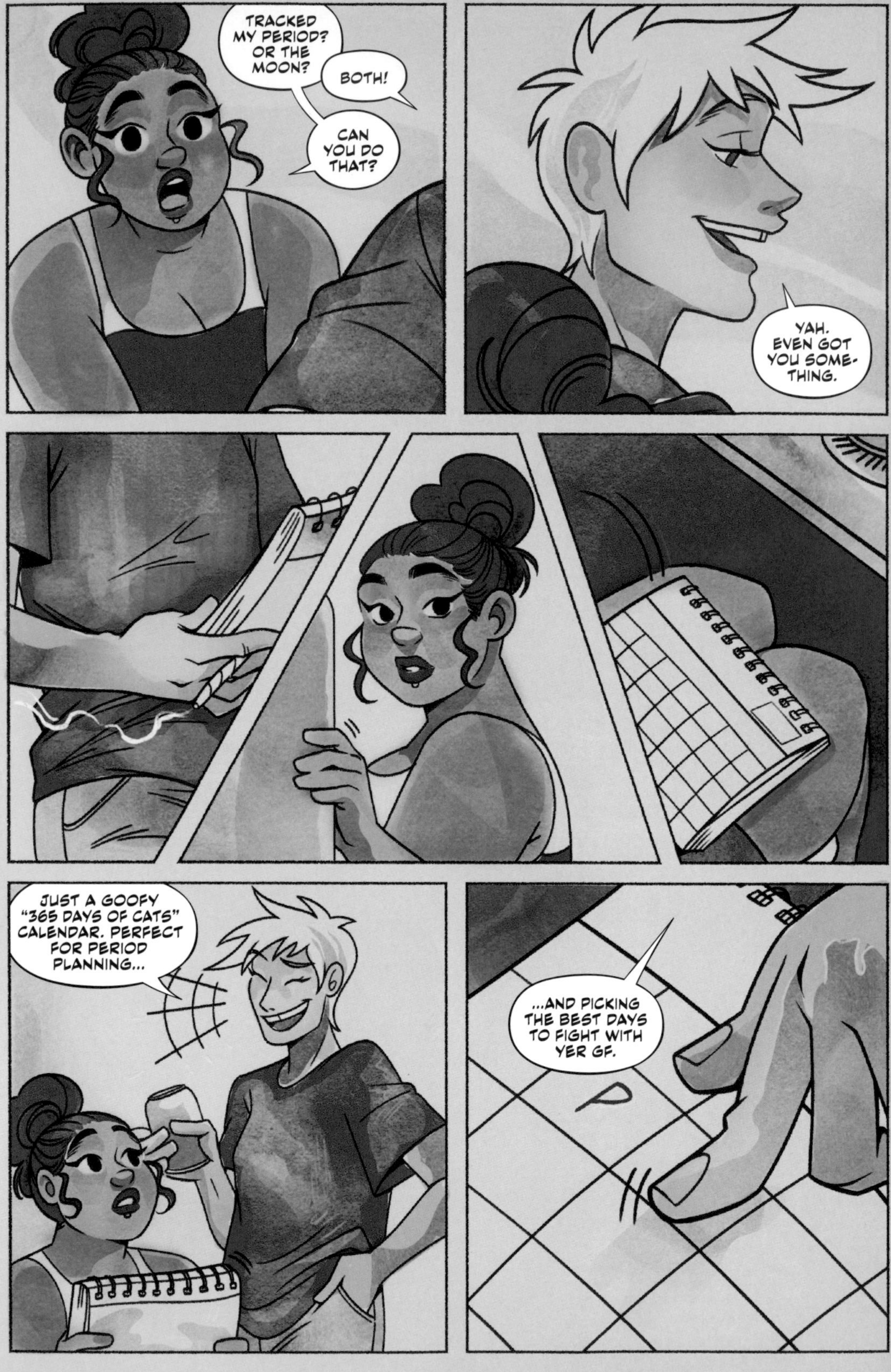
TRACKED MY PERIOD? OR THE MOON?
BOTH!
CAN YOU DO THAT?
YAH. EVEN GOT YOU SOME-THING.
JUST A GOOFY "365 DAYS OF CATS" CALENDAR. PERFECT FOR PERIOD PLANNING...
...AND PICKING THE BEST DAYS TO FIGHT WITH YER GF.
P

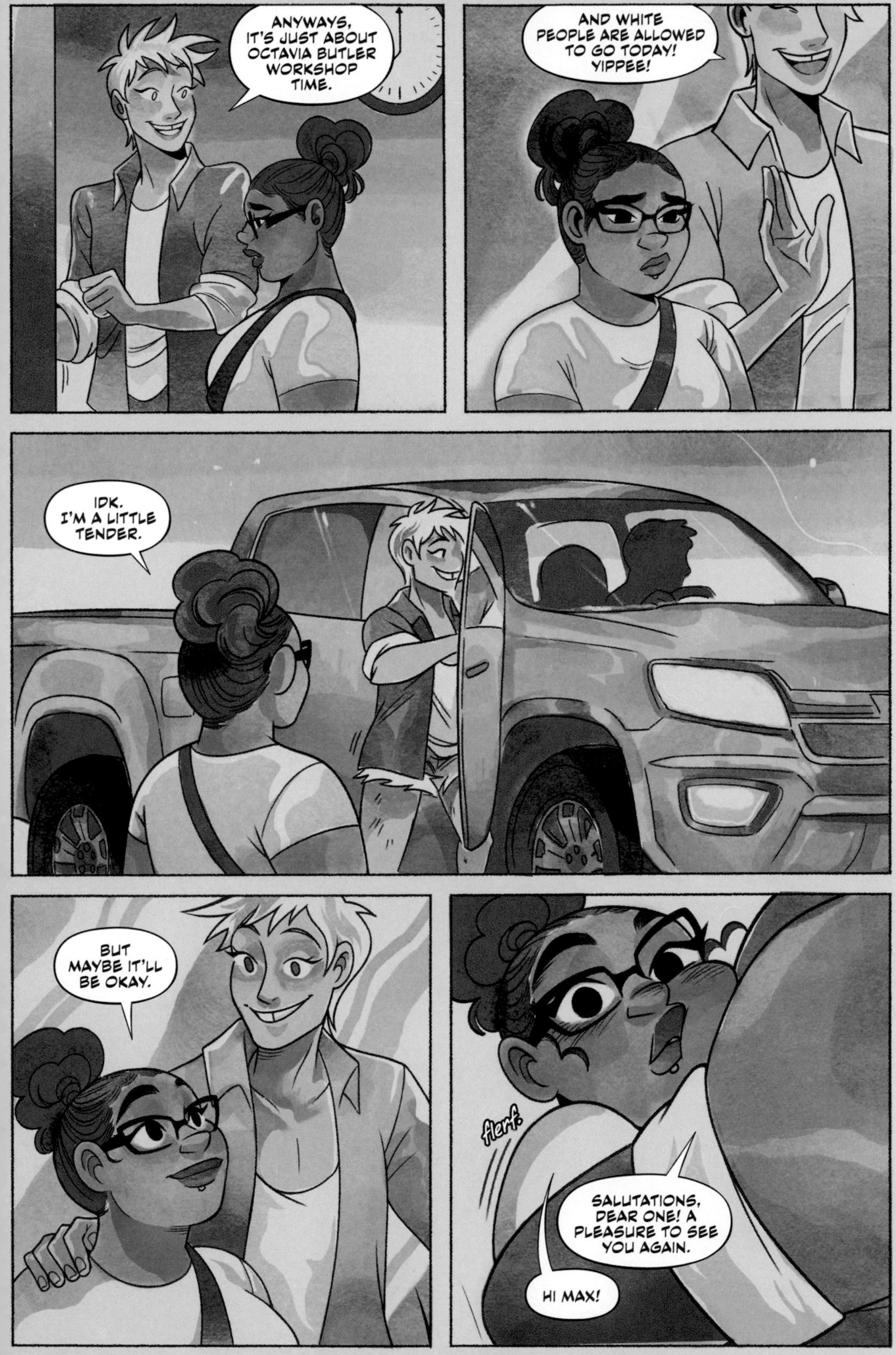
ANYWAYS, IT'S JUST ABOUT OCTAVIA BUTLER WORKSHOP TIME.
AND WHITE PEOPLE ARE ALLOWED TO GO TODAY! YIPPEE!
IDK. I'M A LITTLE TENDER.
BUT MAYBE IT'LL BE OKAY.
flerf.
SALUTATIONS, DEAR ONE! A PLEASURE TO SEE YOU AGAIN.
HI MAX!

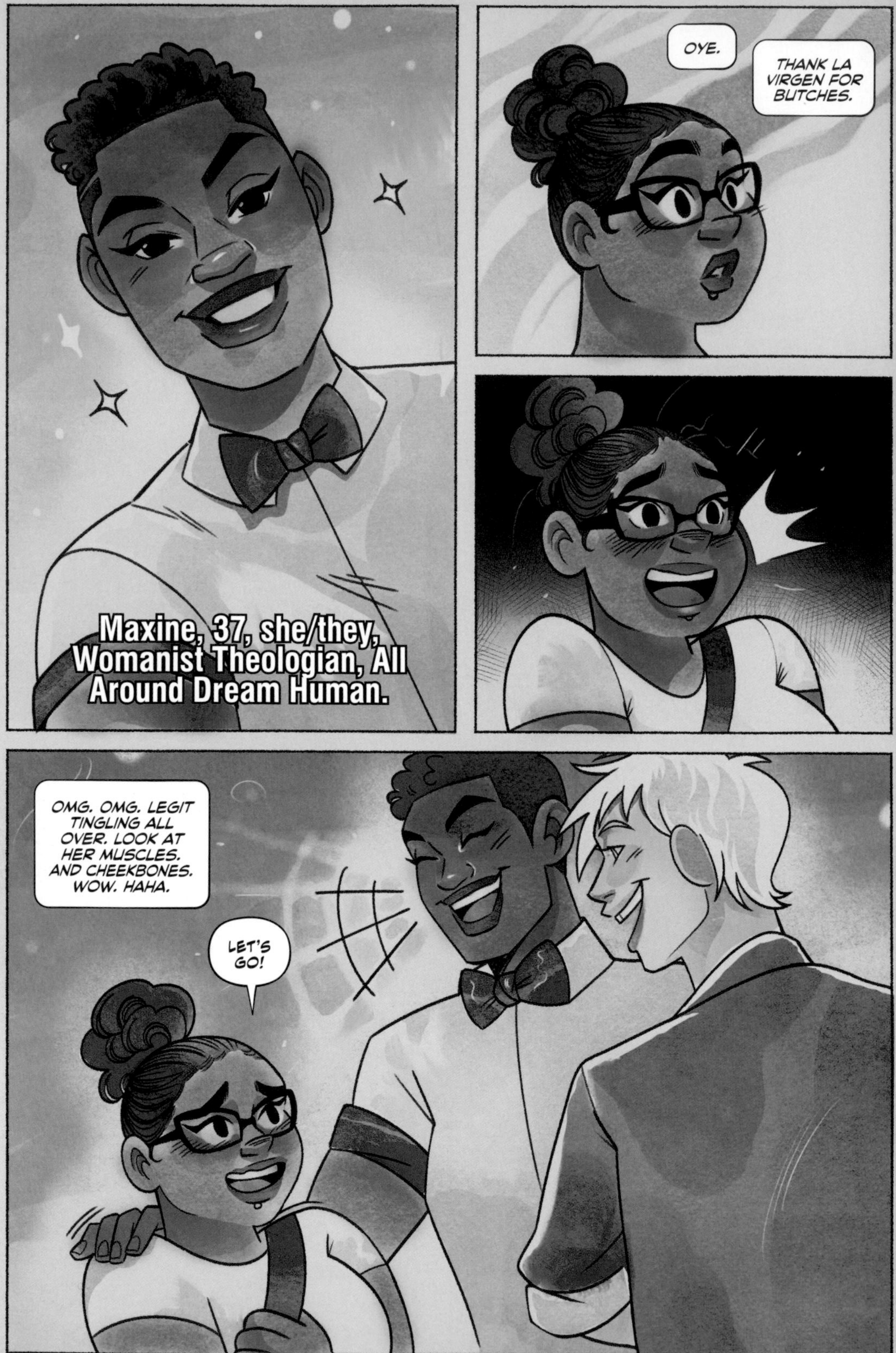
Maxine, 37, she/they, Womanist Theologian, All Around Dream Human.
OYE.
THANK LA VIRGEN FOR BUTCHES.
OMG. OMG. LEGIT TINGLING ALL OVER. LOOK AT HER MUSCLES. AND CHEEKBONES. WOW. HAHA.
LET'S GO!

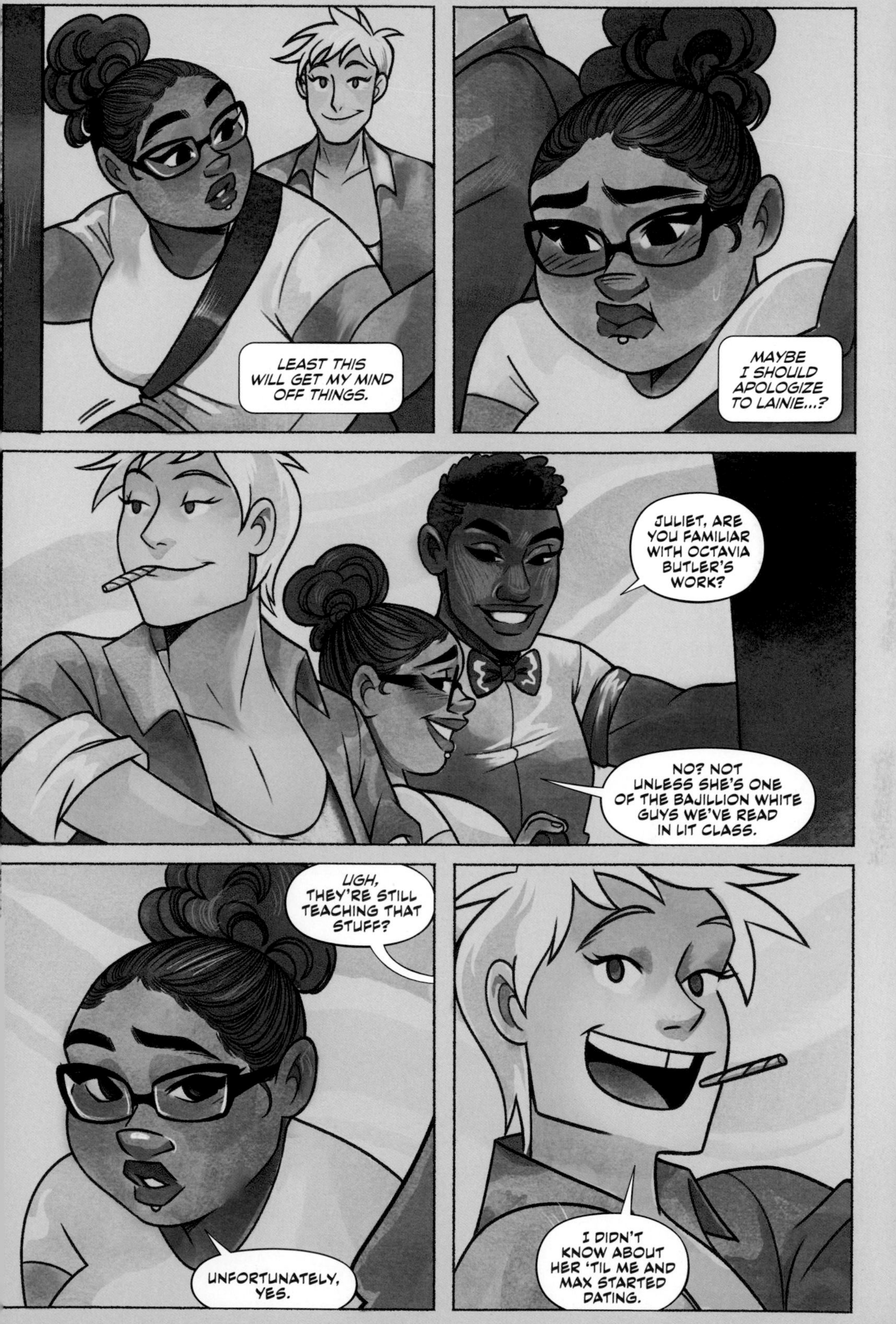
LEAST THIS WILL GET MY MIND OFF THINGS.
MAYBE I SHOULD APOLOGIZE TO LAINIE...?
JULIET, ARE YOU FAMILIAR WITH OCTAVIA BUTLER'S WORK?
NO? NOT UNLESS SHE'S ONE OF THE BAJILLION WHITE GUYS WE'VE READ IN LIT CLASS.
UGH, THEY'RE STILL TEACHING THAT STUFF?
UNFORTUNATELY, YES.
I DIDN'T KNOW ABOUT HER 'TIL ME AND MAX STARTED DATING.

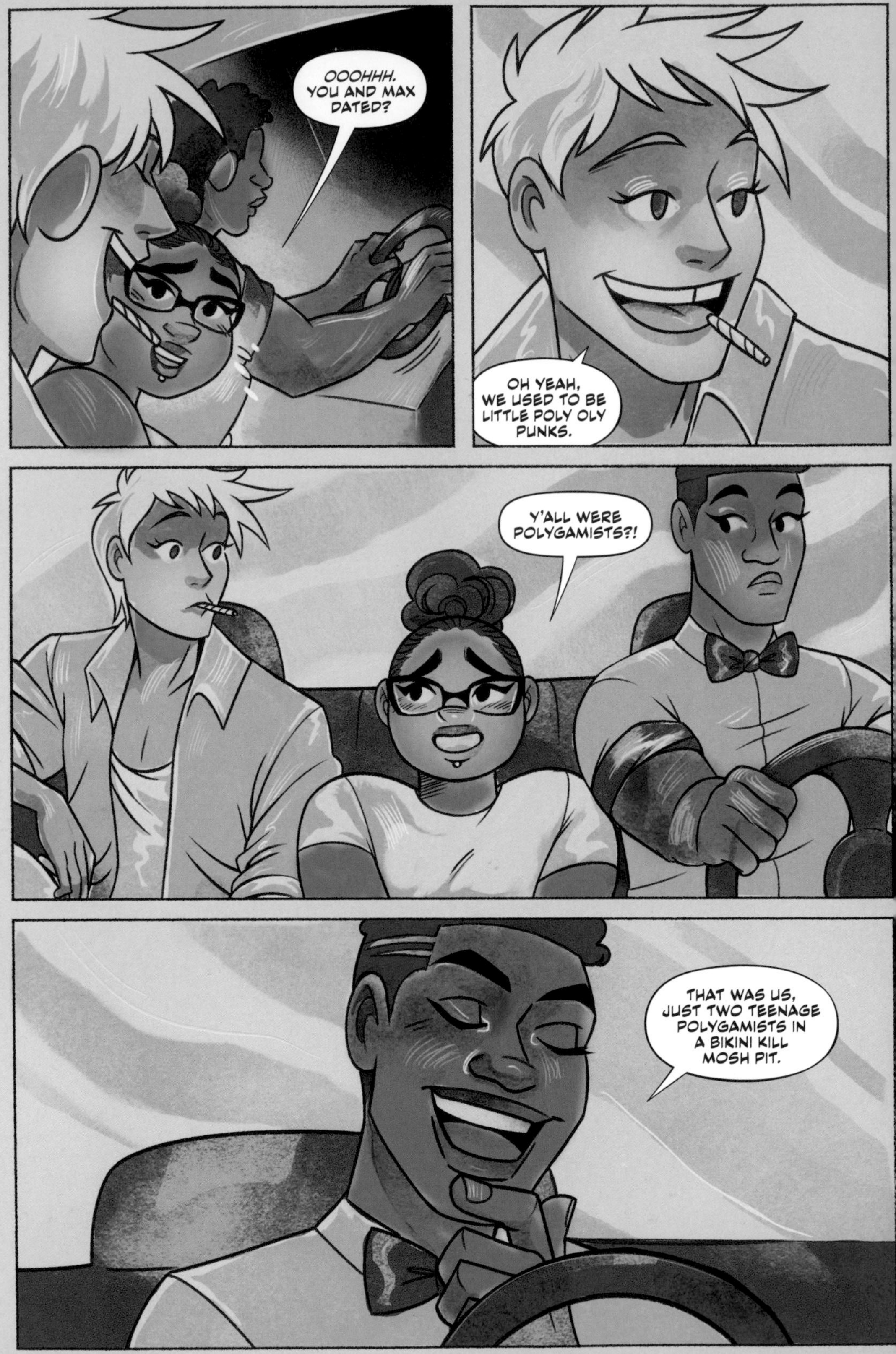
OOOHHH. YOU AND MAX DATED?
OH YEAH, WE USED TO BE LITTLE POLY OLY PUNKS.
Y'ALL WERE POLYGAMISTS?!
THAT WAS US, JUST TWO TEENAGE POLYGAMISTS IN A BIKINI KILL MOSH PIT.

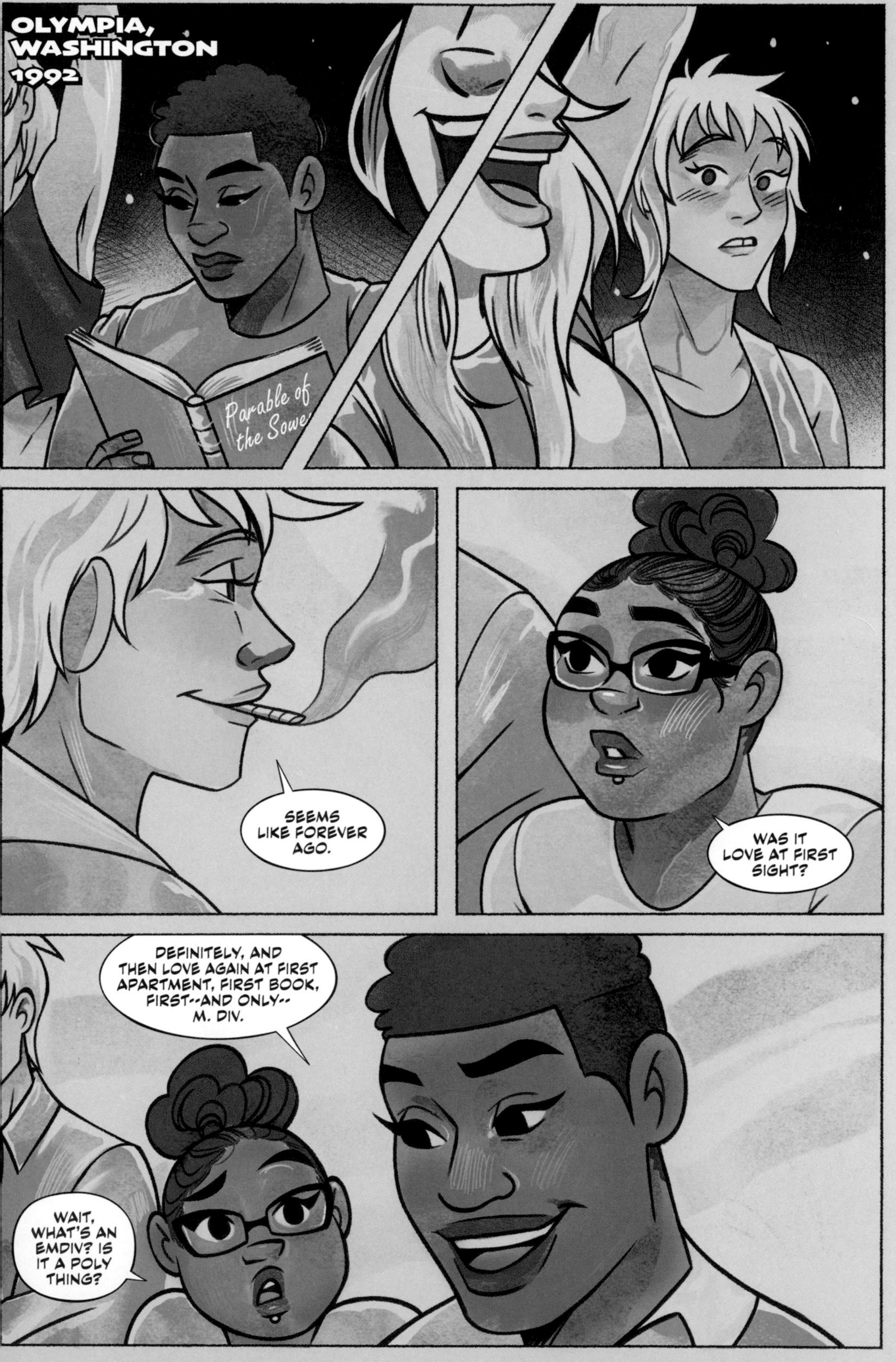
OLYMPIA, WASHINGTON 1992
Parable of the Sowe
SEEMS LIKE FOREVER AGO.
WAS IT LOVE AT FIRST SIGHT?
DEFINITELY, AND THEN LOVE AGAIN AT FIRST APARTMENT, FIRST BOOK, FIRST--AND ONLY-- M. DIV.
WAIT, WHAT'S AN EMDIV? IS IT A POLY THING?

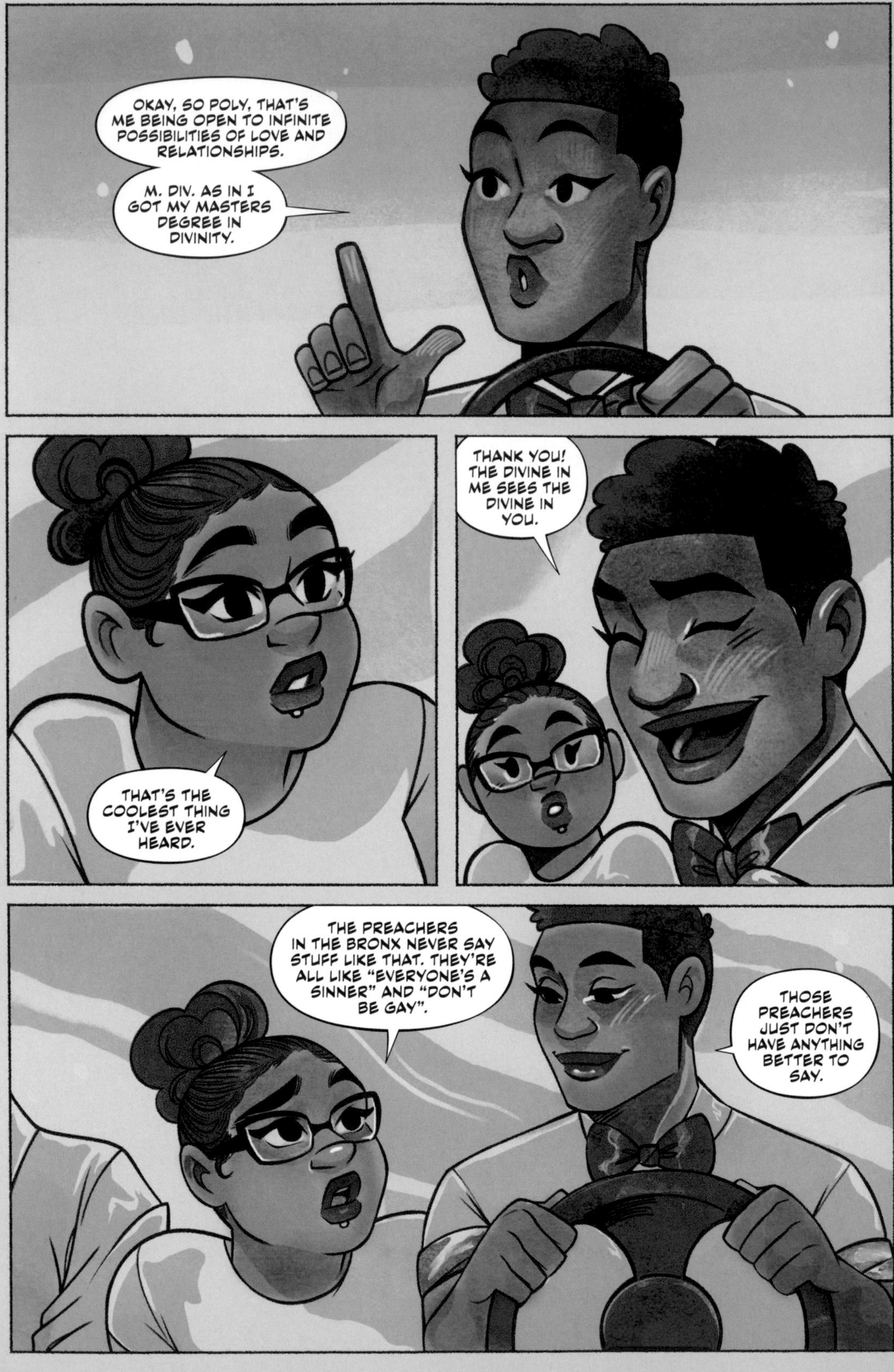
OKAY, SO POLY, THAT'S ME BEING OPEN TO INFINITE POSSIBILITIES OF LOVE AND RELATIONSHIPS.
M. DIV. AS IN I GOT MY MASTERS DEGREE IN DIVINITY.
THAT'S THE COOLEST THING I'VE EVER HEARD.
THANK YOU! THE DIVINE IN ME SEES THE DIVINE IN YOU.
THE PREACHERS IN THE BRONX NEVER SAY STUFF LIKE THAT. THEY'RE ALL LIKE "EVERYONE'S A SINNER" AND "DON'T BE GAY".
THOSE PREACHERS JUST DON'T HAVE ANYTHING BETTER TO SAY.

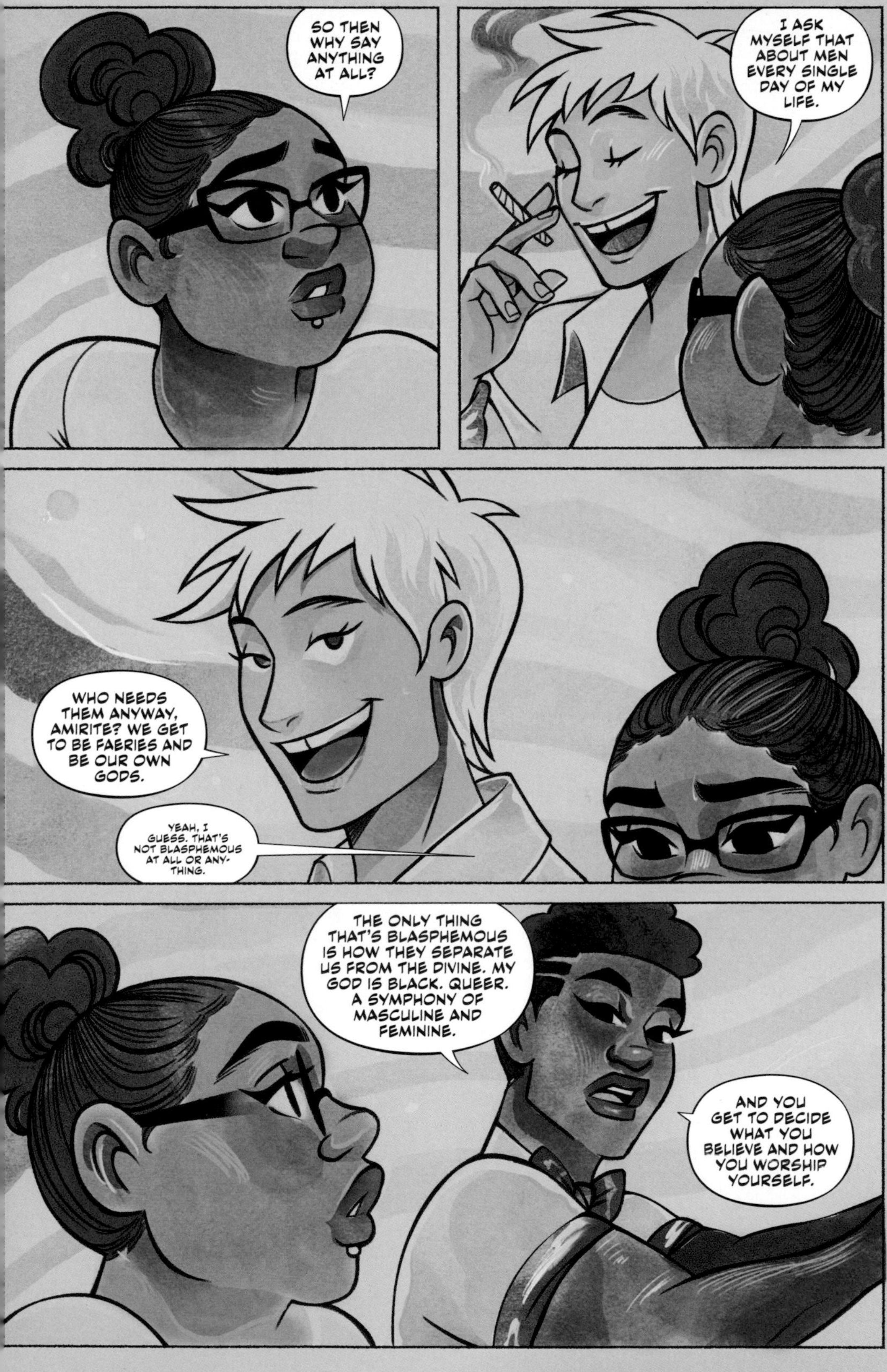
SO THEN WHY SAY ANYTHING AT ALL?
I ASK MYSELF THAT ABOUT MEN EVERY SINGLE DAY OF MY LIFE.
WHO NEEDS THEM ANYWAY, AMIRITE? WE GET TO BE FAERIES AND BE OUR OWN GODS.
YEAH, I GUESS. THAT'S NOT BLASPHEMOUS AT ALL OR ANY-THING.
THE ONLY THING THAT'S BLASPHEMOUS IS HOW THEY SEPARATE US FROM THE DIVINE. MY GOD IS BLACK. QUEER. A SYMPHONY OF MASCULINE AND FEMININE.
AND YOU GET TO DECIDE WHAT YOU BELIEVE AND HOW YOU WORSHIP YOURSELF.

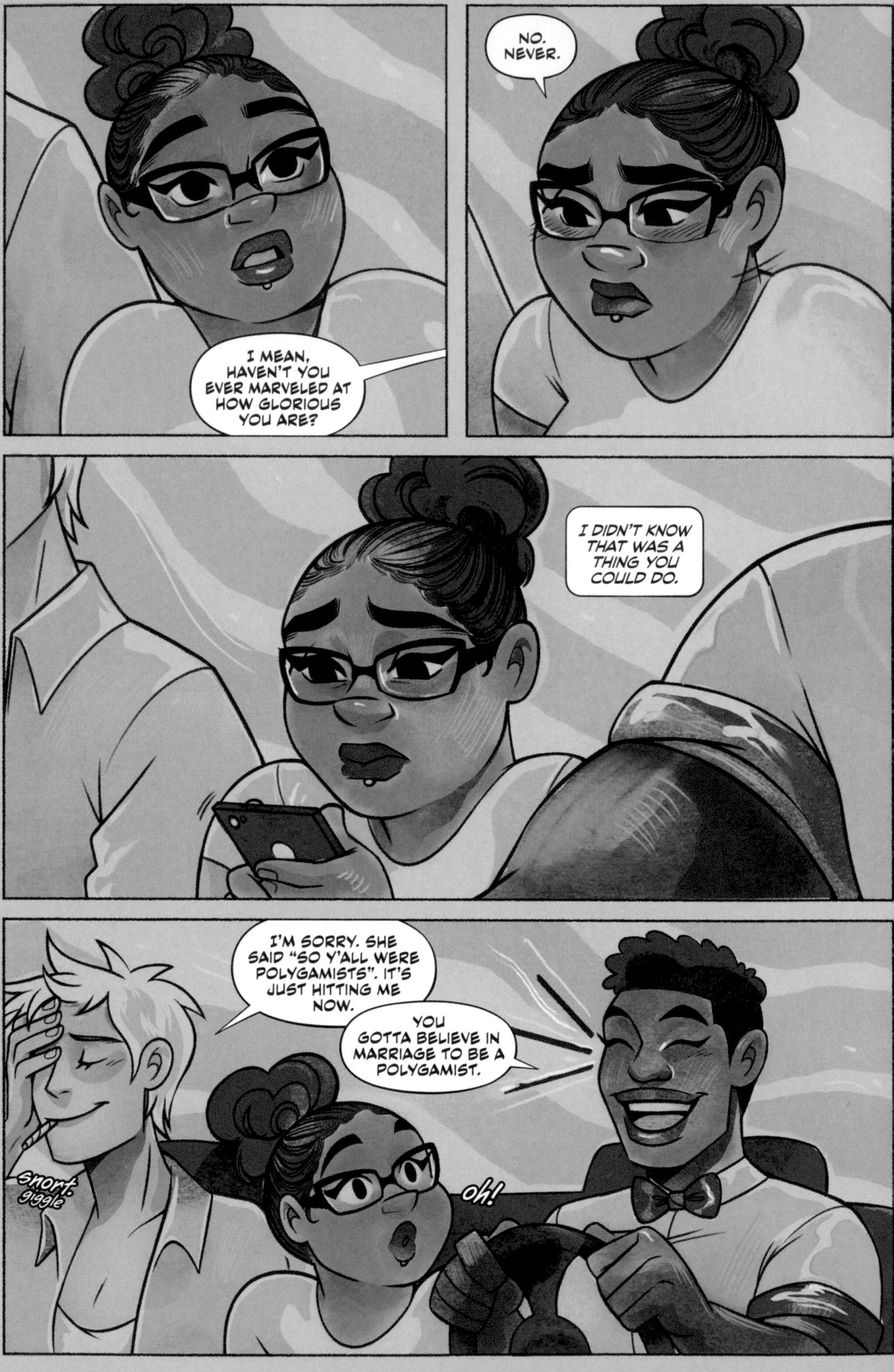
I MEAN, HAVEN'T YOU EVER MARVELED AT HOW GLORIOUS YOU ARE?
NO. NEVER.
I DIDN'T KNOW THAT WAS A THING YOU COULD DO.
I'M SORRY. SHE SAID "SO Y'ALL WERE POLYGAMISTS". IT'S JUST HITTING ME NOW.
YOU GOTTA BELIEVE IN MARRIAGE TO BE A POLYGAMIST.
snort. giggle
oh!

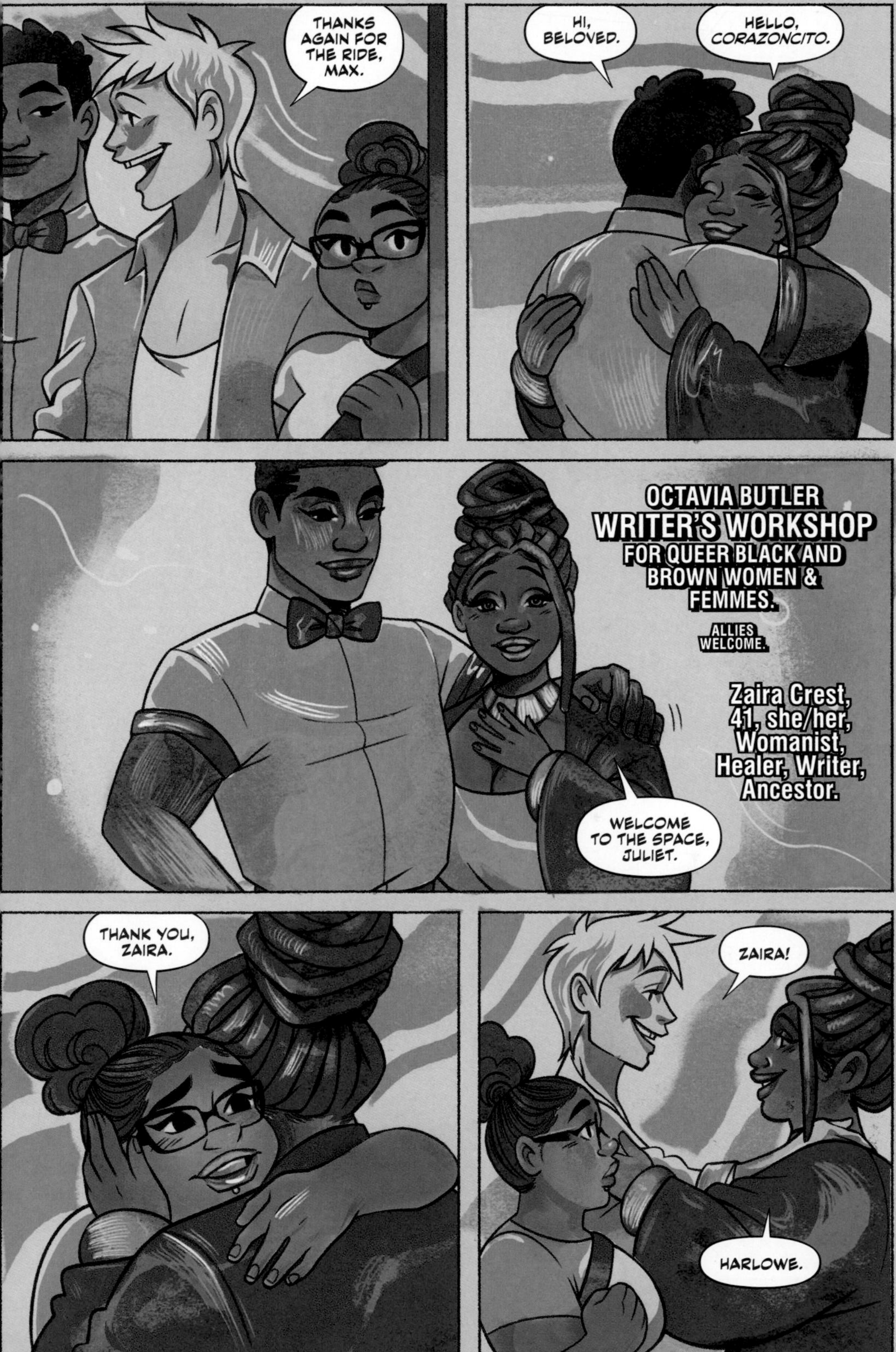
THANKS AGAIN FOR THE RIDE, MAX.
HI, BELOVED.
HELLO, CORAZONCITO.
OCTAVIA BUTLER WRITER'S WORKSHOP FOR QUEER BLACK AND BROWN WOMEN & FEMMES.
ALLIES WELCOME.
Zaira Crest, 41, she/her, Womanist, Healer, Writer, Ancestor.
WELCOME TO THE SPACE, JULIET.
THANK YOU, ZAIRA.
ZAIRA!
HARLOWE.

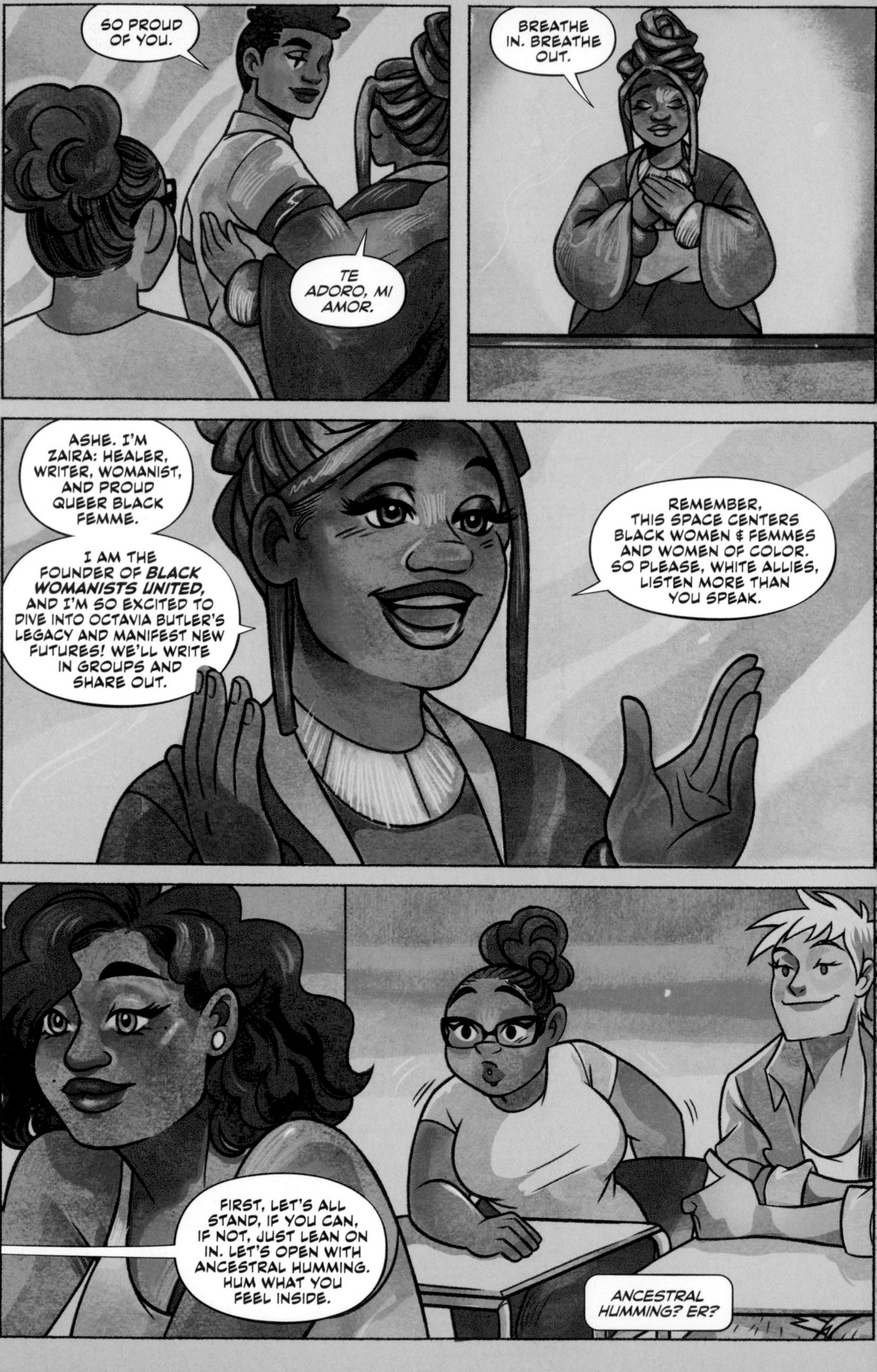
SO PROUD OF YOU.
TE ADORO, MI AMOR.
BREATHE IN. BREATHE OUT.
ASHE. I'M ZAIRA: HEALER, WRITER, WOMANIST, AND PROUD QUEER BLACK FEMME.
I AM THE FOUNDER OF *BLACK WOMANISTS UNITED*, AND I'M SO EXCITED TO DIVE INTO OCTAVIA BUTLER'S LEGACY AND MANIFEST NEW FUTURES! WE'LL WRITE IN GROUPS AND SHARE OUT.
REMEMBER, THIS SPACE CENTERS BLACK WOMEN & FEMMES AND WOMEN OF COLOR. SO PLEASE, WHITE ALLIES, LISTEN MORE THAN YOU SPEAK.
FIRST, LET'S ALL STAND, IF YOU CAN, IF NOT, JUST LEAN ON IN. LET'S OPEN WITH ANCESTRAL HUMMING. HUM WHAT YOU FEEL INSIDE.
ANCESTRAL HUMMING? ER?

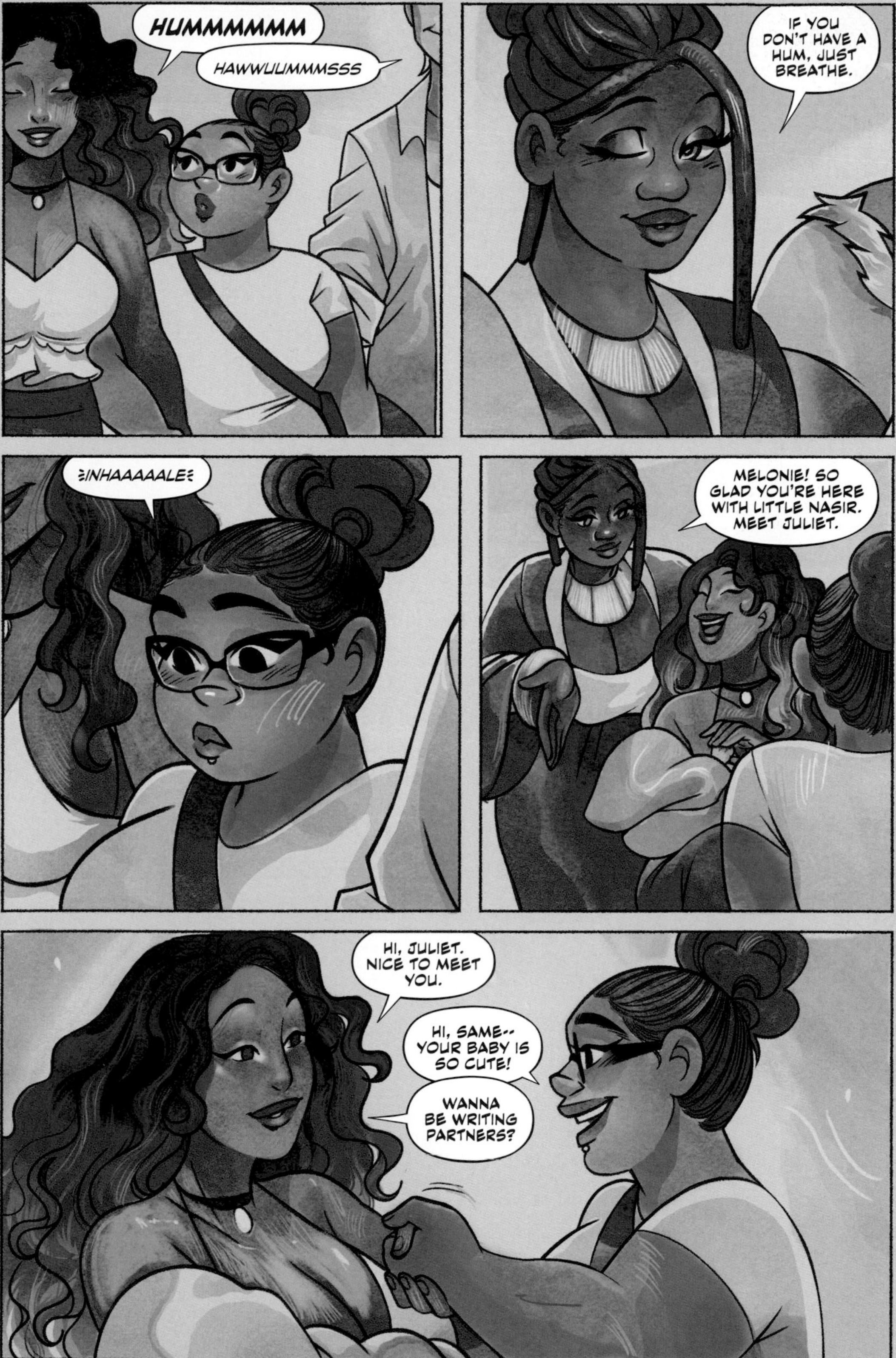
HUMMMMMMM
HAWWUUMMMSSS
IF YOU DON'T HAVE A HUM, JUST BREATHE.
INHAAAAALE
MELONIE! SO GLAD YOU'RE HERE WITH LITTLE NASIR. MEET JULIET.
HI, JULIET. NICE TO MEET YOU.
HI, SAME-- YOUR BABY IS SO CUTE!
WANNA BE WRITING PARTNERS?

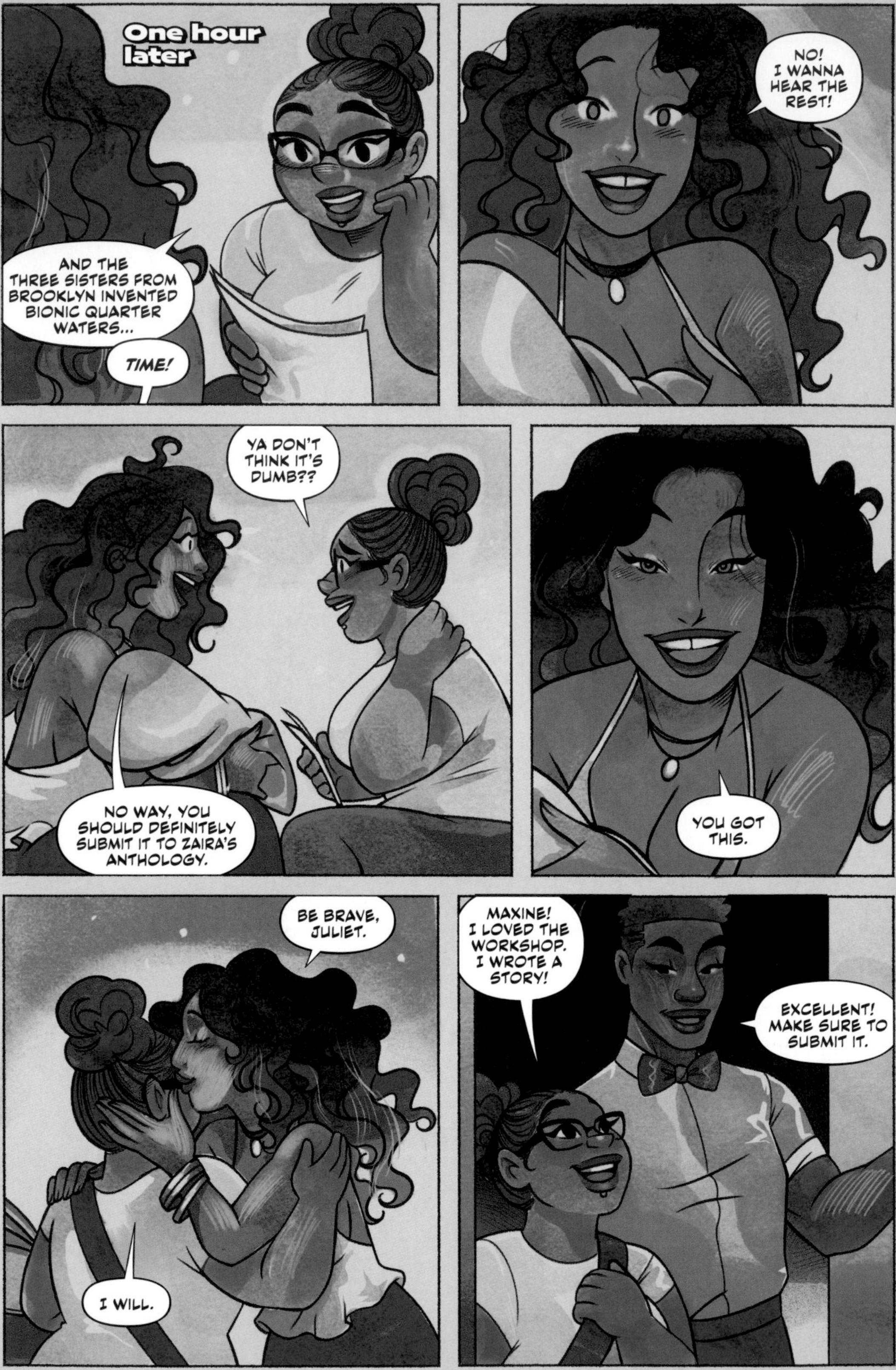
One hour later
AND THE THREE SISTERS FROM BROOKLYN INVENTED BIONIC QUARTER WATERS...
TIME!
NO! I WANNA HEAR THE REST!
YA DON'T THINK IT'S DUMB??
NO WAY, YOU SHOULD DEFINITELY SUBMIT IT TO ZAIRA'S ANTHOLOGY.
YOU GOT THIS.
BE BRAVE, JULIET.
I WILL.
MAXINE! I LOVED THE WORKSHOP. I WROTE A STORY!
EXCELLENT! MAKE SURE TO SUBMIT IT.

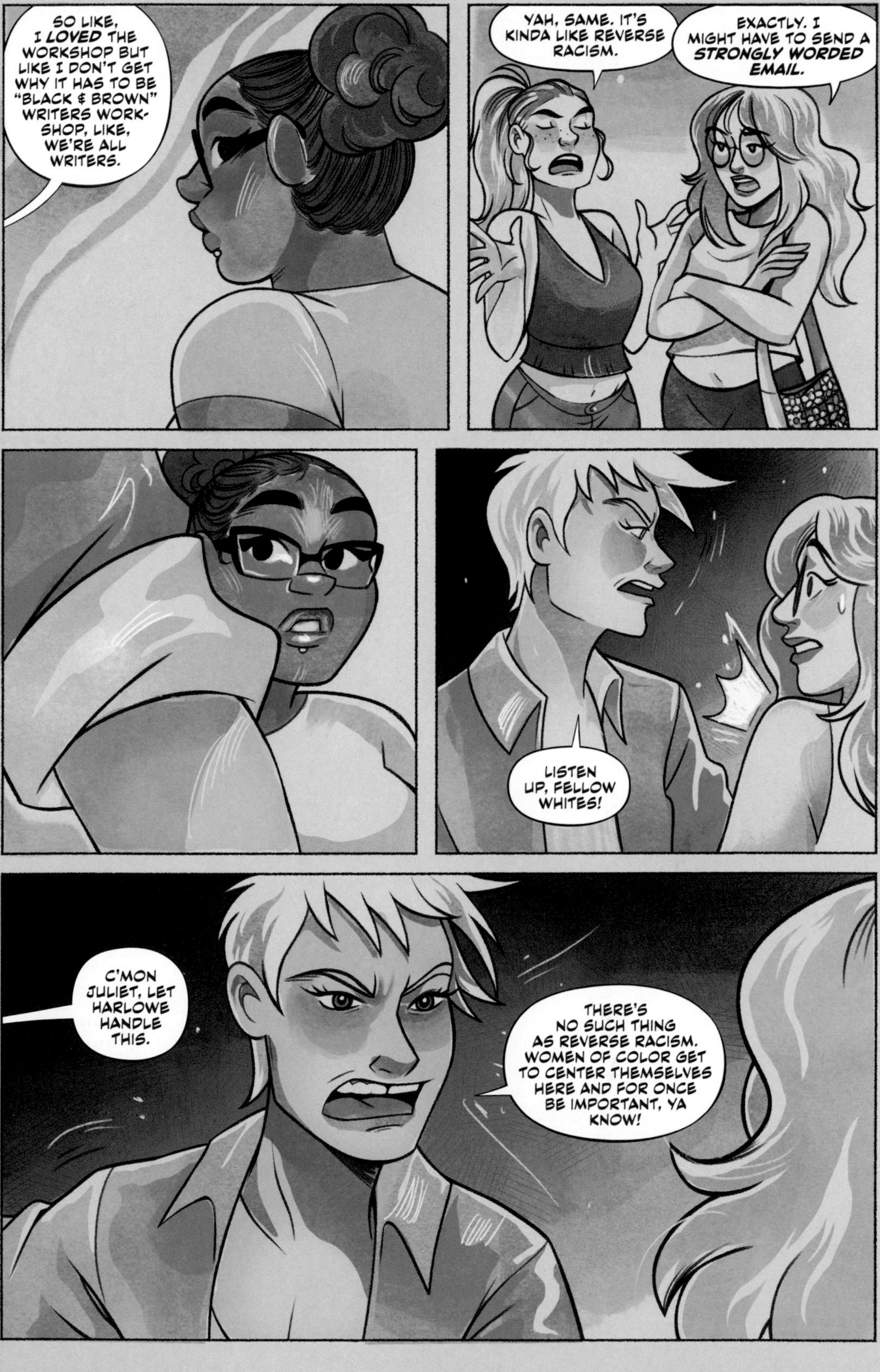
SO LIKE, I LOVED THE WORKSHOP BUT LIKE I DON'T GET WHY IT HAS TO BE "BLACK & BROWN" WRITERS WORKSHOP, LIKE, WE'RE ALL WRITERS.
YAH, SAME. IT'S KINDA LIKE REVERSE RACISM.
EXACTLY. I MIGHT HAVE TO SEND A STRONGLY WORDED EMAIL.
LISTEN UP, FELLOW WHITES!
C'MON JULIET, LET HARLOWE HANDLE THIS.
THERE'S NO SUCH THING AS REVERSE RACISM. WOMEN OF COLOR GET TO CENTER THEMSELVES HERE AND FOR ONCE BE IMPORTANT, YA KNOW!

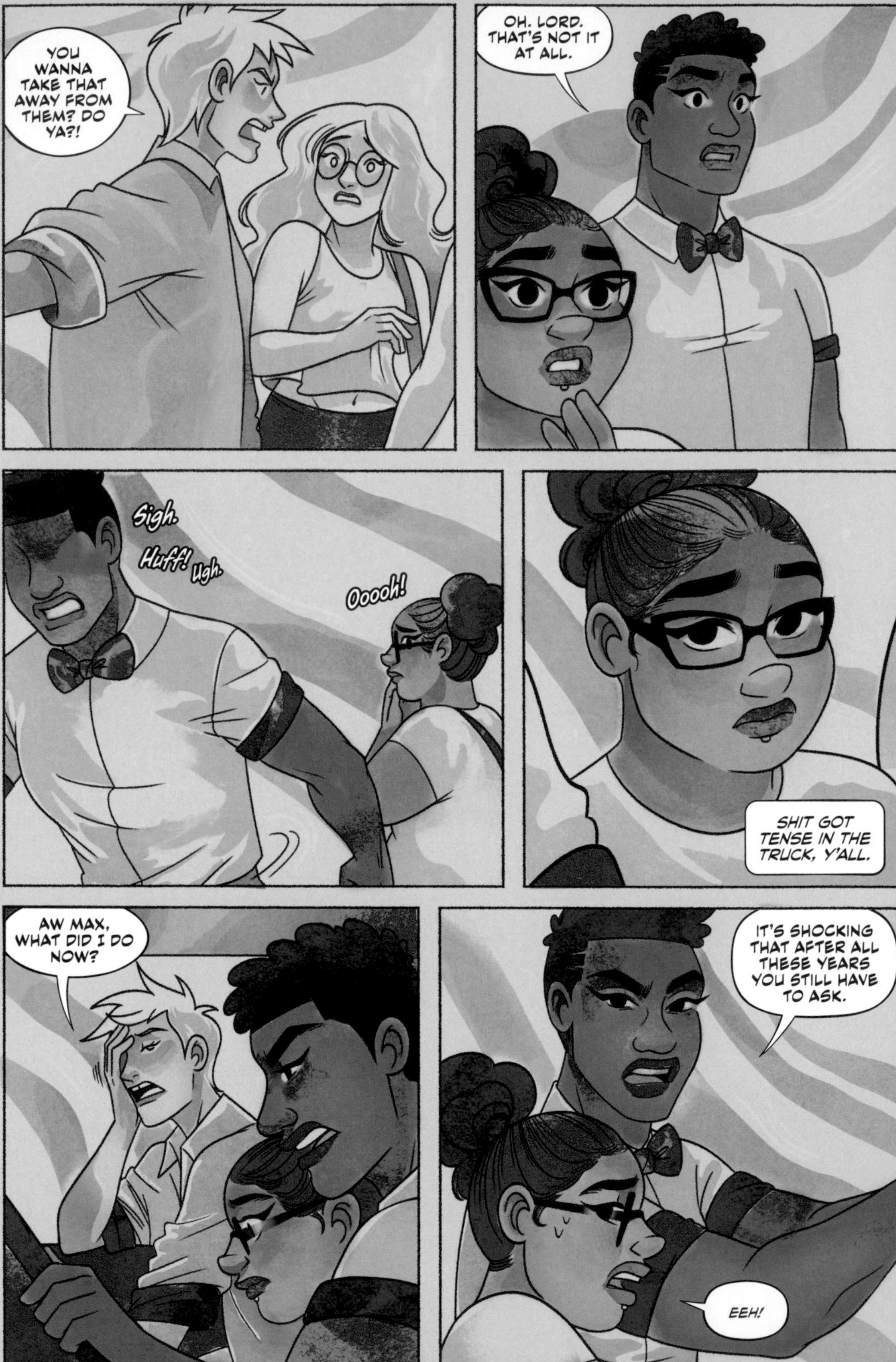
YOU WANNA TAKE THAT AWAY FROM THEM? DO YA?!
OH. LORD. THAT'S NOT IT AT ALL.
Sigh.
Huff! Ugh.
Ooooh!
SHIT GOT TENSE IN THE TRUCK, Y'ALL.
AW MAX, WHAT DID I DO NOW?
IT'S SHOCKING THAT AFTER ALL THESE YEARS YOU STILL HAVE TO ASK.
EEH!

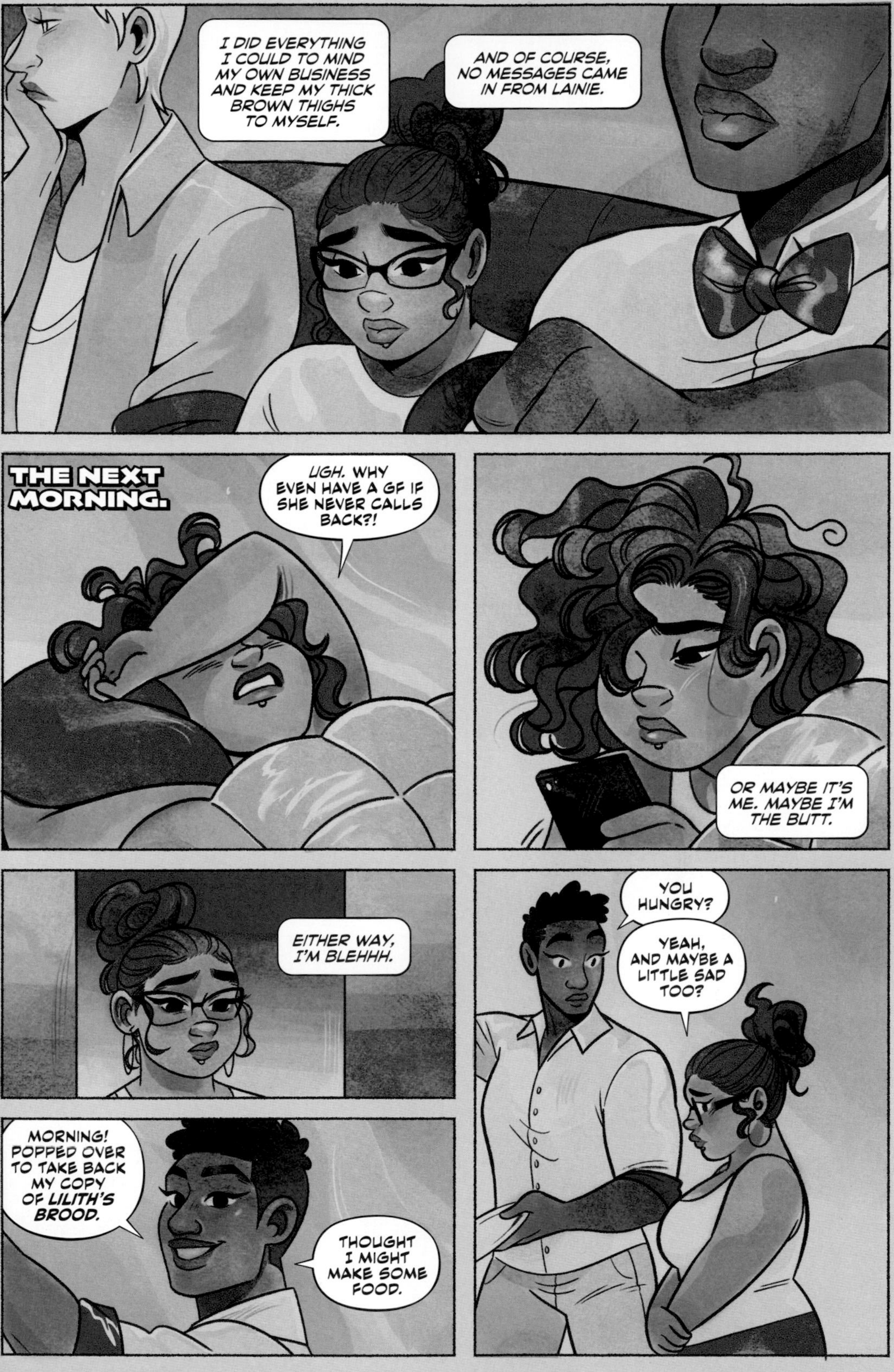
I DID EVERYTHING I COULD TO MIND MY OWN BUSINESS AND KEEP MY THICK BROWN THIGHS TO MYSELF.
AND OF COURSE, NO MESSAGES CAME IN FROM LAINIE.
THE NEXT MORNING.
UGH. WHY EVEN HAVE A GF IF SHE NEVER CALLS BACK?!
OR MAYBE IT'S ME. MAYBE I'M THE BUTT.
EITHER WAY, I'M BLEHHH.
MORNING! POPPED OVER TO TAKE BACK MY COPY OF LILITH'S BROOD.
THOUGHT I MIGHT MAKE SOME FOOD.
YOU HUNGRY?
YEAH, AND MAYBE A LITTLE SAD TOO?

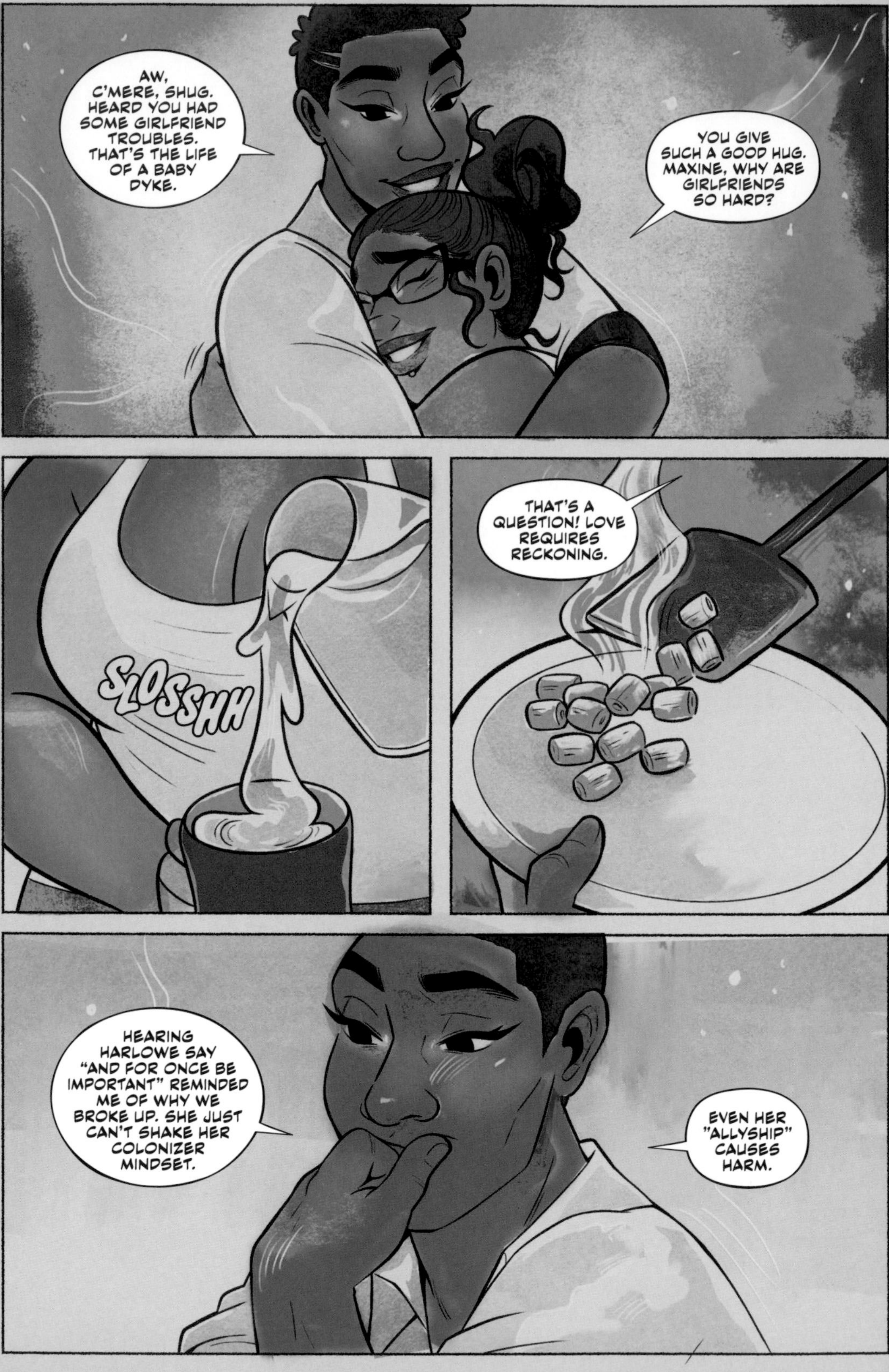
AW, C'MERE, SHUG. HEARD YOU HAD SOME GIRLFRIEND TROUBLES. THAT'S THE LIFE OF A BABY DYKE.
YOU GIVE SUCH A GOOD HUG. MAXINE, WHY ARE GIRLFRIENDS SO HARD?
SLOSSHH
THAT'S A QUESTION! LOVE REQUIRES RECKONING.
HEARING HARLOWE SAY "AND FOR ONCE BE IMPORTANT" REMINDED ME OF WHY WE BROKE UP. SHE JUST CAN'T SHAKE HER COLONIZER MINDSET.
EVEN HER "ALLYSHIP" CAUSES HARM.

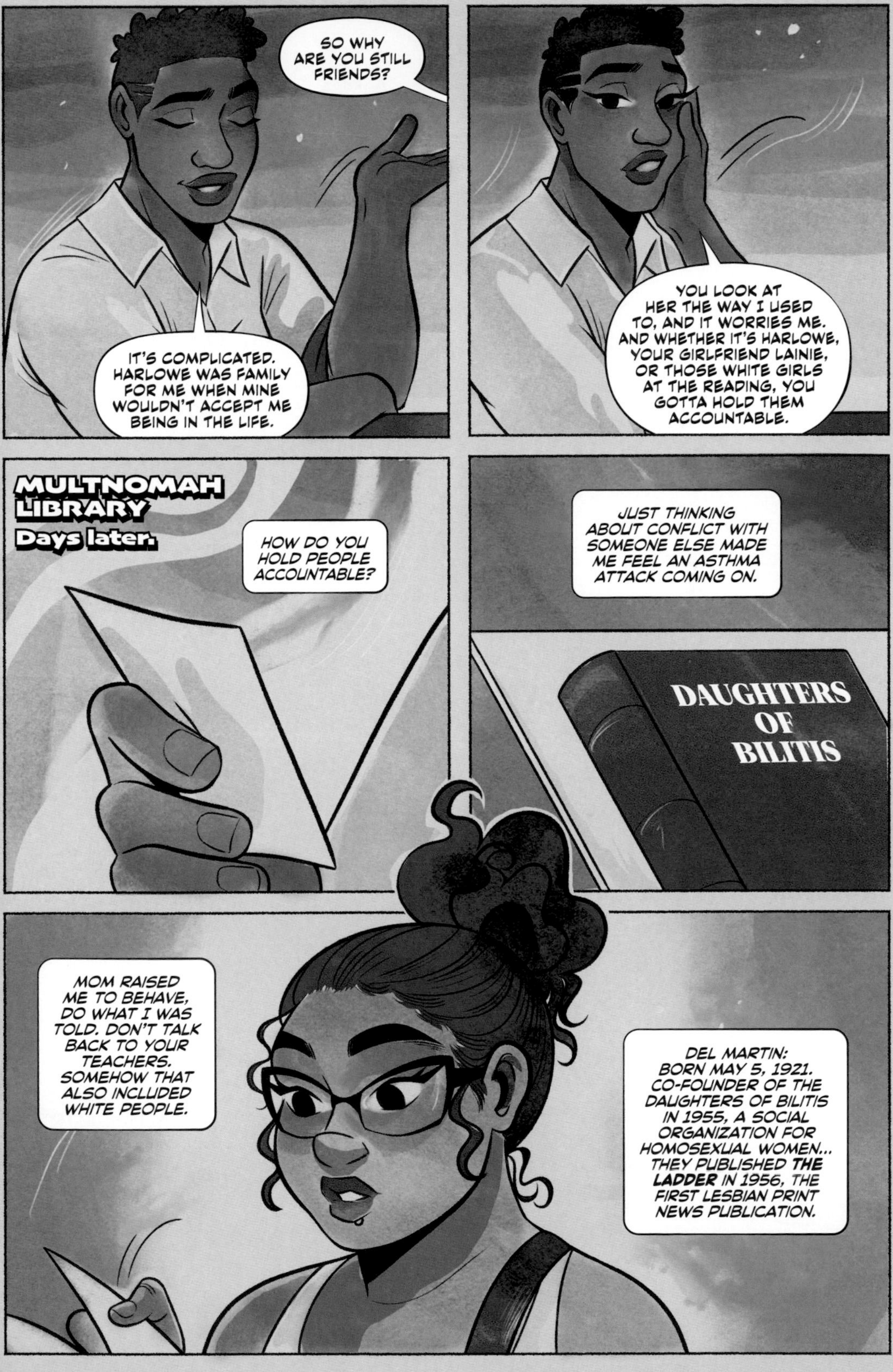

SO WHY ARE YOU STILL FRIENDS?
IT'S COMPLICATED. HARLOWE WAS FAMILY FOR ME WHEN MINE WOULDN'T ACCEPT ME BEING IN THE LIFE.
YOU LOOK AT HER THE WAY I USED TO, AND IT WORRIES ME. AND WHETHER IT'S HARLOWE, YOUR GIRLFRIEND LAINIE, OR THOSE WHITE GIRLS AT THE READING, YOU GOTTA HOLD THEM ACCOUNTABLE.
MULTNOMAH LIBRARY
Days later.
HOW DO YOU HOLD PEOPLE ACCOUNTABLE?
JUST THINKING ABOUT CONFLICT WITH SOMEONE ELSE MADE ME FEEL AN ASTHMA ATTACK COMING ON.
DAUGHTERS OF BILITIS
MOM RAISED ME TO BEHAVE, DO WHAT I WAS TOLD. DON'T TALK BACK TO YOUR TEACHERS. SOMEHOW THAT ALSO INCLUDED WHITE PEOPLE.
DEL MARTIN: BORN MAY 5, 1921. CO-FOUNDER OF THE DAUGHTERS OF BILITIS IN 1955, A SOCIAL ORGANIZATION FOR HOMOSEXUAL WOMEN... THEY PUBLISHED **THE LADDER** IN 1956, THE FIRST LESBIAN PRINT NEWS PUBLICATION.

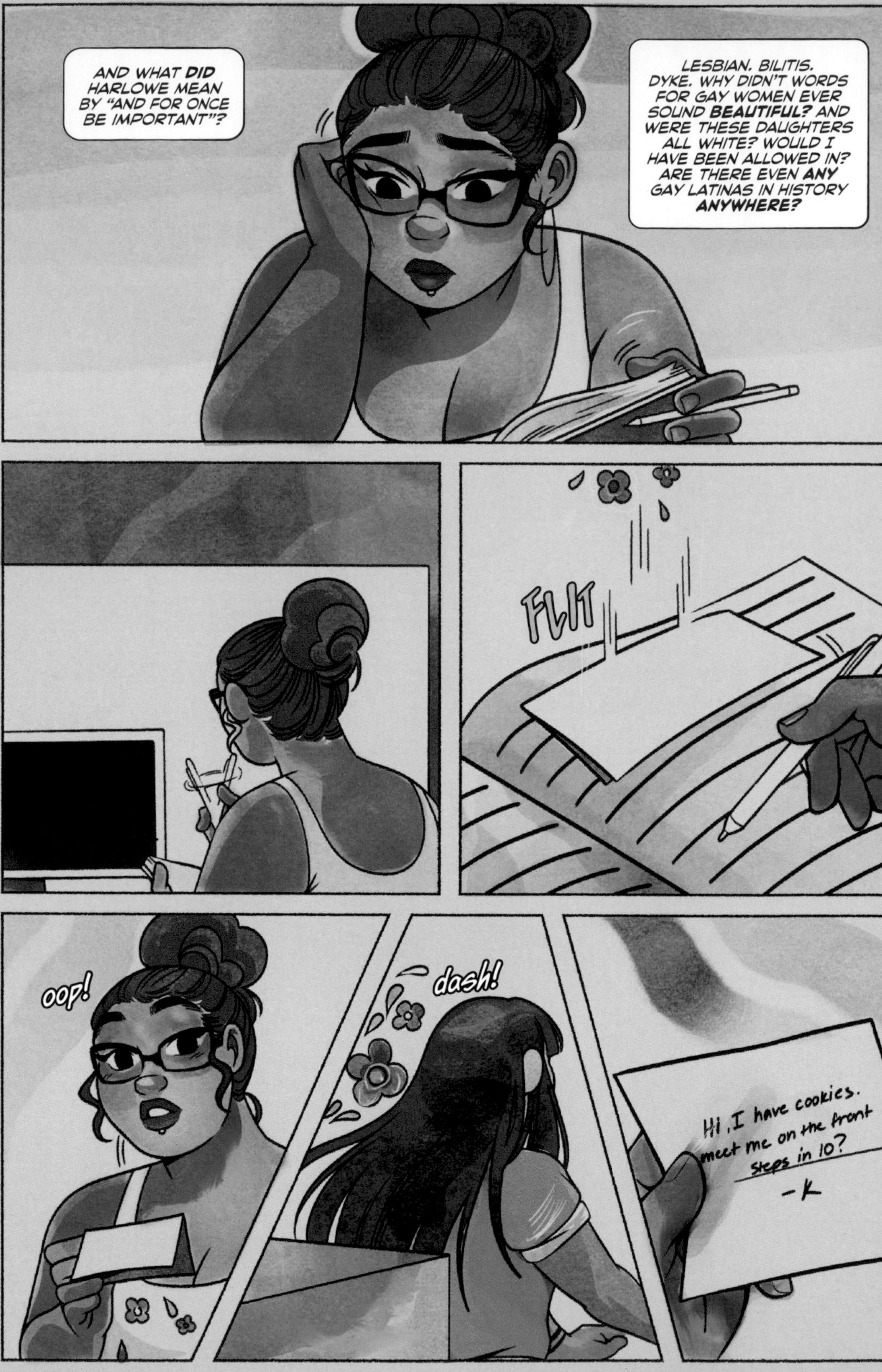
AND WHAT **DID** HARLOWE MEAN BY "AND FOR ONCE BE IMPORTANT"?
LESBIAN. BILITIS. DYKE. WHY DIDN'T WORDS FOR GAY WOMEN EVER SOUND **BEAUTIFUL?** AND WERE THESE DAUGHTERS ALL WHITE? WOULD I HAVE BEEN ALLOWED IN? ARE THERE EVEN **ANY** GAY LATINAS IN HISTORY **ANYWHERE?**
FLIT
oop!
dash!
Hi, I have cookies. meet me on the front steps in 10?
-K

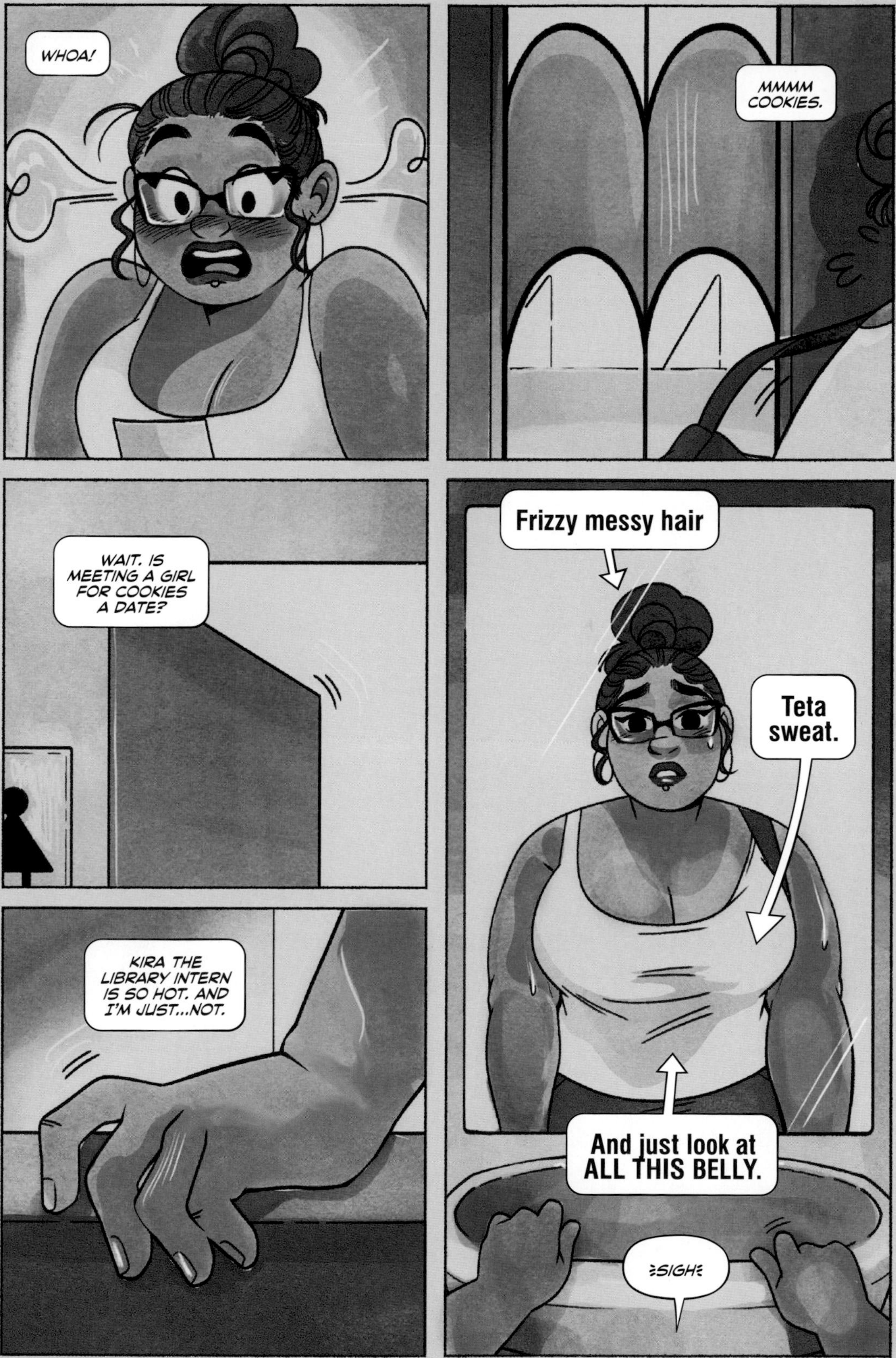
WHOA!
MMMM COOKIES.
WAIT. IS MEETING A GIRL FOR COOKIES A DATE?
KIRA THE LIBRARY INTERN IS SO HOT. AND I'M JUST...NOT.
Frizzy messy hair
Teta sweat.
And just look at ALL THIS BELLY.
SIGH

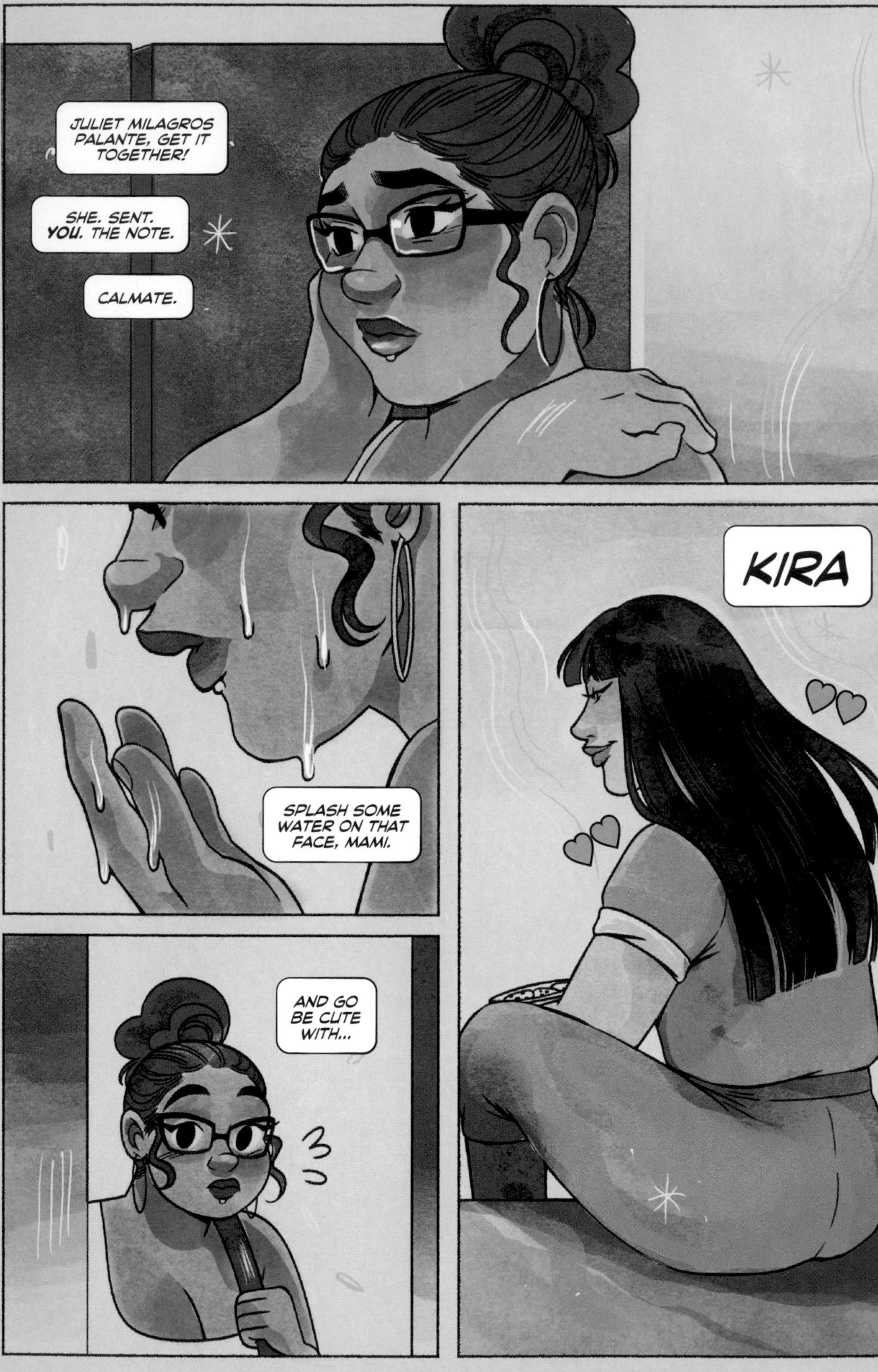
JULIET MILAGROS PALANTE, GET IT TOGETHER!
SHE. SENT. YOU. THE NOTE.
CALMATE.
SPLASH SOME WATER ON THAT FACE, MAMI.
KIRA
AND GO BE CUTE WITH...

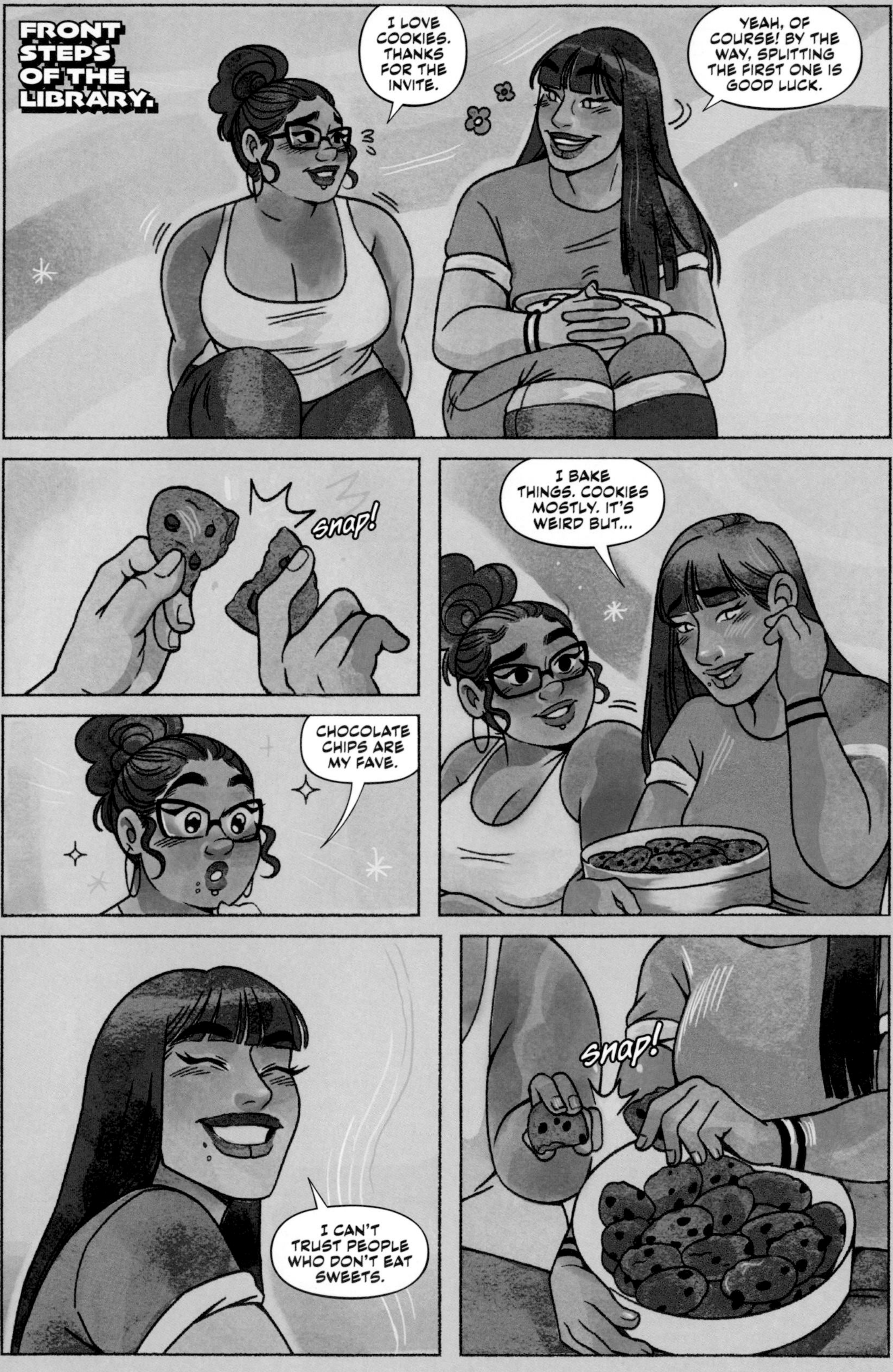
FRONT STEPS OF THE LIBRARY.
I LOVE COOKIES. THANKS FOR THE INVITE.
YEAH, OF COURSE! BY THE WAY, SPLITTING THE FIRST ONE IS GOOD LUCK.
snap!
CHOCOLATE CHIPS ARE MY FAVE.
I BAKE THINGS. COOKIES MOSTLY. IT'S WEIRD BUT...
I CAN'T TRUST PEOPLE WHO DON'T EAT SWEETS.
snap!

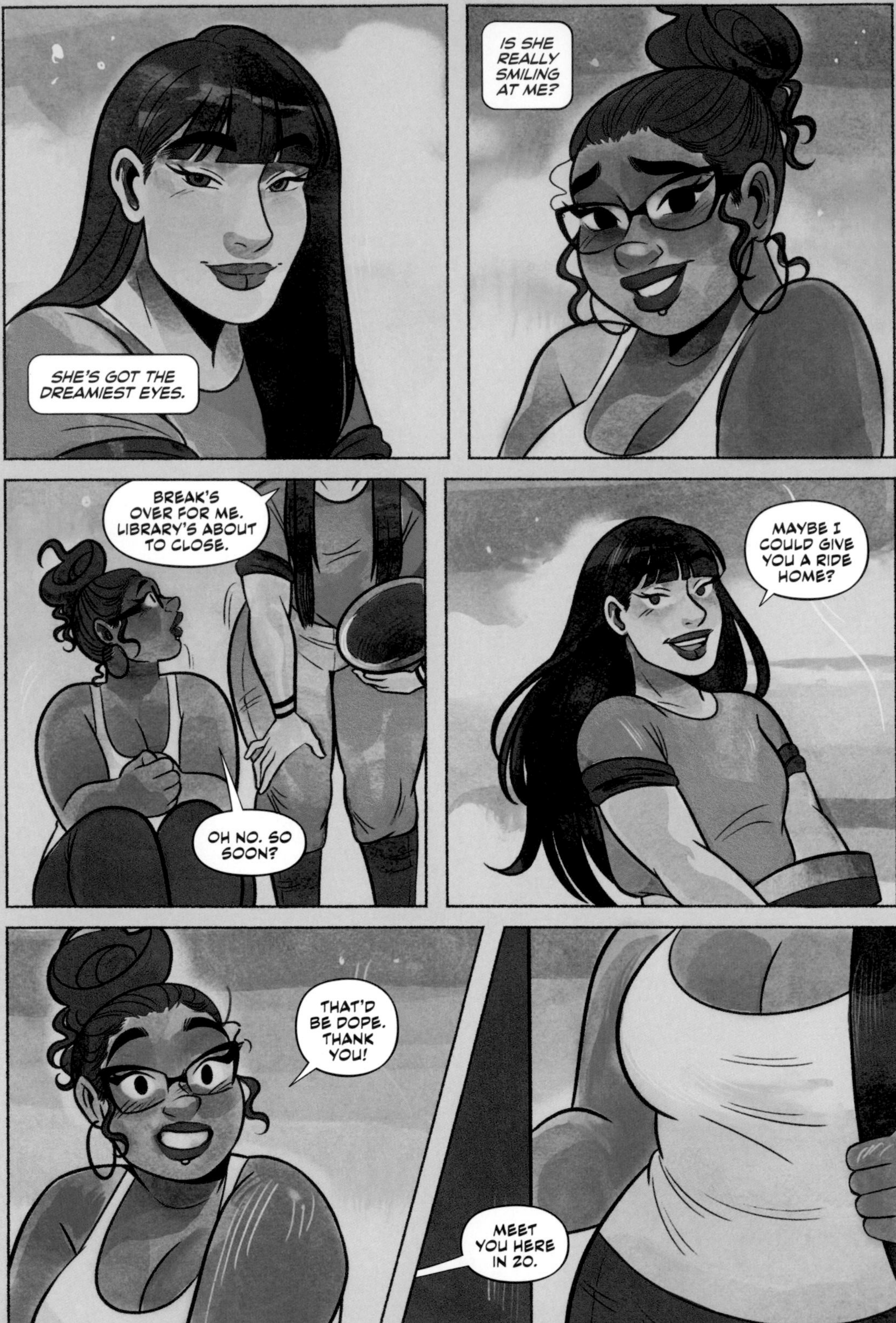
SHE'S GOT THE DREAMIEST EYES.
IS SHE REALLY SMILING AT ME?
BREAK'S OVER FOR ME. LIBRARY'S ABOUT TO CLOSE.
OH NO. SO SOON?
MAYBE I COULD GIVE YOU A RIDE HOME?
THAT'D BE DOPE. THANK YOU!
MEET YOU HERE IN 20.

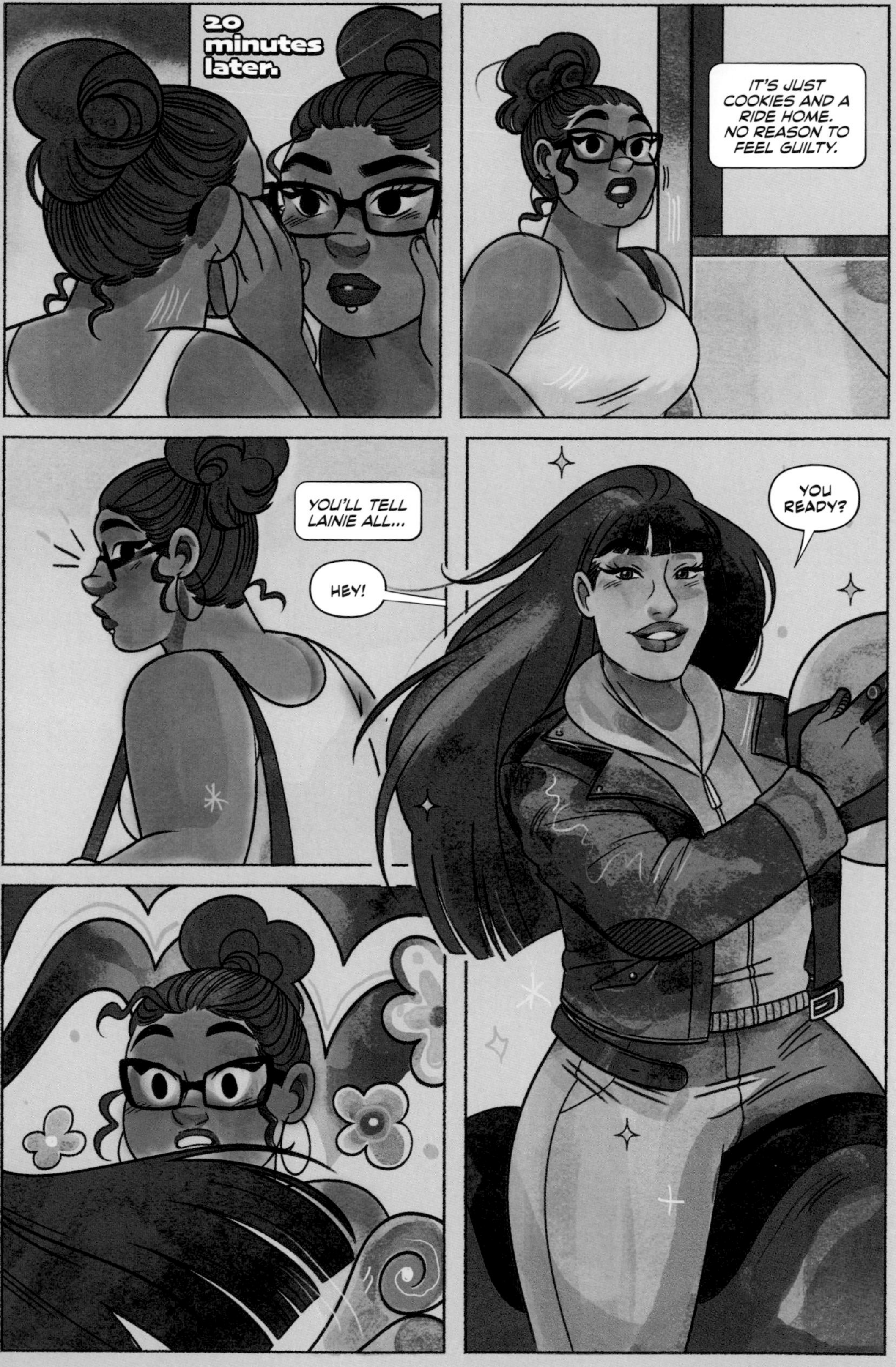
20 minutes later.
IT'S JUST COOKIES AND A RIDE HOME. NO REASON TO FEEL GUILTY.
YOU'LL TELL LAINIE ALL...
HEY!
YOU READY?

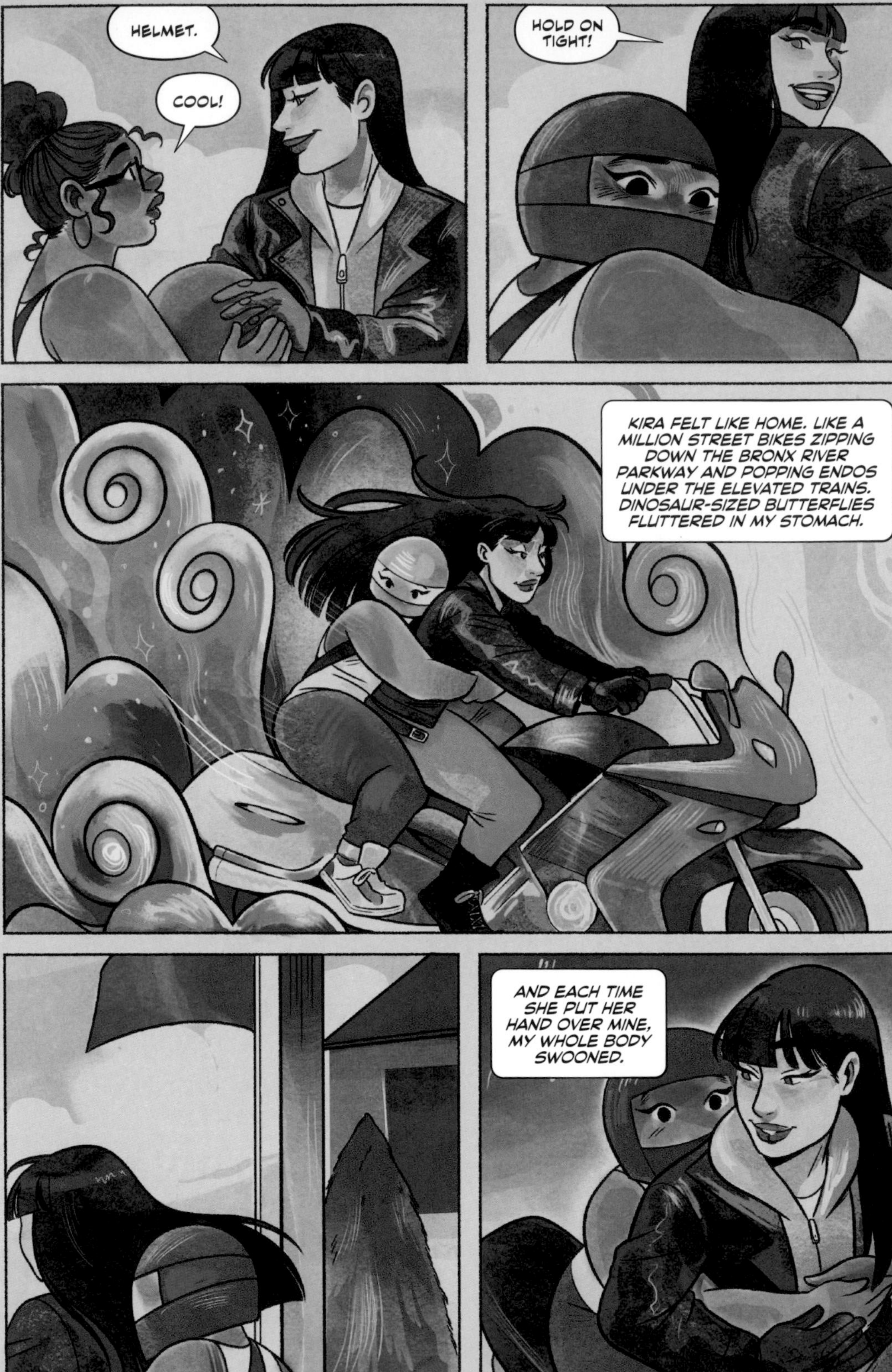
HELMET.
COOL!
HOLD ON TIGHT!
KIRA FELT LIKE HOME. LIKE A MILLION STREET BIKES ZIPPING DOWN THE BRONX RIVER PARKWAY AND POPPING ENDOS UNDER THE ELEVATED TRAINS. DINOSAUR-SIZED BUTTERFLIES FLUTTERED IN MY STOMACH.
AND EACH TIME SHE PUT HER HAND OVER MINE, MY WHOLE BODY SWOONED.

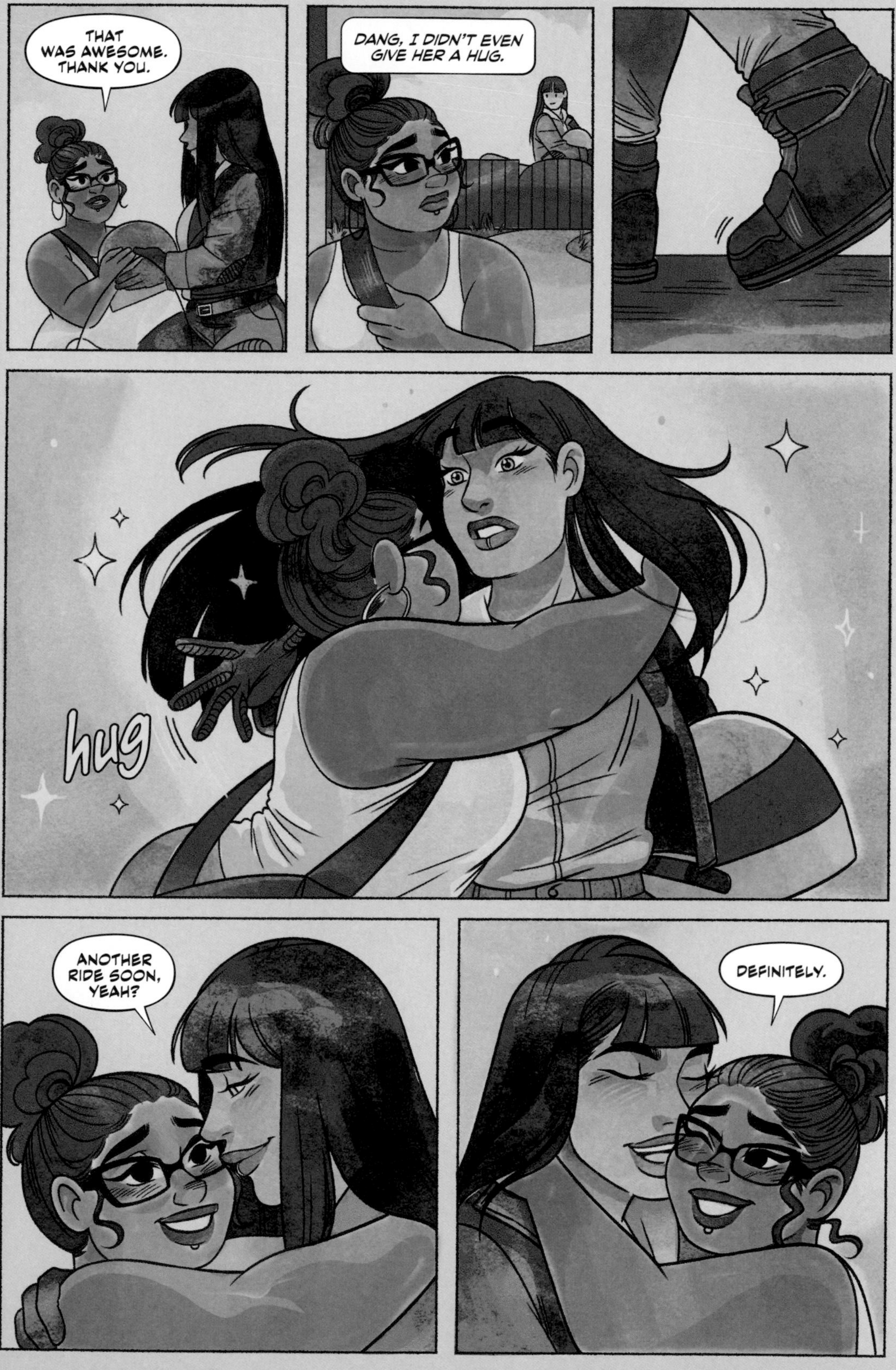
THAT WAS AWESOME. THANK YOU.
DANG, I DIDN'T EVEN GIVE HER A HUG.
hug
ANOTHER RIDE SOON, YEAH?
DEFINITELY.

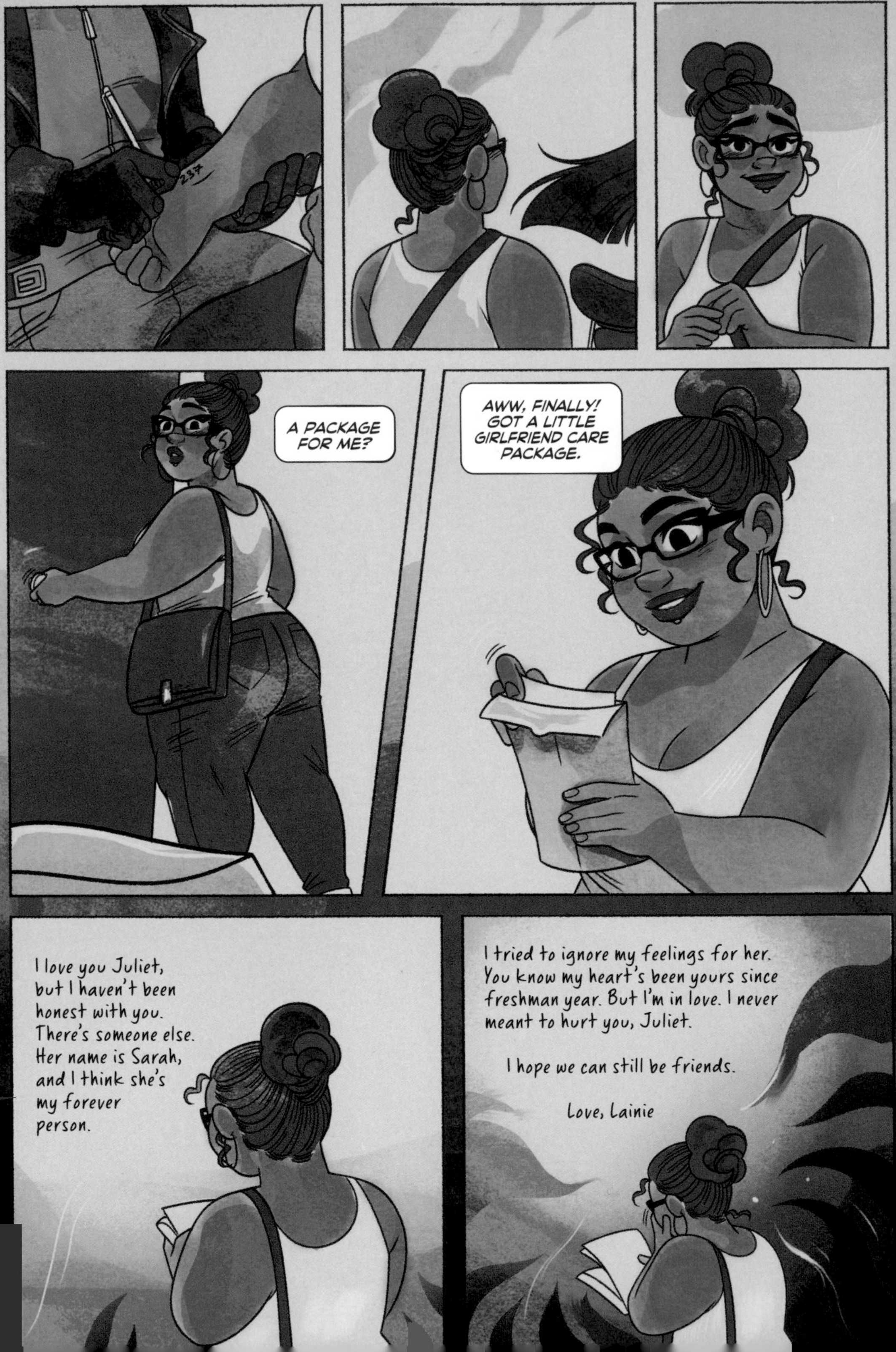
237
A PACKAGE FOR ME?
AWW, FINALLY! GOT A LITTLE GIRLFRIEND CARE PACKAGE.
I love you Juliet, but I haven't been honest with you. There's someone else. Her name is Sarah, and I think she's my forever person.
I tried to ignore my feelings for her. You know my heart's been yours since freshman year. But I'm in love. I never meant to hurt you, Juliet.
I hope we can still be friends.
Love, Lainie

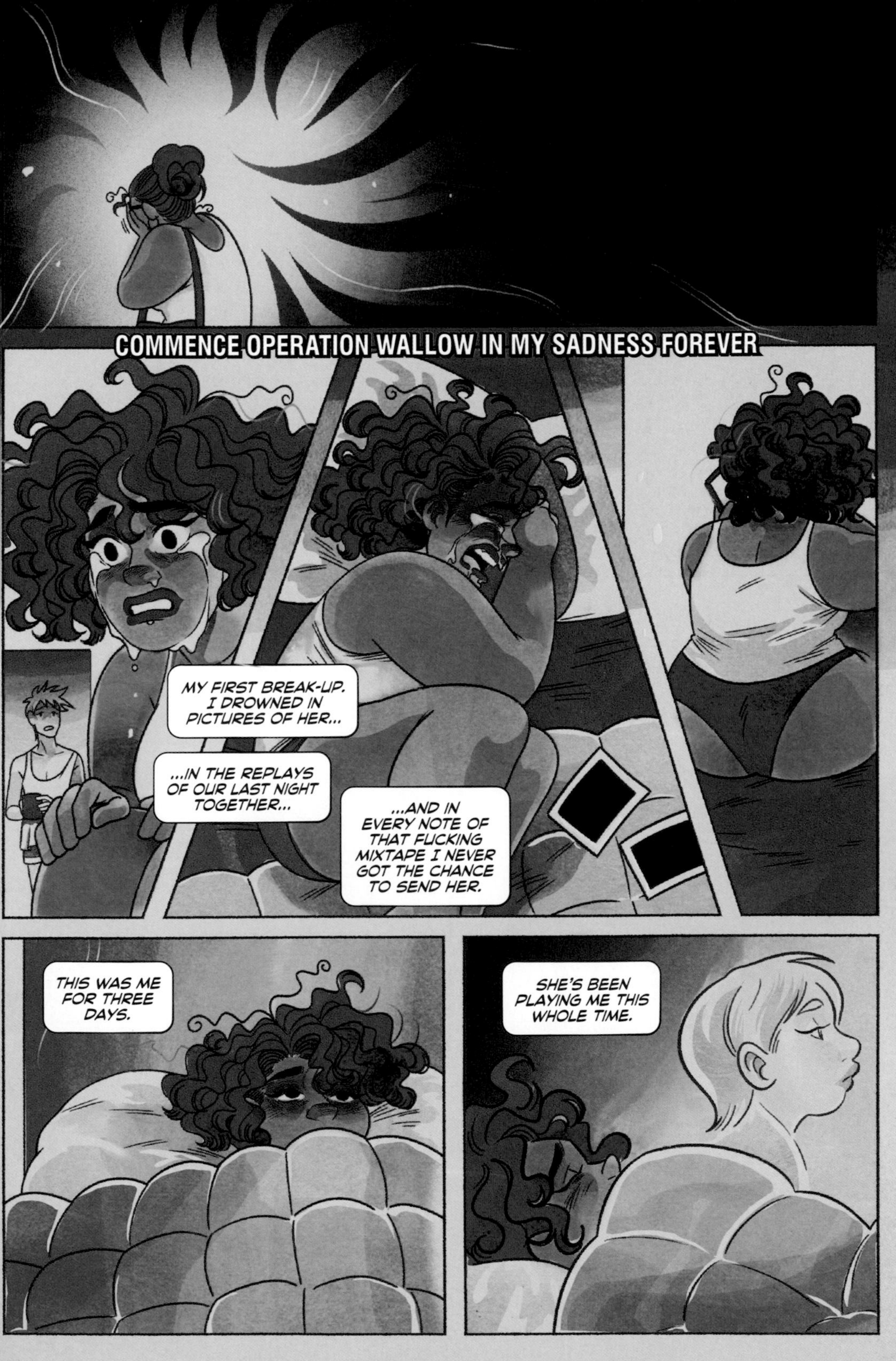
COMMENCE OPERATION WALLOW IN MY SADNESS FOREVER
MY FIRST BREAK-UP. I DROWNED IN PICTURES OF HER...
...IN THE REPLAYS OF OUR LAST NIGHT TOGETHER...
...AND IN EVERY NOTE OF THAT FUCKING MIXTAPE I NEVER GOT THE CHANCE TO SEND HER.
THIS WAS ME FOR THREE DAYS.
SHE'S BEEN PLAYING ME THIS WHOLE TIME.

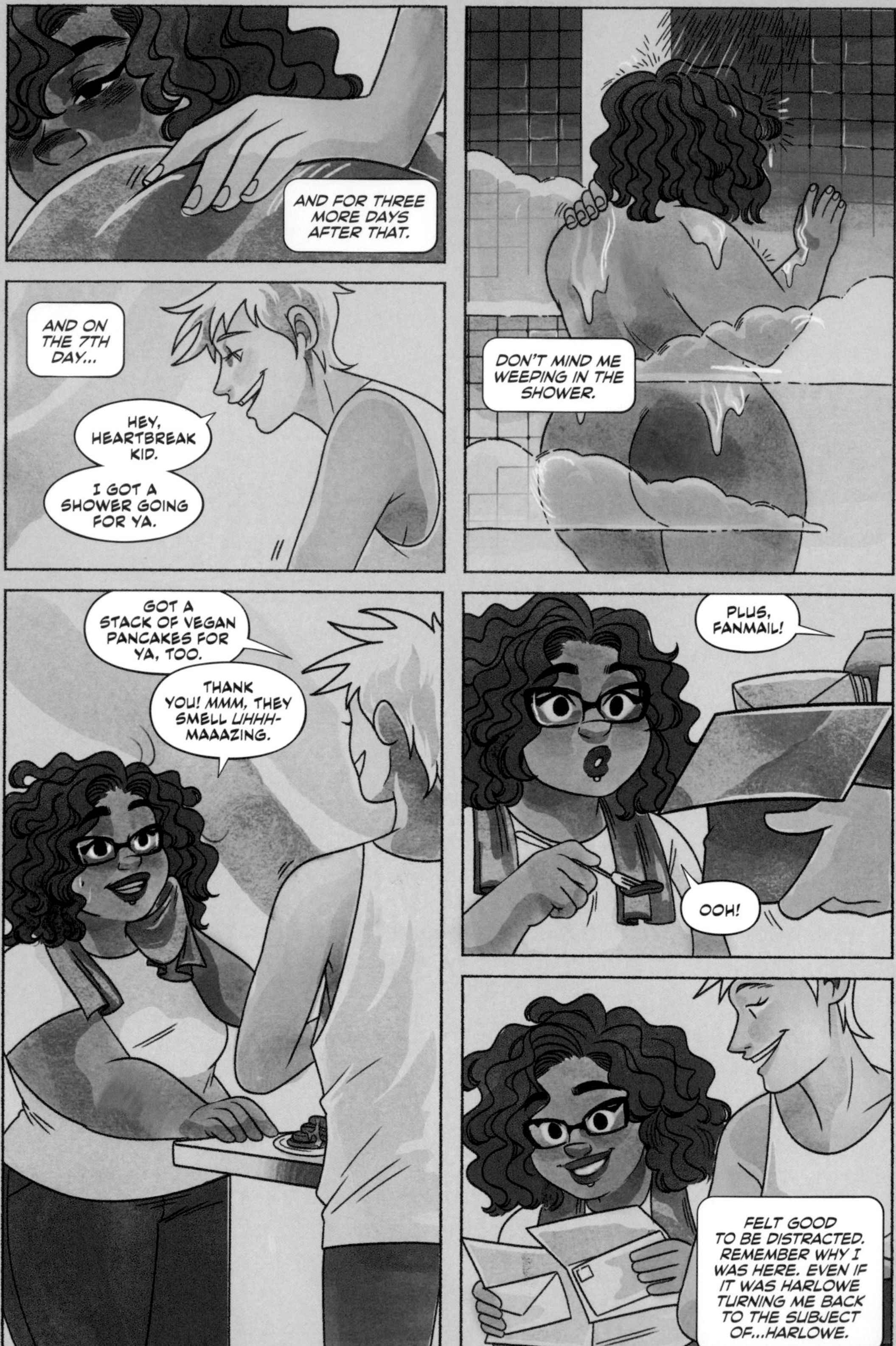
AND FOR THREE MORE DAYS AFTER THAT.
AND ON THE 7TH DAY...
HEY, HEARTBREAK KID.
I GOT A SHOWER GOING FOR YA.
DON'T MIND ME WEEPING IN THE SHOWER.
GOT A STACK OF VEGAN PANCAKES FOR YA, TOO.
THANK YOU! MMM, THEY SMELL *UHHH-MAAAZING.*
PLUS, FANMAIL!
OOH!
FELT GOOD TO BE DISTRACTED. REMEMBER WHY I WAS HERE. EVEN IF IT WAS HARLOWE TURNING ME BACK TO THE SUBJECT OF...HARLOWE.

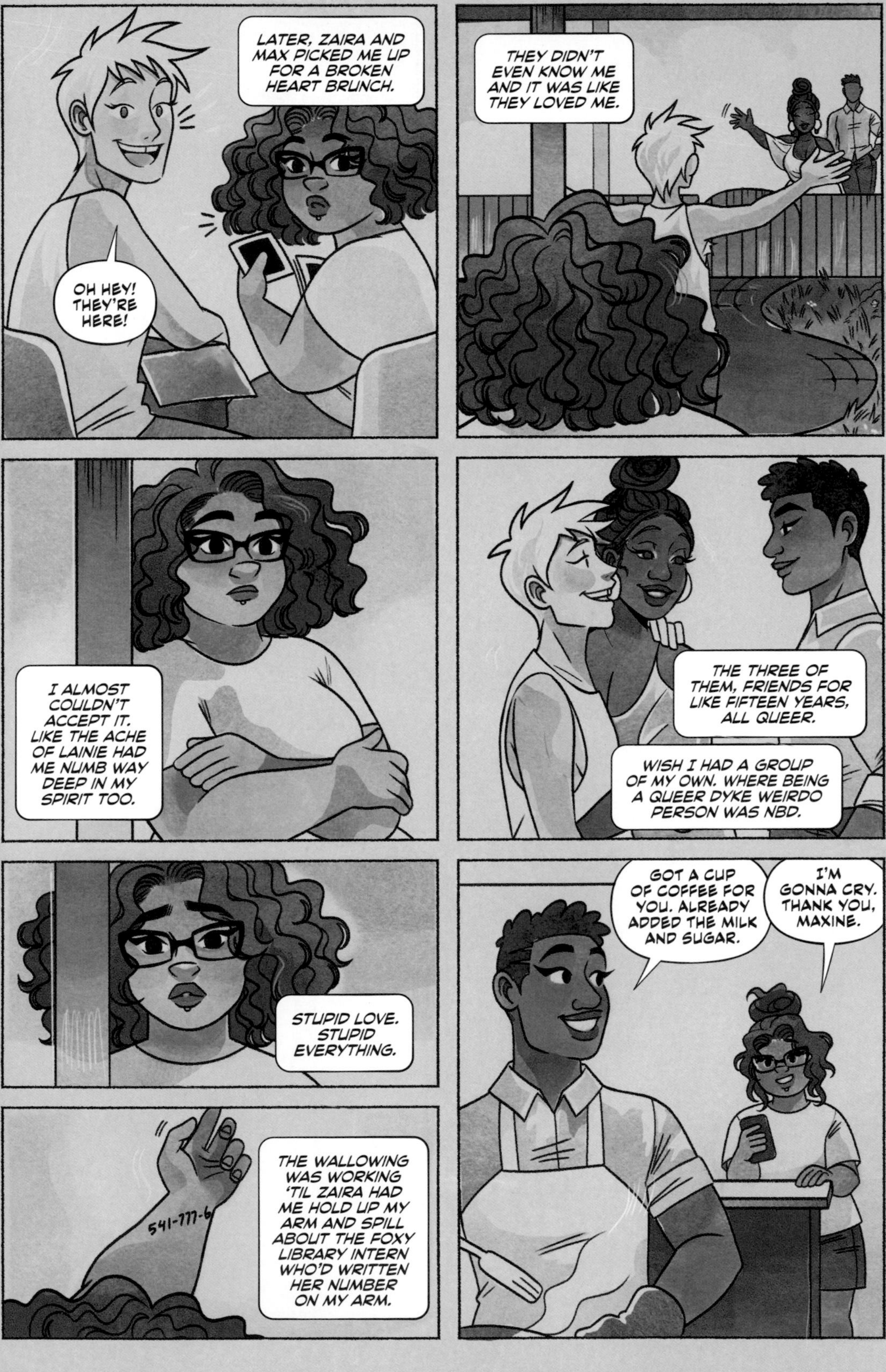
LATER, ZAIRA AND MAX PICKED ME UP FOR A BROKEN HEART BRUNCH.
OH HEY! THEY'RE HERE!
THEY DIDN'T EVEN KNOW ME AND IT WAS LIKE THEY LOVED ME.
I ALMOST COULDN'T ACCEPT IT. LIKE THE ACHE OF LAINIE HAD ME NUMB WAY DEEP IN MY SPIRIT TOO.
THE THREE OF THEM, FRIENDS FOR LIKE FIFTEEN YEARS, ALL QUEER.
WISH I HAD A GROUP OF MY OWN. WHERE BEING A QUEER DYKE WEIRDO PERSON WAS NBD.
STUPID LOVE. STUPID EVERYTHING.
541-777-6
THE WALLOWING WAS WORKING 'TIL ZAIRA HAD ME HOLD UP MY ARM AND SPILL ABOUT THE FOXY LIBRARY INTERN WHO'D WRITTEN HER NUMBER ON MY ARM.
GOT A CUP OF COFFEE FOR YOU. ALREADY ADDED THE MILK AND SUGAR.
I'M GONNA CRY. THANK YOU, MAXINE.

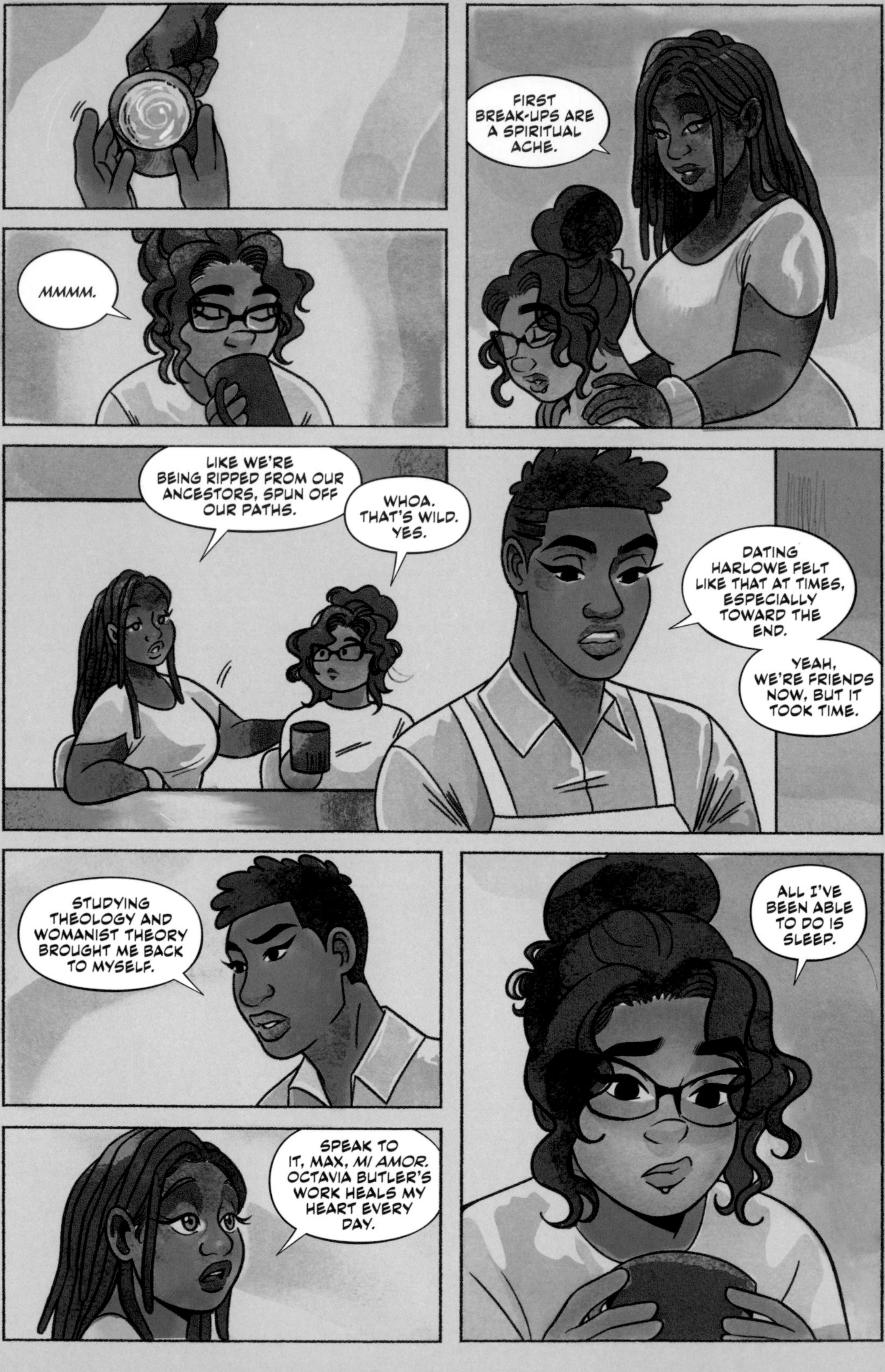
FIRST BREAK-UPS ARE A SPIRITUAL ACHE.
MMMM.
LIKE WE'RE BEING RIPPED FROM OUR ANCESTORS, SPUN OFF OUR PATHS.
WHOA. THAT'S WILD. YES.
DATING HARLOWE FELT LIKE THAT AT TIMES, ESPECIALLY TOWARD THE END.
YEAH, WE'RE FRIENDS NOW, BUT IT TOOK TIME.
STUDYING THEOLOGY AND WOMANIST THEORY BROUGHT ME BACK TO MYSELF.
SPEAK TO IT, MAX, *MI AMOR.* OCTAVIA BUTLER'S WORK HEALS MY HEART EVERY DAY.
ALL I'VE BEEN ABLE TO DO IS SLEEP.

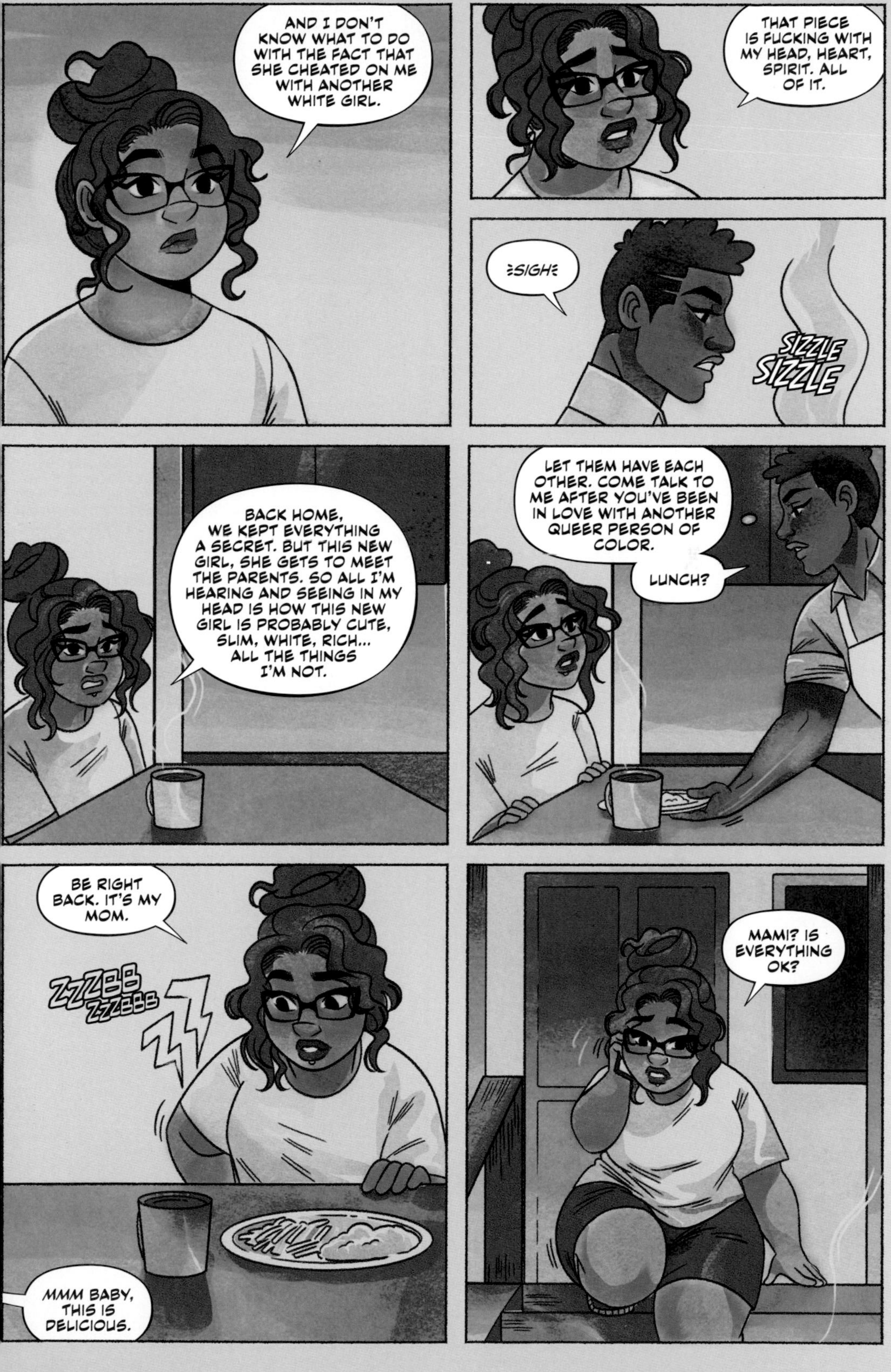
AND I DON'T KNOW WHAT TO DO WITH THE FACT THAT SHE CHEATED ON ME WITH ANOTHER WHITE GIRL.
THAT PIECE IS FUCKING WITH MY HEAD, HEART, SPIRIT. ALL OF IT.
SIGH
SIZZLE SIZZLE
BACK HOME, WE KEPT EVERYTHING A SECRET. BUT THIS NEW GIRL, SHE GETS TO MEET THE PARENTS. SO ALL I'M HEARING AND SEEING IN MY HEAD IS HOW THIS NEW GIRL IS PROBABLY CUTE, SLIM, WHITE, RICH... ALL THE THINGS I'M NOT.
LET THEM HAVE EACH OTHER. COME TALK TO ME AFTER YOU'VE BEEN IN LOVE WITH ANOTHER QUEER PERSON OF COLOR.
LUNCH?
BE RIGHT BACK. IT'S MY MOM.
ZZZBB ZZZBBB
MMM BABY, THIS IS DELICIOUS.
MAMI? IS EVERYTHING OK?

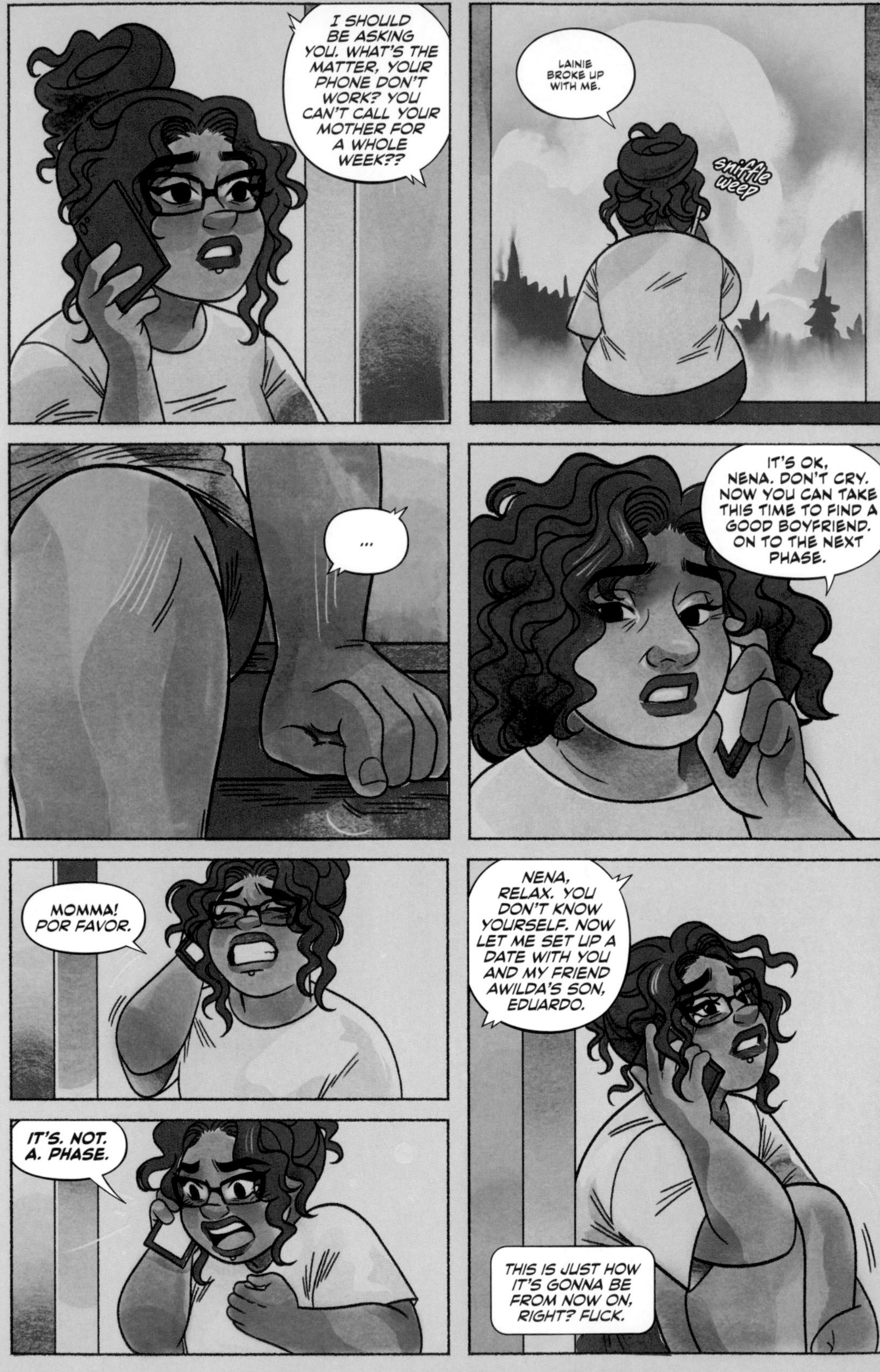
I SHOULD BE ASKING YOU. WHAT'S THE MATTER, YOUR PHONE DON'T WORK? YOU CAN'T CALL YOUR MOTHER FOR A WHOLE WEEK??
LAINIE BROKE UP WITH ME.
sniffle weep
...
IT'S OK, NENA. DON'T CRY. NOW YOU CAN TAKE THIS TIME TO FIND A GOOD BOYFRIEND. ON TO THE NEXT PHASE.
MOMMA! POR FAVOR.
IT'S. NOT. A. PHASE.
NENA, RELAX. YOU DON'T KNOW YOURSELF. NOW LET ME SET UP A DATE WITH YOU AND MY FRIEND AWILDA'S SON, EDUARDO.
THIS IS JUST HOW IT'S GONNA BE FROM NOW ON, RIGHT? FUCK.

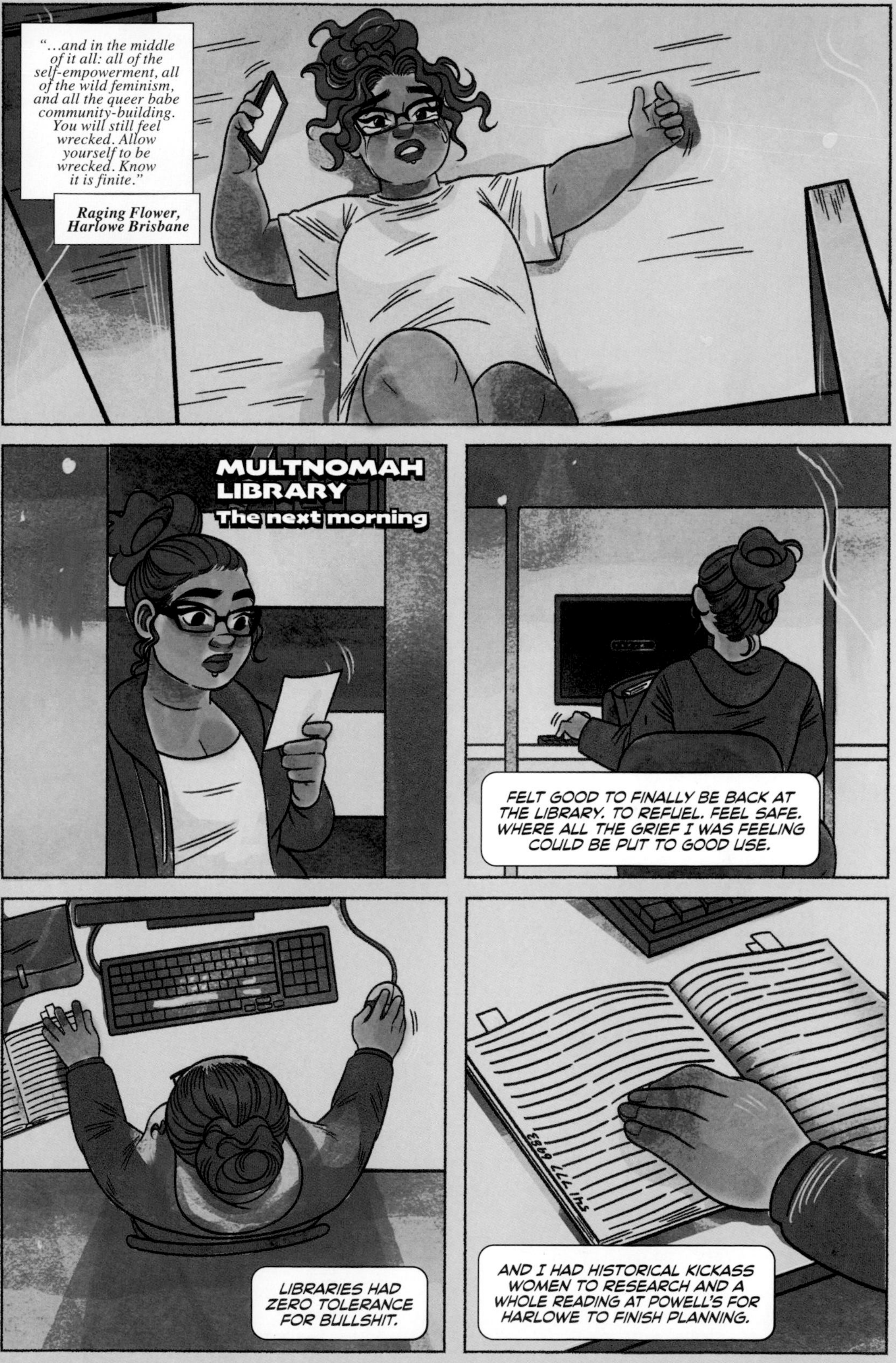
"...and in the middle of it all: all of the self-empowerment, all of the wild feminism, and all the queer babe community-building. You will still feel wrecked. Allow yourself to be wrecked. Know it is finite."
Raging Flower, Harlowe Brisbane
MULTNOMAH LIBRARY
The next morning
FELT GOOD TO FINALLY BE BACK AT THE LIBRARY. TO REFUEL. FEEL SAFE. WHERE ALL THE GRIEF I WAS FEELING COULD BE PUT TO GOOD USE.
LIBRARIES HAD ZERO TOLERANCE FOR BULLSHIT.
AND I HAD HISTORICAL KICKASS WOMEN TO RESEARCH AND A WHOLE READING AT POWELL'S FOR HARLOWE TO FINISH PLANNING.

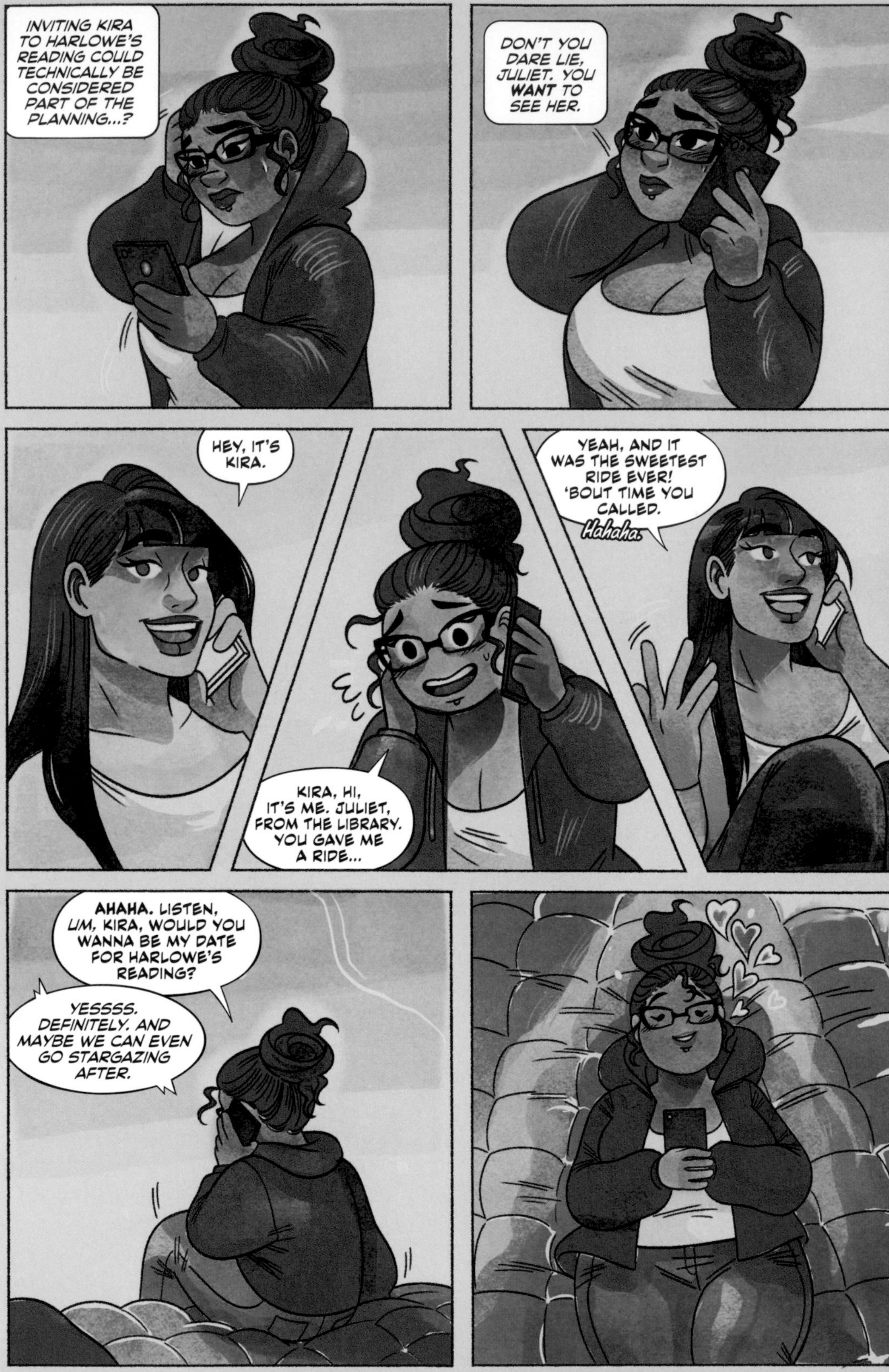
INVITING KIRA TO HARLOWE'S READING COULD TECHNICALLY BE CONSIDERED PART OF THE PLANNING...?
DON'T YOU DARE LIE, JULIET. YOU **WANT** TO SEE HER.
HEY, IT'S KIRA.
KIRA, HI, IT'S ME. JULIET, FROM THE LIBRARY. YOU GAVE ME A RIDE...
YEAH, AND IT WAS THE SWEETEST RIDE EVER! 'BOUT TIME YOU CALLED.
Hahaha.
AHAHA. LISTEN, UM, KIRA, WOULD YOU WANNA BE MY DATE FOR HARLOWE'S READING?
YESSSS. DEFINITELY. AND MAYBE WE CAN EVEN GO STARGAZING AFTER.

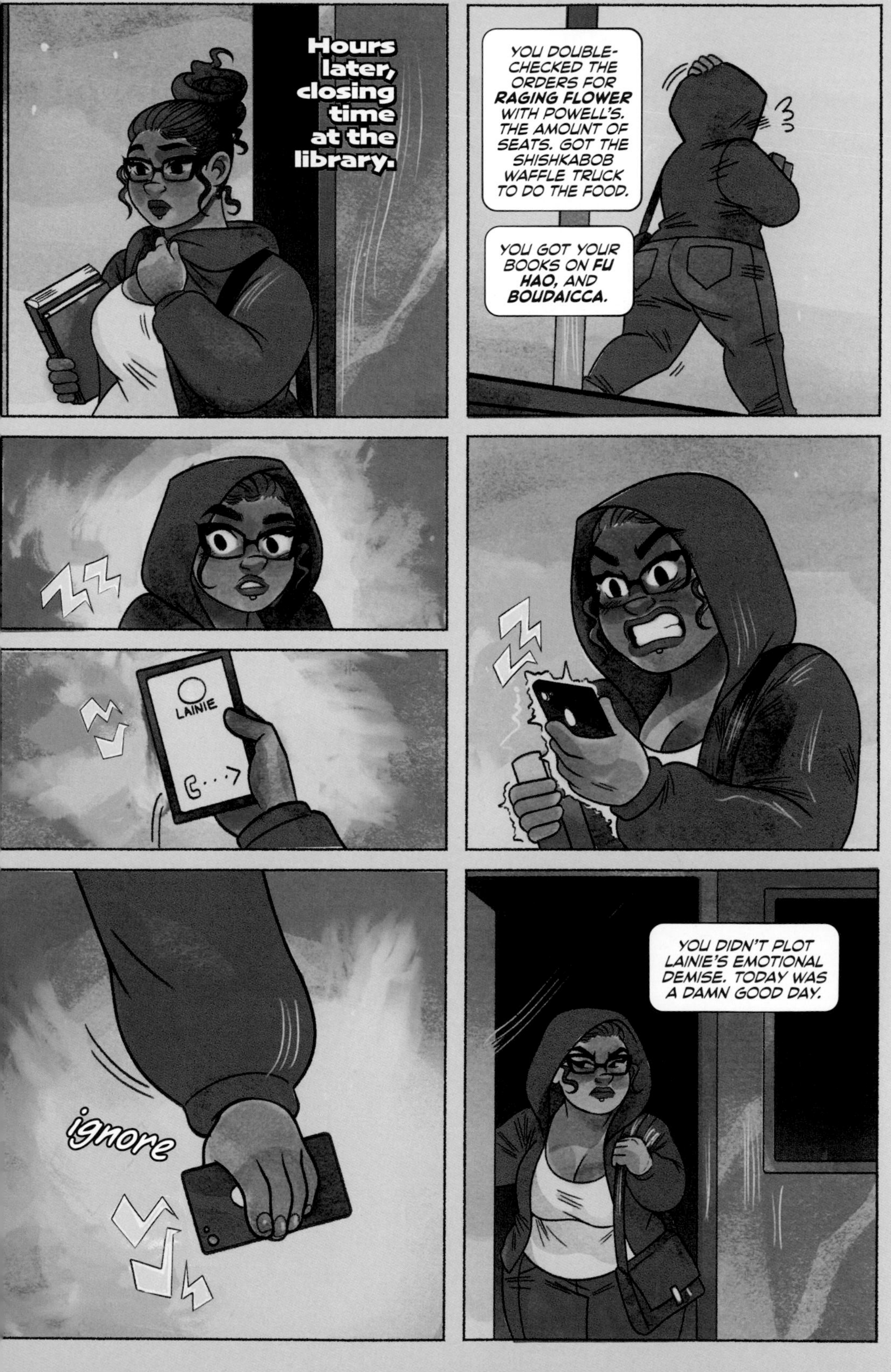
Hours later, closing time at the library.
YOU DOUBLE-CHECKED THE ORDERS FOR RAGING FLOWER WITH POWELL'S. THE AMOUNT OF SEATS. GOT THE SHISHKABOB WAFFLE TRUCK TO DO THE FOOD.
YOU GOT YOUR BOOKS ON FU HAO, AND BOUDAICCA.
LAINIE
ignore
YOU DIDN'T PLOT LAINIE'S EMOTIONAL DEMISE. TODAY WAS A DAMN GOOD DAY.

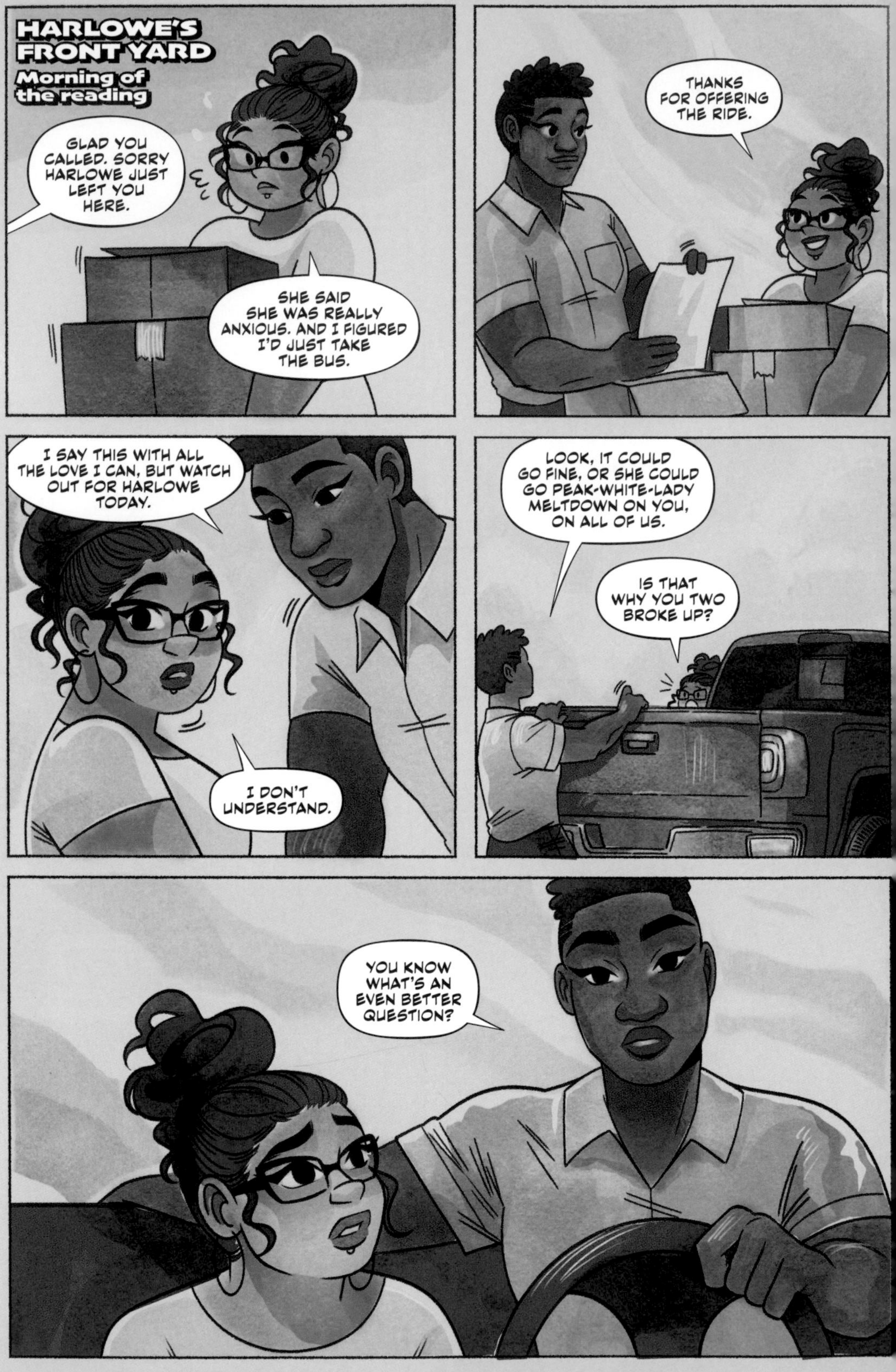
HARLOWE'S FRONT YARD
Morning of the reading
GLAD YOU CALLED. SORRY HARLOWE JUST LEFT YOU HERE.
SHE SAID SHE WAS REALLY ANXIOUS. AND I FIGURED I'D JUST TAKE THE BUS.
THANKS FOR OFFERING THE RIDE.
I SAY THIS WITH ALL THE LOVE I CAN, BUT WATCH OUT FOR HARLOWE TODAY.
I DON'T UNDERSTAND.
LOOK, IT COULD GO FINE, OR SHE COULD GO PEAK-WHITE-LADY MELTDOWN ON YOU, ON ALL OF US.
IS THAT WHY YOU TWO BROKE UP?
YOU KNOW WHAT'S AN EVEN BETTER QUESTION?

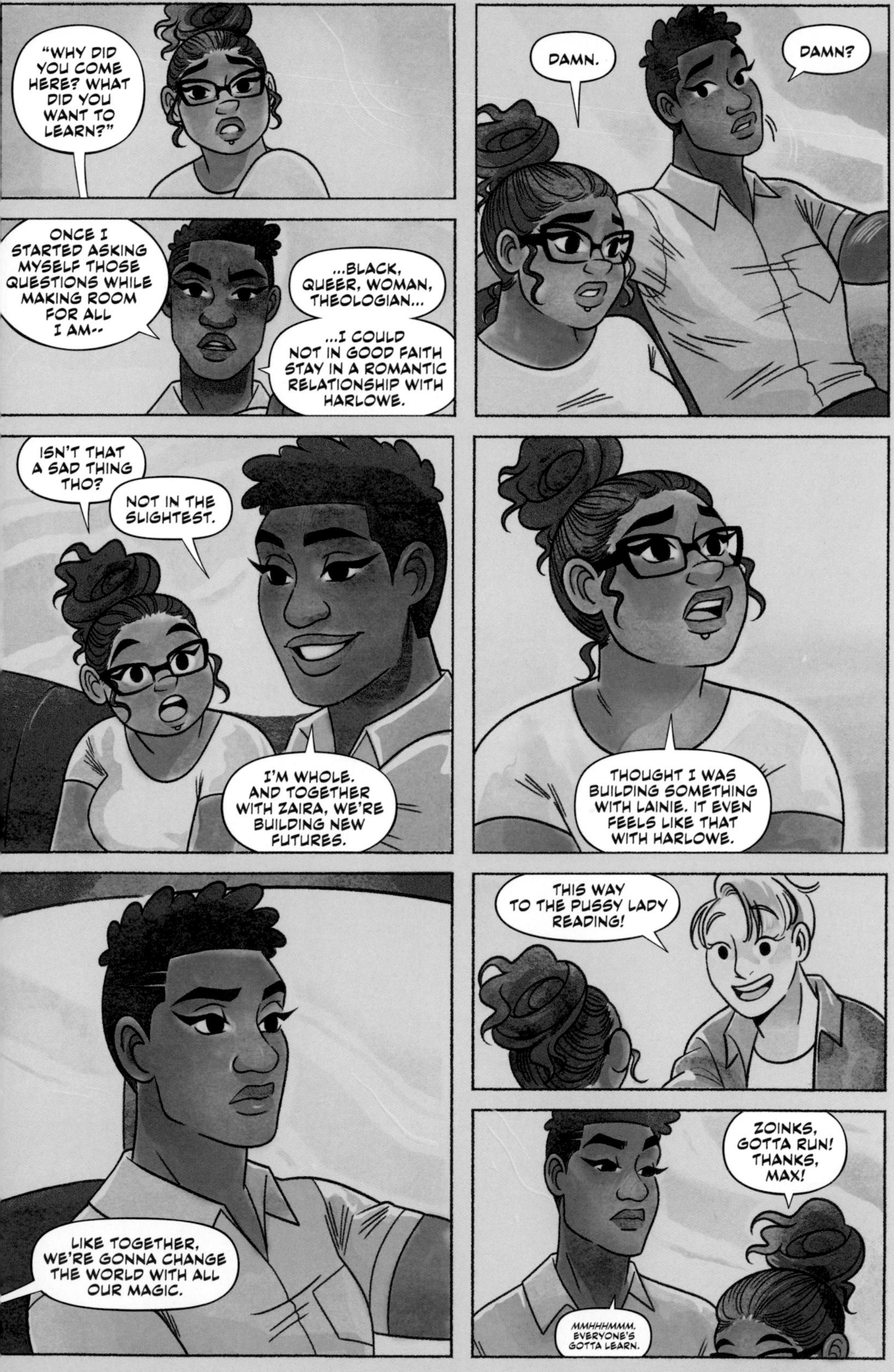
"WHY DID YOU COME HERE? WHAT DID YOU WANT TO LEARN?"
DAMN.
DAMN?
ONCE I STARTED ASKING MYSELF THOSE QUESTIONS WHILE MAKING ROOM FOR ALL I AM--
...BLACK, QUEER, WOMAN, THEOLOGIAN...
...I COULD NOT IN GOOD FAITH STAY IN A ROMANTIC RELATIONSHIP WITH HARLOWE.
ISN'T THAT A SAD THING THO?
NOT IN THE SLIGHTEST.
I'M WHOLE. AND TOGETHER WITH ZAIRA, WE'RE BUILDING NEW FUTURES.
THOUGHT I WAS BUILDING SOMETHING WITH LAINIE. IT EVEN FEELS LIKE THAT WITH HARLOWE.
LIKE TOGETHER, WE'RE GONNA CHANGE THE WORLD WITH ALL OUR MAGIC.
THIS WAY TO THE PUSSY LADY READING!
ZOINKS, GOTTA RUN! THANKS, MAX!
MMHHHMMM. EVERYONE'S GOTTA LEARN.

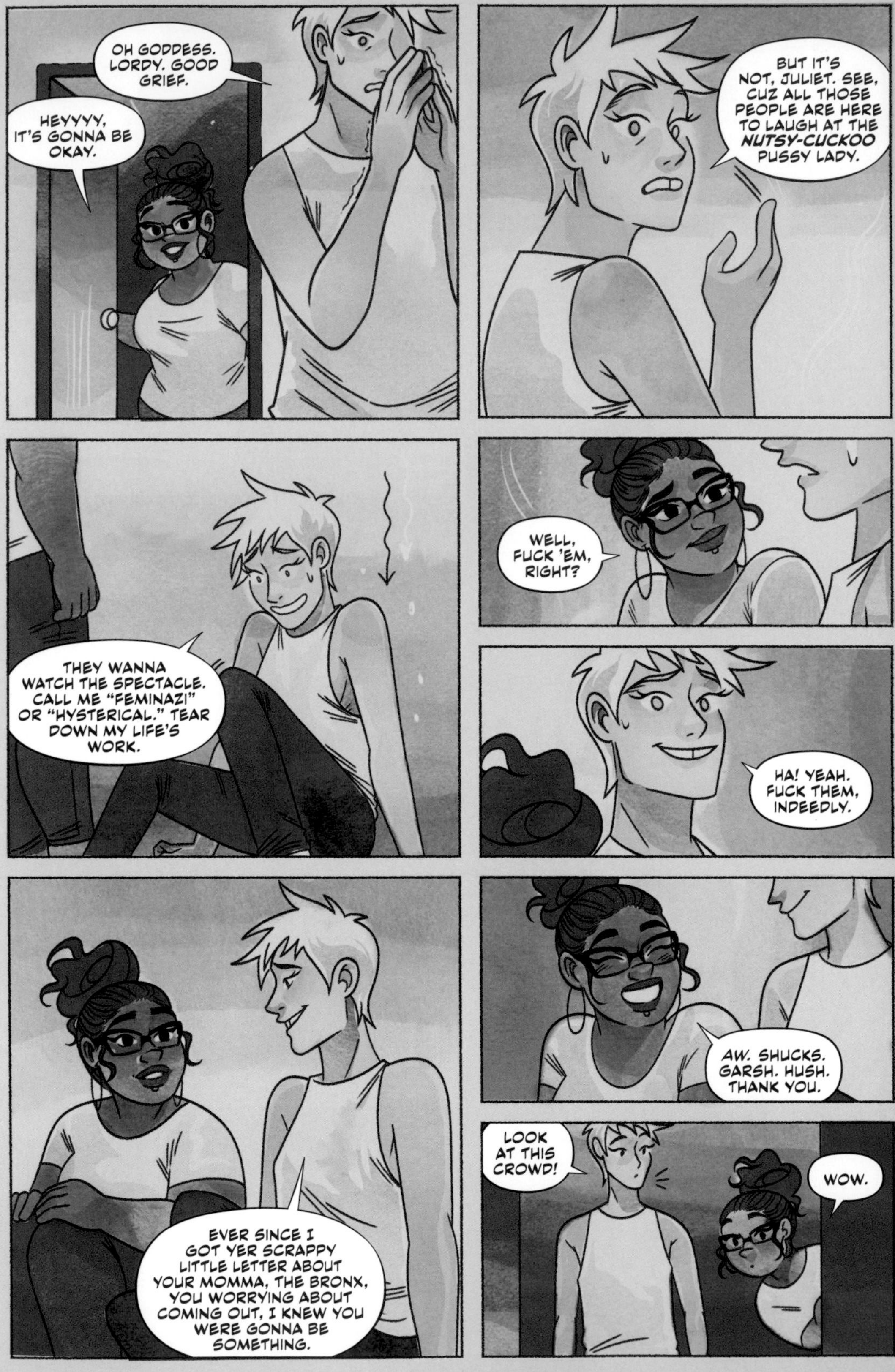
OH GODDESS. LORDY. GOOD GRIEF.
HEYYYY, IT'S GONNA BE OKAY.
BUT IT'S NOT, JULIET. SEE, CUZ ALL THOSE PEOPLE ARE HERE TO LAUGH AT THE *NUTSY-CUCKOO* PUSSY LADY.
THEY WANNA WATCH THE SPECTACLE. CALL ME "FEMINAZI" OR "HYSTERICAL." TEAR DOWN MY LIFE'S WORK.
WELL, FUCK 'EM, RIGHT?
HA! YEAH. FUCK THEM, INDEEDLY.
EVER SINCE I GOT YER SCRAPPY LITTLE LETTER ABOUT YOUR MOMMA, THE BRONX, YOU WORRYING ABOUT COMING OUT, I KNEW YOU WERE GONNA BE SOMETHING.
AW. SHUCKS. GARSH. HUSH. THANK YOU.
LOOK AT THIS CROWD!
WOW.

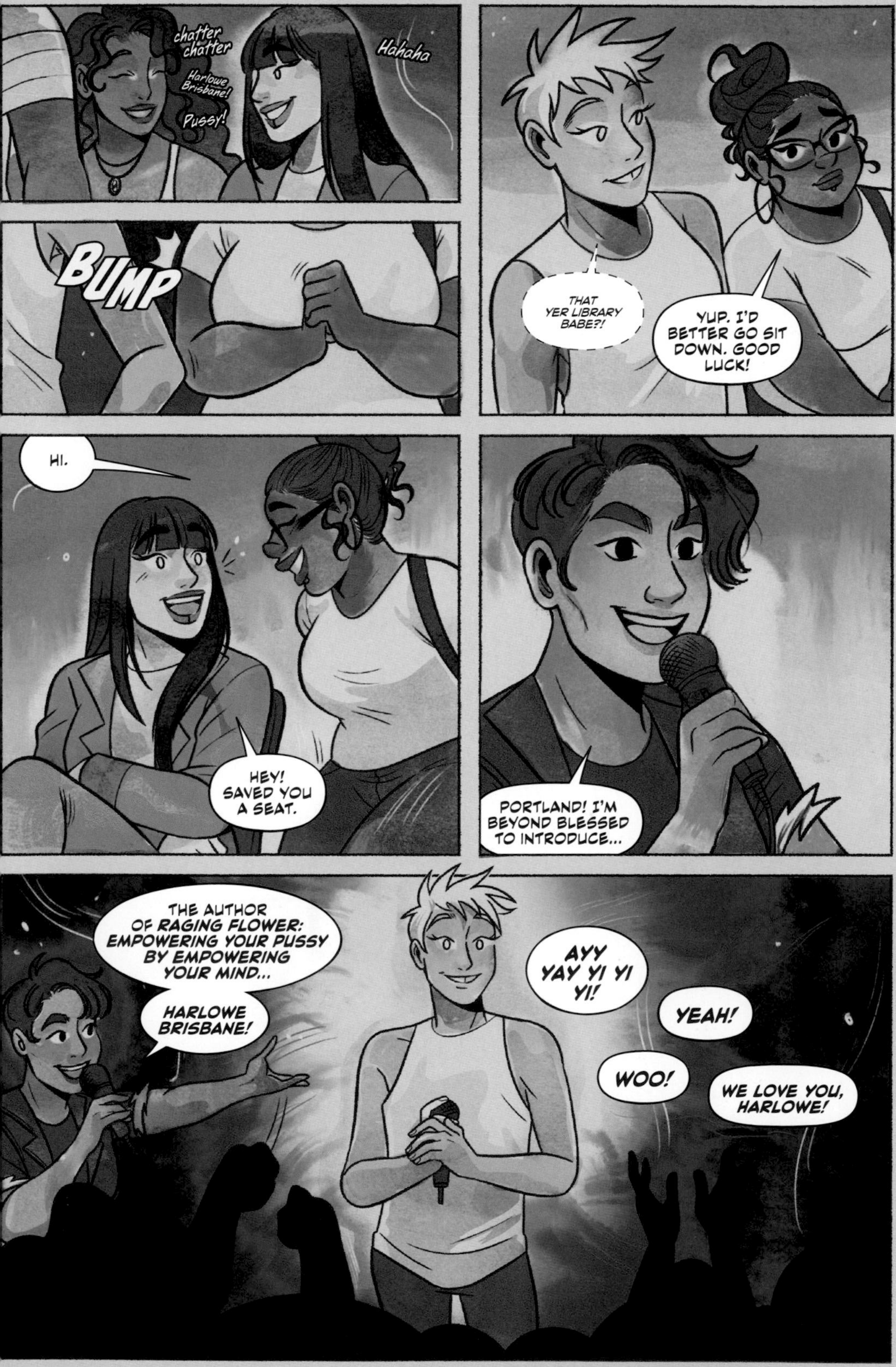
chatter chatter
Harlowe Brisbane!
Pussy!
Hahaha
BUMP
THAT YER LIBRARY BABE?!
YUP. I'D BETTER GO SIT DOWN. GOOD LUCK!
HI.
HEY! SAVED YOU A SEAT.
PORTLAND! I'M BEYOND BLESSED TO INTRODUCE...
THE AUTHOR OF RAGING FLOWER: EMPOWERING YOUR PUSSY BY EMPOWERING YOUR MIND...
HARLOWE BRISBANE!
AYY YAY YI YI YI!
YEAH!
WOO!
WE LOVE YOU, HARLOWE!

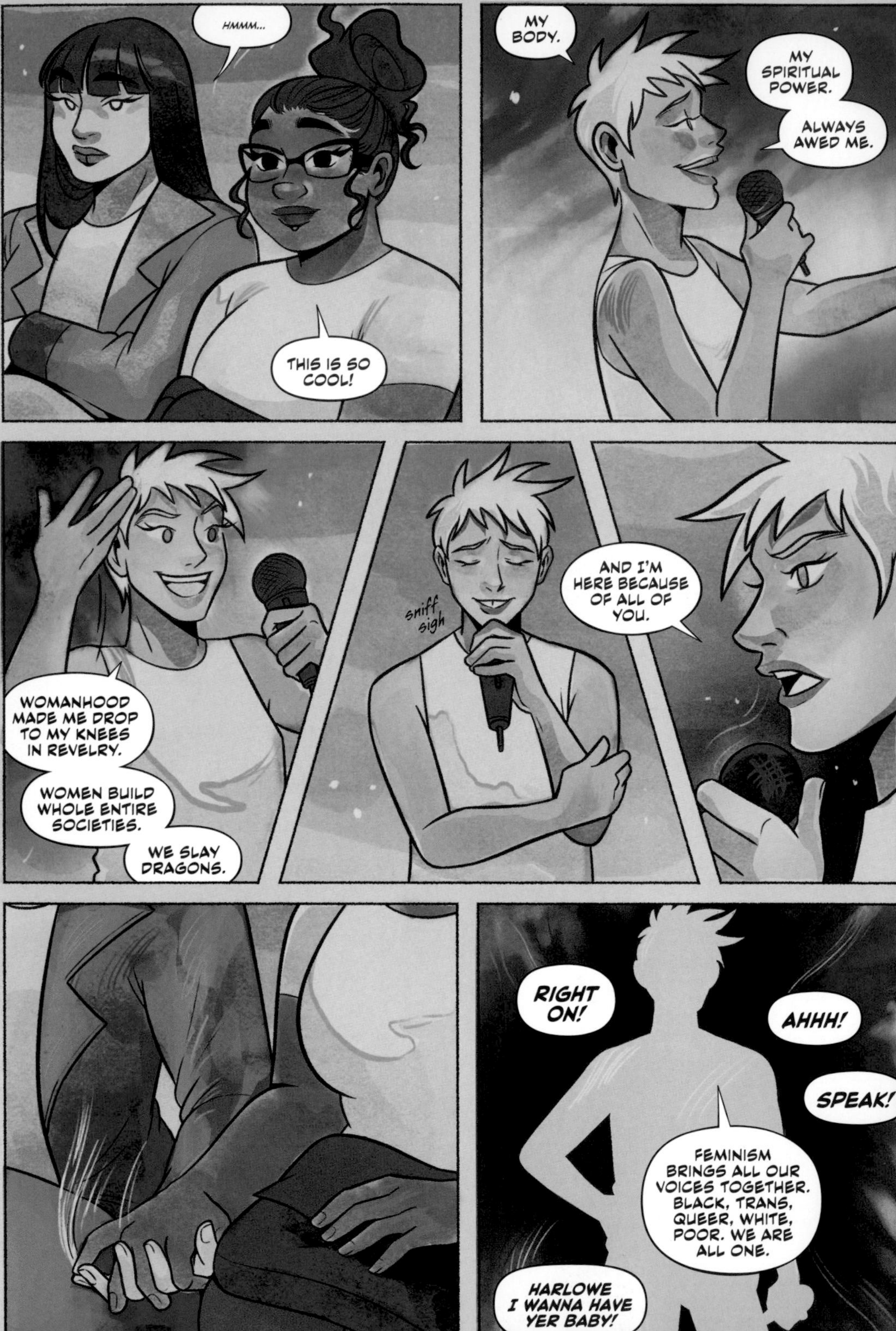
HMMM...
THIS IS SO COOL!
MY BODY.
MY SPIRITUAL POWER.
ALWAYS AWED ME.
WOMANHOOD MADE ME DROP TO MY KNEES IN REVELRY.
WOMEN BUILD WHOLE ENTIRE SOCIETIES.
WE SLAY DRAGONS.
sniff sigh
AND I'M HERE BECAUSE OF ALL OF YOU.
RIGHT ON!
AHHH!
SPEAK!
FEMINISM BRINGS ALL OUR VOICES TOGETHER. BLACK, TRANS, QUEER, WHITE, POOR. WE ARE ALL ONE.
HARLOWE I WANNA HAVE YER BABY!

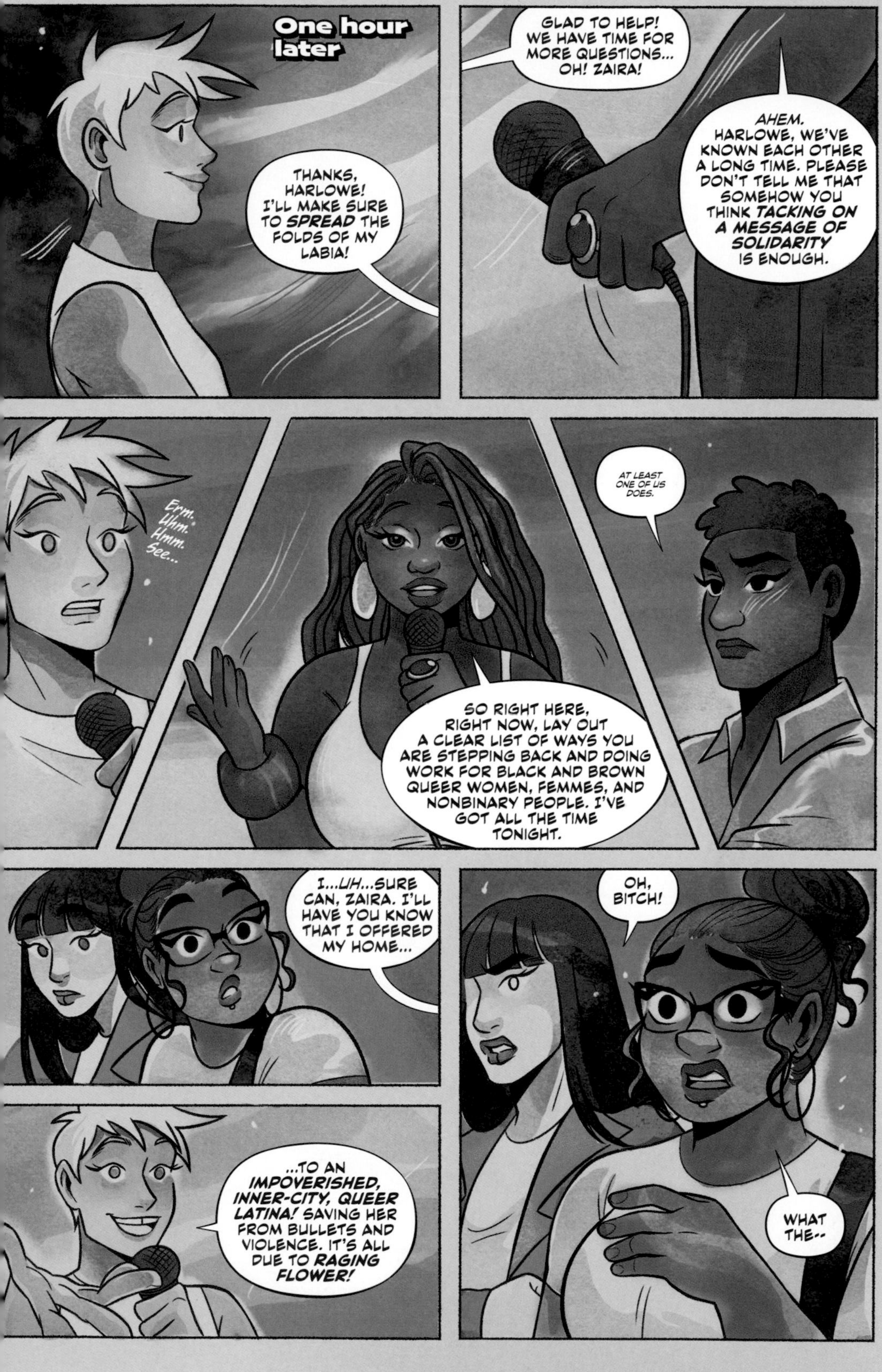
One hour later
THANKS, HARLOWE! I'LL MAKE SURE TO SPREAD THE FOLDS OF MY LABIA!
GLAD TO HELP! WE HAVE TIME FOR MORE QUESTIONS... OH! ZAIRA!
AHEM. HARLOWE, WE'VE KNOWN EACH OTHER A LONG TIME. PLEASE DON'T TELL ME THAT SOMEHOW YOU THINK TACKING ON A MESSAGE OF SOLIDARITY IS ENOUGH.
Erm. Uhm. Hmm. See...
SO RIGHT HERE, RIGHT NOW, LAY OUT A CLEAR LIST OF WAYS YOU ARE STEPPING BACK AND DOING WORK FOR BLACK AND BROWN QUEER WOMEN, FEMMES, AND NONBINARY PEOPLE. I'VE GOT ALL THE TIME TONIGHT.
AT LEAST ONE OF US DOES.
I...UH...SURE CAN, ZAIRA. I'LL HAVE YOU KNOW THAT I OFFERED MY HOME...
...TO AN IMPOVERISHED, INNER-CITY, QUEER LATINA! SAVING HER FROM BULLETS AND VIOLENCE. IT'S ALL DUE TO RAGING FLOWER!
OH, BITCH!
WHAT THE--

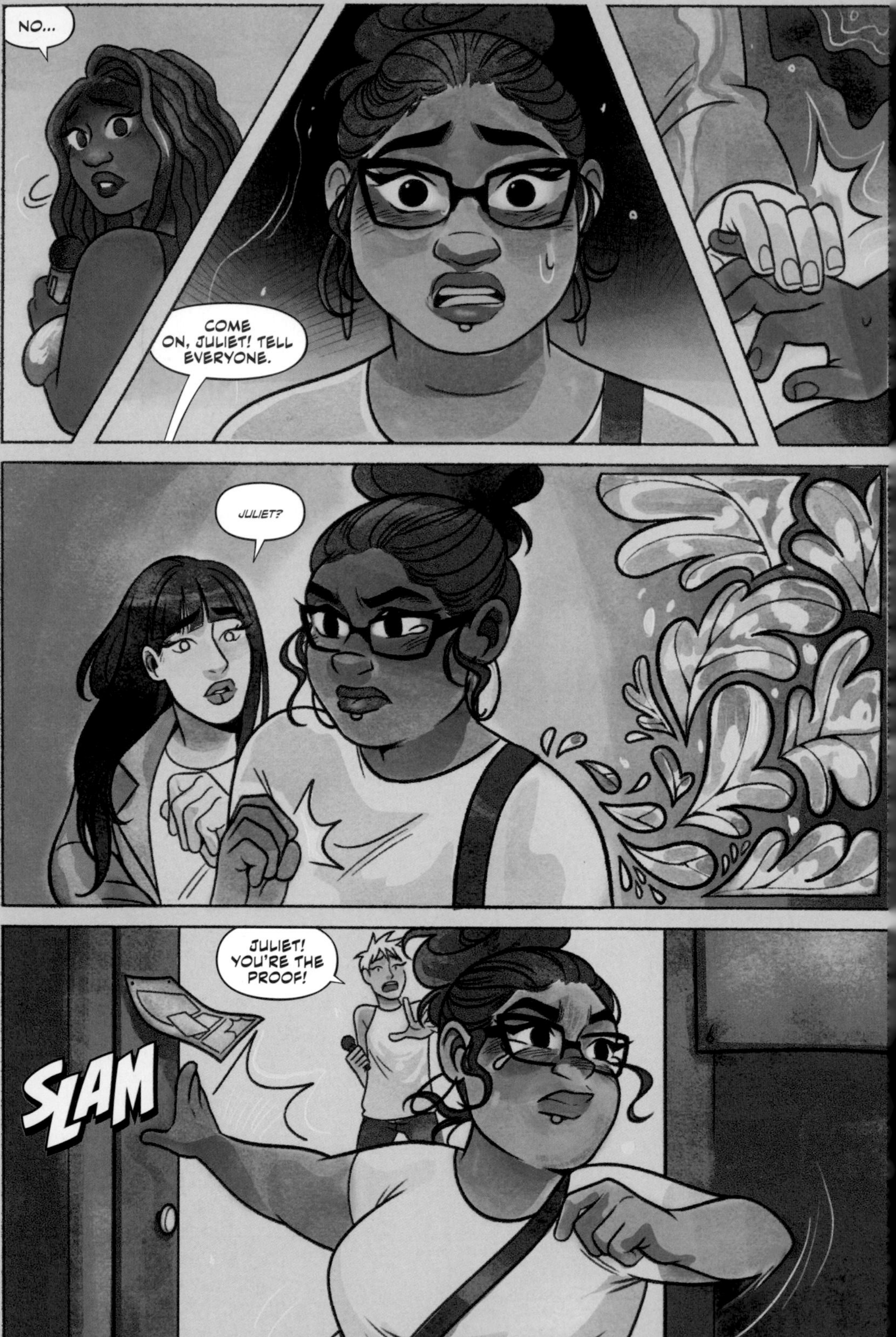
NO...
COME ON, JULIET! TELL EVERYONE.
JULIET?
JULIET! YOU'RE THE PROOF!
SLAM

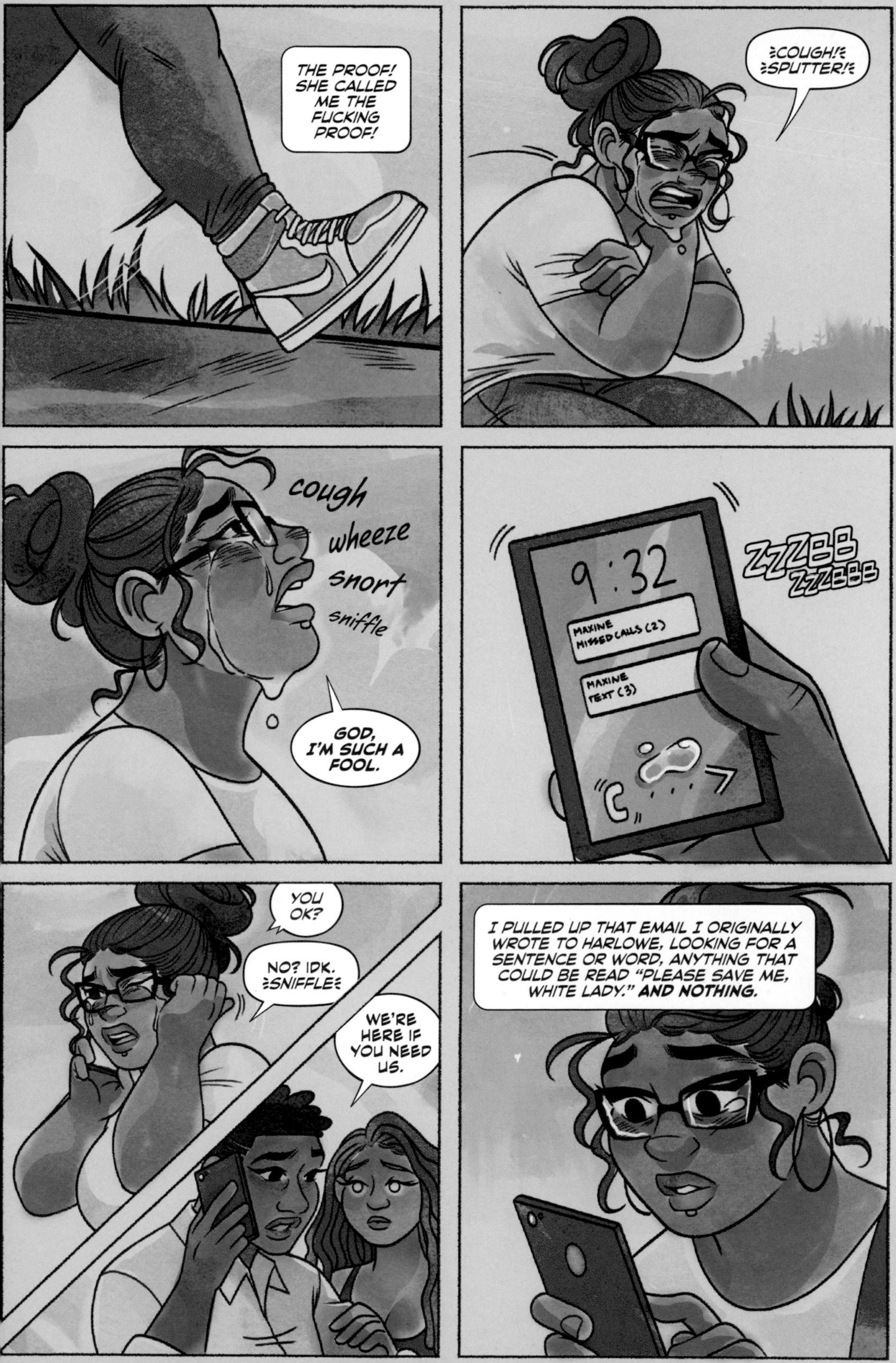
THE PROOF! SHE CALLED ME THE FUCKING PROOF!
COUGH! SPUTTER!
cough
wheeze
snort
sniffle
GOD, I'M SUCH A FOOL.
9:32
MAXINE MISSED CALLS (2)
MAXINE TEXT (3)
ZZZBB ZZZBBB
YOU OK?
NO? IDK. SNIFFLE
WE'RE HERE IF YOU NEED US.
I PULLED UP THAT EMAIL I ORIGINALLY WROTE TO HARLOWE, LOOKING FOR A SENTENCE OR WORD, ANYTHING THAT COULD BE READ "PLEASE SAVE ME, WHITE LADY." AND NOTHING.

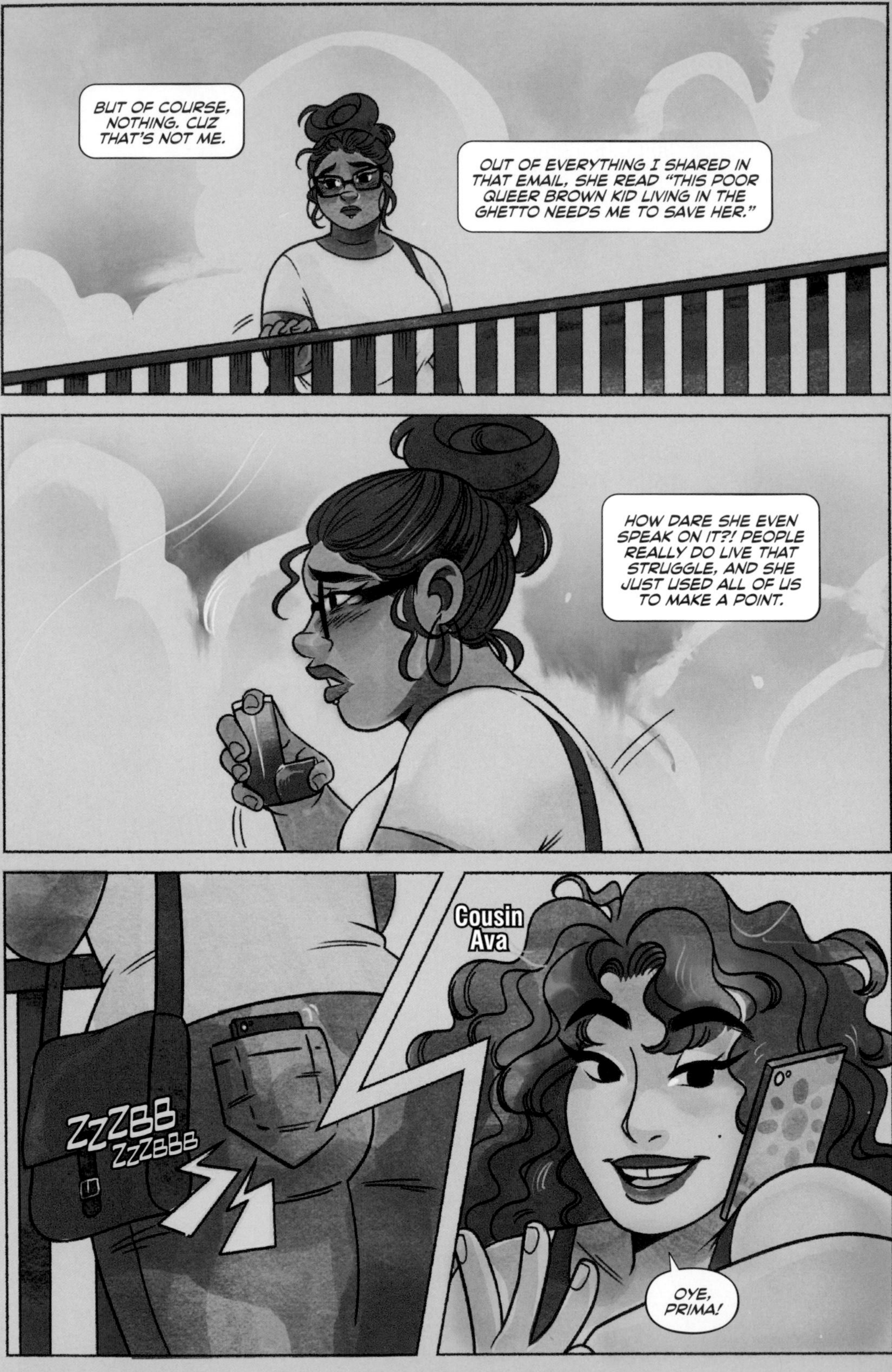
BUT OF COURSE, NOTHING. CUZ THAT'S NOT ME.
OUT OF EVERYTHING I SHARED IN THAT EMAIL, SHE READ "THIS POOR QUEER BROWN KID LIVING IN THE GHETTO NEEDS ME TO SAVE HER."
HOW DARE SHE EVEN SPEAK ON IT?! PEOPLE REALLY DO LIVE THAT STRUGGLE, AND SHE JUST USED ALL OF US TO MAKE A POINT.
ZZZBB
ZZZBBB
Cousin Ava
OYE, PRIMA!

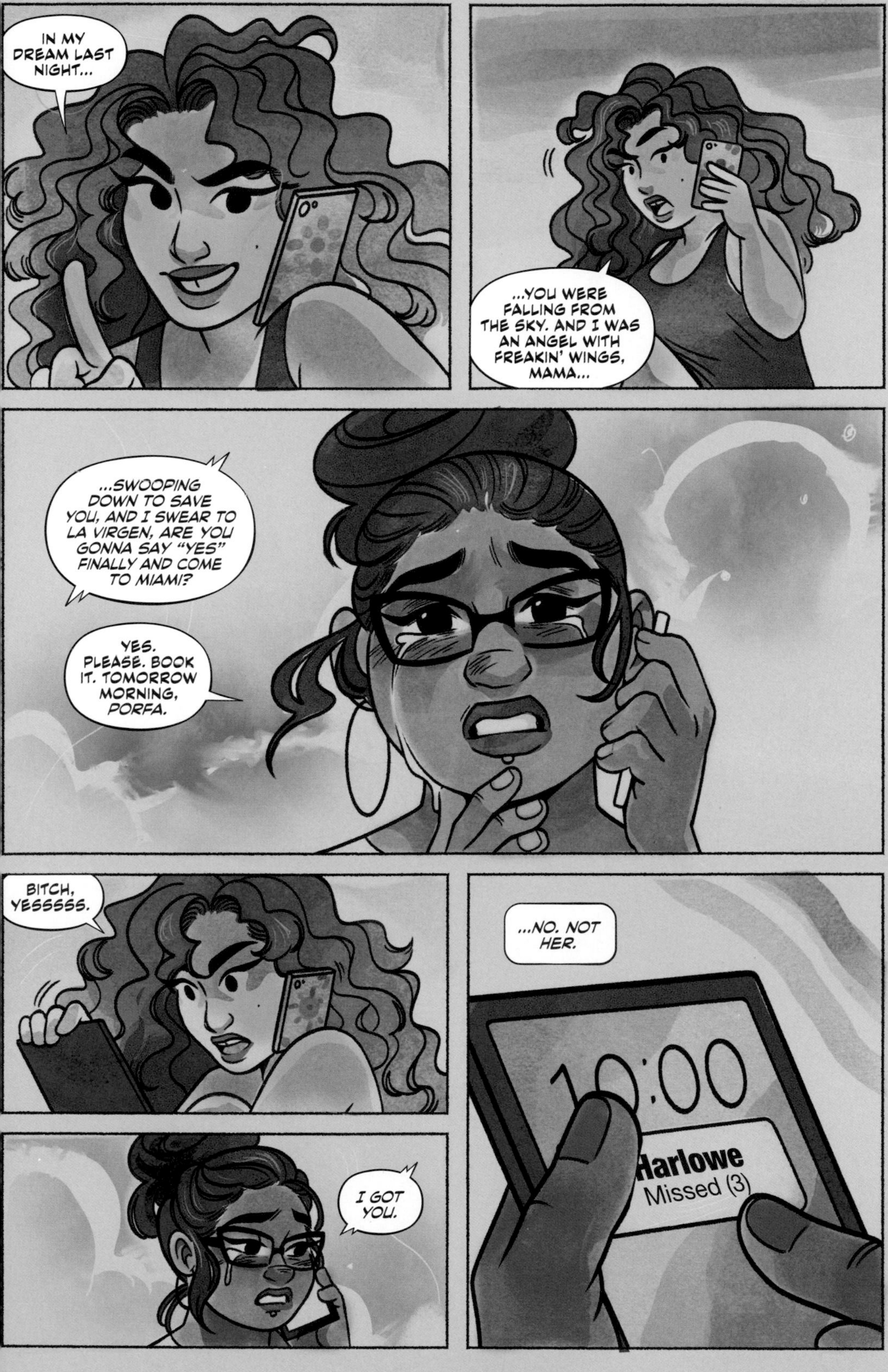
IN MY DREAM LAST NIGHT...
...YOU WERE FALLING FROM THE SKY. AND I WAS AN ANGEL WITH FREAKIN' WINGS, MAMA...
...SWOOPING DOWN TO SAVE YOU, AND I SWEAR TO LA VIRGEN, ARE YOU GONNA SAY "YES" FINALLY AND COME TO MIAMI?
YES. PLEASE. BOOK IT. TOMORROW MORNING, PORFA.
BITCH, YESSSSS.
I GOT YOU.
...NO. NOT HER.
10:00
Harlowe
Missed (3)

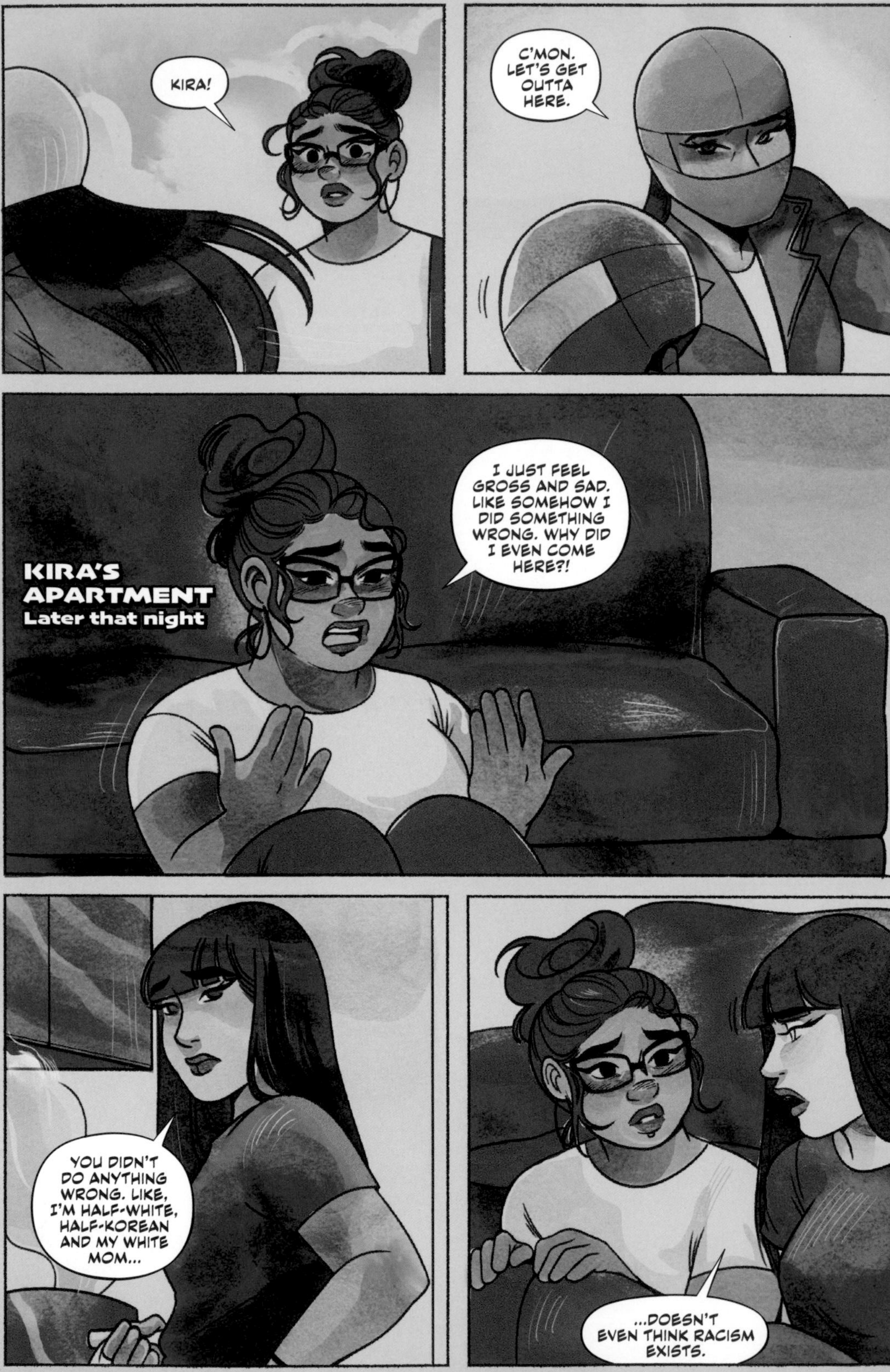
KIRA!
C'MON. LET'S GET OUTTA HERE.
KIRA'S APARTMENT
Later that night
I JUST FEEL GROSS AND SAD. LIKE SOMEHOW I DID SOMETHING WRONG. WHY DID I EVEN COME HERE?!
YOU DIDN'T DO ANYTHING WRONG. LIKE, I'M HALF-WHITE, HALF-KOREAN AND MY WHITE MOM...
...DOESN'T EVEN THINK RACISM EXISTS.

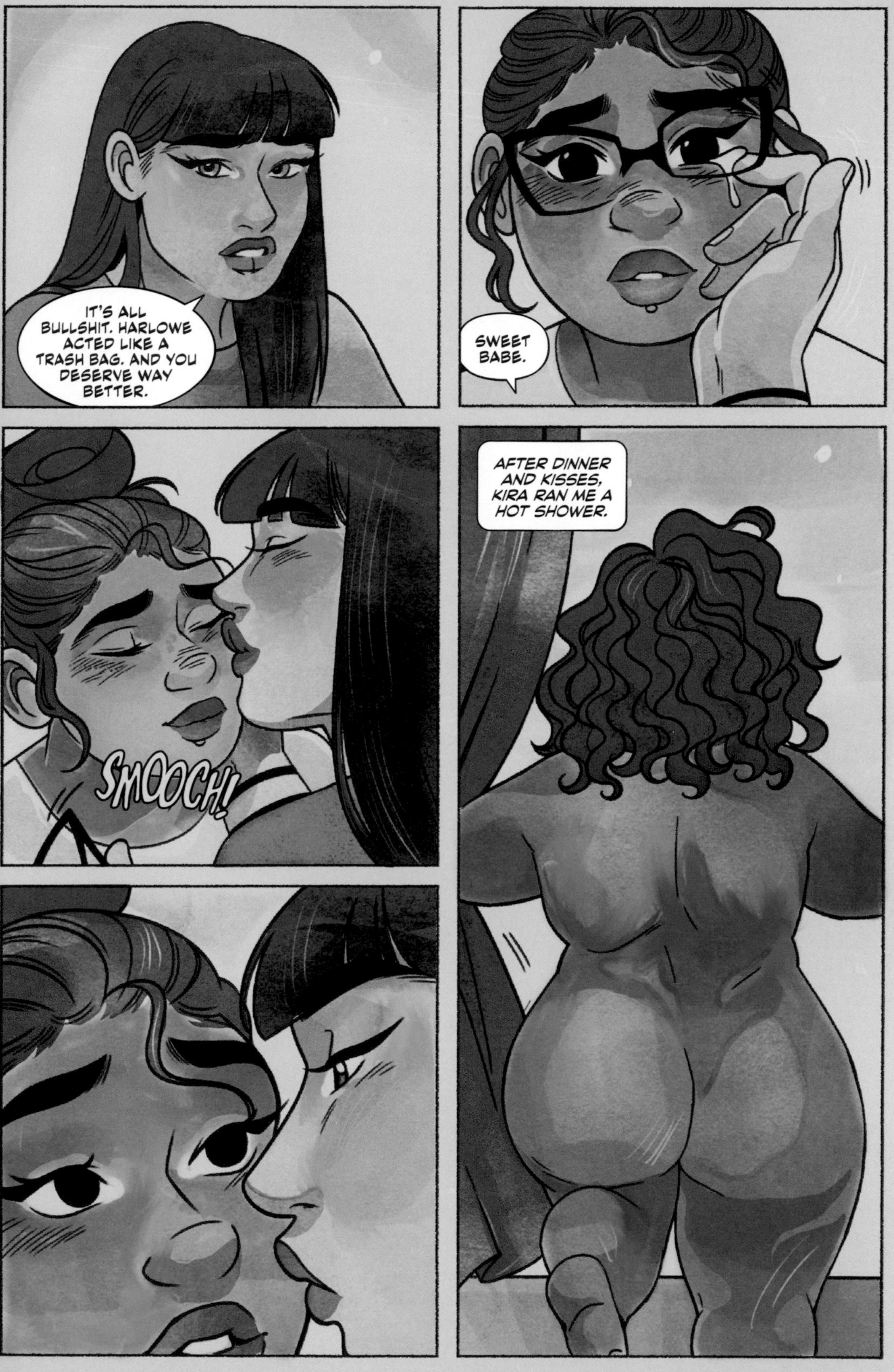
IT'S ALL BULLSHIT. HARLOWE ACTED LIKE A TRASH BAG. AND YOU DESERVE WAY BETTER.
SWEET BABE.
SMOOCH!
AFTER DINNER AND KISSES, KIRA RAN ME A HOT SHOWER.

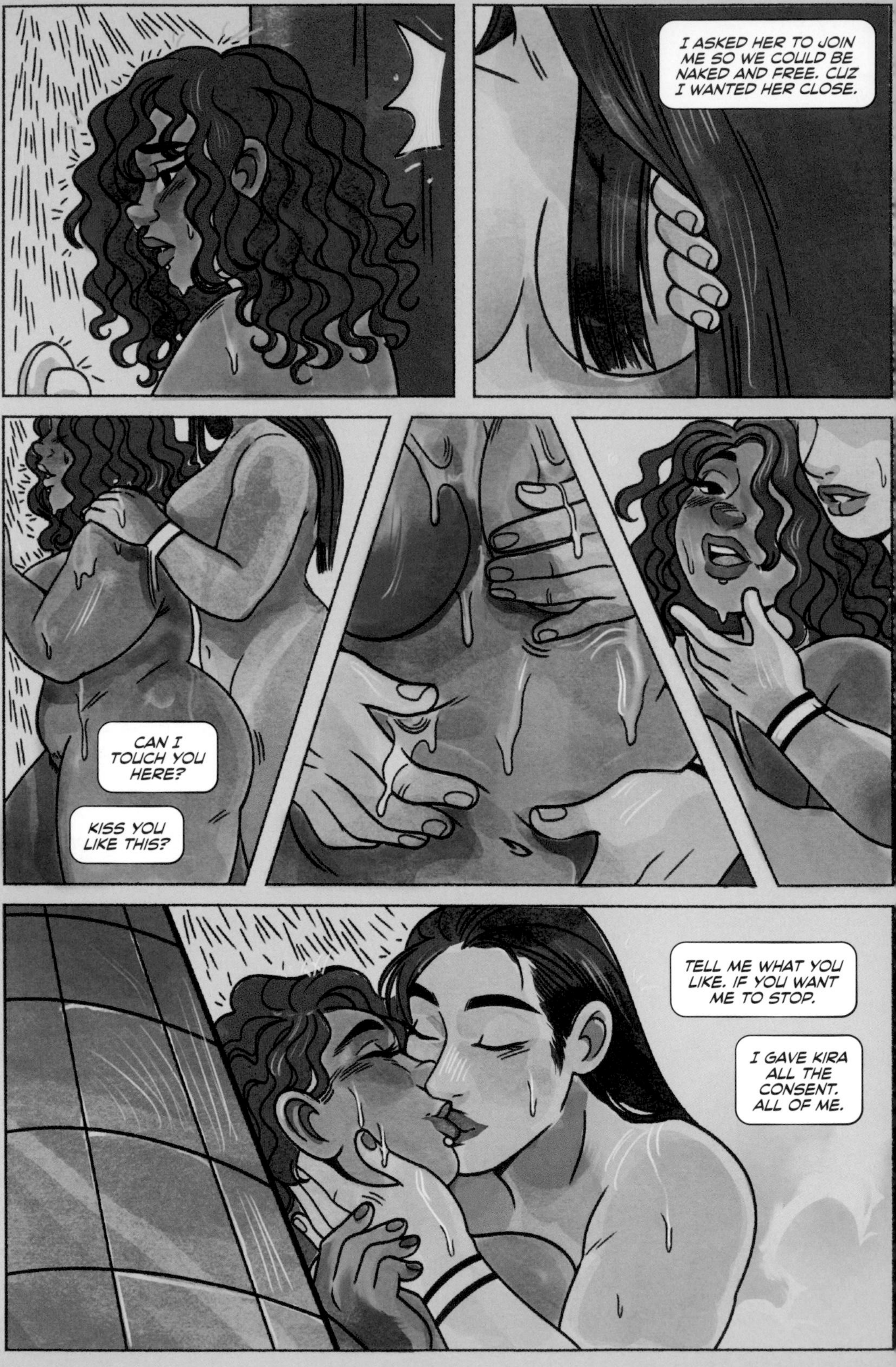
I ASKED HER TO JOIN ME SO WE COULD BE NAKED AND FREE. CUZ I WANTED HER CLOSE.
CAN I TOUCH YOU HERE?
KISS YOU LIKE THIS?
TELL ME WHAT YOU LIKE. IF YOU WANT ME TO STOP.
I GAVE KIRA ALL THE CONSENT. ALL OF ME.

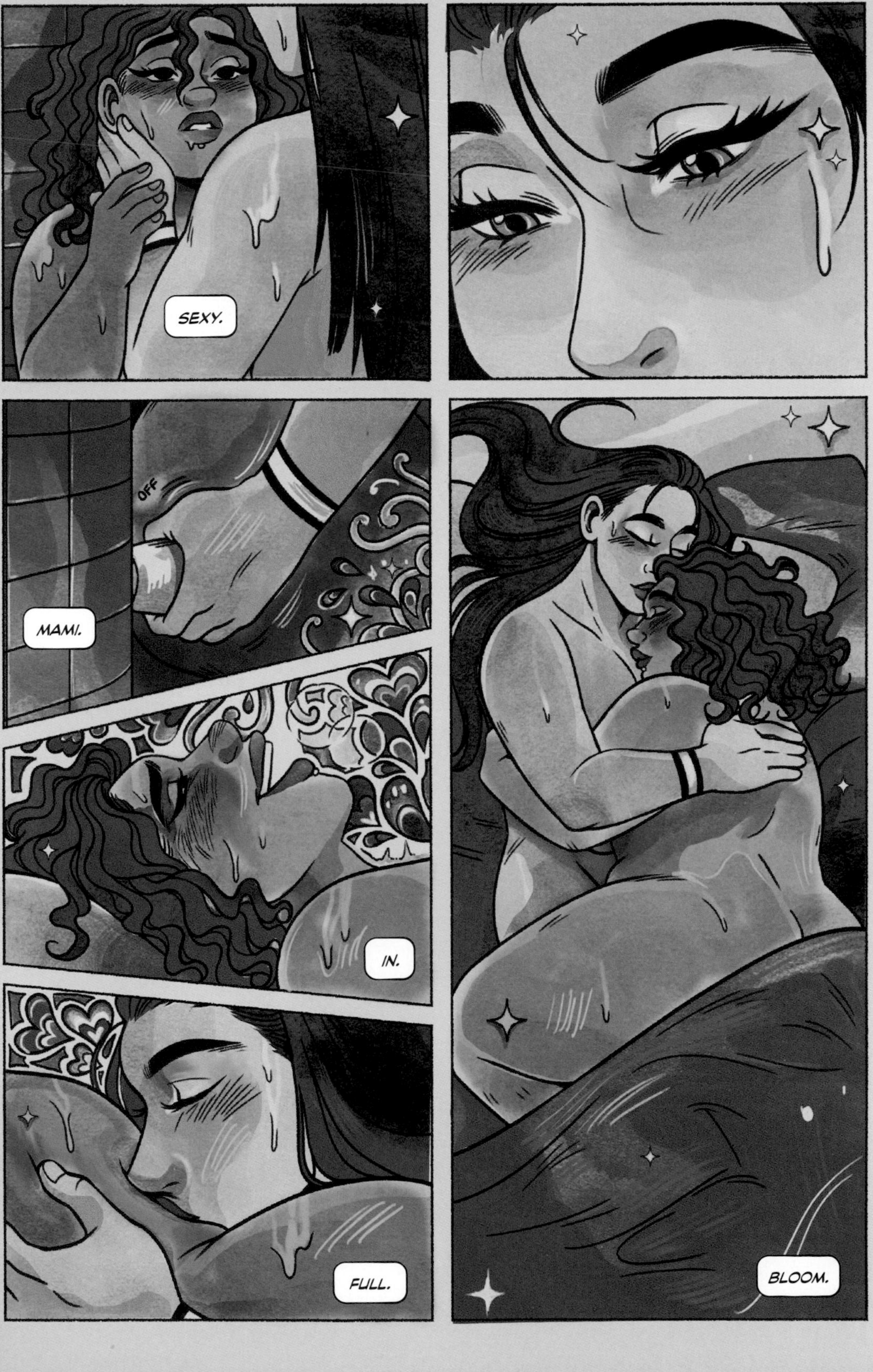
SEXY.
OFF
MAMI.
IN.
FULL.
BLOOM.

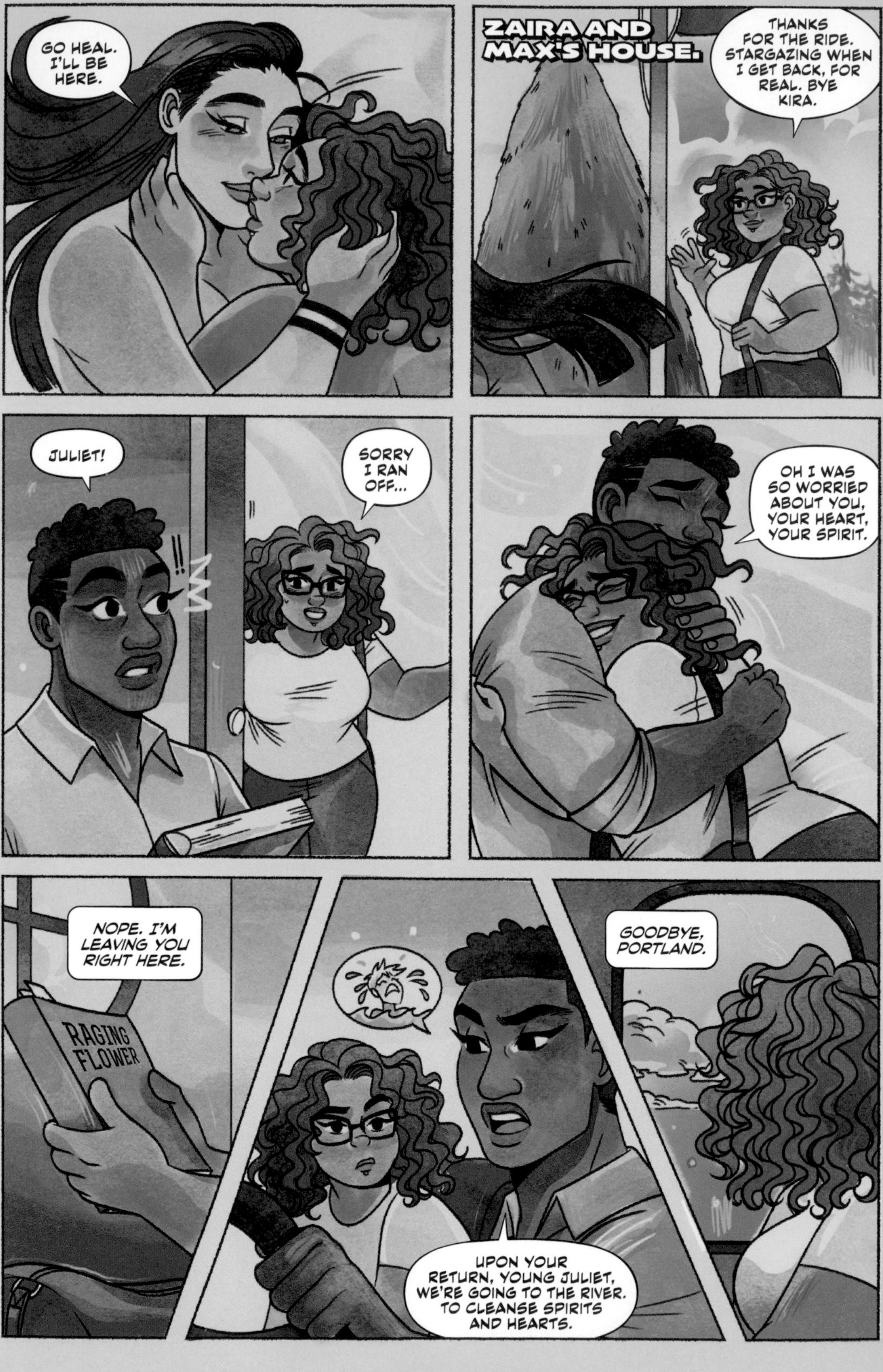
GO HEAL. I'LL BE HERE.
ZAIRA AND MAX'S HOUSE.
THANKS FOR THE RIDE. STARGAZING WHEN I GET BACK, FOR REAL. BYE KIRA.
JULIET!
SORRY I RAN OFF...
OH I WAS SO WORRIED ABOUT YOU, YOUR HEART, YOUR SPIRIT.
NOPE. I'M LEAVING YOU RIGHT HERE.
RAGING FLOWER
UPON YOUR RETURN, YOUNG JULIET, WE'RE GOING TO THE RIVER. TO CLEANSE SPIRITS AND HEARTS.
GOODBYE, PORTLAND.

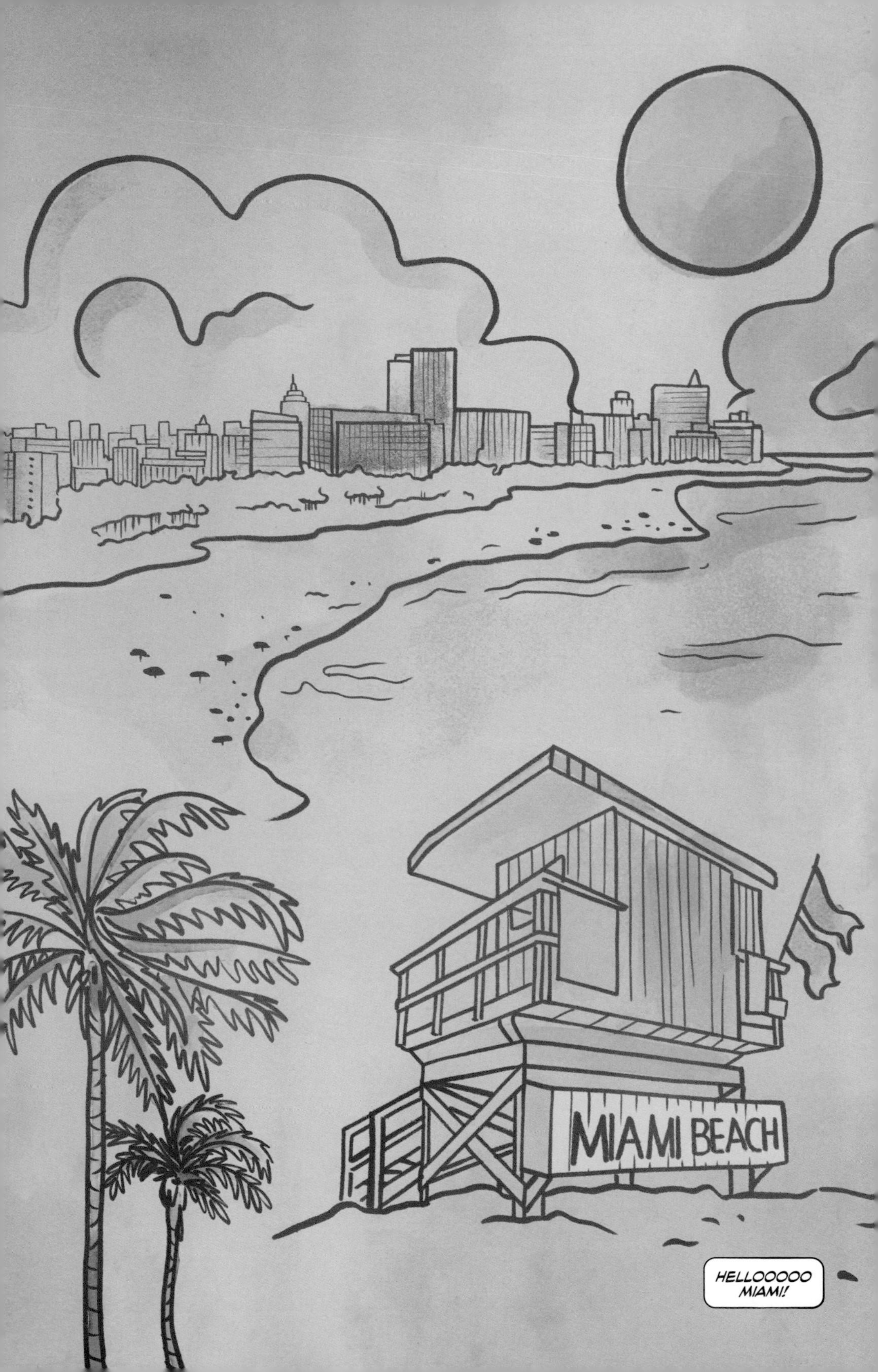
MIAMI BEACH
HELLOOOOO MIAMI!

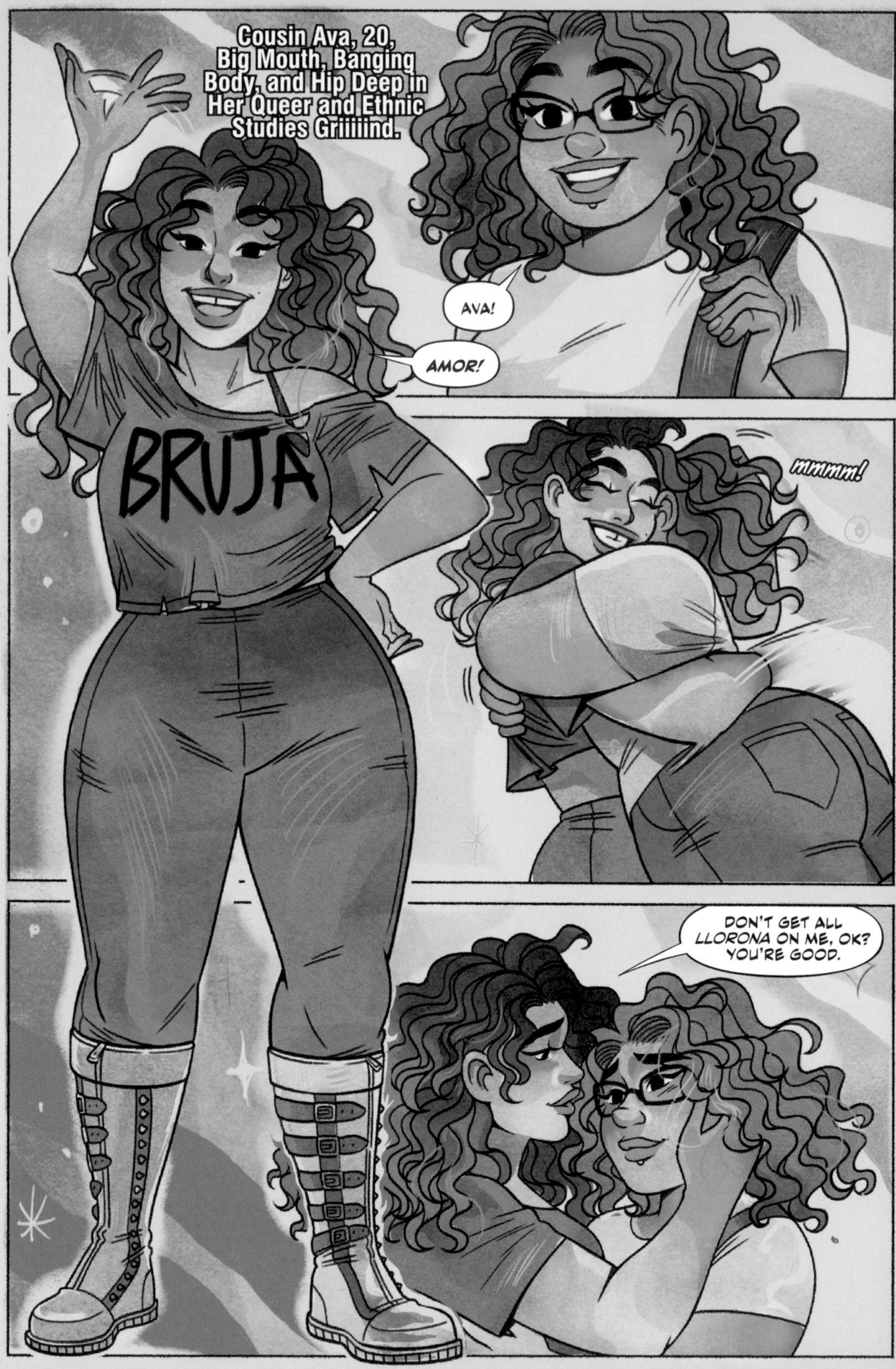
Cousin Ava, 20, Big Mouth, Banging Body, and Hip Deep in Her Queer and Ethnic Studies Griiiiind.
AVA!
AMOR!
BRUJA
mmmm!
DON'T GET ALL LLORONA ON ME, OK? YOU'RE GOOD.

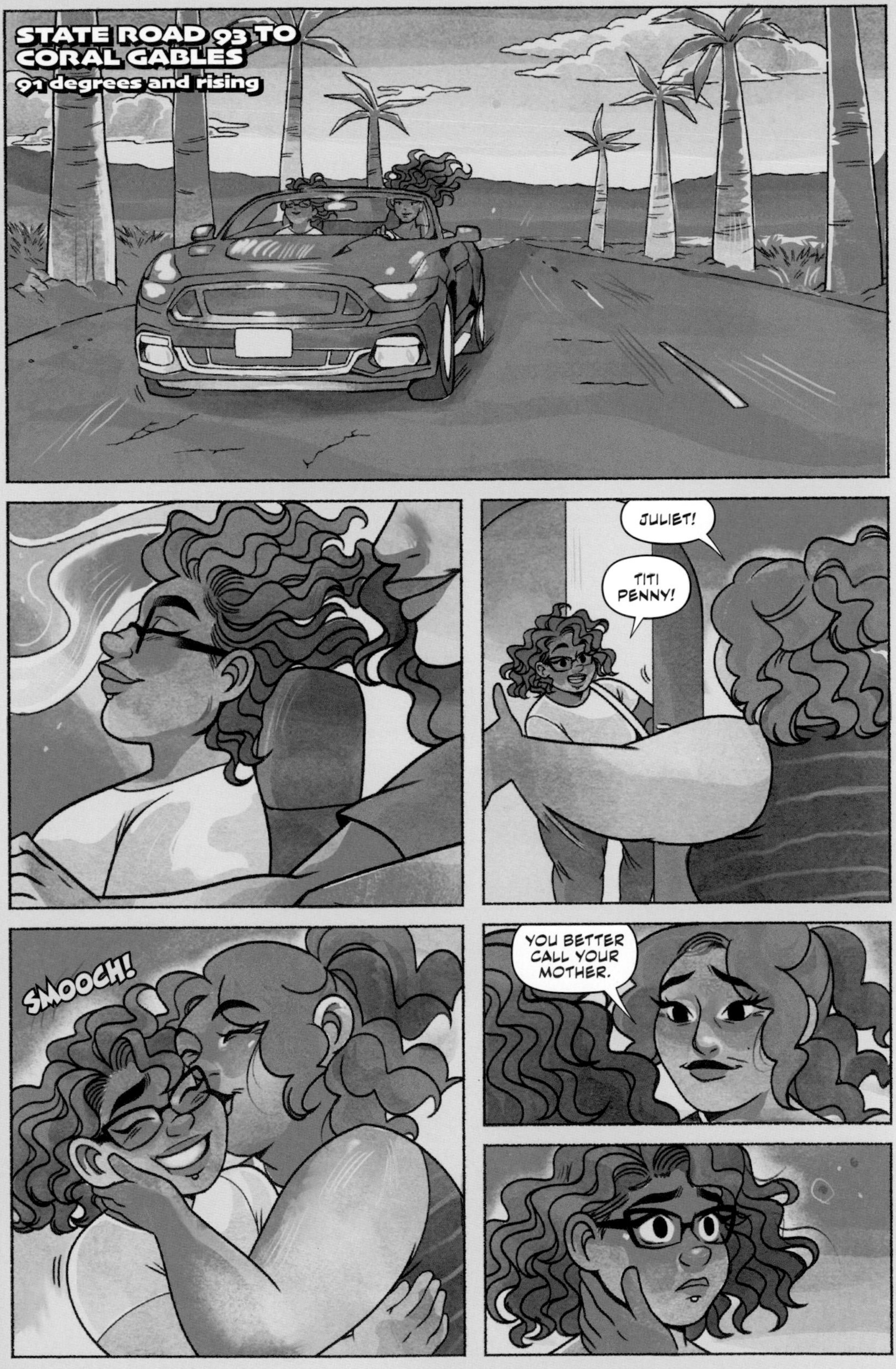
STATE ROAD 93 TO CORAL GABLES
91 degrees and rising
JULIET!
TITI PENNY!
SMOOCH!
YOU BETTER CALL YOUR MOTHER.

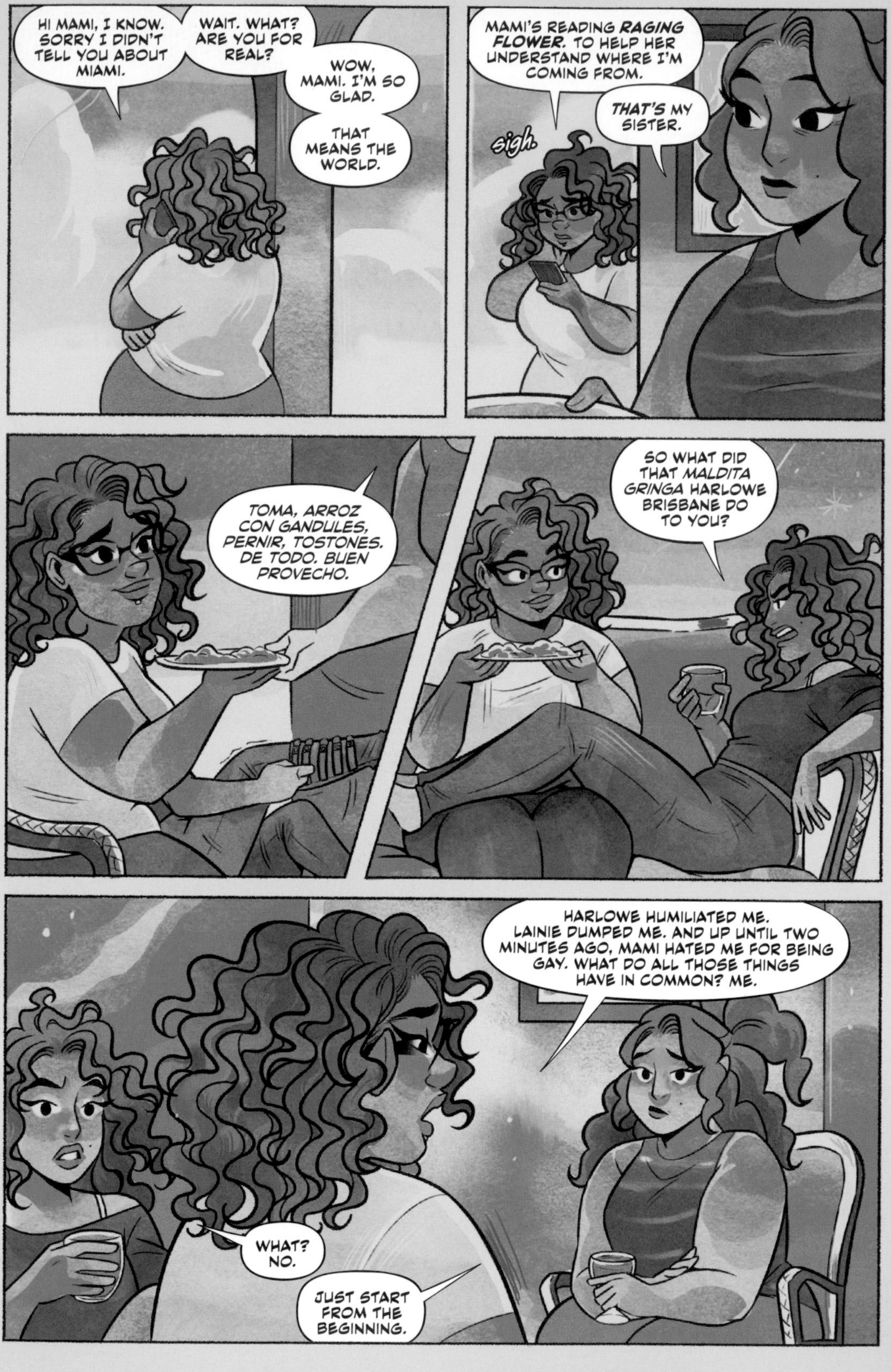
HI MAMI, I KNOW. SORRY I DIDN'T TELL YOU ABOUT MIAMI.
WAIT. WHAT? ARE YOU FOR REAL?
WOW, MAMI. I'M SO GLAD.
THAT MEANS THE WORLD.
MAMI'S READING *RAGING FLOWER*. TO HELP HER UNDERSTAND WHERE I'M COMING FROM.
sigh.
THAT'S MY SISTER.
TOMA, ARROZ CON GANDULES, PERNIR, TOSTONES. DE TODO. BUEN PROVECHO.
SO WHAT DID THAT *MALDITA GRINGA* HARLOWE BRISBANE DO TO YOU?
HARLOWE HUMILIATED ME. LAINIE DUMPED ME. AND UP UNTIL TWO MINUTES AGO, MAMI HATED ME FOR BEING GAY. WHAT DO ALL THOSE THINGS HAVE IN COMMON? ME.
WHAT? NO.
JUST START FROM THE BEGINNING.

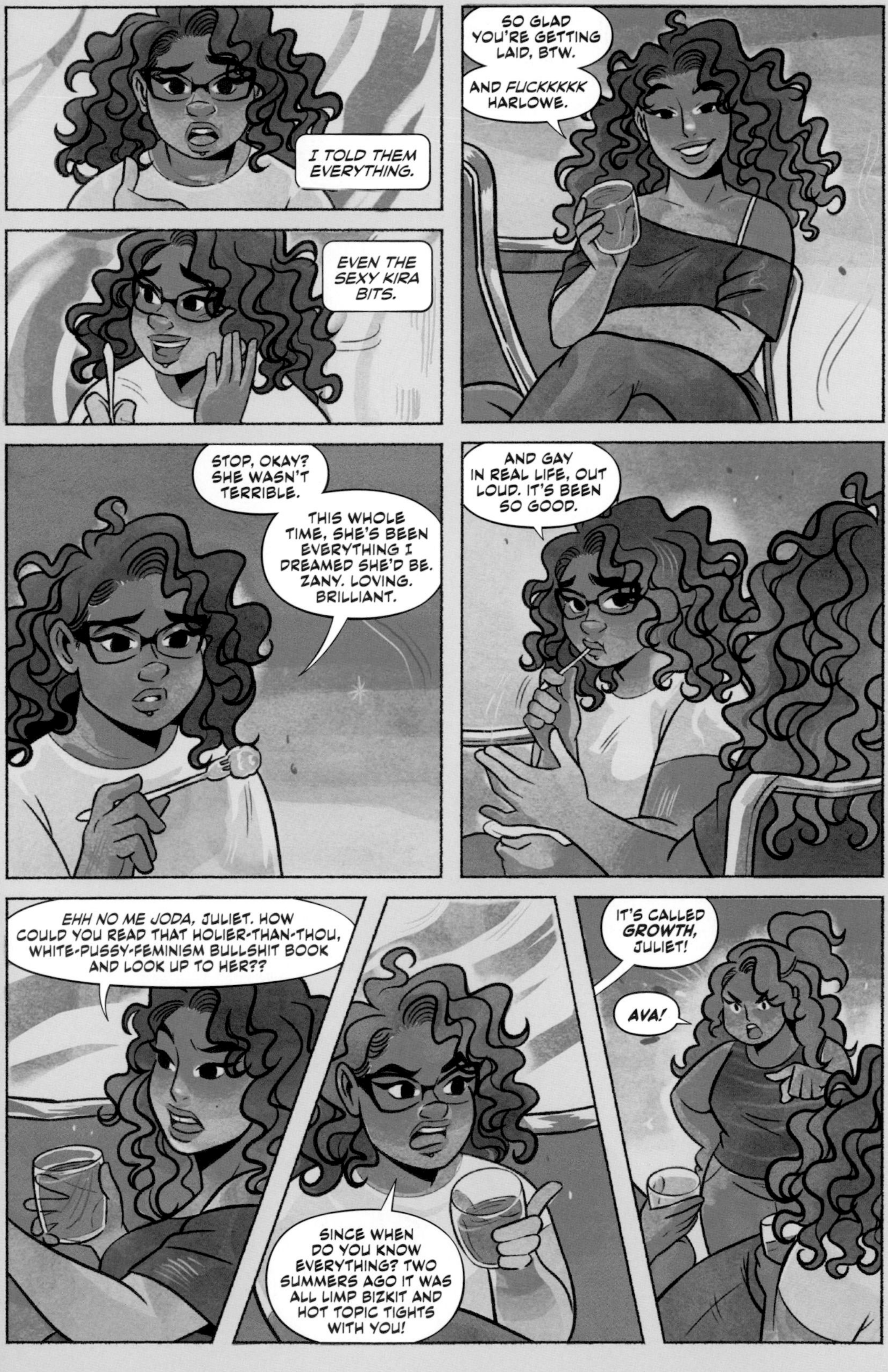
I TOLD THEM EVERYTHING.
EVEN THE SEXY KIRA BITS.
SO GLAD YOU'RE GETTING LAID, BTW.
AND FUCKKKKK HARLOWE.
STOP, OKAY? SHE WASN'T TERRIBLE.
THIS WHOLE TIME, SHE'S BEEN EVERYTHING I DREAMED SHE'D BE. ZANY. LOVING. BRILLIANT.
AND GAY IN REAL LIFE, OUT LOUD. IT'S BEEN SO GOOD.
EHH NO ME JODA, JULIET. HOW COULD YOU READ THAT HOLIER-THAN-THOU, WHITE-PUSSY-FEMINISM BULLSHIT BOOK AND LOOK UP TO HER??
SINCE WHEN DO YOU KNOW EVERYTHING? TWO SUMMERS AGO IT WAS ALL LIMP BIZKIT AND HOT TOPIC TIGHTS WITH YOU!
IT'S CALLED GROWTH, JULIET!
AVA!

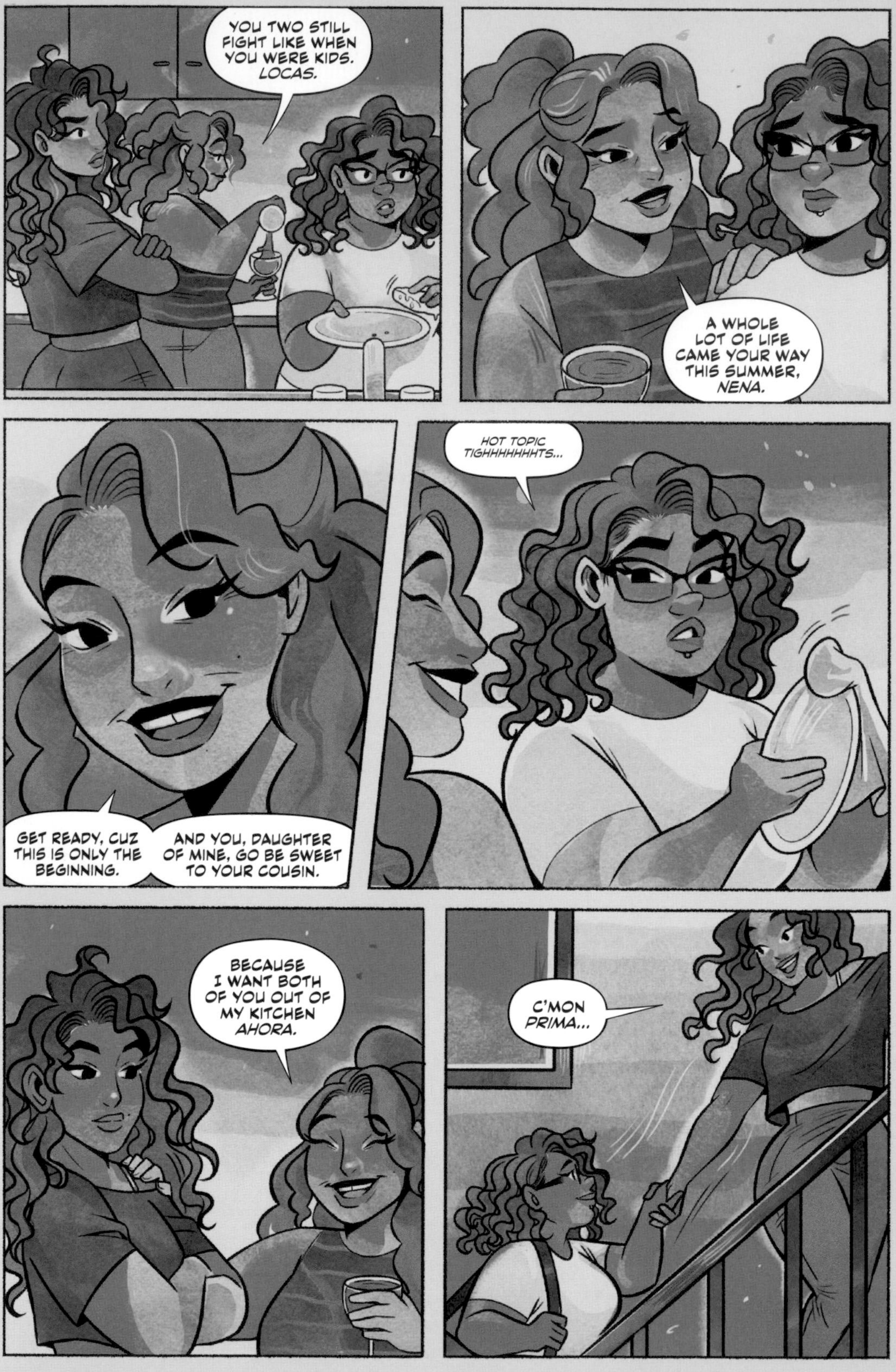
YOU TWO STILL FIGHT LIKE WHEN YOU WERE KIDS. *LOCAS.*
A WHOLE LOT OF LIFE CAME YOUR WAY THIS SUMMER, *NENA.*
HOT TOPIC TIGHHHHHHHTS...
GET READY, CUZ THIS IS ONLY THE BEGINNING.
AND YOU, DAUGHTER OF MINE, GO BE SWEET TO YOUR COUSIN.
BECAUSE I WANT BOTH OF YOU OUT OF MY KITCHEN *AHORA.*
C'MON *PRIMA...*

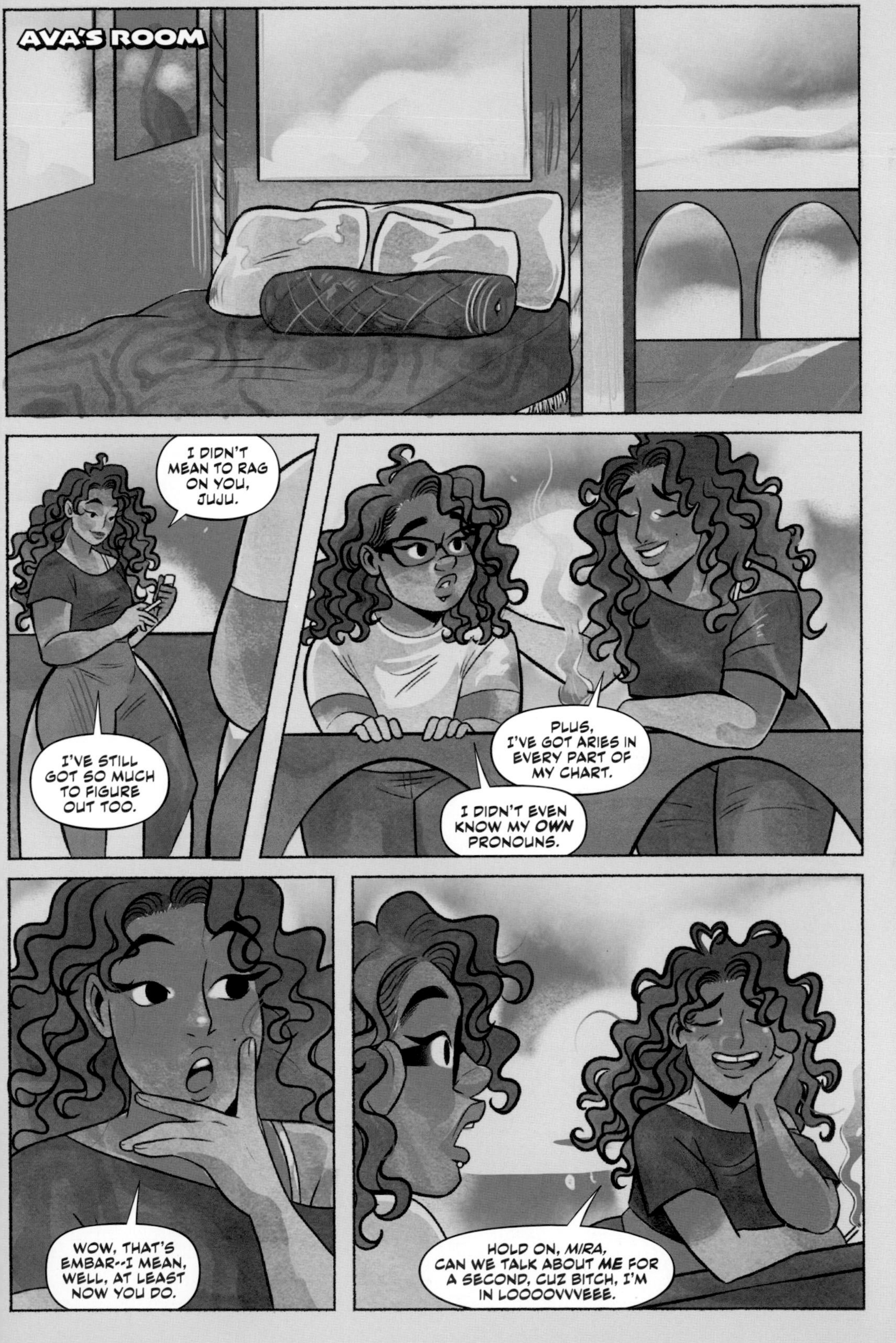
AVA'S ROOM
I DIDN'T MEAN TO RAG ON YOU, JUJU.
I'VE STILL GOT SO MUCH TO FIGURE OUT TOO.
PLUS, I'VE GOT ARIES IN EVERY PART OF MY CHART.
I DIDN'T EVEN KNOW MY *OWN* PRONOUNS.
WOW, THAT'S EMBAR--I MEAN, WELL, AT LEAST NOW YOU DO.
HOLD ON, *MIRA*, CAN WE TALK ABOUT **ME** FOR A SECOND, CUZ BITCH, I'M IN LOOOOVVVEEE.

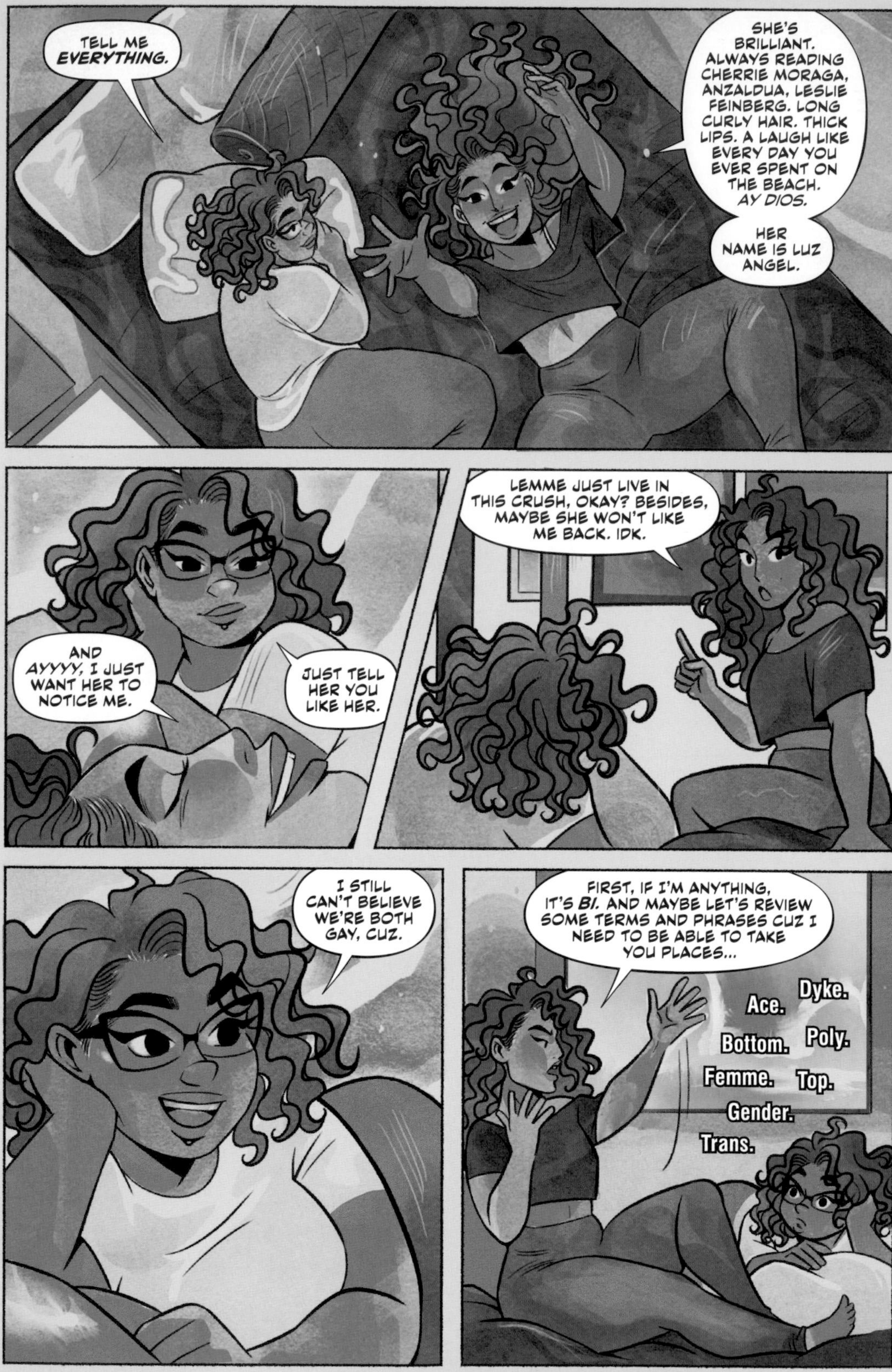
TELL ME *EVERYTHING.*
SHE'S BRILLIANT. ALWAYS READING CHERRIE MORAGA, ANZALDUA, LESLIE FEINBERG. LONG CURLY HAIR. THICK LIPS. A LAUGH LIKE EVERY DAY YOU EVER SPENT ON THE BEACH. *AY DIOS.*
HER NAME IS LUZ ANGEL.
AND *AYYYY,* I JUST WANT HER TO NOTICE ME.
JUST TELL HER YOU LIKE HER.
LEMME JUST LIVE IN THIS CRUSH, OKAY? BESIDES, MAYBE SHE WON'T LIKE ME BACK. IDK.
I STILL CAN'T BELIEVE WE'RE BOTH GAY, CUZ.
FIRST, IF I'M ANYTHING, IT'S *BI.* AND MAYBE LET'S REVIEW SOME TERMS AND PHRASES CUZ I NEED TO BE ABLE TO TAKE YOU PLACES...
Ace.
Dyke.
Bottom.
Poly.
Femme.
Top.
Gender.
Trans.

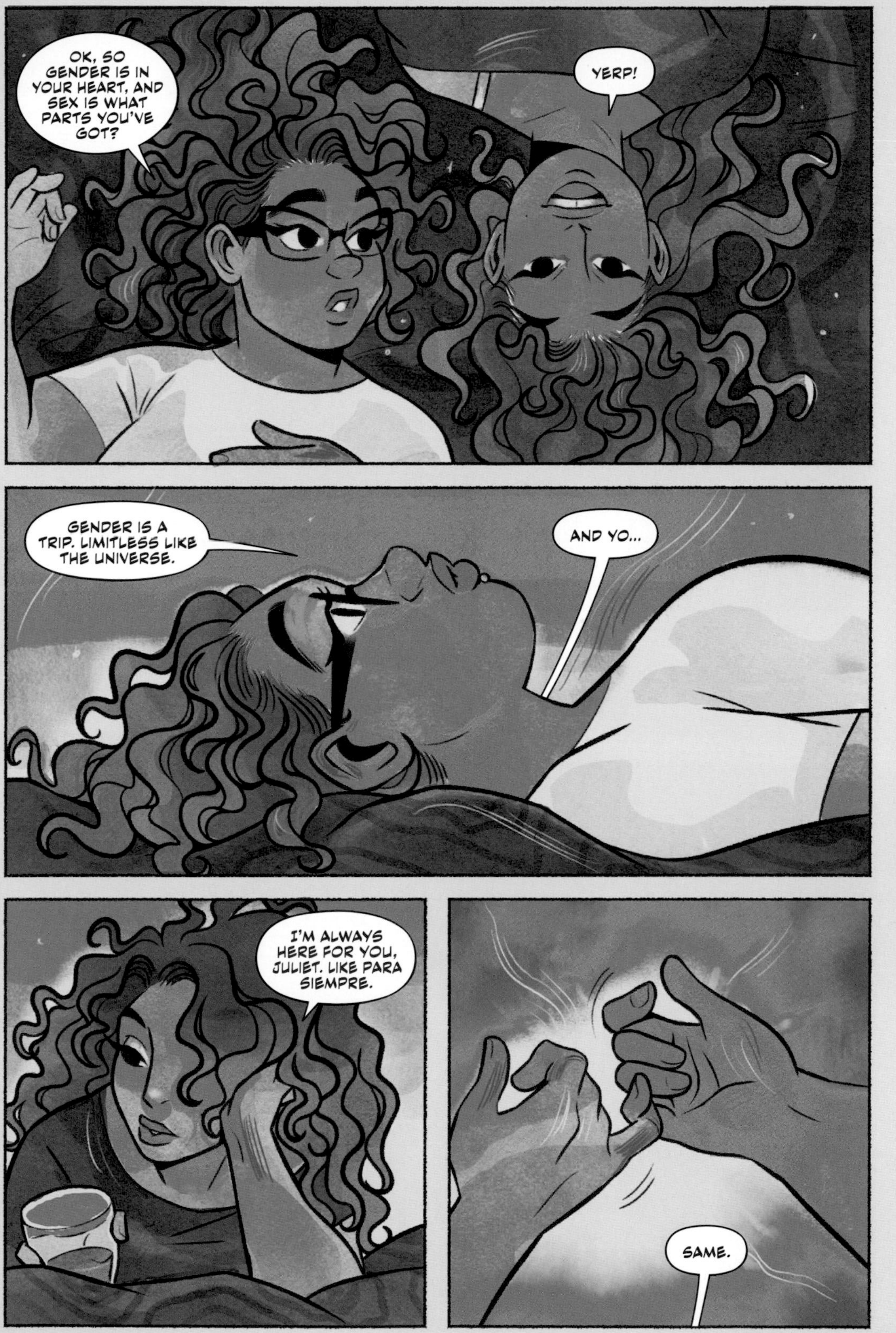
OK, SO GENDER IS IN YOUR HEART, AND SEX IS WHAT PARTS YOU'VE GOT?
YERP!
GENDER IS A TRIP. LIMITLESS LIKE THE UNIVERSE.
AND YO...
I'M ALWAYS HERE FOR YOU, JULIET. LIKE PARA SIEMPRE.
SAME.

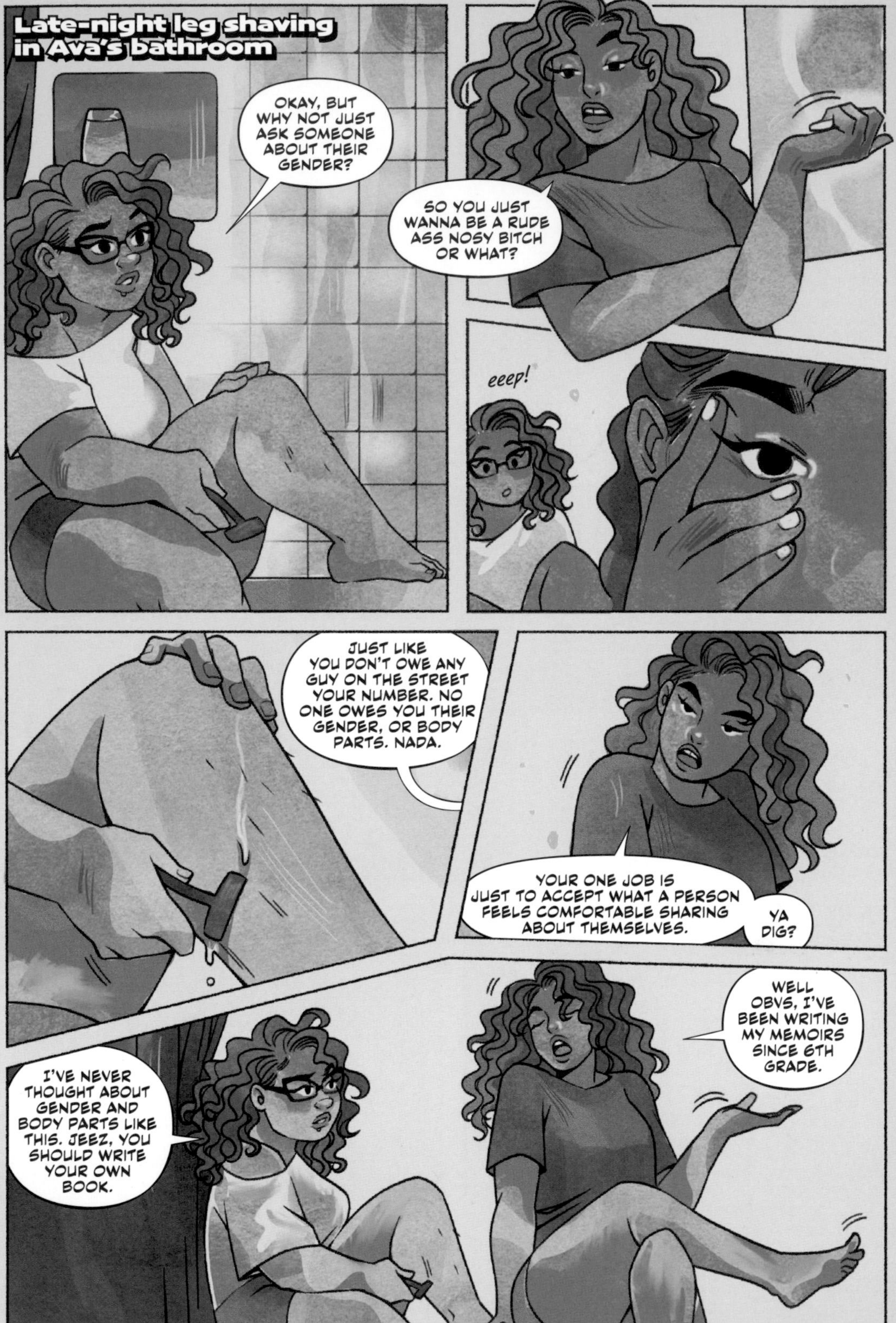
Late-night leg shaving in Ava's bathroom
OKAY, BUT WHY NOT JUST ASK SOMEONE ABOUT THEIR GENDER?
SO YOU JUST WANNA BE A RUDE ASS NOSY BITCH OR WHAT?
eeep!
JUST LIKE YOU DON'T OWE ANY GUY ON THE STREET YOUR NUMBER. NO ONE OWES YOU THEIR GENDER, OR BODY PARTS. NADA.
YOUR ONE JOB IS JUST TO ACCEPT WHAT A PERSON FEELS COMFORTABLE SHARING ABOUT THEMSELVES.
YA DIG?
I'VE NEVER THOUGHT ABOUT GENDER AND BODY PARTS LIKE THIS. JEEZ, YOU SHOULD WRITE YOUR OWN BOOK.
WELL OBVS, I'VE BEEN WRITING MY MEMOIRS SINCE 6TH GRADE.

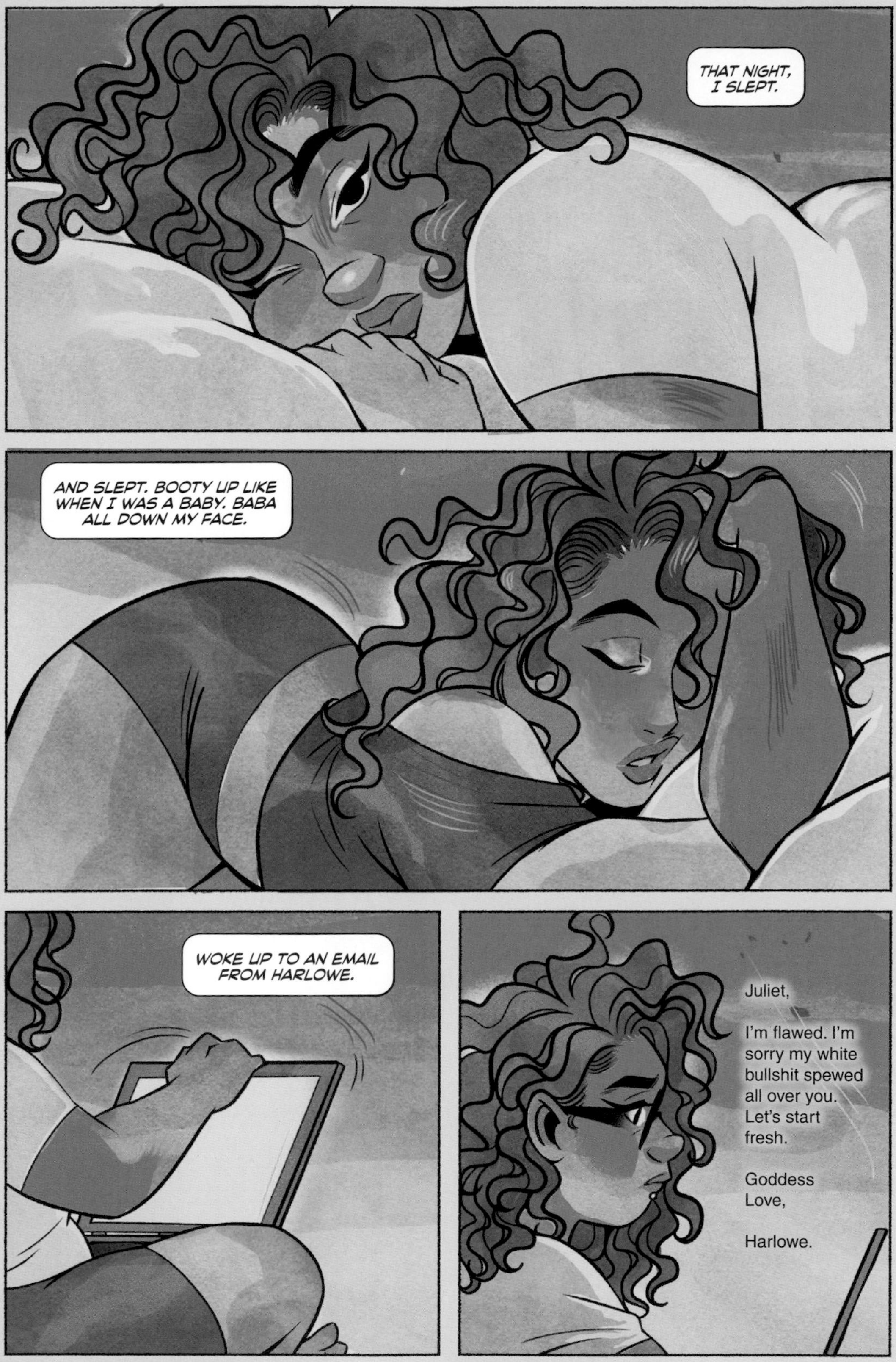
THAT NIGHT, I SLEPT.
AND SLEPT. BOOTY UP LIKE WHEN I WAS A BABY. BABA ALL DOWN MY FACE.
WOKE UP TO AN EMAIL FROM HARLOWE.
Juliet,
I'm flawed. I'm sorry my white bullshit spewed all over you. Let's start fresh.
Goddess Love,
Harlowe.

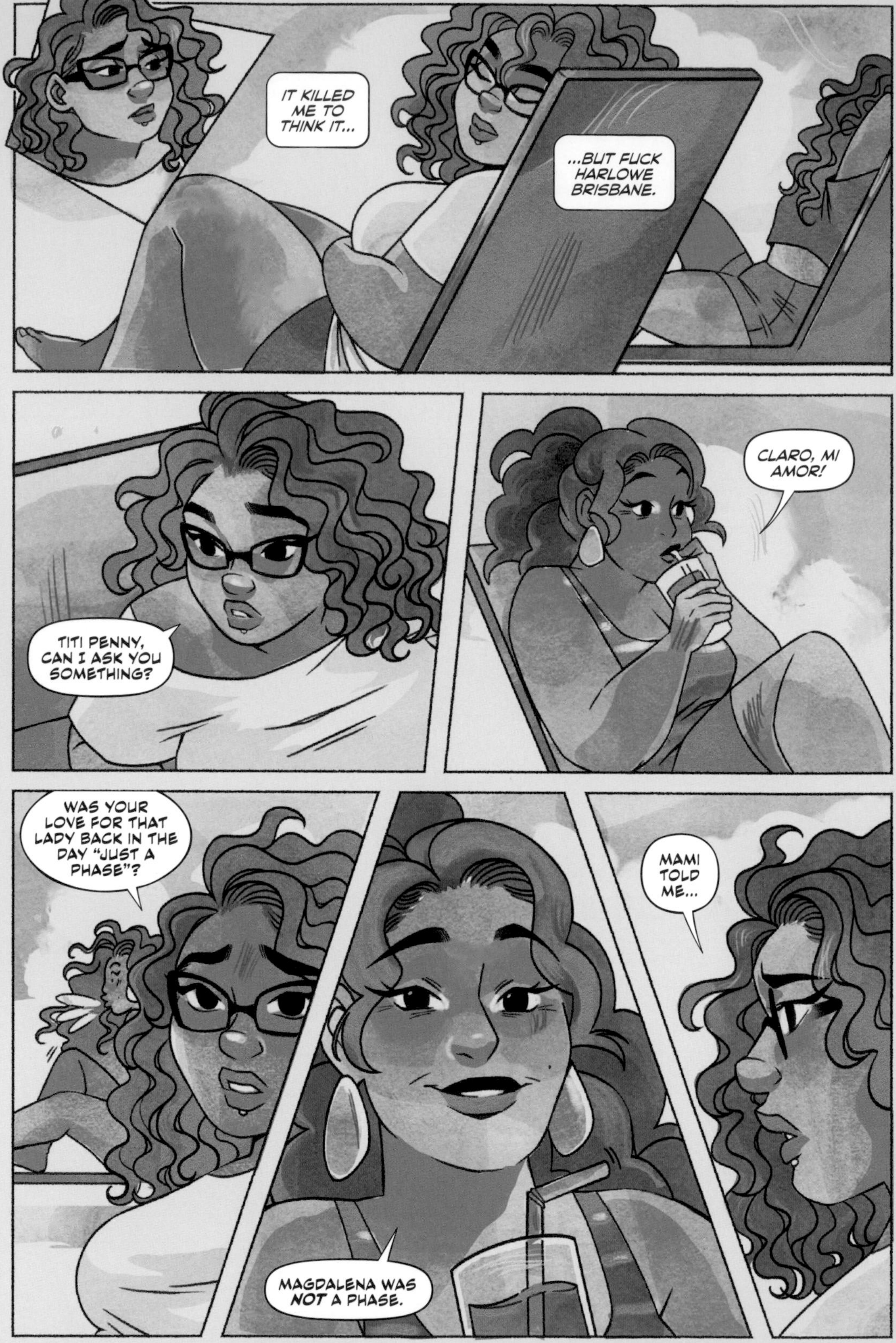
IT KILLED ME TO THINK IT...
...BUT FUCK HARLOWE BRISBANE.
TITI PENNY, CAN I ASK YOU SOMETHING?
CLARO, MI AMOR!
WAS YOUR LOVE FOR THAT LADY BACK IN THE DAY "JUST A PHASE"?
MAMI TOLD ME...
MAGDALENA WAS *NOT* A PHASE.

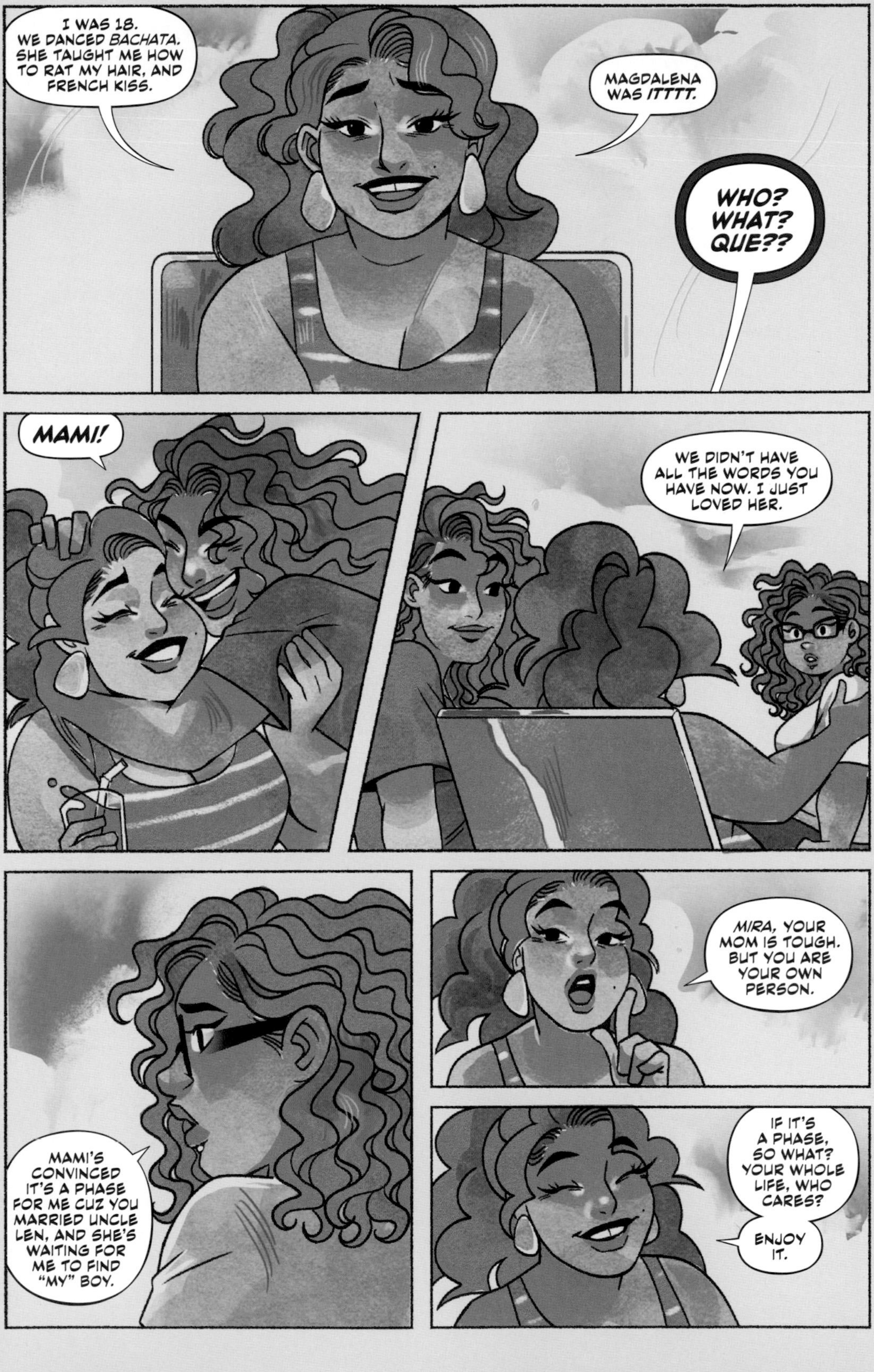
I WAS 18. WE DANCED *BACHATA*. SHE TAUGHT ME HOW TO RAT MY HAIR, AND FRENCH KISS.
MAGDALENA WAS *ITTTT.*
WHO? WHAT? QUE??
MAMI!
WE DIDN'T HAVE ALL THE WORDS YOU HAVE NOW. I JUST LOVED HER.
MAMI'S CONVINCED IT'S A PHASE FOR ME CUZ YOU MARRIED UNCLE LEN, AND SHE'S WAITING FOR ME TO FIND "MY" BOY.
MIRA, YOUR MOM IS TOUGH. BUT YOU ARE YOUR OWN PERSON.
IF IT'S A PHASE, SO WHAT? YOUR WHOLE LIFE, WHO CARES?
ENJOY IT.

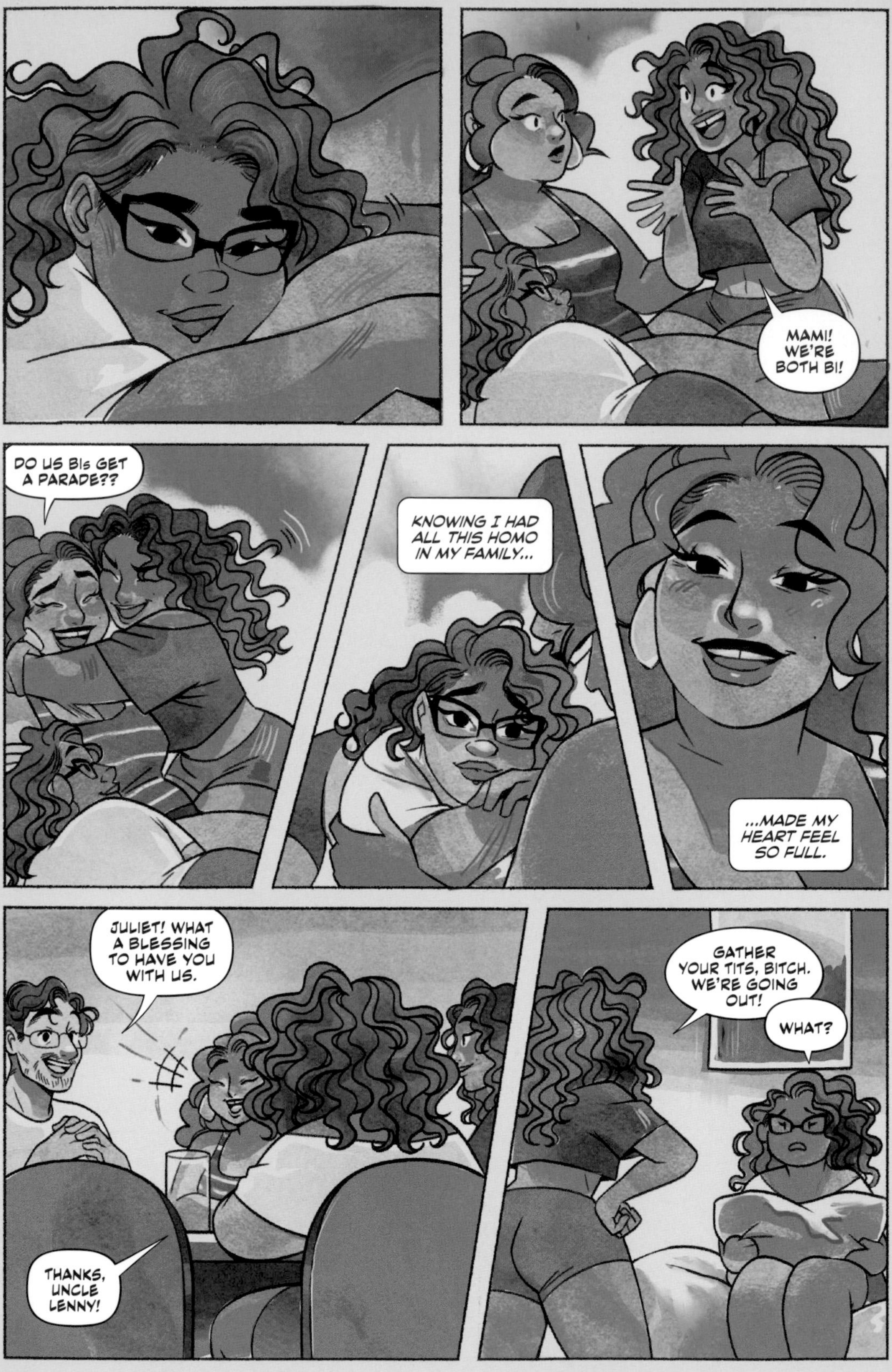
MAMI! WE'RE BOTH BI!
DO US BIs GET A PARADE??
KNOWING I HAD ALL THIS HOMO IN MY FAMILY...
...MADE MY HEART FEEL SO FULL.
JULIET! WHAT A BLESSING TO HAVE YOU WITH US.
THANKS, UNCLE LENNY!
GATHER YOUR TITS, BITCH. WE'RE GOING OUT!
WHAT?

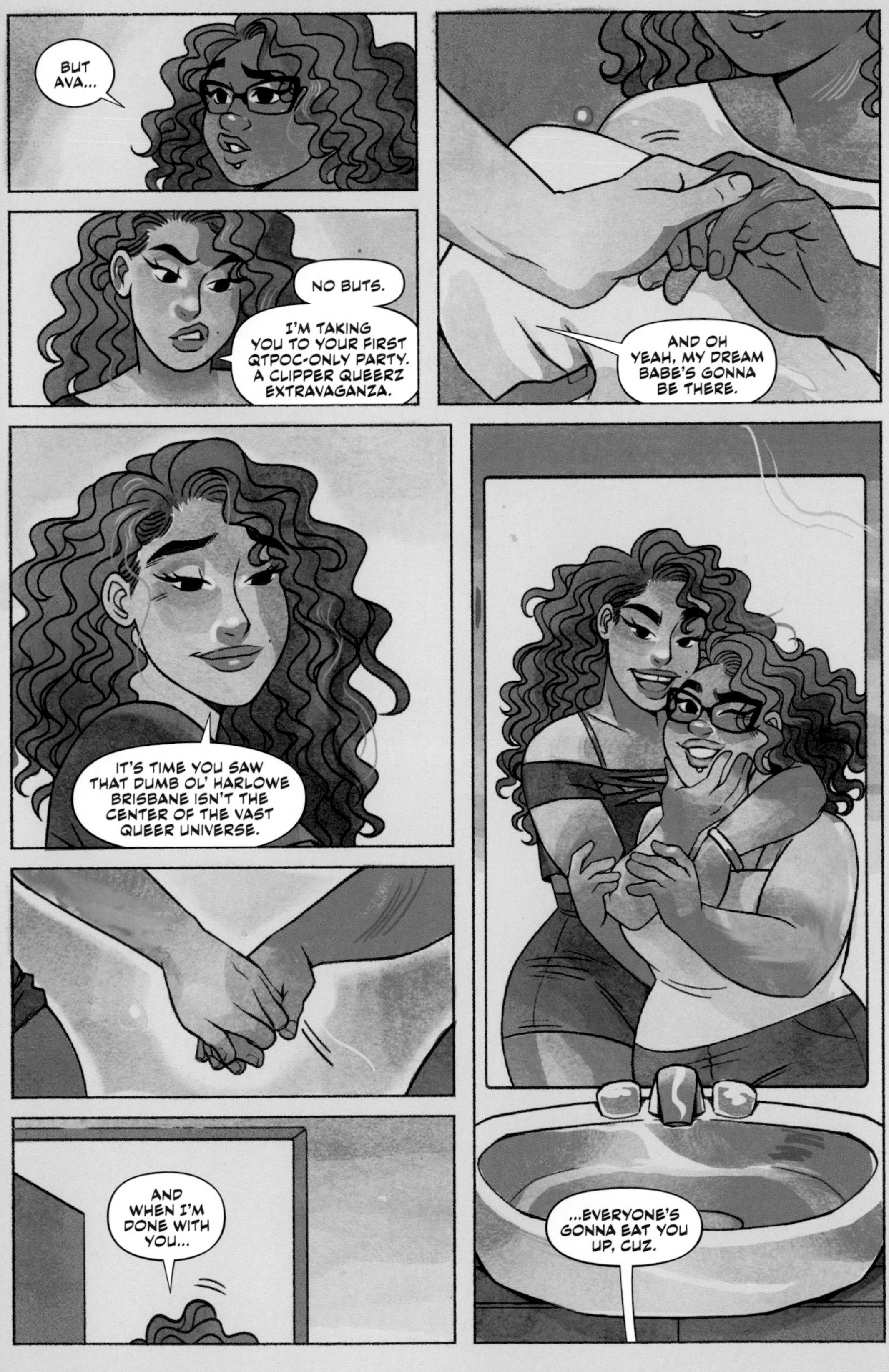
BUT AVA...
NO BUTS.
I'M TAKING YOU TO YOUR FIRST QTPOC-ONLY PARTY. A CLIPPER QUEERZ EXTRAVAGANZA.
AND OH YEAH, MY DREAM BABE'S GONNA BE THERE.
IT'S TIME YOU SAW THAT DUMB OL' HARLOWE BRISBANE ISN'T THE CENTER OF THE VAST QUEER UNIVERSE.
AND WHEN I'M DONE WITH YOU...
...EVERYONE'S GONNA EAT YOU UP, CUZ.

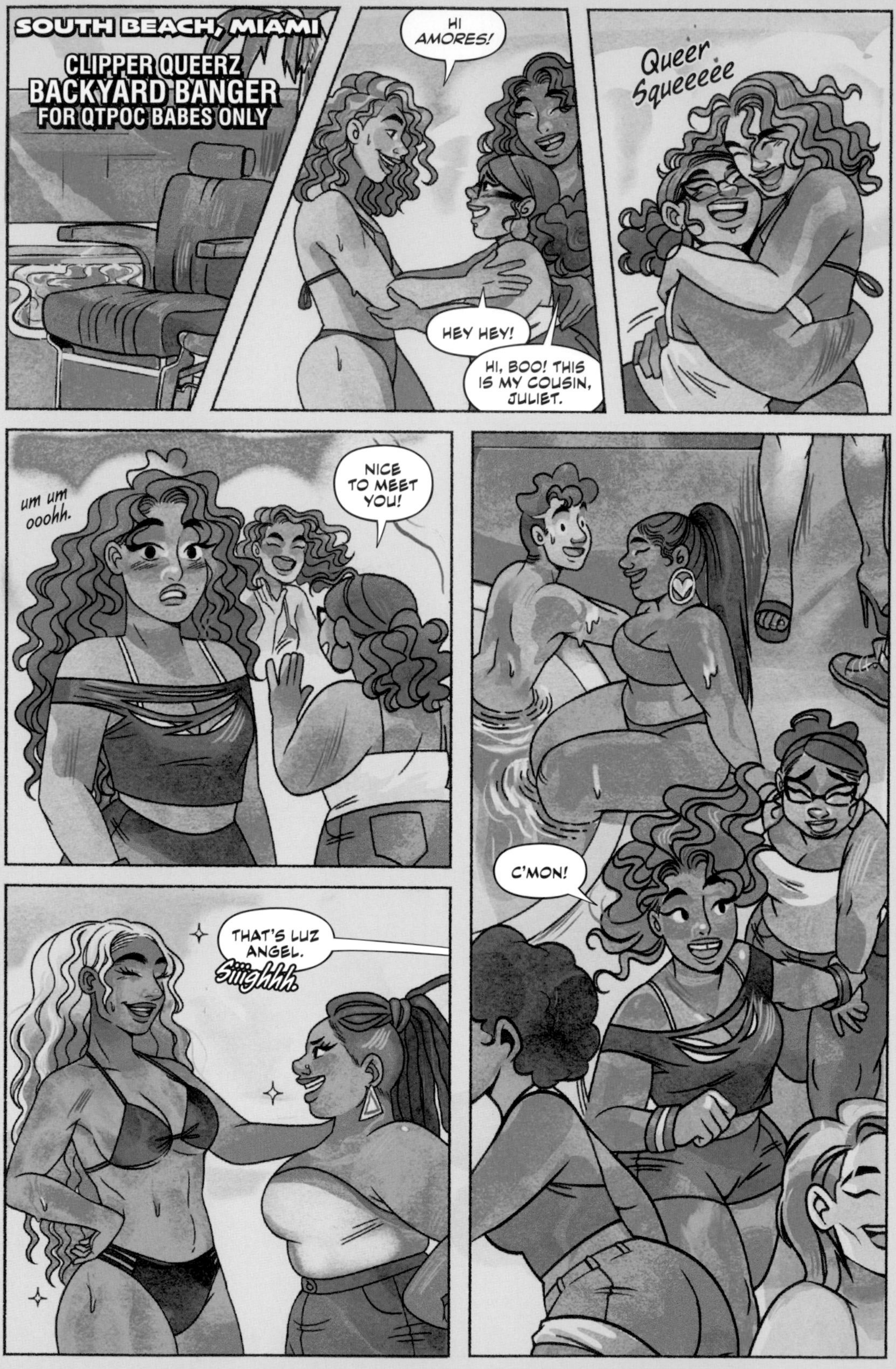
SOUTH BEACH, MIAMI
CLIPPER QUEERZ
BACKYARD BANGER
FOR QTPOC BABES ONLY
HI AMORES!
HEY HEY!
HI, BOO! THIS IS MY COUSIN, JULIET.
Queer Squeeeee
um um ooohh.
NICE TO MEET YOU!
THAT'S LUZ ANGEL.
Siiighhh.
C'MON!

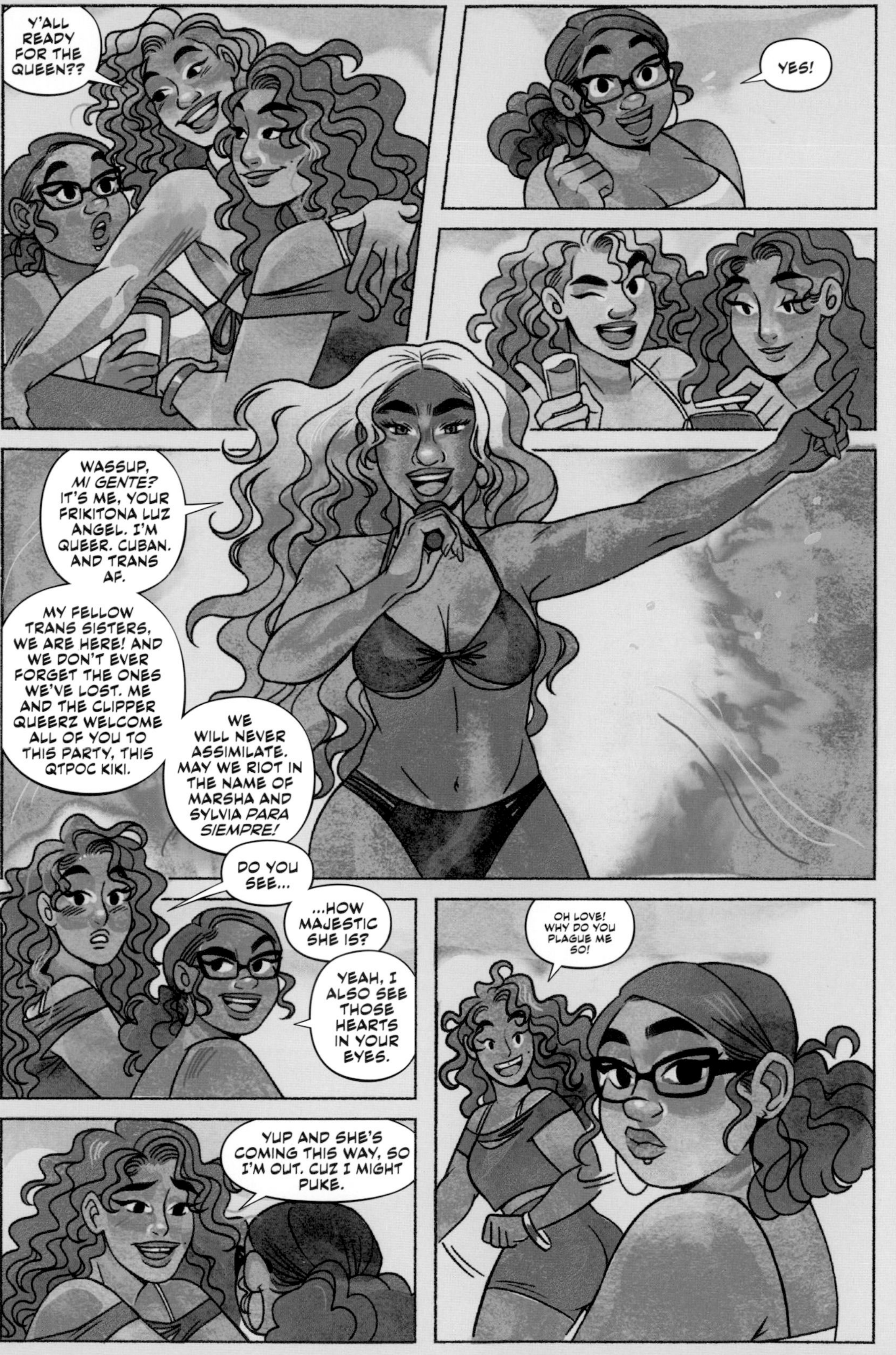
Y'ALL READY FOR THE QUEEN??
YES!
WASSUP, *MI GENTE?* IT'S ME, YOUR FRIKITONA LUZ ANGEL. I'M QUEER. CUBAN. AND TRANS AF.
MY FELLOW TRANS SISTERS, WE ARE HERE! AND WE DON'T EVER FORGET THE ONES WE'VE LOST. ME AND THE CLIPPER QUEERZ WELCOME ALL OF YOU TO THIS PARTY, THIS QTPOC KIKI.
WE WILL NEVER ASSIMILATE. MAY WE RIOT IN THE NAME OF MARSHA AND SYLVIA *PARA SIEMPRE!*
DO YOU SEE...
...HOW MAJESTIC SHE IS?
YEAH, I ALSO SEE THOSE HEARTS IN YOUR EYES.
YUP AND SHE'S COMING THIS WAY, SO I'M OUT. CUZ I MIGHT PUKE.
OH LOVE! WHY DO YOU PLAGUE ME SO!

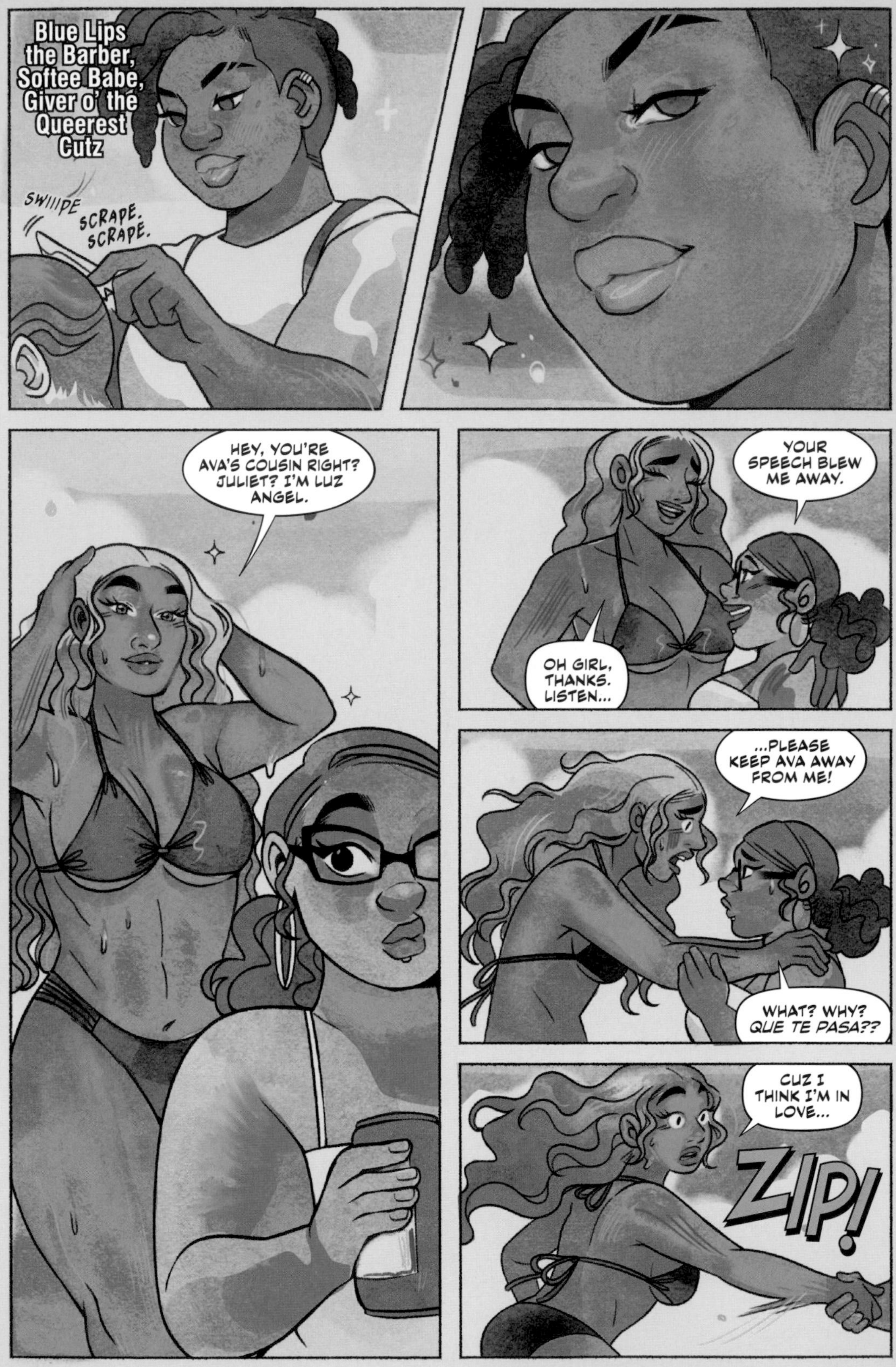
Blue Lips the Barber, Softee Babe, Giver o' the Queerest Cutz
SWIIIPE
SCRAPE. SCRAPE.
HEY, YOU'RE AVA'S COUSIN RIGHT? JULIET? I'M LUZ ANGEL.
YOUR SPEECH BLEW ME AWAY.
OH GIRL, THANKS. LISTEN...
...PLEASE KEEP AVA AWAY FROM ME!
WHAT? WHY? QUE TE PASA??
CUZ I THINK I'M IN LOVE...
ZIP!

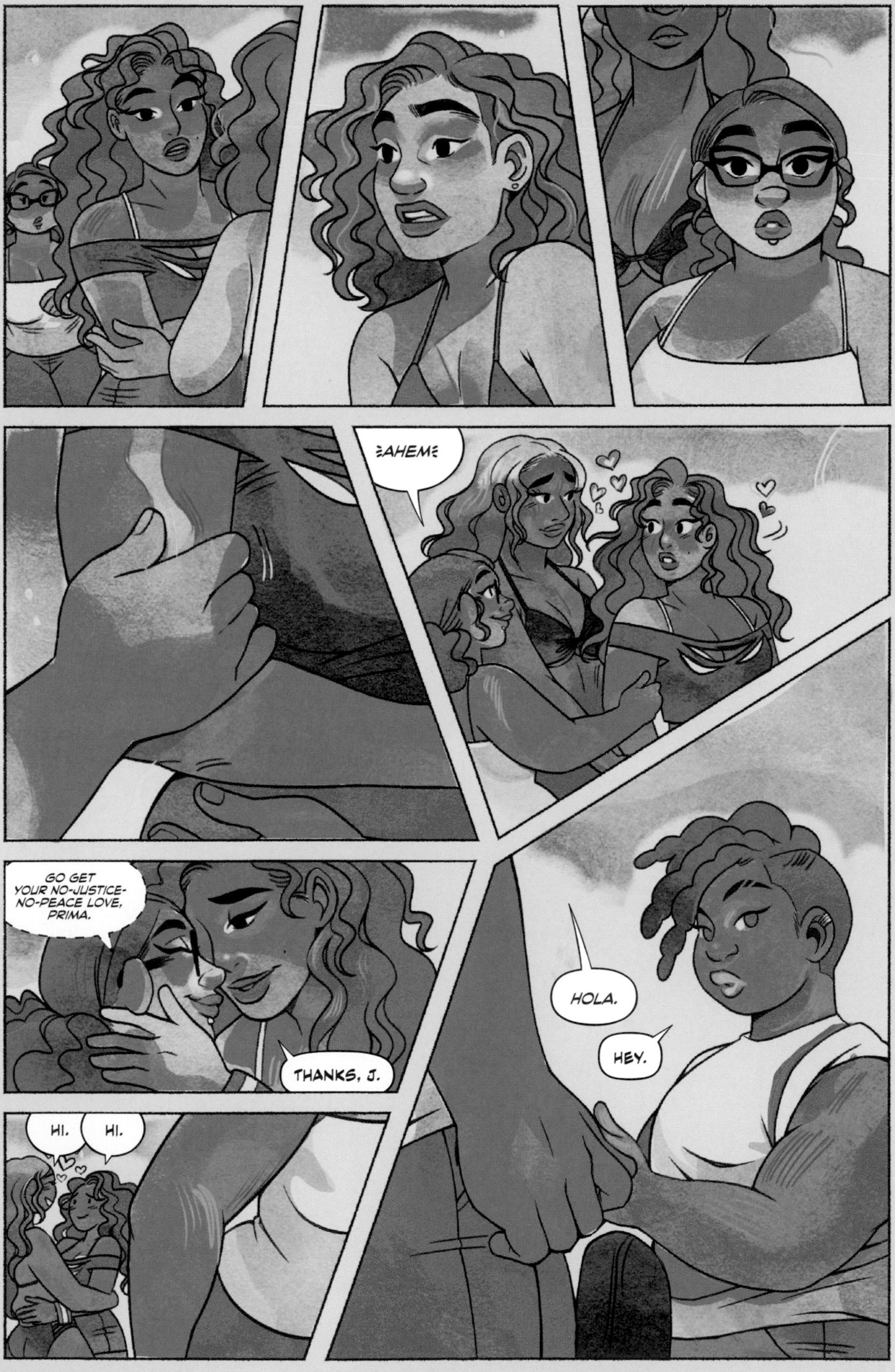
AHEM
GO GET YOUR NO-JUSTICE-NO-PEACE LOVE, PRIMA.
THANKS, J.
HOLA.
HEY.
HI.
HI.

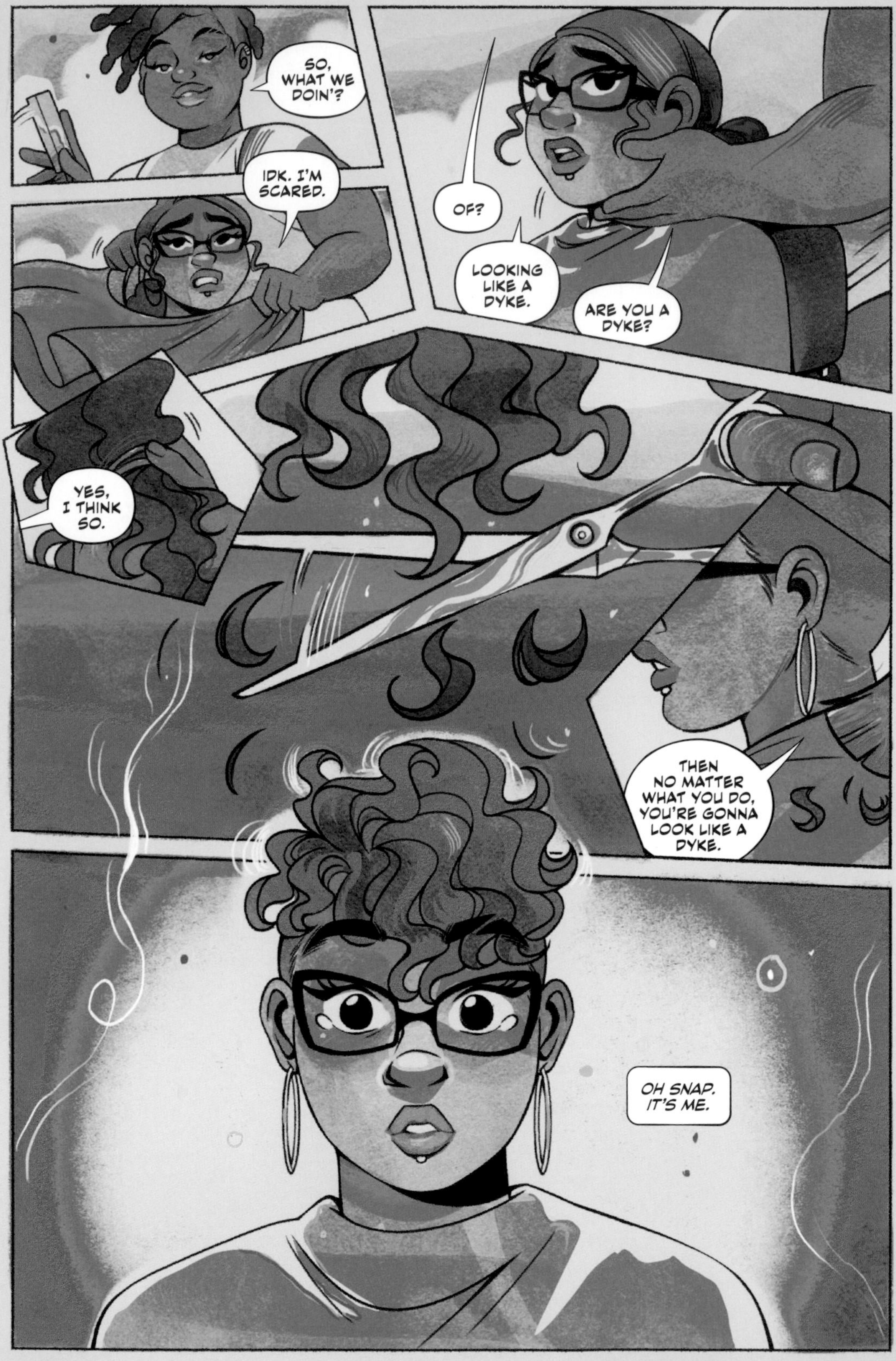
SO, WHAT WE DOIN'?
IDK. I'M SCARED.
OF?
LOOKING LIKE A DYKE.
ARE YOU A DYKE?
YES, I THINK SO.
THEN NO MATTER WHAT YOU DO, YOU'RE GONNA LOOK LIKE A DYKE.
OH SNAP. IT'S ME.

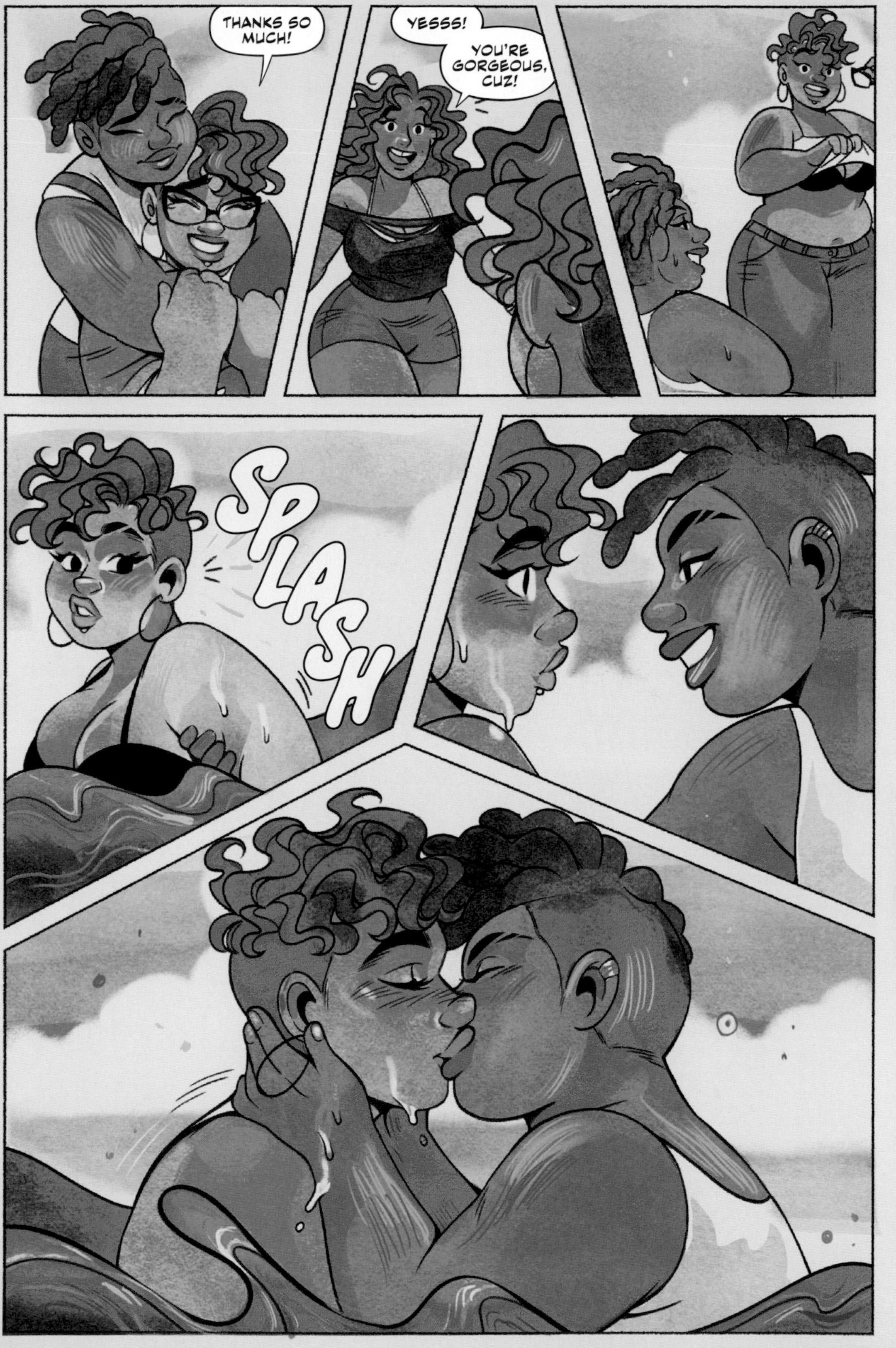
THANKS SO MUCH!
YESSS!
YOU'RE GORGEOUS, CUZ!
SPLASH

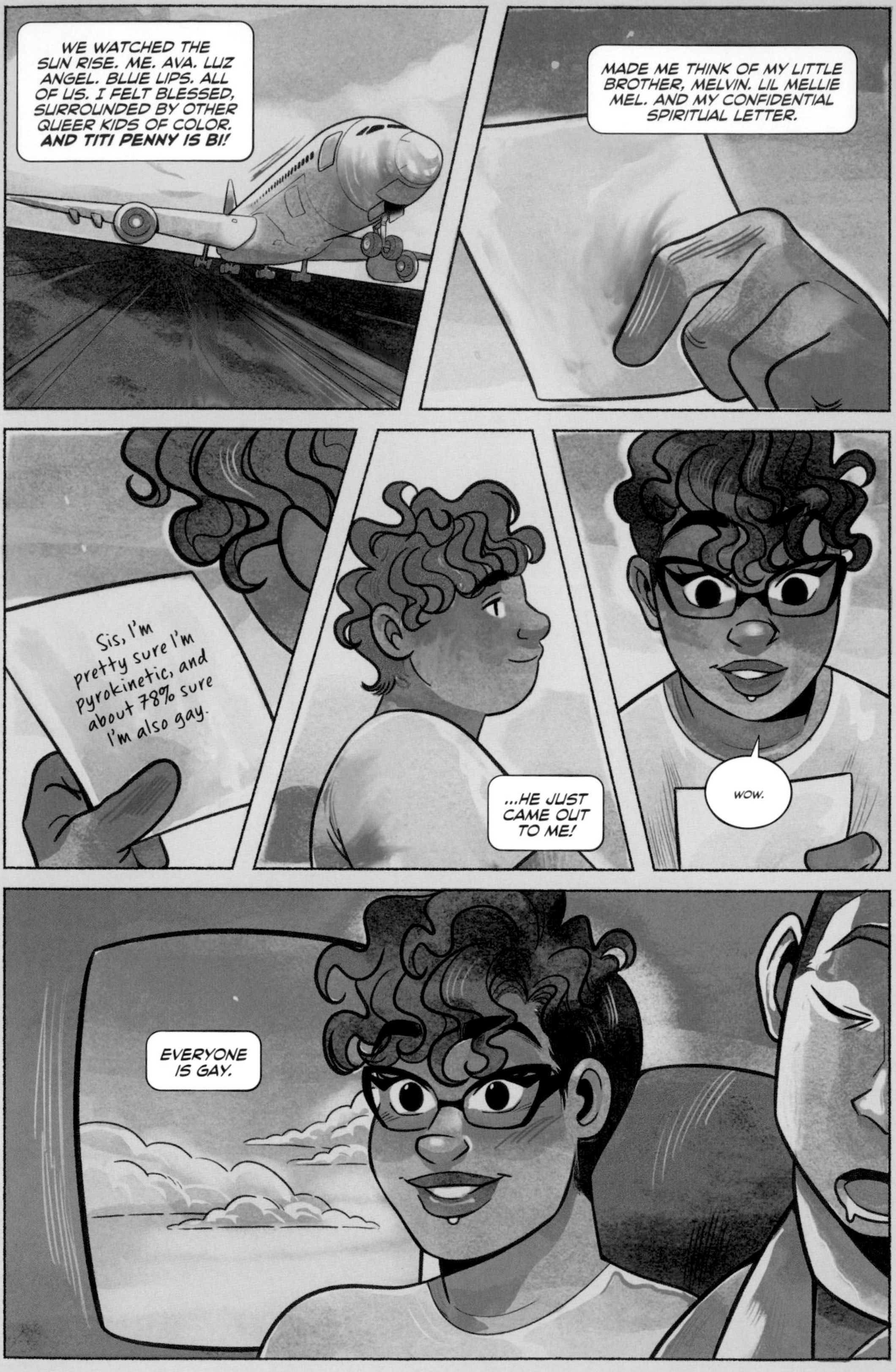
WE WATCHED THE SUN RISE. ME. AVA. LUZ ANGEL. BLUE LIPS. ALL OF US. I FELT BLESSED, SURROUNDED BY OTHER QUEER KIDS OF COLOR. **AND TITI PENNY IS BI!**
MADE ME THINK OF MY LITTLE BROTHER, MELVIN. LIL MELLIE MEL. AND MY CONFIDENTIAL SPIRITUAL LETTER.
Sis, I'm pretty sure I'm pyrokinetic, and about 78% sure I'm also gay.
...HE JUST CAME OUT TO ME!
WOW.
EVERYONE IS GAY.

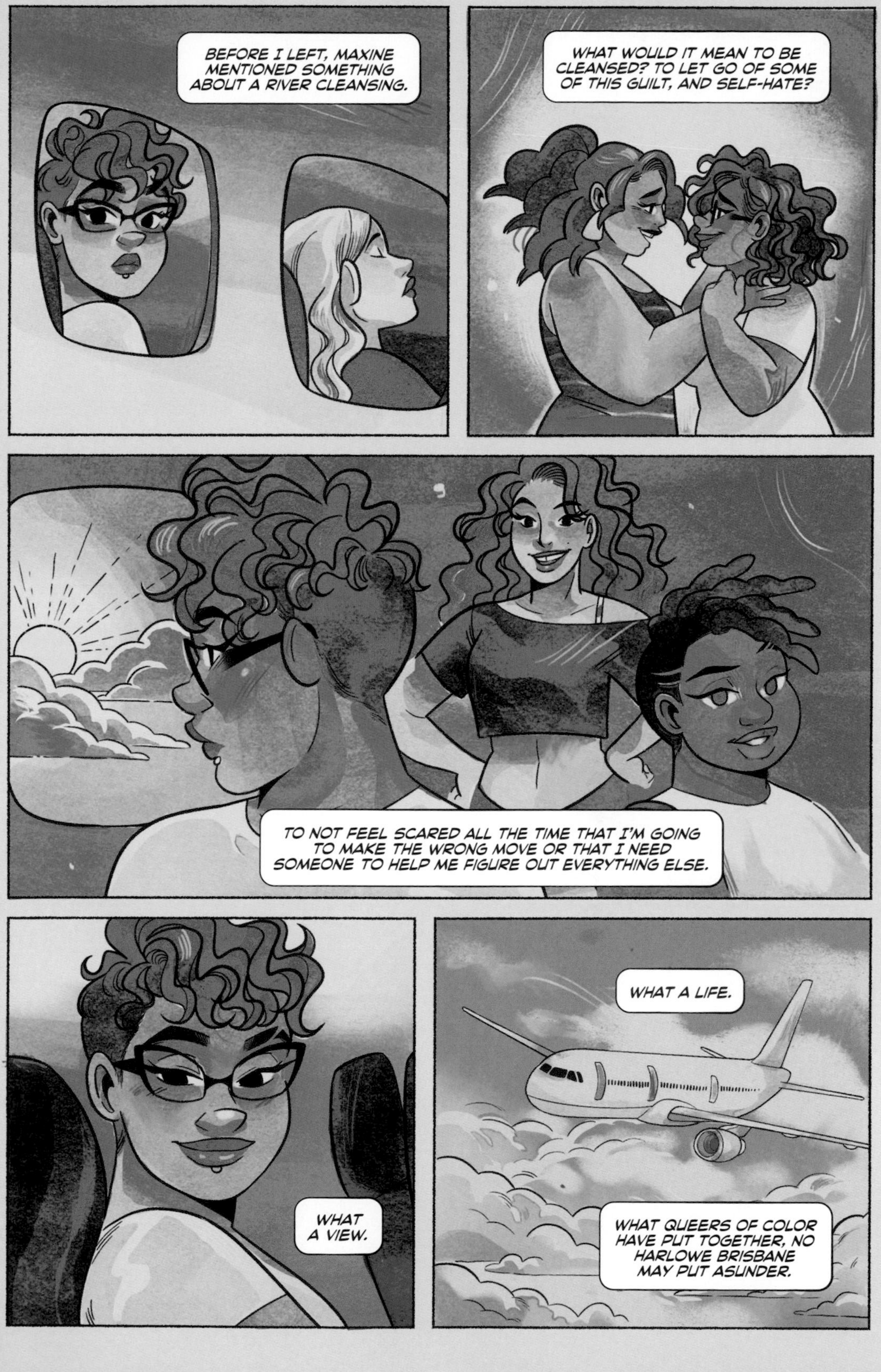
BEFORE I LEFT, MAXINE MENTIONED SOMETHING ABOUT A RIVER CLEANSING.
WHAT WOULD IT MEAN TO BE CLEANSED? TO LET GO OF SOME OF THIS GUILT, AND SELF-HATE?
TO NOT FEEL SCARED ALL THE TIME THAT I'M GOING TO MAKE THE WRONG MOVE OR THAT I NEED SOMEONE TO HELP ME FIGURE OUT EVERYTHING ELSE.
WHAT A VIEW.
WHAT A LIFE.
WHAT QUEERS OF COLOR HAVE PUT TOGETHER, NO HARLOWE BRISBANE MAY PUT ASUNDER.

IF EVER YOU GET THE CHANCE TO RIDE BIKES...

...WITH DYKES...

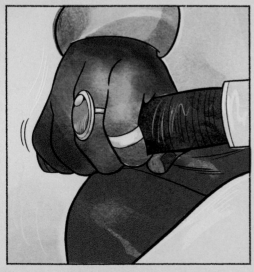

...FUCKING GO!

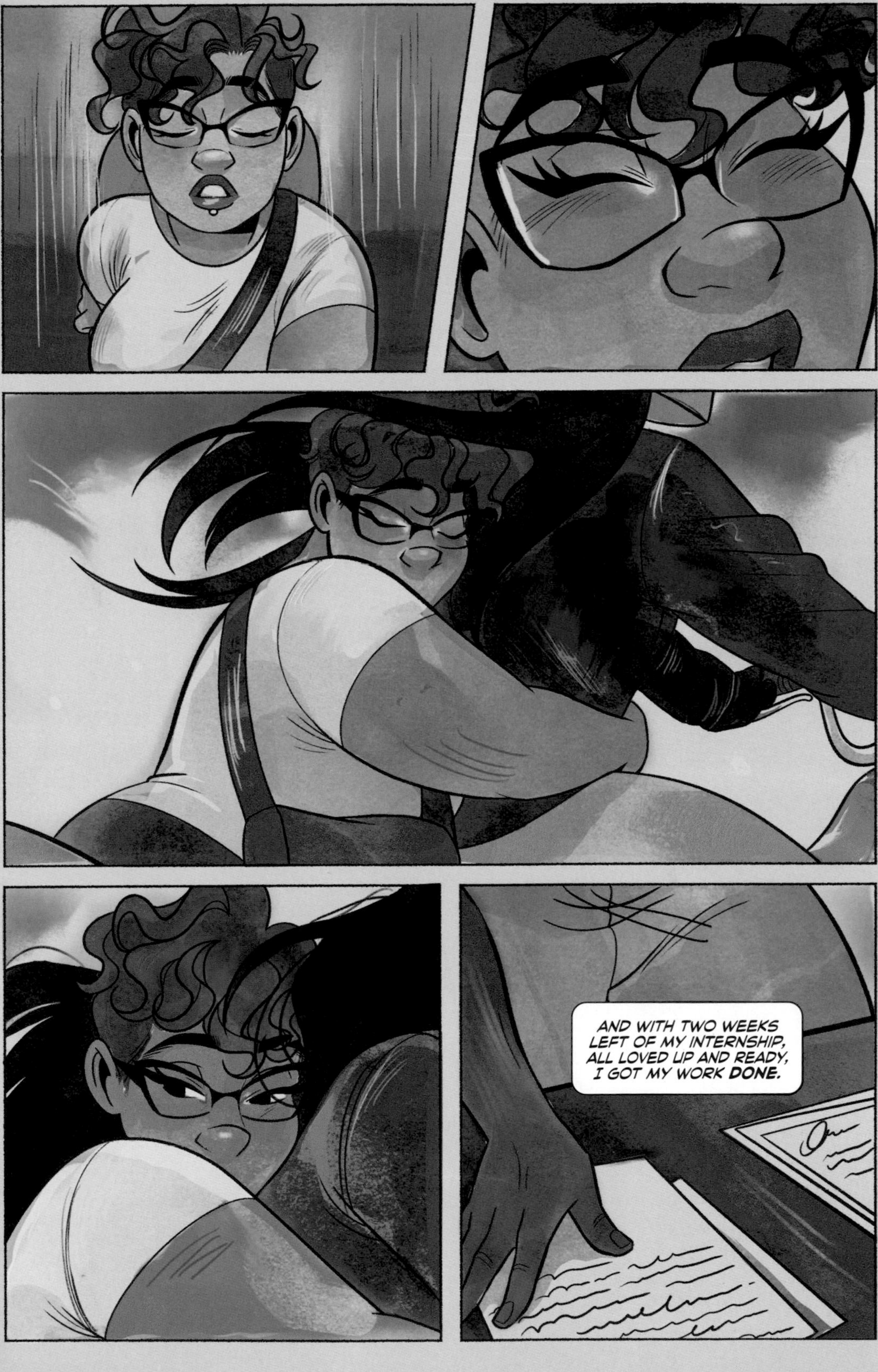
AND WITH TWO WEEKS LEFT OF MY INTERNSHIP, ALL LOVED UP AND READY, I GOT MY WORK **DONE.**

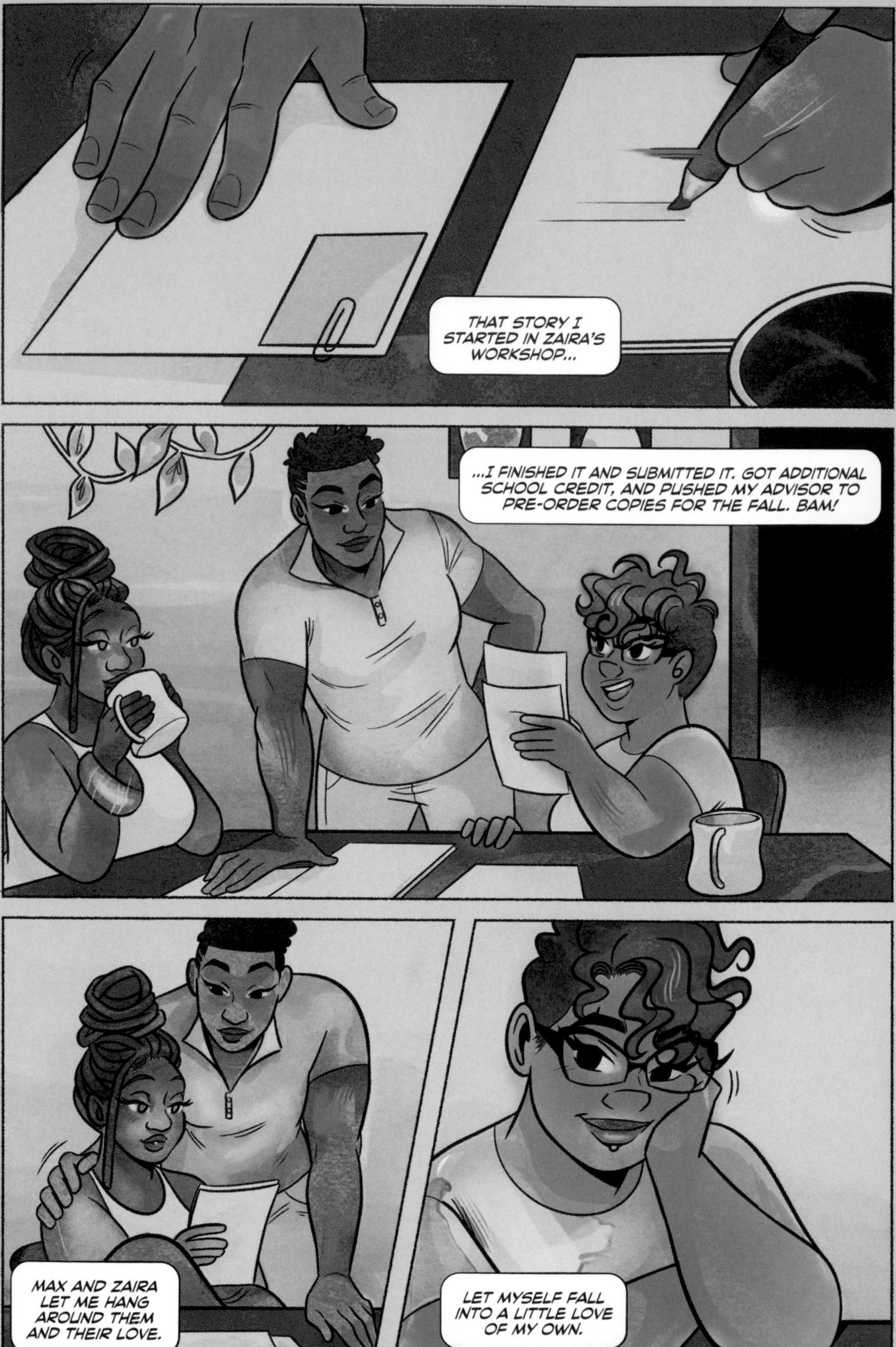
THAT STORY I STARTED IN ZAIRA'S WORKSHOP...
...I FINISHED IT AND SUBMITTED IT. GOT ADDITIONAL SCHOOL CREDIT, AND PUSHED MY ADVISOR TO PRE-ORDER COPIES FOR THE FALL. BAM!
MAX AND ZAIRA LET ME HANG AROUND THEM AND THEIR LOVE.
LET MYSELF FALL INTO A LITTLE LOVE OF MY OWN.

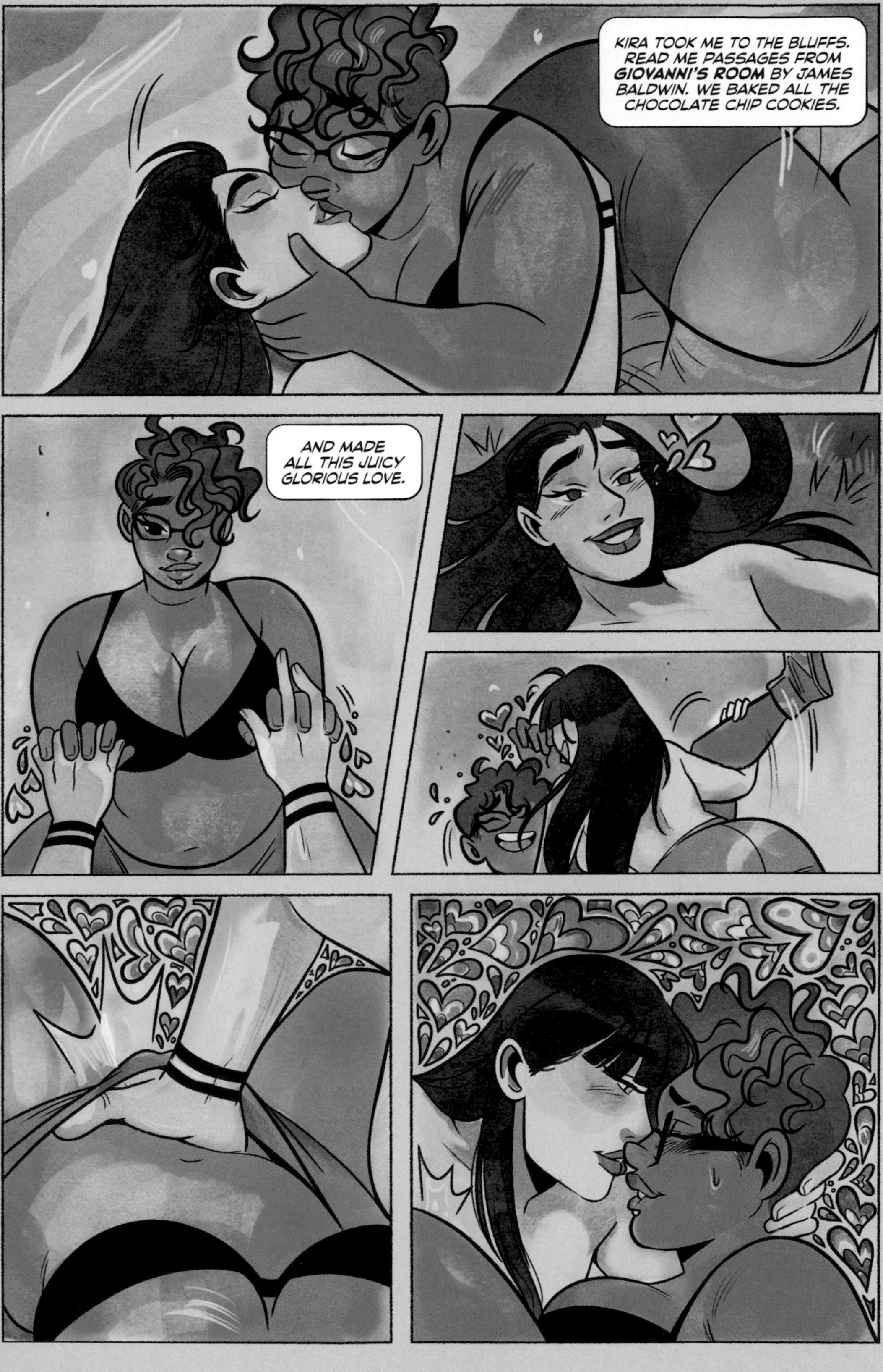
KIRA TOOK ME TO THE BLUFFS. READ ME PASSAGES FROM GIOVANNI'S ROOM BY JAMES BALDWIN. WE BAKED ALL THE CHOCOLATE CHIP COOKIES.
AND MADE ALL THIS JUICY GLORIOUS LOVE.

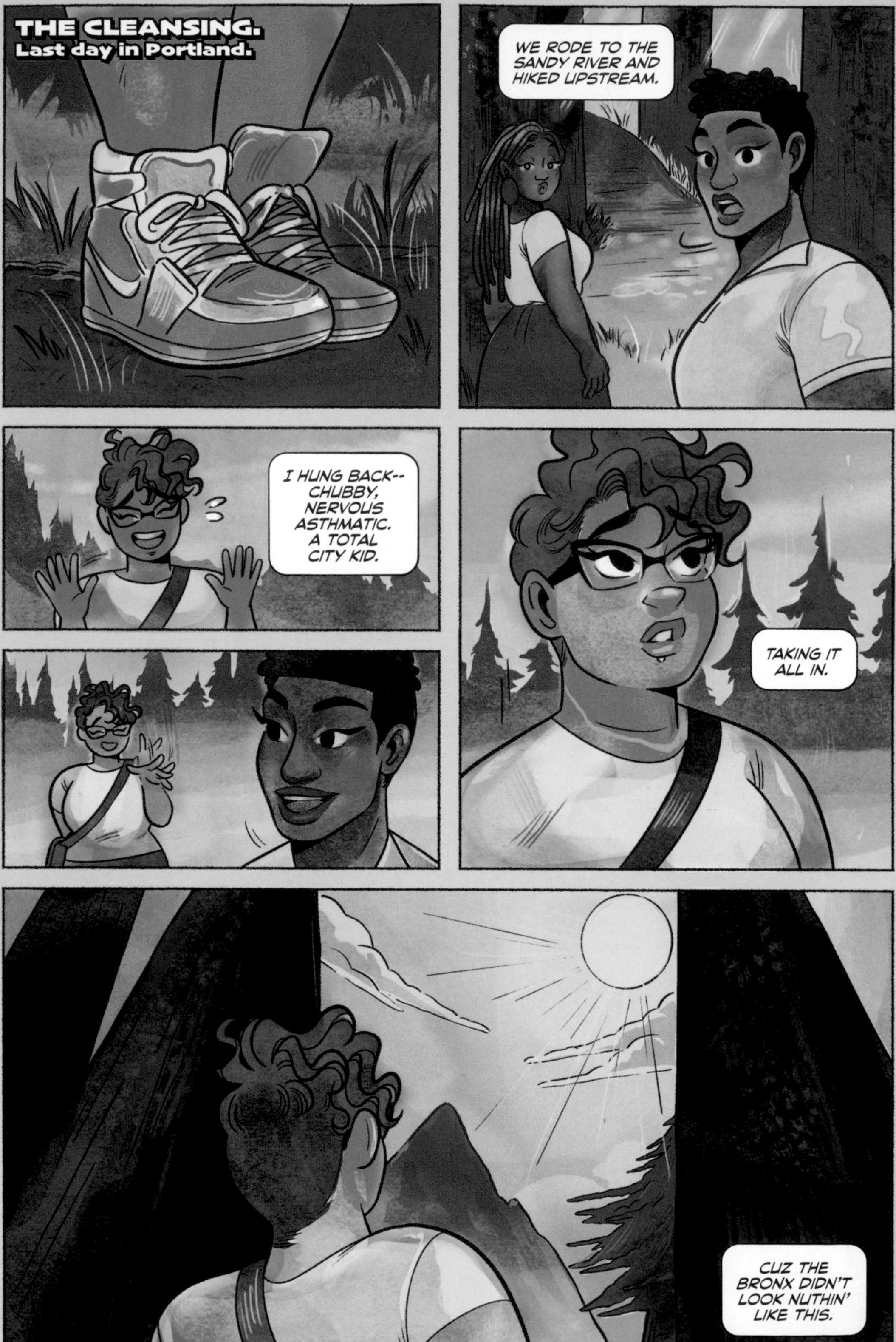
THE CLEANSING.
Last day in Portland.
WE RODE TO THE SANDY RIVER AND HIKED UPSTREAM.
I HUNG BACK-- CHUBBY, NERVOUS ASTHMATIC. A TOTAL CITY KID.
TAKING IT ALL IN.
CUZ THE BRONX DIDN'T LOOK NUTHIN' LIKE THIS.

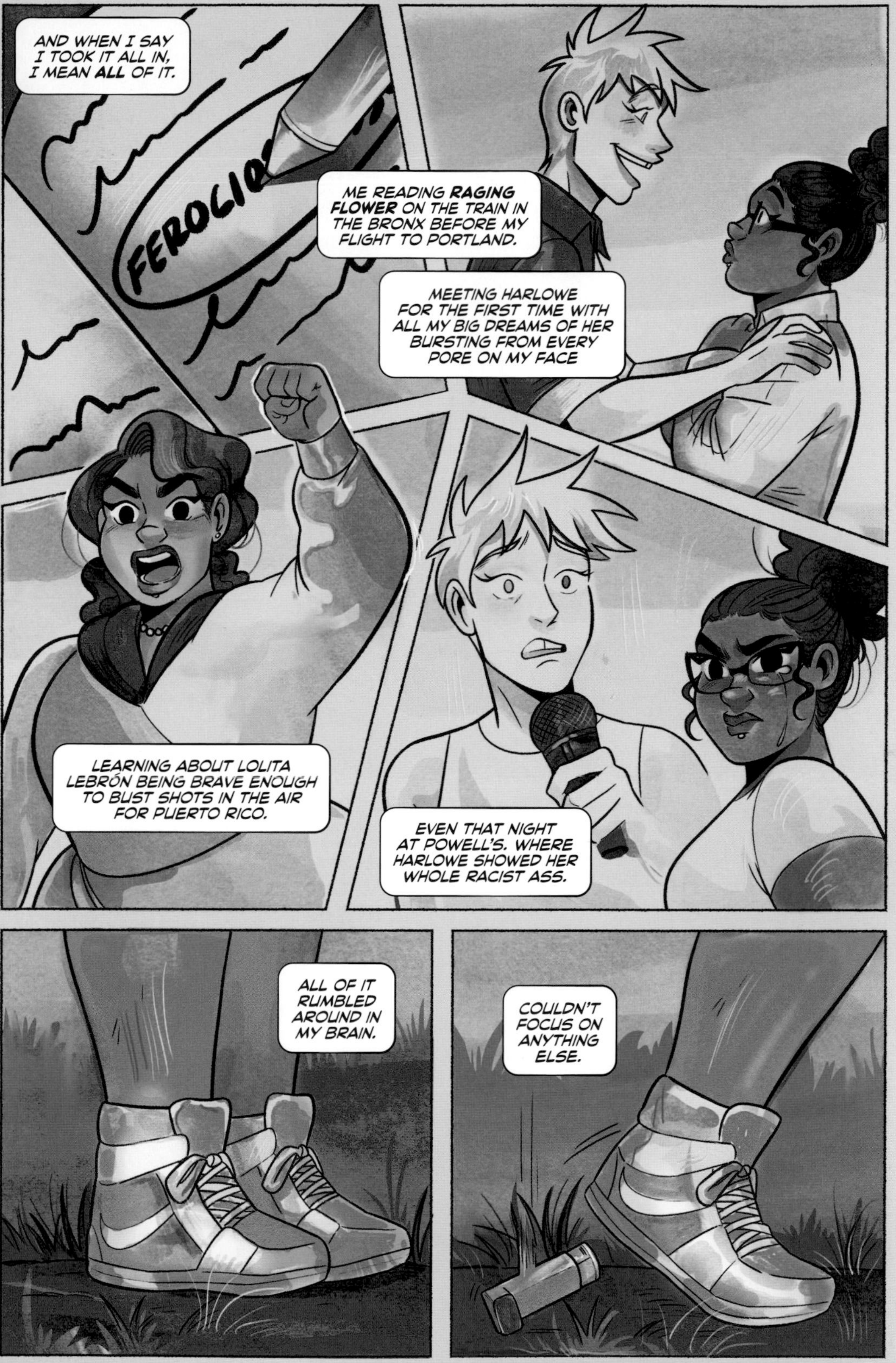

AND WHEN I SAY I TOOK IT ALL IN, I MEAN **ALL** OF IT.
FEROCIO
ME READING **RAGING FLOWER** ON THE TRAIN IN THE BRONX BEFORE MY FLIGHT TO PORTLAND.
MEETING HARLOWE FOR THE FIRST TIME WITH ALL MY BIG DREAMS OF HER BURSTING FROM EVERY PORE ON MY FACE
LEARNING ABOUT LOLITA LEBRÓN BEING BRAVE ENOUGH TO BUST SHOTS IN THE AIR FOR PUERTO RICO.
EVEN THAT NIGHT AT POWELL'S. WHERE HARLOWE SHOWED HER WHOLE RACIST ASS.
ALL OF IT RUMBLED AROUND IN MY BRAIN.
COULDN'T FOCUS ON ANYTHING ELSE.

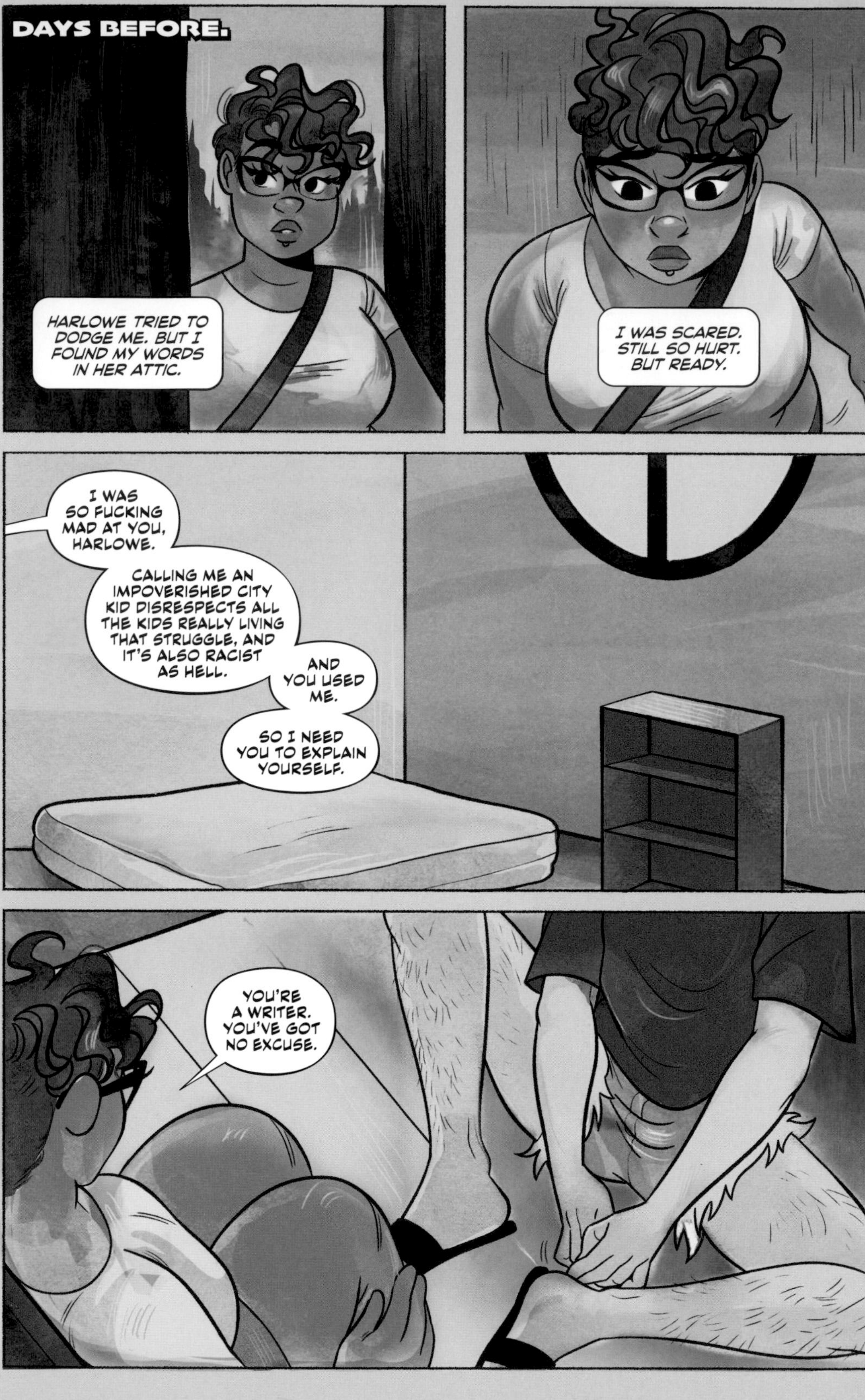
DAYS BEFORE.
HARLOWE TRIED TO DODGE ME. BUT I FOUND MY WORDS IN HER ATTIC.
I WAS SCARED. STILL SO HURT. BUT READY.
I WAS SO FUCKING MAD AT YOU, HARLOWE.
CALLING ME AN IMPOVERISHED CITY KID DISRESPECTS ALL THE KIDS REALLY LIVING THAT STRUGGLE, AND IT'S ALSO RACIST AS HELL.
AND YOU USED ME.
SO I NEED YOU TO EXPLAIN YOURSELF.
YOU'RE A WRITER. YOU'VE GOT NO EXCUSE.

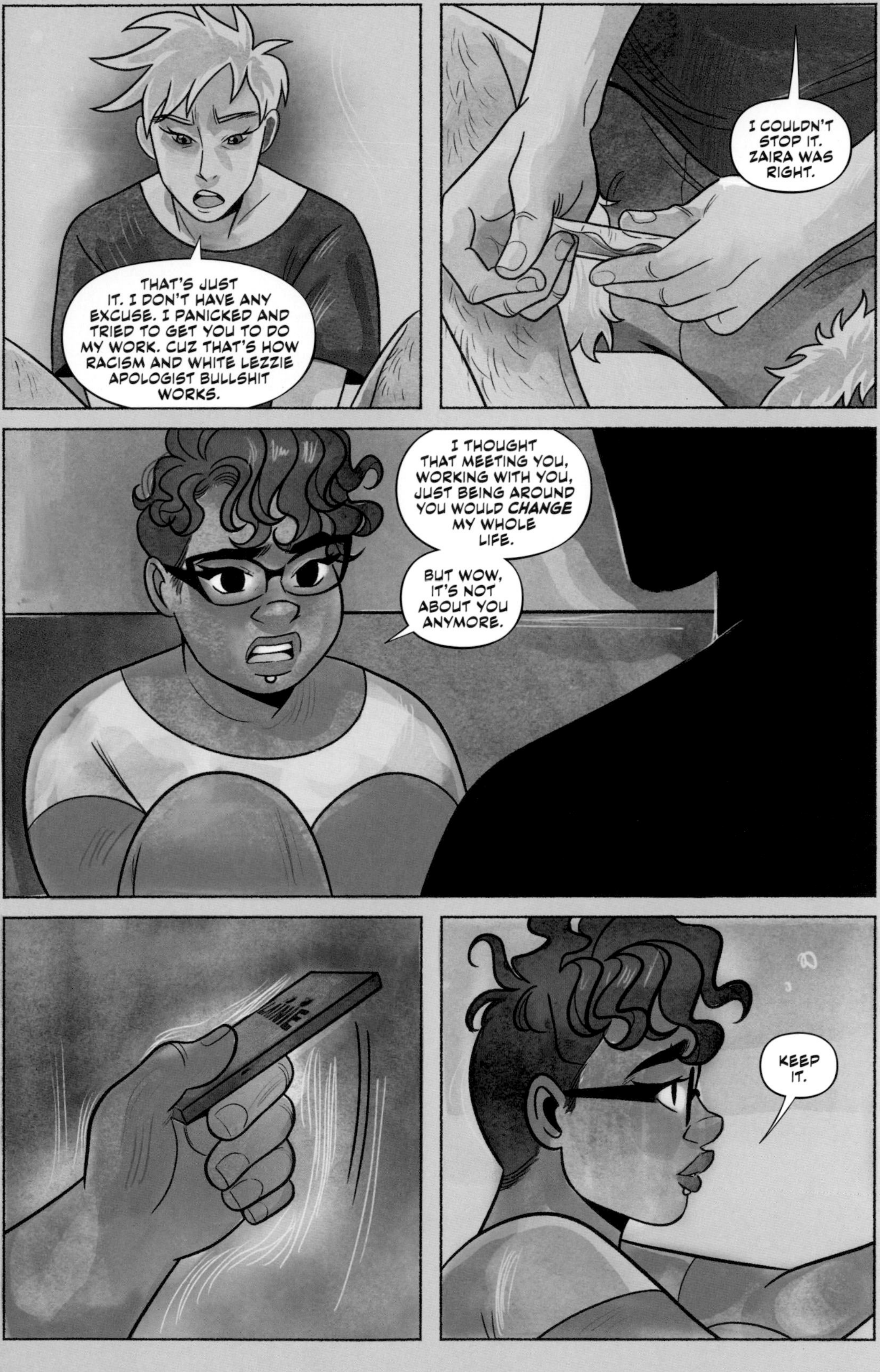

THAT'S JUST IT. I DON'T HAVE ANY EXCUSE. I PANICKED AND TRIED TO GET YOU TO DO MY WORK. CUZ THAT'S HOW RACISM AND WHITE LEZZIE APOLOGIST BULLSHIT WORKS.
I COULDN'T STOP IT. ZAIRA WAS RIGHT.
I THOUGHT THAT MEETING YOU, WORKING WITH YOU, JUST BEING AROUND YOU WOULD *CHANGE* MY WHOLE LIFE.
BUT WOW, IT'S NOT ABOUT YOU ANYMORE.
KEEP IT.

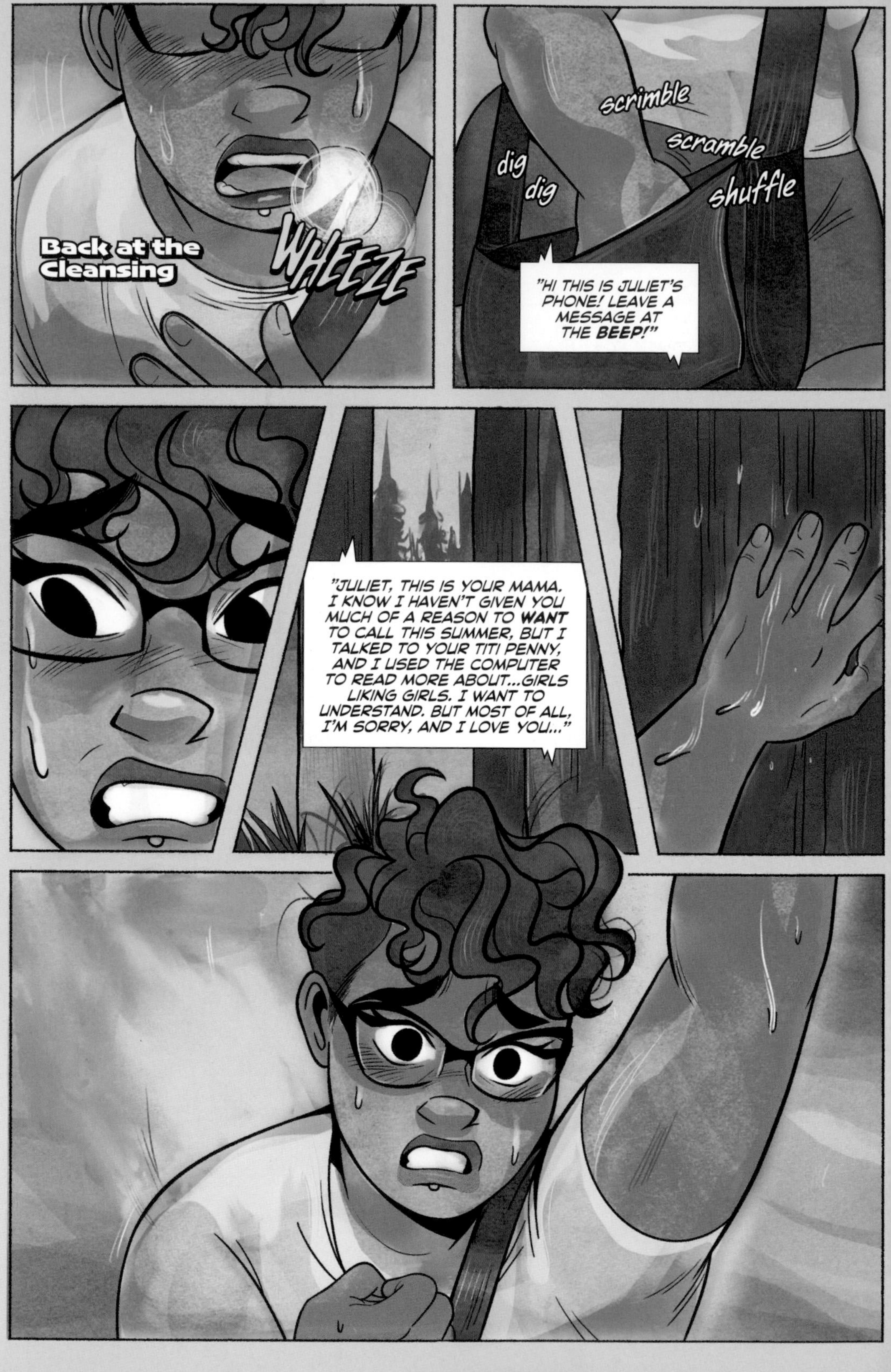
Back at the Cleansing
WHEEZE
scrimble
scramble
dig
dig
shuffle
"HI THIS IS JULIET'S PHONE! LEAVE A MESSAGE AT THE BEEP!"
"JULIET, THIS IS YOUR MAMA. I KNOW I HAVEN'T GIVEN YOU MUCH OF A REASON TO WANT TO CALL THIS SUMMER, BUT I TALKED TO YOUR TITI PENNY, AND I USED THE COMPUTER TO READ MORE ABOUT...GIRLS LIKING GIRLS. I WANT TO UNDERSTAND. BUT MOST OF ALL, I'M SORRY, AND I LOVE YOU..."

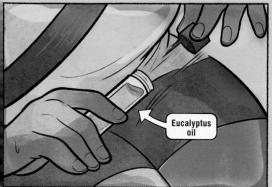

Eucalyptus oil

sana sana

TRUST YOUR LUNGS.

TRUST THE UNIVERSE.

TRUST YOUR DAMN SELF.

ALL I AM IS ALL I NEED.

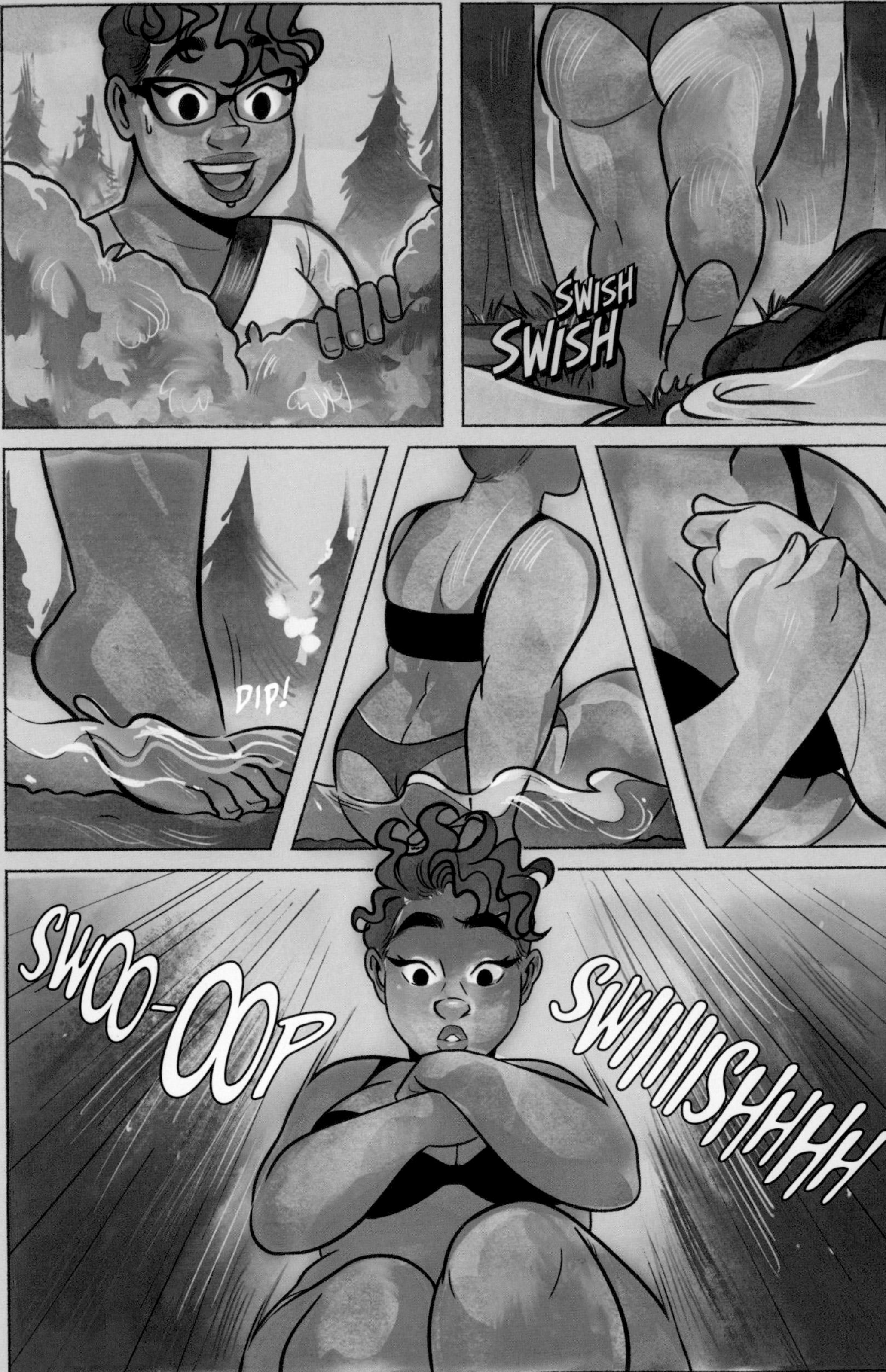
SWISH
SWISH
DIP!
SWOO-OOP
SWIIIISHHHH

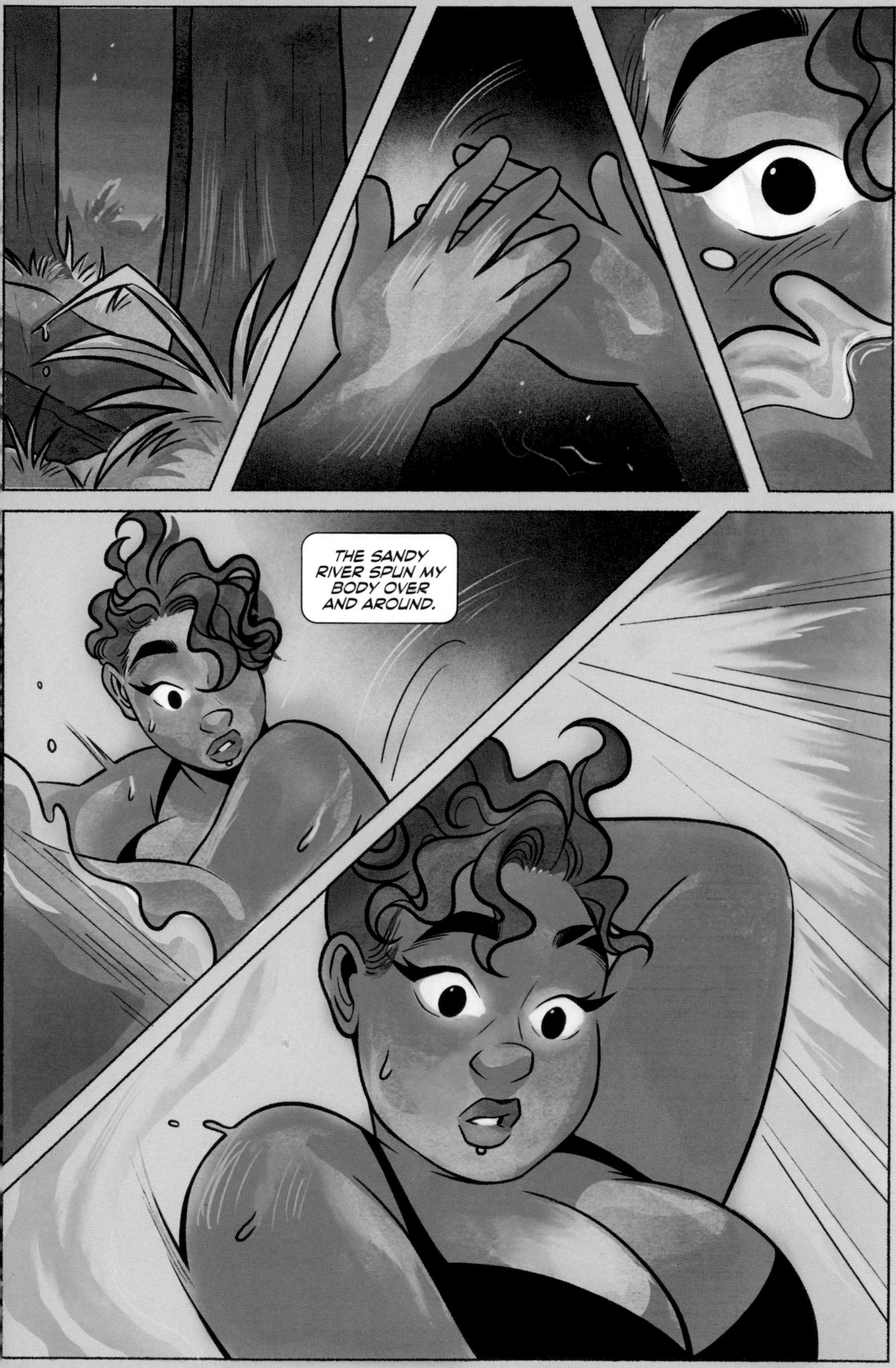
THE SANDY RIVER SPUN MY BODY OVER AND AROUND.

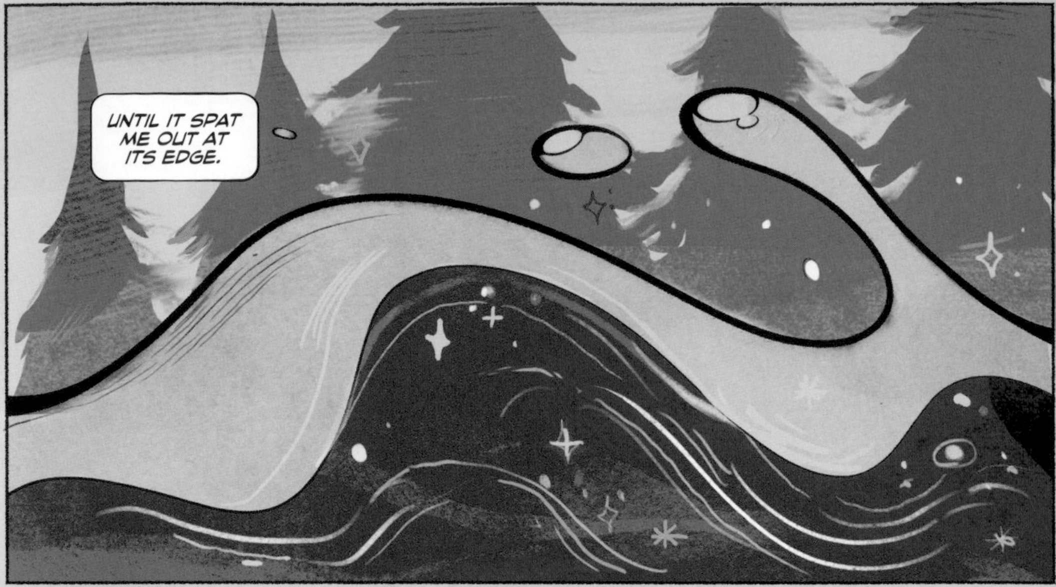
UNTIL IT SPAT ME OUT AT ITS EDGE.

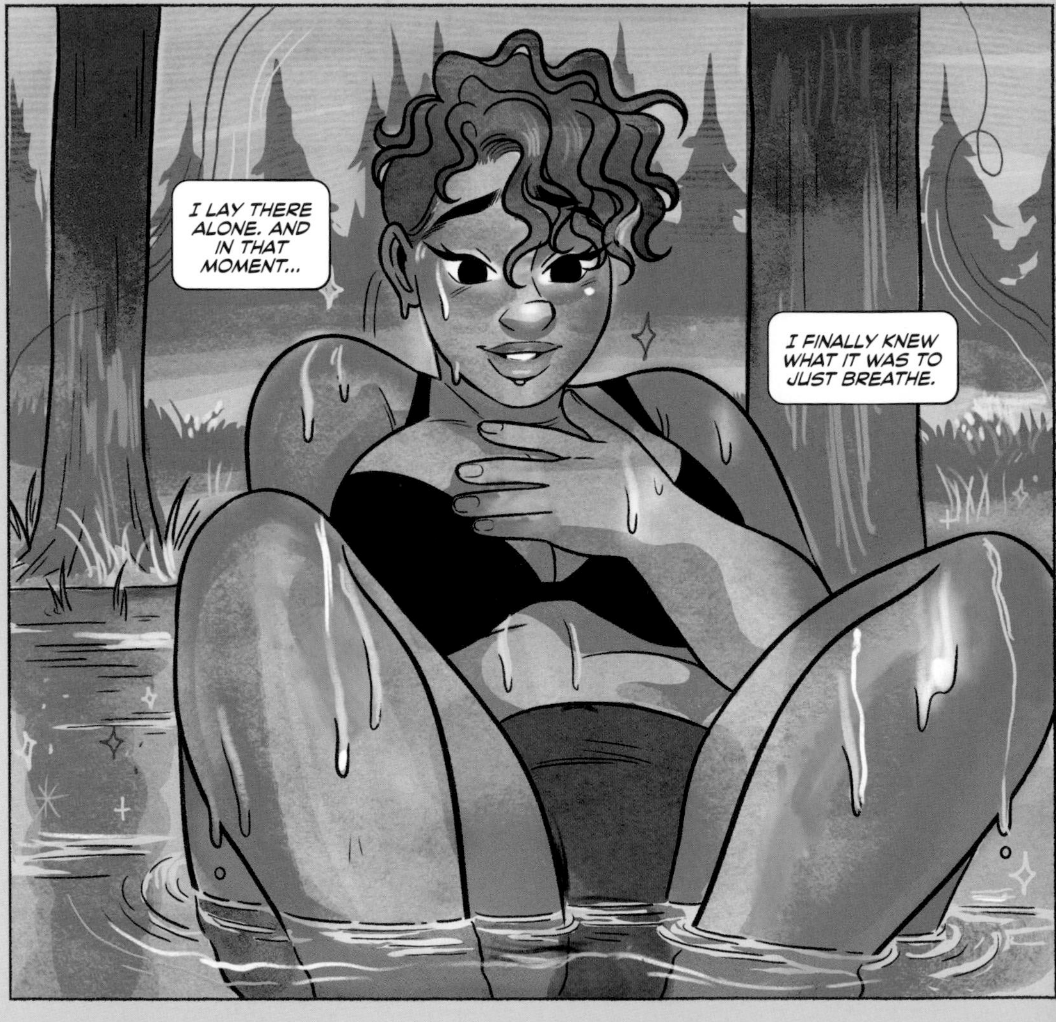
I LAY THERE ALONE. AND IN THAT MOMENT...
I FINALLY KNEW WHAT IT WAS TO JUST BREATHE.

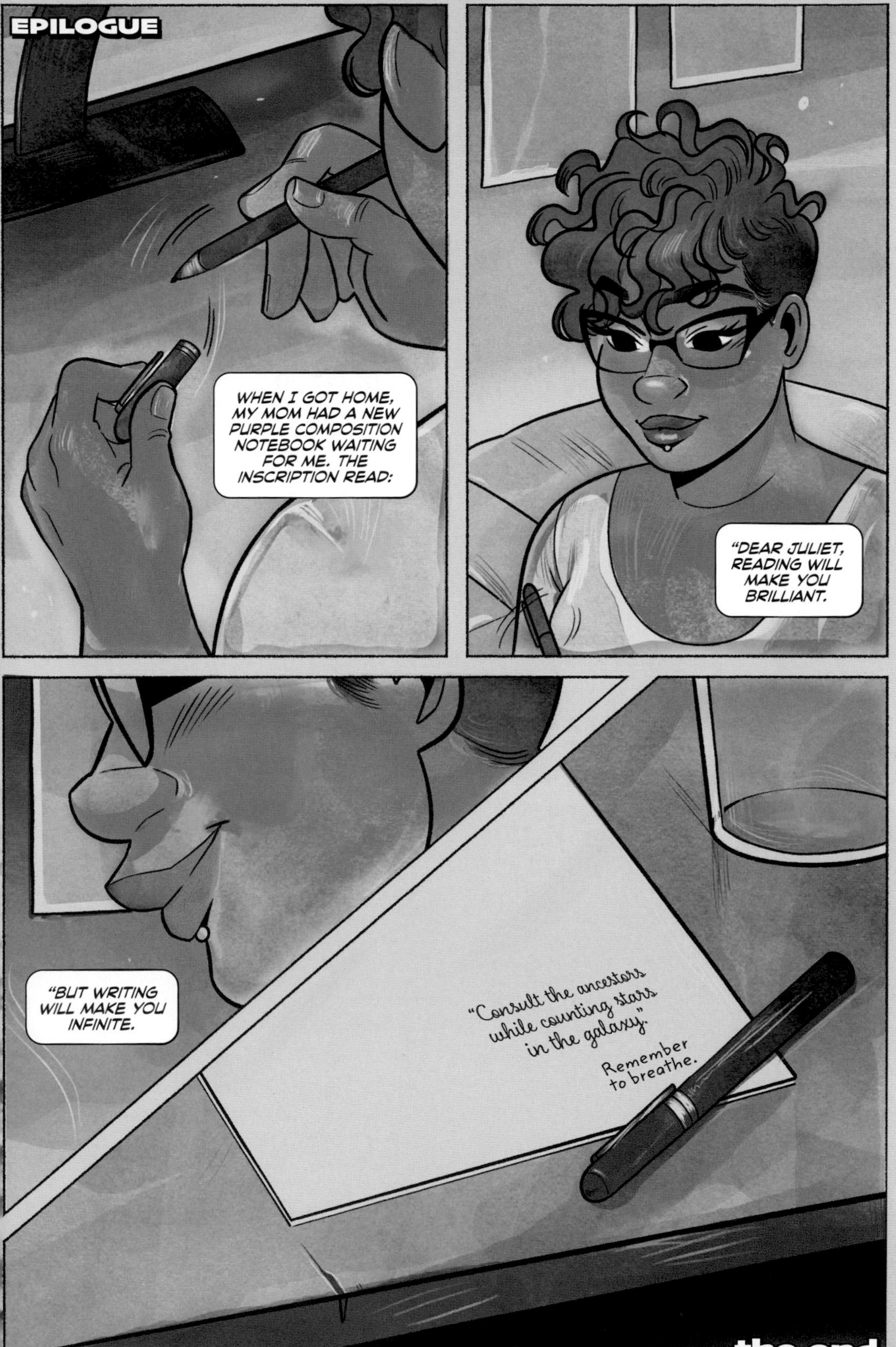
EPILOGUE
WHEN I GOT HOME, MY MOM HAD A NEW PURPLE COMPOSITION NOTEBOOK WAITING FOR ME. THE INSCRIPTION READ:
"DEAR JULIET, READING WILL MAKE YOU BRILLIANT.
"BUT WRITING WILL MAKE YOU INFINITE.
"Consult the ancestors while counting stars in the galaxy."
Remember to breathe.
the end.

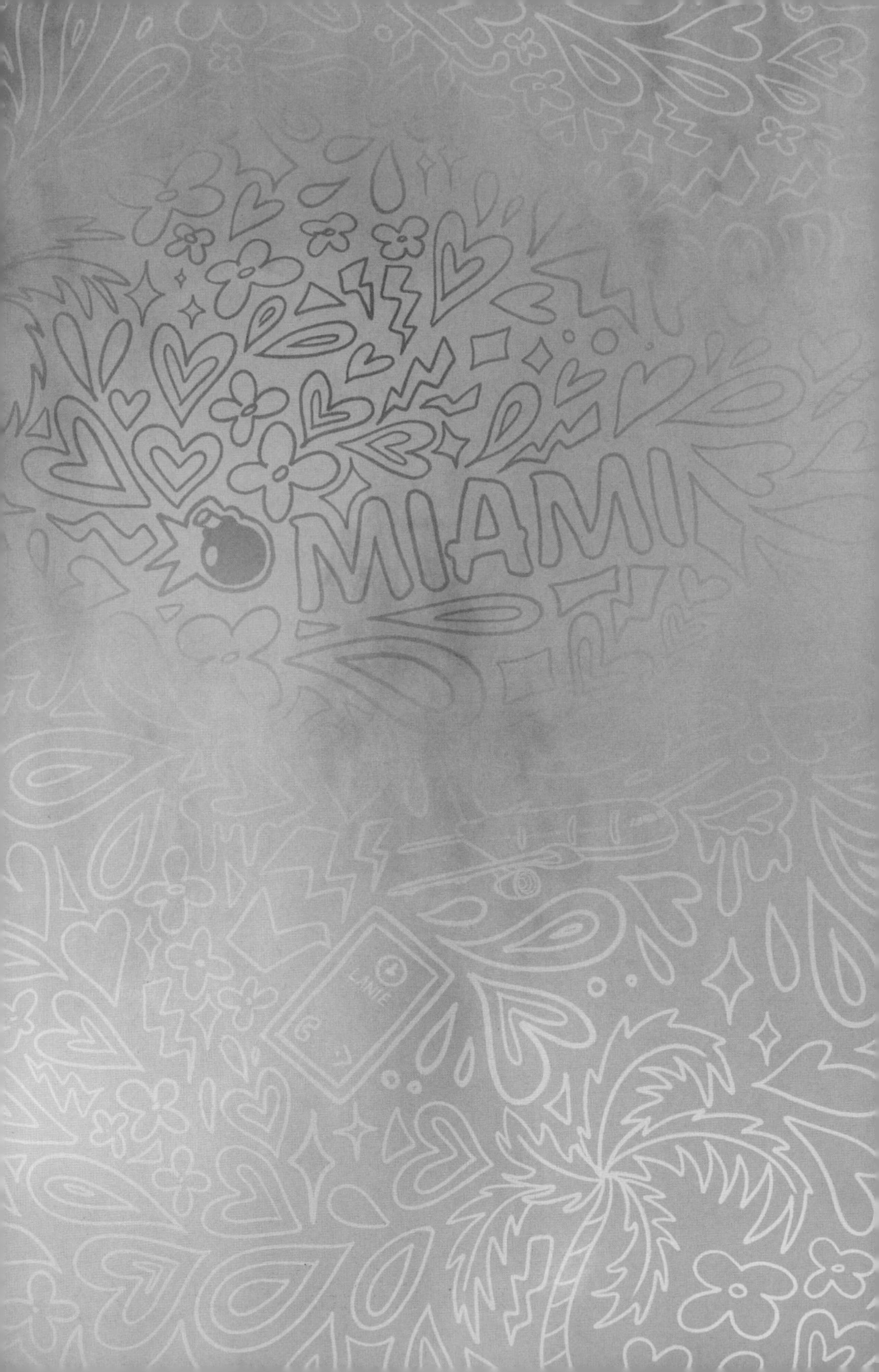
MIAMI
LANIE

DISCOVER
ALL THE HITS

STEVENSON · ELLIS · WATTERS · ALLEN
LUMBERJANES
BEWARE THE KITTEN HOLY
NEW YORK TIMES
BESTSELLING SERIES

Allison + Treiman + Cogar
GIANT
DAYS
VOLUME ONE

From a writer of Disney's Moana
RIBON • FISH • PEER
SLAM!

Hope Larson • Brittney Williams • Sarah Stern
GOLDIE VANCE
Volume One

THE BACKSTAGERS

TYSON HESSE'S
DIESEL
IGNITION

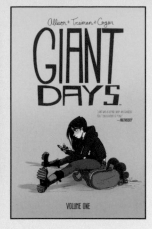

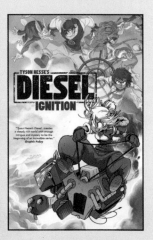

Lumberjanes
Noelle Stevenson, Shannon Watters, Grace Ellis, Brooklyn Allen, and Others
Volume 1: Beware the Kitten Holy
ISBN: 978-1-60886-687-8 | $14.99 US
Volume 2: Friendship to the Max
ISBN: 978-1-60886-737-0 | $14.99 US
Volume 3: A Terrible Plan
ISBN: 978-1-60886-803-2 | $14.99 US
Volume 4: Out of Time
ISBN: 978-1-60886-860-5 | $14.99 US
Volume 5: Band Together
ISBN: 978-1-60886-919-0 | $14.99 US

Giant Days
John Allison, Lissa Treiman, Max Sarin
Volume 1
ISBN: 978-1-60886-789-9 | $9.99 US
Volume 2
ISBN: 978-1-60886-804-9 | $14.99 US
Volume 3
ISBN: 978-1-60886-851-3 | $14.99 US

Jonesy
Sam Humphries, Caitlin Rose Boyle
Volume 1
ISBN: 978-1-60886-883-4 | $9.99 US
Volume 2
ISBN: 978-1-60886-999-2 | $14.99 US

Slam!
Pamela Ribon, Veronica Fish, Brittany Peer
Volume 1
ISBN: 978-1-68415-004-5 | $14.99 US

Goldie Vance
Hope Larson, Brittney Williams
Volume 1
ISBN: 978-1-60886-898-8 | $9.99 US
Volume 2
ISBN: 978-1-60886-974-9 | $14.99 US

The Backstagers
James Tynion IV, Rian Sygh
Volume 1
ISBN: 978-1-60886-993-0 | $14.99 US

Tyson Hesse's Diesel: Ignition
Tyson Hesse
ISBN: 978-1-60886-907-7 | $14.99 US

Coady & The Creepies
Liz Prince, Amanda Kirk, Hannah Fisher
ISBN: 978-1-68415-029-8 | $14.99 US

BOOM! BOX™

AVAILABLE AT YOUR LOCAL COMICS SHOP AND BOOKSTORE
WWW.**BOOM-STUDIOS**.COM